D0816018

THE UNBELIEVABLE

It was only as Robert was stumbling back toward the kitchen table that he realized there was a light coming from the living room. The living room that had been in darkness when he'd passed through it fifteen minutes ago.

He moved toward the doorway and peeked around the edge. There was a small fire burning in the fireplace.

He very slowly, very quietly moved back into the kitchen and pulled open the cutlery drawer, wincing at the way it groaned. He removed the largest knife he could find.

Exhaling a breath he wasn't aware he'd been holding, he moved back toward the living room. The fire popped loudly, then hissed and sizzled.

Keeping his back pressed against the wall and wishing he owned a gun, Robert moved left, toward the fireplace and the sofa—which had been moved, turned around so that if one were to sit on it they would face the fireplace and not the other, smaller sofa that sat six feet across from it.

He wondered if it had been moved earlier, while he was still in the hospital.

Gripping the handle with as much strength as he could muster, he moved onward, closer to the sofa and sizzling fire, crackling like the sound of delicate bones snapping, and now—breathe, c'mon, that's it—he was facing the side of the sofa, and so moved forward, closer to it.

Unbelieving of the sight before him, Robert dropped the knife.

Stood staring at the Impossibility that lay so peaceful before him.

And slowly raised both hands to cover his mouth before any sound could escape.

In Silent Graves

Gary A. Braunbeck

LEISURE BOOKS   **B**   NEW YORK CITY

LEISURE BOOKS ®

April 2004

Published by

Dorchester Publishing Co., Inc.
200 Madison Avenue
New York, NY 10016

ISBN 0-8439-5329-2

The name "Leisure Books" and the stylized "L" with design are trademarks of Dorchester Publishing Co., Inc.

Printed in the United States of America.

Introduction
by Michael Marano

I'm usually allergic to introductions that kick off with invocations of Proust, but this quote is such a good'un, I'm going to ask you to bear with me: "As long as reading is for us the instigator whose magic keys have opened the door to those dwelling places deep within us that we would not otherwise have known how to enter, its role in our lives is salutary. It becomes dangerous, on the other hand, when, instead of awakening us to the personal life of the mind, reading tends to take its place."

Can I get an *Amen!* for Brother Marcel? (Remember the *Monty Python* skit in which John Cleese, while asking for a fish license for his pet halibut, said: "Marcel Proust had an haddock! So, if you're calling the author of 'A la recherche du temps perdu' a looney, I shall have to ask you to step outside!"?)

Due to the sadisms of the book business today (publishers bark "realities of the market" to justify the buying strategies of the week, thereby exonerating themselves from any aesthetic or moral responsibility for what they do, or don't do), you'll notice a prevalence of books that seem to exist for the specific purpose

1

of taking the place of "the personal life of the mind." These salable units, er, I mean, *books*, instead seem to offer a refuge from the terrors of inner life, to paraphrase Christopher Lasch, author of *The Culture of Narcissism*. It's easier to stock the shelves of chain stores with Sarah Jessica-esque "chick lit" whelped as book club fodder, the primary purpose of which is to be yakked about rather than read and thought about or even just *enjoyed*. Then of course there are the "thrillers" that do not thrill, but reassure; anything with the sense of true cold-sweat danger that Mickey Spillane or Ian Fleming could barrel down on you like the grill of a truck wouldn't fly today. There're legal melodramas shilled to the cubicle set about vitally important missing "McGuffin" files that are just like the stacks of files on the desks of the books' targeted buyers, which thereby comfort the buyers into thinking that the drudge forms they fill out with hundreds of keystrokes and mouse clicks each day are vitally important, too. There're "epic" fantasies written not with the all-knowing voice of the true ancient or medieval epic, but with the wish-fulfilling camera lens of withered imaginations given form not by myth but by TV and movies; these books feature heroes with far fewer facets than the twenty-sided dice with which they were plotted. There's pastiche masquerading as postmodernism—books that are fashion accessories for the soul-patched, patchouli-reeking, frayed-black-sweater-wearing Starbucks pseudointelligentsia. And there're technothrillers with brand-name authors emblazoned on the covers who did not actually write the books sandwiched by those covers.

We live in a publishing world in which character depth is often no more than a list of possessions the reader is expected to covet, or a prose collection of Pavlov cues implanted by other media. I tried to read one retina-scrapingly bad mystery in which Handsome-Craggy-Rugged-Older-Stud-Number-thirty-two-in-a-Series was flat-out described as looking "a lot like Harrison Ford." That's not even *trying*, guys. One writer of easy-to-read best-smellers admitted he created one hero specifically with

Introduction

Bruce Willis in mind. Chain bookstores demand product, er, I mean, books, that are "easy sells" to attractive marketing niches. This tends to mean shelves are crowded with items that are marketed to the point that they can't, as per Brother Marcel, "open the door to those dwelling places deep within us that we would not otherwise have known how to enter" any more than an SUV ad can. When something is that much of a commodity, it can't really challenge the reader. And if a book doesn't challenge, it usually flatters and reassures.

Cripes, I'm not even certain chain bookstores really mean to sell *books*, anymore. I look around them, and the feeling I get is that the stores are mainly selling *themselves*, their *ambience*, and that the books are much like the cheaply priced DVDs at high-end appliance stores; just as big appliance stores stock price-gouged DVDs to lure you in so they can sell you a fridge, so do big chain bookstores seem to stock bait, er, I mean books, to lure you in to sell you coffee, CDs, knickknacks, pens, lamps, pastry, candy, mugs, novelty doormats, picture frames, and, uhmmmm, DVDs. Ya don't lure people with doubt, worry, deep emotions, deep thought, empathy, compassion, the sublime, joy, or any of the other things that form the backbone of literature. Fiction stocked to lure you into buying a DVD, a Garfield travel mug, and a Darth Maul key ring can't do a Proust and awaken you to the personal life of the mind if it coddles you into a happy consumerist fog.

It's because of these factors that you now hold in your hands the equivalent of a ticket to see *Easy Rider* on the opening day of its release, or a copy of *Horses* still warm from the record press. I've never met Gary Braunbeck, but I got a feeling he'd get a chuckle outta being compared to Dennis Hopper and Patti Smith. Any culture vulture, reader of entertainment magazines, or regular watcher of *Bravo*, *IFC*, or *A&E* could tell you about the doldrums of Hollywood movies in the sixties (which told us how much we were supposed to love unchallenging drivel starring Doris Day and Rock Hudson) and of the record industry in

3

Introduction

the seventies (which told us we were to think of The Starland Vocal Band and The Captain and Tennille as "rockin' ").

In my humble yet unimpeachable opinion, books of the aughts are in the same kind of morass. The market is too inflexible. The outlets too limited. Too few publishers are left, and these are owned by too few megacorporations. Something's gotta give. Voices that challenge, that feel, that care, can barely be heard through the fortress walls of the unyielding market. *In Silent Graves* might be the first blow of the battering ram. It's as dramatic in its implications as *Easy Rider* was to the movies of the late sixties and the seventies, and as Patti Smith was to the New York music scene of the CBGBs era. It's an important book because of Gary's passion, and passion is something a lot of people seem to fear more than any undead bugaboo usually associated with books about the supernatural.

About eight decades ago, Eliot wrote in "Gerontion," a poem about a kind of living death:

"I have lost my passion: why should I need to keep it
Since what is kept must be adulterated?"

The absence and dilution of passion is that which brings on living death, the squandering of feeling, the smothering of a person's soul to embers. Gary's book bursts with passion, and thus, life. It scalds with it. He's not afraid to feel the hurt of existence and to make you feel it, too. If you embrace life, you have to embrace loss and emptiness and grief. Yeah, this means embracing darkness, but isn't confronting darkness and making your peace with it a way to cherish light all the more? Complacent numbness is a living death: *"a dull head among windy spaces."* Any schmuck can write about unpleasant things and call it horror. Just look back at the myriad books published in the eighties with those annoying gerund titles: *The Searing, The Plunging, The Flaying,* et al. But only a guy like Gary can bull-grapple the supernatural, the unreal, and force it to feel like the mundane

Introduction

earthbound terror we've been crushed by in hospital waiting rooms while a loved one is sick.

In Silent Graves is a work of towering imagination; its blending of preexisting folklore into a new mythology against which Gary can place his heartbreaking narrative is comparable to Tolkien's and Lewis's created mythologies. But *In Silent Graves* is much closer than Narnia or Middle-earth. It's as close as Ohio, or the next county over or the house next door. Gary's passion and compassion are infectious. You feel this book, and you're made to feel in new ways because of it. It exists to be read and experienced and it exists to take you into those places deep within us most books are too afraid let us acknowledge even exist. *In Silent Graves* does not take you to those deep places to languish like some stunted solipsist. It takes us to those deep places to more thoroughly draw us out of ourselves. In its original edition, *In Silent Graves* was read only by a handful of people. That's being rectified, now, and it's a reason to rejoice. Maybe, along with the crack in the fortress walls of publishing, we can see the crack where the mountain opens up, too.

Michael Marano is a horror critic and sometime writer of horror fiction.

5

" 'A fine setting for a fit of despair,' it occurred to him. 'If only I were standing here by accident instead of design.' "

—*Kafka,* The Castle

"My neighbors' bodies are neat and clean, but their brains are caked with the dust of generations of low hopes and ignorant fear their lives were fossilized well before birth."

—*Lucy A. Snyder,* "Permian Basin Blues"

"Man has places in his heart which do not yet exist, and into them enters suffering, in order that they may have existence."

—*Leon Bloy*

Invocation

. . . later—*after the sirens died down and the area was cordoned off, after the strobing lights blinked out and everyone was questioned, after shock and horror slowly transformed into disgust and grief, after the crowd was dispersed and the coroner's wagon pulled away with its grotesque, grim cargo—one of the officers made a last sweep of the scene and found a neatly folded sheet of stationery tucked into a corner of the bureau's chipped and dingy mirror. This discovery would lead detectives to search the ruins of the motel room again, this time to find a thick envelope taped to the underside of a drawer in the writing table. Inside this envelope were hundreds of pages, both hand-written and typed, which would answer all of their questions—forget that the answers did not fit neatly into the cubically contained prison of their consensual reality.*

But, for the moment, there was only this small, neatly folded piece of paper, taken from the corner of the chipped and dingy mirror.

The script was delicate and exquisitely feminine, the spaces between each word painstakingly exact, the angle of her slant almost Elizabethan in its fluid grace, each letter a blossom, each word a bouquet, the sentence itself a breathtaking garland: Send me a picture of the daughter we never had, the bright little girl with chubby pink cheeks and wistful smile and wide gray eyes that say, I used to feel lonely but it's all better now . . .

Most of the world thinks that's where Robert Londrigan's story came to its end, but we know better, don't we?

It's time now. The moon is full and high above; there are sounds out there beyond this warm firelight, lonely and semi-human; and around your feet swirls the fog, night breath of the river, come to hide you from the things making those lonely sounds.

Don't be afraid. Remember the words you were taught? They'll protect you, if in your heart you truly believe.

Do you remember?

Fine; all together, now:

Come forward, Robert Londrigan, and bring your memories and the gods and heroes of your childhood with you; come forward for the wonder of men and women cleaving to one another and the children who spring forth from the coupling; step from the shadows of the past and tell us what the good American man you once were did that was so bad in the eyes of God and humankind that you were forced to flee the company of people; come forward, eager to cast light all about in the dark corners of the last thirty-seven days of your life and make clear to us what happened once upon a time; you don't need a muse to tell your story, you need a voice that stands in front of you like a sign marking the end of your journey, one filled with compassion and some touch of pity and hardened with anger to a shine; come forward and give body and entitlement and boldness to your tale before it falls victim to those who would make it myth, give it life with a voice that now takes its place in front of you, ready to begin, to weave the strands together, to paint your portrait in just detail, to reveal with which doll the nesting set truly begins; come forward! Let us speak the man you once were back into existence.

Part One
Pretty Pictures

"Perhaps more of her still moves
in the scattered elements her soul shed;
she's in the ground, she's in the air,
and as her blood once thrilled
at hearing exotic tales of travel
to places that she could never see,
now she travels in a slow, millenial
circulation around the continents,
pulled by the sun and moon, and now
she knows what Ocean really means."

—Lucy A. Snyder, *"Photograph of a Lady, Circa 1890"*

February 13

Cedar Hill Division of Police
Homicide Unit
Inter-Office Memo

From: Bill Emerson
To: Ben Littlejohn

Hey, Pard:

First of all, happy Valentine's Day. Sorry I don't
have a box of chocolates for you, but here's a little
present, nonetheless. Montrose homicide decided to
overnight this to us instead of faxing it piecemeal like
they've been doing. I guess they were sick of me calling
them half a dozen times a day (I can be a big pain in
the you-know-what, no surprise to you, I'm guessing).
I have their guarantee that this is a "full and complete
copy" of the contents of the envelope they found taped
to the bottom of the desk drawer. Tell you the truth,
after reading this I don't know what the hell to think.
I should also warn you that they had extra sets of photographs made, and the Polaroids are even worse than
the few they made public right after it happened.
Cap'n Goldstein informs me that after we all have ourselves a look-see, this stuff is to be sealed and never
opened again, case closed, cha-cha-cha. The investigation is now officially in limbo and, considering what
you're going to find in here, maybe it's best that some
cases be left alone. I don't know. Didn't sleep too well
last night after finishing it. The Polaroids in particular
are pretty gruesome. Considering that you and Cheryl
just found out about her being preggies (congratula-
tions, by the way!), it maybe wouldn't be the greatest

idea for you to look at them. But you're a big boy, you can make your own decisions. Okay, that's it for me, pal; by the time you're reading this tomorrow, Eunice and me will be on our way to London. She's really looking forward to the trip and keeps reminding me that I haven't had a vacation in four years. I hope I enjoy it; from what I understand, they serve their beer room-temperature over there. Oh, joy.

You know what gets to me the most? I talked with this guy maybe four, five times and not once did my yo-yo alarm go off.

Maybe, to quote Danny Glover from any of the *Lethal Weapon* movies, I'm getting too old for this s—t.

Bill

Chapter One

To whoever eventually finds this, please understand this one thing above all else: I never intended to do harm.

But I guess that Philosophy 101 adage is true: No snowflake in an avalanche ever feels responsible.

When I was a young boy and sick with fever my mother would sit at my bedside and read stories, usually fairy tales or mysteries. I preferred fairy tales but she liked mysteries the best—especially Sherlock Holmes and Raymond Chandler—because they were, she said, like a flower: "Imagine that the solution is what's at the center of the flower, but you can't get to it yet because the bell has to bloom and the petals have to open one by one. I always like to think of it that way: The truth is the fruit in the middle of the flower."

Whenever she said that, my gaze would inevitably wander to the various sets of nesting dolls that she collected and that littered my childhood home; if there was an empty space on the mantel, a bureau, table, or bookshelf, my mother would fill that space with her nesting dolls.

It wasn't until later, after I had grown into something resembling a responsible adult and gotten married to a woman who shared my mother's fascination with the *little mothers*, that I learned the proper term for them was *matryoshka* dolls.

Still, the more I thought about it while sick with fever (and I had been a sickly child, seemingly always in bed with a fever, infection, migraine, or some injury sustained during a game of football or tag of simply tossing a Frisbee), I realized that my mother's interpretation of the mystery flower could just as well be applied to her *matryoshka* dolls: Imagine the solution is the final, smallest doll contained within all the others, but you can't yet get to it because the rest of them have to be disassembled one by one.

Such taxing metaphors often proved to be too much for my young mind, so I would ask her to read something from the Brothers Grimm or Hans Christian Andersen and would lose myself in the worlds of *Once Upon a Time*.

The myriad deceptions inherent in "Once Upon a Time" are seductive even to adults, for the phrase implies no boundaries to the possibilities of events. In a "Once Upon a Time" world anything can happen . . . except, of course, to you. I used to wonder at what point in our childhoods we came to realize and accept that those four words led us into worlds that never existed, introduced us to people who never were, and described adventures that never happened, and so had no significant bearing on our actual lives.

As a child I longed for "Once Upon a Time."

As an adult I dismissed it.

Now I have no choice but to embrace it.

Look, over there, and whisper to yourself: *Once Upon a Time* . . .

* * *

In Silent Graves

A small group of ghost children moved across the street under the diffuse silver light of the October moon, bags in one hand, flashlights in the other, each giggling in anticipation at the treasures waiting for them—the chocolate bars, the bubble gum, the licorice sticks, and the who-can-imagine-what wonders—as they chanted: "Tonight is the night when dead leaves fly/Like witches on switches across the sky. . . ."

The man in the park stared at them, then shook his head and glared downward as if the ground were the sole source of his troubles.

Of all the lamebrained and half-assed pearls of so-called wisdom that turned a person's intellectual landscape into the razed ruins of Dresden after the war, none, the man decided, was more imbecilic than "You have to take the bad with the good"—may the person or persons who dreamed up *that* one languish in Purgatory or wherever it was God (or whoever was in charge of this freak show) sent those whose propensity for new buzzwords and catchphrases reduced the mass IQ to less than a child's shoe size.

The bad with the good. Uh-huh.

And so he sat on this bench in Dell Memorial Park on this Halloween night stewing over the argument he'd found waiting for him when he arrived home from work forty minutes ago, trying his best not to get annoyed with the sights and sounds of the trick-or-treaters as they made their happy way from house to house, noting with amusement that there were even some adults and teenagers who'd donned masks and costumes, much to the delight of the younger ones.

He watched them for a few moments, his annoyance transforming into gratitude; at least they gave him something else with which to occupy his thoughts for the moment.

And now as I look on that still figure, the me of a mere thirty-seven days ago, as I look down through the darkening tunnel of nearly 3,200,000 seconds, I cannot smile at him. He embarrasses me. He fills me with sorrow. He shames me. I regret the things he did and the things he did not do; I shake my head in pity for the things he didn't see happening and for the things he should have seen coming. I blush at his desires. I can no longer share—let alone understand—most of his dreams. The child may be the father of the man but who is to say we must love our children, even as we sit next to their sick bed reading flower mysteries or fairy tales?

I wish I could say that I miss him.

How to convey some sense of what he was like?

His name was Robert Alan Londrigan. He was two months shy of his thirty-ninth birthday. He made his living as a television news reporter at a local network affiliate station. He liked pepperoni and extra cheese on his pizzas, when he had them. He had never once cheated on his wife, even though a few women had made offers (and despite his having been dangerously tempted once). He used to play the flute in his high school orchestra. He didn't like the smell of onions. Physically, he was in better condition than were most men in their late thirties. He was neither as handsome as he wished nor as homely as he feared. He had never killed anyone or anything, save for the occasional spider or silverfish that found its way into the house.

But enough of this; it's best we return to *Once Upon a Time* and join him as . . .

. . . the first group of ghost children disappeared behind a row of trees that lined the sidewalk, another, smaller group of creatures emerged and moved stealthily along; there were devils in this batch, werewolves and misshapen monstrosities from recent horror movies followed by a princess or two who looked over their shoulders at the fast-approaching vampire brigade, all of them continuing the previous chant: "Tonight is the night when pumpkins stare/Through sheaves and leaves everywhere . . ."

Deciding to wish them joy and many happy frights, unaware of the dozens of glowing pumpkin eyes that watched him from a distance, Robert turned his attention back to the irritations at hand.

Denise had been livid about the lead story for the six P.M. broadcast: An anencephalic baby had been born to a young couple in Florida who wanted the infant taken off life support, but then the Adopters—a fanatical fringe group who claimed association with the local Pro-Life organization—had petitioned the courts to stop the parents from doing so, their justification being that the baby could not speak for itself so they, being Good Christians With A Conscience, would speak on its behalf. The court decreed that the baby could only be taken off life support if officially pronounced brain-dead; the hospital's legal spokesperson pointed out that in order for the baby to be pronounced brain-dead it first had to *physically possess* a brain. The parents were both zombies at this point and the doctors were screaming for immediate action so the baby's organs could be harvested for desperately needed transplant material; if that weren't enough, attorneys for the Pro-Life organization emphatically denied that the petitioners were in any way affiliated with their organization and filed for a restraining order to stop ". . . the damaging, unsolicited, ill-advised, and potentially life-threatening actions" of the Adopters. Yes, it was a perverted circus but it was also a golden story, a heaven-sent ratings grabber if ever there was one, and though Robert's heart broke for the poor child and its parents, he was enough of a news professional to know an opportunity when one presented itself.

Vulture Culture; show the viewing public photographs of a mass slaughter and convince them they were looking at pretty pictures drawn by their kindergarten child.

In this business, you either accepted that or staked out your spot on the unemployment line.

No sooner had he come through the door than Denise was in his face:

"*Why* didn't you call and warn me?"

19

"There wasn't time. The story broke fifteen minutes before we went on air."

"Goddammit, Bobby, you *know* how that sort of thing upsets me!" This said not with whining self-pity but a hard edge of disgust that betrayed the fear both of them had been living with ever since the doctor had given them the news.

Denise was in her sixth month of pregnancy. Robert made it a point to call her every night before the six P.M. broadcast (the only one she ever watched) and warn her if there were any stories about abandoned babies or abused children or any such prime-news-time horrors. Her pregnancy had not, thus far, been an easy one; on top of the hormonal typhoon rampaging through her body, she was saddled with an all too delicate frame and an even more tenuous immune system that was often forced to critical mass just to fight off a mild cold; the last thing she needed was any type of news story to remind her just how terrible life could be to a helpless child. Sure, maybe he was being a little overprotective of her—or maybe he was just a closet sexist jerk who believed that a pregnant woman was incapable of handling any amount of stress—but her mood swings were becoming so abrupt and fiercely extreme that he was afraid to tell her anything even *remotely* unpleasant.

This baby was too important to both of them: In the six years they had been married, Denise had suffered two miscarriages, both in the fourth month. Robert would have swum a hundred raging rivers and then walked across a field of broken glass in bare feet to make sure she carried this baby to term.

They both so wanted a family.

He'd looked at her and sighed. "I'm sorry, all right? I know that doesn't make things easier for you—and I sure as hell know it doesn't do anything to lessen the shock of seeing us lead with that story—but I swear, hon, I *swear* to you there wasn't time for me to call."

She sat down at the kitchen table, her hands clasped tightly together as if in prayer, and took several deep, calming breaths. "Why did you have to lead with it?"

"You're kidding, right?"

"Three guesses."

"We couldn't *not* lead with it! It's not every day that a baby is born without a brain and—"

"And it's *sick*, Bobby! The way everyone pounces on this sort of thing, cheapening someone's tragedy like that."

"It's *news*, Denise, okay? Look, I don't dictate human nature—"

"I never said you did."

He paused, taking a deep breath, calming himself. "Don't you think something like this breaks my heart, too? Christ, hon, if you think the video we used was bad, you should've seen the stuff we *didn't* run. The affiliate station in Florida actually managed to get tape of the baby itself, and it was . . ." He shook his head. "It was awful, just . . . awful."

"Vulture Culture?" she whispered.

"You know it."

"Then why not just slap a keyhole-shaped lens onto the camera? It's the same principle. You've said yourself that it's not really news anymore, it's showbiz, entertainment, the more shocking, the better. God! Don't you ever feel like you're helping to create a nation of voyeurs?"

"People were voyeuristic long before I started in this business."

"You want to argue semantics now? Fine, you may not have *created* the status quo, but I don't see you doing anything to stop perpetuating it."

"Like what? Refuse to do the piece? You looked at our bills lately? This house? You think you could live any other way than to what you've become accustomed?"

She glared at him. "Don't make this about money, Bobby. I grew up poor and so did you—"

"That's *right!* That is *absolutely* right! I *did* grow up poor and I have no passionate desire to return to the government cheese

21

line or to hunker down to protect the family's food stamps like they were the fucking Rosetta Stone!"

Denise shook her head. "Are you ever going to let go of that? You think it cloaks you in some kind of saintly nobility that you grew up in near poverty? Maybe once, a long time ago, sure, maybe, but *now* . . . now you're just like me, Bobby—*spoiled.* More than spoiled—jaded, when you get right down to it. Maybe even worse than jaded . . . indifferent . . . numb. I can't tell anymore and at times like this I'm not sure I should even care."

That one hurt, but he didn't want to let it show. Why had the argument even gone *this* far? She knew (didn't she?) how much he loved her, how much her just *existing* made him joyous over every morning, every breath.

"Don't upset yourself like this, Denise, all right? You know what the doctor said about stress and—"

"And there's my loving husband right there in high-definition digital, in front of God and everyone, well groomed and oh, so handsome, inviting us all to come and gawk . . ."

He tried explaining to her about Jeffries, how central Ohio's most popular news icon was in New York interviewing for a network position (one he would certainly be offered, judging from the way the network had been courting him), and how his departure would leave the weeknight anchor position wide open; even though the station was trying out various reporters in different slots, it was common knowledge that Robert was the front-runner to step into Jeffries's shoes—providing that he used this week to show his Stuff.

"Denise, honey, please—don't look away, okay? Please, listen to me. Look, the first three stories of the night were the anencephalic baby, then a couple in Mount Vernon who spent their last five dollars on lottery tickets and hit the twenty-seven-million-dollar jackpot, and the city council zoning vote. Openings like that are the equivalent of handing an anchor the Holy Grail because those three stories, in *that* order, gave me the chance to go from deadly serious to annoyingly light to professionally efficient—all in under six minutes! An anchorman *has* to be able to turn it on and off like that, to make those quick transitions—studies show that viewers' moods while watching the news are often shaped by the tone of voice the newscaster uses. And I showed 'em, hon—God, how I showed them! It was the best news broadcast I've ever done and everyone at the station tonight *knew it*. This may sound crass, but in a twisted way that poor baby's pathetic plight may be one of the best things that ever happened to us."

He knew those last words were a mistake even as they were coming out of his mouth, but he'd been too full of himself to stop talking.

Denise didn't buy his spin on the baby's plight and accused him once again of not wanting to have a child with her—an old chestnut that she'd been pulling out since the third month whenever she wanted to get his attention.

Robert—tired, hungry, with the beginnings of a monster headache—snapped back at her: "You think I don't want us to have a family? God! Okay, you want to start throwing around accusations? Try this—why didn't you tell me you'd stopped taking the pill?"

"So I was right, you don't want this baby!"

"*Of course* I want it, I want us to have a family, but I thought it was something we were trying for *together*. You're the one who stopped taking the pill and then sprung it on me—"

"I wanted it to be a surprise!"

"I hate surprises—you could have at least let me know that you were off it, then maybe—ah, hell, this is getting nowhere. Believe it or not, I love you more than God—I know it's kind of hard to tell right now but let's face it, you're not exactly all warm fuzziness yourself."

Then things went from bad to worse when one of the cats rubbed up against his leg: "And what about the *cats*, huh? You *know* I'm allergic to them but you chose to keep them anyway

23

and now I have to take so much goddamn allergy medication every day I feel like a walking pharmacy!"

"Don't you *dare* throw that back at me again! I was willing to get rid of them but you said no!"

"I would've felt guilty, you know that!"

On and on and on, spite and hurtful words standing in for reason and emotional support while they fought about everything except what was truly bothering them: *Six months and counting, fingers crossed and a prayer on the lips* . . .

Finally it got so damned ridiculous they couldn't stand the sight of each other, so Robert grabbed his coat, stormed out of the house, and after two drinks on an empty stomach at a favorite neighborhood watering hole, found himself here, at the park, on a bench, stewing at the sight and sounds of the Halloween trick-or-treaters as they made their happy way from house to house.

A group of costumed teens were taking a shortcut through the park. Robert took little notice of them, only looking up when a lone straggler, evidently in no hurry to catch up with his friends, made his way past. The kid's mask was a macabre delight; it looked as if someone had cleaved his skull open with an axe, then reassembled bone fragments from his shattered face into a crazy-quilt, jigsaw-puzzle grotesquerie that bore only the most passing resemblance to a human face. It was actually kind of impressive, if you went in for that sort of thing.

"That's a helluva mask," Robert said as the kid strode past.

"Go fuck yourself, Willy," snarled the kid, then sprinted away.

Robert was frozen with, of all things, embarrassment.

Damnit to hell—maybe he hadn't fallen under the moon spell of the Halloween around him, but that kid had now shattered *any* hope of enjoying things.

So Robert went back to his stewing.

In less tense times, Denise would have called it pouting, then told him how much his pouting turned her on, so go 'head, pout some more, oh, yeah, baby, *pout* for me. . . .

He almost laughed but stopped himself from doing so, a form of punishment for the abominable way he'd behaved toward her; so he leaned forward, elbows on his knees, face in his hands: Portrait of a Would-Be Celebrity Contemplating His Sins.

"A goblin lives in our house, in *our* house, in OUR house," sang another group of ghost children.

Robert paid them no mind.

Was he really being so selfish? He'd worked his ass off to get this far; the fluff pieces used as filler at noon and five-thirty, filling in at the weekend and late-night desks, biting the bullet, and learning how to engage in "friendly banter" with the various (and usually vapid) coanchors like some sort of acting-class improvisation exercise . . . he *deserved* this shot. Okay, yeah, maybe there was an element of ego fulfillment involved here—how *couldn't* there be?—but mostly he wanted the anchor job because it would ensure a good life for his wife and child, for *his family*.

So why did he feel like some kind of peep-show barker?

He sat up straight, stared across the park at another group or trick-or-treaters, and cursed himself for trying to reconcile his desire for advancement with the tragedy of that baby and its parents. But reporting the news was his job; how could Denise blame him for wanting to make maximum impact? Okay, he could have had one of the interns give her a call when he realized he wouldn't have time to do so himself, but things had been so hectic and wired and he'd been so *pumped* for the broadcast, psyching himself up for what he knew might be one of the most important hours of his career and—

—and you just didn't think about her, admit it.

"Selfish, stupid *prick*," he said, evidently a bit too loud for the old woman on the footpath a few yards away, out for a pleasant October evening stroll to watch the young ones and remember when she herself had gone joyously from house to house, bag and flashlight in hand; she stopped at the sound of Robert's voice, frowned at him, then, with a disapproving shake of her head, continued on.

Gary A. Braunbeck

Just a fount of charm today, aren't you, Bobby-Boy?

Then: *Good thing she wasn't around when Split-Face wished me a good evening.*

He rose to his feet, turned in her direction, and opened his mouth to offer an apology but it stuck in his throat.

He blinked, looked away, then back.

There was now more than one sad and stooped old woman ambling along the footpath; trailing behind her like a succession of ghosts were other women, some older, some younger, each dimly visible, each more diaphanous than the last.

One used a walker, one didn't; one wore tattered clothes that looked to have been purchased at a Goodwill store while the next was adorned in sable and pearls; trailing behind her, so confident and healthy that her bloom was still visible, another woman—this one obviously younger than the others—strode with jaunty energy, her eyes filled with mischief and wonder; the woman after, pitiful and emaciated, shambled slowly forward, brittle hands knotted against aged, sagging breasts, eyes unfocused, lines on her face harshened by shadows and age spots; sauntering dreamily behind her, arm in arm with a true love only she could see, the next lady smiled as she stared adoringly at the invisible gentleman with her, obviously still in love with him after so many, many years; then came women who were younger, still, though Robert could only tell this by their shapes rather than visible features because the parade was becoming more and more indistinct, bits of mist, until, at last, small shapes, delicate shapes, ghost-children shapes trailed at the end, more wisps of memory than anything else.

Yet Robert could tell there was something *uniform* about all the women and shapes, a similarity in the facial structure of those whose features he could see, a sameness in stride and gesture in those whose forms became less corporeal.

Sisters, maybe?

Before logic could kick in and remind him that several of the shapes were more spirit than sisterlike (and therefore probably a construct of a mind and body that had consumed only two Crown Royals in the last nine hours), the first woman, the old woman who'd been so offended at Robert's calling himself a prick, stopped on the footpath and turned to face the others.

The air changed—nothing cataclysmic, mind you, no great wind suddenly thundered across the park, assaulting everything in its path and howling with Wagnerian might—but there was nonetheless a sudden sense of *density* in the atmosphere; Robert was suddenly *too* aware of the sound made by the October leaves as the wind scattered them across the footpath; the dry whisper of sorrow, the crackle of old regrets stepping out of dark corners and pulling at him with skeletal fingers, all of it cast in shimmering silver by the moonlight of a cold, cold heaven: Everything around him appeared inverted suddenly, inside out and upside down, a reflection trapped in the arc of a polished spoon—

—and the first old woman was no longer at the end of the footpath but right next to him, with the rest of the spirit parade approaching her, and Robert grew dizzy and disoriented as the procession dwindled by degrees with each step they took until, at last, they dissolved into the flesh of the disapproving old woman—yet her face, like some holograph, held traces of all of them: A slight tilt of her head, and there was the fourth old woman; a subtle nod, and one of the younger women was there, along with the older, decrepit ones and the wisps of memory that were the little-mist girls.

Robert was too stunned and too frightened to move, speak, or even breathe; when his chest tightened and his lungs threatened to implode, when his legs began to buckle, when his vision began to blur and the park spin, only then did he look away from the impossible spectacle and grab the back of the bench to cement himself in what he hoped was still reality.

You're tired, your conscience is playing tricks on you, and you're also a bit drunk and don't want to admit it and this is just your body's way of telling you to get your sad act together, pal.

He felt as if he had not moved in a very long time and began to stir but his head felt light and as distant as his hands and feet, each perceived action so slow and murky it seemed to never end. He felt as if he were sending signals to his limbs while standing outside himself. Something hitched deep inside, he felt it, and for a moment was shocked by an image of himself running through heavy air, the neighborhood a passing blur, his features contorted into a mask of fear that would have made even Split-Face turn away in revulsion. He blinked, bit down on his lip, and saw the hazy silhouette of the old woman standing in front of him.

Everywhere in his body there was sudden, extravagant pain, more pain than he thought he could ever endure without succumbing to death or unconsciousness, but that wasn't the worst of it, no, not by a long shot; embracing this pain, enshrouding it, sepulcherlike and impervious and tinged with despair, was a wishfulness, a longing, a *want* beyond comprehension; a need so desolate, fed by a loneliness so absolute and merciless that he would almost rather have died than endure one more millisecond of it.

He struck out, blindly.

He cried out, silently.

The density surrounding him disappeared, wrenching the pressure from his chest and allowing him to fall onto the bench, pulling in great, liberating breaths of crisp autumn-night air.

Shuddering and groaning, he blinked tears from his eyes and doubled over, pressing his arms against his stomach.

". . . a goblin lives in our house, in *our* house, in OUR house . . ."

He looked up and caught sight of some tiny trick-or-treaters across the street.

". . . a goblin lives in *our* house, all the year round . . ."

There.

The world had righted itself.

And there was only one old woman, alone, stoop-shouldered

28

and smiling to herself as she made her way along the footpath to the far end of the park, out for a pleasant evening stroll and enjoying the sights and sounds of the young ones.

As if sensing his gaze, she turned and gave him a small, almost imperceptible wave, the kind that, between close friends, says, *We have a secret, you and I, and with this gesture I seal our bond.* Then she went about her pleasant, stoop-shouldered, Halloween-night business.

Of all things, it was the wave that set off an alarm in Robert's head; there was something *cold* about it, distant and pitiless—

". . . he bumps and he jumps and he thumps right at midnight . . ."

—and maybe he was just having a panic attack for no god-damned good reason but he could swear there had been something almost *threatening* in the gesture—

". . . a goblin lives in *our* house . . ."

—the old woman disappeared along a curve in the footpath that wound behind some trees—

". . . all the year round . . ."

—and a moment later Split-Face stepped onto the exact same spot in the path—

—and waved.

"So, Willy," said Split-Face, "let you and me be wipers of scores out with all men . . ."

And with those words there came to Robert a vision, brief and hallucinatory, of dozens, maybe hundreds of children, all of them wearing masks even more grotesque than the one Split-Face wore, and they were surrounding him, reaching for him, calling for him, crushing him under their Need—

—somewhere in the darkness, a child let fly with three whistled notes, each more discordant and shrill than the one before—

—and with the fading of the third note, the vision abandoned him.

Panic seized Robert, pulled him to his feet and slapped his

face, then kicked him in the ass and sent him half stumbling, half running out of the park toward his house four blocks away.

The neighborhood blurred as he sped along.

The air was thick and weighty.

Heart trip-hammering against his chest, Robert took the front steps three at a time and discovered that Denise had turned off all the lights to keep away the trick-or-treaters and then locked the door, engaging the dead bolt, as well. Sweating and shaking, Robert fumbled his keys from his pocket, dropped them, cursed under his breath, and grabbed them off the porch; then it was inside, the door left standing open behind him, through the hallway, banging his leg against the phone stand and calling her name, hearing a weak, ragged reply from upstairs.

He ran up to her, almost skidding into the wall when he hit the landing, and slammed open the bedroom door.

Denise lay half on the floor, half on the bed, sweating and convulsing, dressed only in a thin nightshirt, her skin a hideous ashen shade. She looked at him and coughed up a small spray of blood and mucus that slopped onto her cheek. Robert ran over to her and knelt down, trying to be gentle as he cradled her in his arms and tried to get her either fully on the floor or back onto the bed, but she shook her head and placed a trembling hand against his chest, her eyes moving to the phone receiver that swung back and forth from the bedside table, and as he began moving her Robert asked, "Did you call already?" and she nodded, slowly, wincing from the pain as he touched her face; he felt how cold she was, then kissed her forehead and made the last series of movements that would have her back on the bed but he was too panicked, he didn't quite have the balance he thought, the angle was all wrong and he slipped and both of them tumbled to the floor and Denise threw back her head to scream but couldn't, all that emerged was a sickening sound like a deflating balloon that turned her face red the pain was so intense, and as the sound of sirens sliced through the night Robert stared helplessly at his wife's gaping mouth and straining vocal cords and thought, *If she can just scream she'll be all right, I know it, so please, please scream,* but no further sounds came from her as she hitched, spasmed, spat up more blood, then lost consciousness. A few moments later there was the sound of several pairs of feet on the porch and a voice calling into the house and Robert screamed, "Get in here—*Jesus God,* get in here *now!*" and it seemed like an eternity before the paramedics made it up the stairs and came into the room and shoved him aside, two of them going to work on Denise while a third readied the gurney and radioed in Denise's vitals.

We have a secret, you and I, and with this gesture . . .

Robert ran outside and down the steps behind them, oblivious of the small crowd of costumed shadows that had gathered to look on, then jumped in his car, gunned the engine, and followed the ambulance as it sped toward the hospital. Once there, he tried to get to her as she was rolled through the automatic doors; he tried to get a glimpse of Denise's face, hoping that she could see him here and know that he would not leave her alone, not during a time like this, but he only saw the IV and EKG hookups that the paramedics had connected en route.

Inside, it was a storm of rushing white lab coats and powder-blue uniforms as the doctors and nurses rolled her into an exam room. Her EKG was erratic as hell and Robert felt less than useless as he watched the team go at his wife with such skill, efficiency, and speed it seemed unreal; before he could regroup and register what was happening a piercing, keening noise sounded and was quickly muted by a nurse as a sweating doctor in the middle of the group yelled for a crash cart and then Robert was shoved aside by another nurse who rolled the machine past him and the doctor in the middle of the chaos grabbed the defibrillator paddles. "Clear!" Then Robert was pressing fisted hands against his mouth as the electricity shot through Denise's body, causing her to jerk and wriggle and bounce in a way that might have been comical if he was watching it in some movie comedy or television show but here only made him want to scream. He didn't understand enough about emergency medical procedures to know if what they were doing was safe for the baby—unless it had been decided that the child was a lost cause and they were doing everything they could to save the mother, instead—but he suddenly, more than anything in the world, more than anything ever in his life, wanted Denise and the baby to live, to be all right, to be his family so he could make up for all the little selfish acts that had made her feel she was peripheral to his world rather than intrinsic to it. Please live, *please*, and he asked forgiveness for all the small, everyday, thoughtless hurts he'd inflicted on her, be they real or imagined, begged forgiveness and salvation from a God he wasn't sure he believed in anymore, just, *please*, he needed them, needed for them to be allowed to live so he could make everything up to her, to them, he'd no longer ignore her needs, he'd even find a new line of work if she wanted him to, they'd be okay, they'd get by, they could make new plans, together, as a family, just let them live and—

"Do you really think we're ready to be parents?" he heard the ghost of his voice ask her after they'd gotten the news. "I don't know about you, but after the last couple of times . . . well, you know, that kind of responsibility scares holy hell out of me."

"Oh, no, you don't," Denise replied, playfully smacking his arm. "A little late for that now. All my life I've dreamed of meeting a man I'd love enough to want to have children with; just my luck that when I do, he develops a retroactive case of Peter Pan Syndrome."

"It'll be fine this time."

"I hope so. I'll pray for it."

"I know you will."

She took his hand in hers. "You'll come around someday. Meantime, I think I've got enough faith to cover both of us in that department."

He hadn't been able to tell her, then, that he was worried he'd make the same thoughtless mistakes with their child that both of their parents had made with—

"Flatline."

An unseen saber slashed open Robert's center.

The doctor applied the paddles again—nothing. Robert felt a cry clog the back of his throat and fought to swallow it down, down, down, *calm down, breathe steady, that's it, c'mon, Doc, do it again, make it work this time, c'mon, c'mon . . .*

He watched, numbed and horrified, as a gleaming scalpel appeared in someone's hand and swooped down like a bird of prey, the incision made, the blood flowing, and suddenly the doctor had his hand inside Denise's opened chest, massaging her heart, and Robert caught a glimpse of white vein beneath membrane—

"Oh, *God*," someone said.

Oozing, something was oozing from between Denise's legs; a dense, sickening, clotted glop of pinkish red meat trapped in a crawling flow of black blood, water, and something that had the texture and consistency of cottage cheese.

Robert glimpsed part of a tiny face, then another doctor was bending down between Denise's legs, gloved hand reaching inside her.

The other doctor slumped his shoulders, then pulled his hands from Denise's chest—

—sudden but slow movement, and suddenly Robert saw between Denise's legs—

—the silhouette of a nose, a section of what might have been its chin—

the EKG was snapped off—

—Denise's body began to deflate, it seemed—

—the room spun—

—and Robert elbowed his way through the ER staff toward his wife and child.

He could hear the voice of a news announcer as somewhere in the waiting room a television set blared away: ". . . in Florida born without a brain died a little after nine-thirty this evening. Doctors say that, due to the spread of infection, its organs are now useless and so they will not attempt to harvest . . ."

Gary A. Braunbeck

Robert saw his child, its impossibly large head, and heard himself whisper, "It's got two brains, that's why it's like that, you see." He looked around at the staring eyes of the doctors and nurses. "There's been a screwup somewhere, you understand, and my—*our* baby, it has the Florida baby's brain, too, you know?" He approached the doctor who'd given Denise open-heart massage and gripped one of his bloody-gloved hands. "It . . . it has an extra brain, see, so all you have to do is just . . . just take it out, okay? Everything will be fine if you'll just take out that extra brain. Please? Just take it out. Just . . . take . . . it . . . *out.* . . ."

Someone gently took his arm, leading him to an office near the end of the corridor; once inside, they shoved a Styrofoam cup filled with hot, bitter coffee into his hands and eased him down into a cushioned chair as a solemn-faced doctor entered and looked at him with something that was supposed to be sympathy but more resembled pity.

Robert sipped at his coffee and wept quietly. He felt as if his metabolism had somehow been altered in these last few minutes. His body was slow, heavy, awkward, cold—as if the force of gravity had been increased slightly. His face felt like a pillow attached to the front of his head, with small tubes placed for his eyes and mouth. He had no peripheral vision whatsoever, and when he heard himself mumble something—who knew what?—his voice sounded at first densely muffled and then hollow and echoing. Voices surrounded him as if there were people in another room adjacent to this one, separated only by a thin paper wall. Foregrounds and backgrounds shifted erratically, making him dizzy, confused, wanting desperately to go back and find Denise sitting up and very much alive so he could touch her, kiss her cheek, take her hand, and apologize for all the things he promised her that never saw fruition, but most of all he wanted to go back and take away the fear and pain of her last moments; she'd died alone and confused, with no familiar face near and that seemed so cruel . . .

So, as the doctor talked, Robert cried; for all the holidays he and Denise would never celebrate, for every disappointment she'd ever experienced, every joy that was dampened, every hope that was spoiled, all the things she wanted to do but never did and now never would . . . he cried for all of it.

A cough, a sniff, a deep breath, and he fumbled the half-crumpled pack of cigarettes from his pocket. He'd sworn to Denise that he'd quit weeks ago—and he'd had every intention of quitting before the baby was born—but he'd been so anxious lately, what with the baby coming and all the brouhaha over Jeffries leaving and who was going to get the anchor slot . . . Besides, he never smoked around Denise, he wasn't that self-absorbed. She'd understand, he was sure of that.

He stared at the cigarette he held between his index and middle fingers. Across the desk, the doctor nodded his head and produced an ashtray from a drawer, along with a half-empty bottle of some single-malt scotch. As Robert lit his cigarette the doctor—whose nameplate identified him as D.S. Steinman—poured a dash of liquor into Robert's coffee, cleared his throat, and said, "We have a secret, you and I."

Robert started, blinked, spluttered out a stream of smoke, and said, "Wh-what? What'd you say?"

"I asked if you're willing to sign the necessary forms."

Robert took a sip of the scotch-laced coffee, then looked at his hands and for some reason thought of the Florida baby's parents. What was there for them to cling to now? All that suffering, and what good did any of it do? Whose pain was eased? What purpose was served?

"It looked like something that floats," he said.

Steinman remained silent.

Robert swallowed. Twice. Very hard. "What forms?"

"Organ donation consent."

He glared at the doctor.

Vulture Culture. You learned to live with it.

Steinman chewed on one of his thumbnails for a moment,

then pulled his hand away and said, "We're a little pressed for time, Mr. Londrigan. I don't mean to seem morbid or cold-hearted—and I can't even begin to imagine the pain you're in right now—but there are people who urgently need what only you can give them right now. What this could do for the children on the list *alone* . . ." He held up a computer printout. "There's a one-month-old girl in Philadelphia who needs a liver transplant, another baby that was seriously burned in Bloomington needs a skin graft, another has to have—"

"Enough. God, enough," said Robert, wiping his eyes.

Steinman tapped a finger against his watch. "I don't mean to pressure you, Mr. Londrigan, but—look, fetal tissue is the perfect transplant material; it bonds instantly and the body won't reject it, but it's useless once infection sets in. In a case of hydrocephalus, that happens very, very quickly. I am more sorry than I can possibly express about your loss, and I know how crass I must appear—if not outright ghoulish—at this moment, but please understand that there are adults and children who've been waiting months—often years—for donors such as your wife and daughter and—"

"It was a girl?"

Steinman paused, then sadly nodded his head.

Robert felt one corner of his mouth start to turn upward. "Denise wanted a girl. Huh. Whatta you know."

Steinman flexed his right hand, obviously impatient and trying not to show it. "Look, Mr. Londrigan, I—"

"Do it. Do it. Cut them open and take whatever you need, whatever's useful—skin, bones, eyes—it had her eyes, did you see that? Take whatever you want. I'll sign the forms." A pause, then: "Denise'd kick my ass up between my shoulders if I didn't."

"Are you certain?"

"Yes, goddammit! And don't look at me like that; I'm not acting under duress and there are no visions of malpractice suits dancing in my head. I know you did everything you could to save her—to save *them*. Dr. Bishop told us it was going to be a rough pregnancy, what with the two previous miscarriages. I just never thought that . . . Ah, hell, never mind. Gimme the things."

Steinman, grim-faced but relieved, pushed the papers toward him.

Robert, deadened, signed them all.

"This is a wonderful thing you're doing," said the doctor. "Think of it as keeping some part of your wife and child alive."

"Take the bad with the good, huh?" Robert shoved the signed forms across the desk, threw down the pen, and stood—albeit unsteadily. "I want to see my family."

But they had already been taken away.

Robert wandered out into the ER's waiting room and sat down, too stunned to think. People moved by him one minute as if in slow motion, the next as if in double time. It occurred to him that he really ought to be calling people—his sister, his parents (Denise had been an only child, and both her parents were gone, her mother having died just after last Thanksgiving), the station, *someone*—but, just as in the park earlier, he couldn't get his body to obey his brain's commands. What the hell could anyone do about it now, anyway? Denise would have waited until morning to start making the necessary calls. "No use in ruining their evening," she'd say, always considerate of others, even if they did not show the same concern for her.

Robert sat back in the chair, took a few more swigs of the scotch and coffee, and stared up at the television mounted on the wall. Some mystery movie was playing now; Andy Griffith (as yet another small-town sheriff) was in a graveyard with several deputies, none of them Don Knotts. The camera moved in for a close-up of a headstone whose inscription could not be read.

That'll be all of us someday, he thought. Sure, there would be mourners at the end, friends, family, old lovers you thought had forgotten about you, maybe someone you once had a crush on in ninth grade, and they would gather, and they would weep, and they would talk among themselves afterward and say, "I remember the way he used to . . ." Your belongings would be divided, given away, or tossed on a fire, your picture moved to the back of a dusty photo album, and, eventually, those left behind would die too, and no one would remain to remember your face, your middle name, even the location of your grave. The seasons would change, the elements would set to work, rain and heat and cold and snow would smooth away the inscription on the headstone until it was no longer legible, and then, later—days, weeks, decades—someone who happened by for whatever reason would glance down, see the faded words and dates, mutter, "I wonder who's buried here," then go on about their business. No one would be left to say that this man was important, or this woman was kind, or that anything they strove for was worthwhile.

He had no idea how long he'd been sitting there when Steinman came up to him and wordlessly put a hand on his shoulder.

Robert took a last sip of his now ice-cold coffee, then looked up. He opened his mouth to speak—he was certain of that, of opening his mouth . . . yes, of that much he was sure—but nothing would come out; it was still as if every functioning organ in his body had been stolen away without his noticing, leaving only this ineffective, meaningless shell.

"One of the nurses paged me when she saw you were still here," said Steinman.

Robert managed to stammer: "Wh-what . . . what time . . . How long have I been here?"

"It's been about two hours since your wife and daughter were sent down."

Sent down. What a nebulous way to put it.

Robert wiped his eyes, then began patting himself down in search of his car keys. "I, uh . . . I'm sorry, it's just that I . . ."

Steinman took a seat next to him. "Take all the time you need, Mr. Londrigan."

Robert nodded his head, not really hearing Steinman's words.

"You know, I told her that I loved her more than God, then had the nerve to feel hurt when it didn't make her swoon. If I'd've been thinking, I would have realized that she knew I don't really believe in God, so I was basically telling her that I loved her more than nothing." A bitter laugh, tinged with anger. "Am I every woman's dream hubby, or what?"

The two men sat in silence for another minute, perhaps two, and then Steinman slowly got to his feet, pulling Robert up with him. "Don't say anything or make a scene, Mr. Londrigan, please."

"You throwing me out?"

"Not at all, just . . . Look, please follow me, all right?"

"Where—"

"Please. Just come with me. Now."

It took every last ounce of strength he could muster to get fully to his feet and follow Steinman, but it was something to do, a purpose of sorts, a direction for a directionless soul to take, forcing him to concentrate on physically getting himself from one place to another. As they walked, he now and again was moved to reflect on his situation—to the effect that he already regarded himself as half removed, as partially absent, from the activity (life?) going on around him. He tried to get himself to believe that it was literally true, that if at this moment he were to be photographed, when the film was developed it would probably reveal only his outline, or maybe it would show him to be merely a gray, semitransparent shadow.

They stopped outside of Steinman's office. "Please wait here," said the doctor, then went inside and closed the door most of the way. Robert leaned against the wall and closed his eyes. He wanted to just slump to floor and fall asleep right here, just a quick nap, that's all, forty winks, no more and no less, just enough to regroup so that he could awaken refreshed and ready to do all of the responsible things that needed doing.

He became aware of Steinman's voice inside the office: "Oh, don't tell me that you're actually reciting policy to *me?*" The man sounded irritable, downright testy. Probably needed to catch forty winks himself, no more, no less. "Yes, I'll assume full responsibility, just have everything ready. We're on our way." The sound of a receiver being slammed none too gently into its cradle, and then there was the good doctor, right next to Robert there in the hallway. "Please follow me."

He guided Robert through a maze of doors and corridors until they reached a final door that required both Steinman's card key and his entering a security code in order to get through. They then got onto an elevator that slowly took them down, down, down.

"Alice in the rabbit's hole, huh?" said Robert. He looked at Steinman. "Denise's favorite book."

The good doctor remained silent.

The elevator stopped just three floors above the Gates of Hell and the two men emerged into a long, dimly lit hallway whose floors shone like black glass. They went straight for several moments, then turned right and walked toward a slash of too-bright light that spilled from the small crack of space between two swinging aluminum doors.

Robert slowed his steps. "Is that . . . *Jesus*, is this what I think it is?"

Steinman came to a full stop and turned to face him. "Yes, Mr. Londrigan, it's exactly what you think it is."

"But why do I—"

Steinman raised one hand, palm out, silencing the question. "Wait here for just a moment." He quickly went through the doors. Robert leaned against the wall, noting that the walls down here were much cooler than those up top. He closed his eyes and listened to the muted voices beyond the door. A few moments later two men dressed in lab coats stepped out into the hallway, eyeing him. Steinman came out behind them and pointed to an exit. "Go outside, take fifteen minutes on me. Smoke 'em if you got 'em."

"I don't got 'em," said one of the men.

"Oh, here," said Robert, reaching into his coat pocket and removing the crumpled pack of cigarettes. He offered them to the two men. "You can, uh . . . you can keep 'em." A shrug and an attempt at a smile. "I promised the wife I'd quit."

The men looked at Steinman, then one of them accepted the smokes with a perfunctory "Thanks," and they were gone.

Steinman waved Robert over, putting a hand firmly against the square of his back and helping him get through the swinging doors; then it was past a pair of gunmetal desks and through another set of swinging doors—these much heavier than the others—into a chilly room where the walls were shiny metal doors. In the center of the room was a series of metal tables with drains. At the end of the row was a plastic curtain that had been pulled across the length of its track to shield whatever lay behind it.

"I want to apologize again," said Steinman, "about my being so abrupt with you earlier. As I said, we were quite pressed for time."

"Were you able to—"

"Yes, Mr. Londrigan. It was an unusually successful harvesting. Because of what you've done, a lot of lives are going to be saved and made fuller. I hope you'll find some measure of comfort in that in the days to come."

Robert nodded his head and stared at the curtain. "But for the moment . . ."

"Yes," repeated Steinman. "But for the moment." He patted Robert's shoulder and gestured for him to move forward. "Go on, Mr. Londrigan. I've arranged for you to have ten minutes alone in here. Go and say good-bye to your family. I'll be out in the corridor if you need . . . I'll just be right outside."

Robert waited until Steinman left, then took a deep breath, looked at his shaking hands, wiped the perspiration from his forehead, stepped through the opening, and—

—and if the man I once was were here now, I suspect he would deny what went through his mind in those few seconds

41

it took for him to step forward, but *I* know what was going through his mind, and he's not here to stop me from telling you:

He was remembering one night when he was home with Denise, the two of them sitting in bed, she with one of many baby books she'd been reading since the doctor had given them the news, he with some novel he'd been trying to read—a best-selling legal thriller that read like any other best-selling legal thriller—and he realized that Denise was talking to him and he hadn't been listening.

"What was that?" he asked.

"I asked if you remembered that story you guys ran a few weeks ago, about that behavior modification seminar at OSU."

He shrugged. "Vaguely."

"Well, I remember it. I thought it was interesting, especially that whole concept of consensual reality—the fact that we're trained from infancy to see the same world our parents see? I even went to the library and found a couple of books about it." She then grabbed up a thick textbook and flipped open to a previously marked section, her voice taking on the tone of a teacher when next she spoke: "Did you know that babies make every conceivable sound in their goo-goo-ing? Impossible Russian vowels, countless different clicks, multitones of Chinese, guttural tones of Basque—you name the language, it's there in those sounds. So how come it finally settles on its parents' language?"

He smiled at her—God, she was beautiful—and touched her cheek. "I give up, Teach, why do they settle?"

She grinned at him, proud of herself for grasping this theory. "Extinction."

"Say what?"

"That's what the process is called, 'extinction.' If a baby makes a sound that isn't positively reinforced, it stops making that sound. It will repeat the sounds it hears, but it drops all others, then eventually loses them altogether. And most of these 'extincted' sounds can't be relearned as an adult. Isn't that something? You know, I remember reading once in Sunday school that when a child is born, it possesses

the knowledge of the one language that was originally spoken by mankind before that whole Tower of Babel thing, only it has to teach itself that language by combining all the sounds it makes—the multitones of Chinese, the Basque—"

"The clicks and what have you," said Robert.

"Yes! Only we—parents—make them stop it. Wouldn't it be interesting if all parents were to let their newborns just go on making those noises? Maybe we'd get back mankind's original one language."

Robert nodded. "I guess maybe so, hon, but I don't see what this has to do with—"

"It has everything to do with it, because extinction isn't just restricted to the sounds a baby makes; it can be applied to behavioral patterns, too. Don't you see how easy it can be to use consensual reality against a child? To take a first smile, a first kiss, a first laugh, and make them seem unacceptable? It's too easy to ruin all the things that keep a child's wonder alive. It's too easy to taint a child's view of the world and itself. Do you realize how easy it is to take a child—a helpless, trusting child—and twist its view of reality?"

He opened his mouth to speak but she placed two of her fingers against his lips and shook her head. "Shhh. Listen. I want to tell you about this daydream I've been having lately, okay? In it, I'm still myself as a child, sometimes a teenage girl, sometimes stuck in that horrible land of twelve years old, but the point is, wherever it is that I start, I always come to this point in my life where things are about to go terribly wrong—you know, that moment when you realize that childhood wonder has no place in your grown-up world? But in this daydream, I hear this voice—like in that old Monty Python sketch!—that says, 'Start again!' and I'm sent right back to the moment before the veil of wonder is lifted from my eyes, right? Only this time I know it's about to happen and I take action to make sure that I don't lose that spark of childhood wonder. Cool, huh? Instant karma."

"More like dharma for one."

Her eyes narrowed. "Don't make fun of me. Can't you see why

43

Gary A. Braunbeck

I brought all this up? So you'll understand why I get so angry sometimes.

"I think about the life you had as a child, and the life I had, and realize that more than our baby sounds were extincted—we were trained to see the same world our parents saw, all right. My mother's a manic-depressive who drove my father to an early grave while I was still a baby, and your dad was an alcoholic who'd pound you and your mother into hamburger any time he got too drunk. So what do we have? An emotional black hole on my side, fear and violence on yours."

"You saw your share of violence, too," said Robert, suddenly very much afraid for his wife. "C'mon, hon, I've seen those scars on you."

"And there's our consensual reality—no treehouses or tea parties with dolls or ghost stories told by your friends around a campfire, none of those things that showed you it was all right to laugh, to have fun and enjoy being a kid. We were saddled with problems no kid should've had to deal with, and by the time we'd either gotten a handle on things or gotten the hell out of those environments, our childhoods were over. Bang. Gone. Extincted. We were robbed, and it pisses me off because I'm afraid that we'll . . ."

"We'll what?" said Robert, tenderly.

When Denise spoke again her voice was thick with dread; she sounded so tiny, so distant, a faraway echo dwindling into nothingness.

"Mother's got two pictures that she always hangs together. One's a photograph of her and my father on their wedding day. The other is a small painting of a battlefield. There were bodies and parts of bodies scattered everywhere, a lot of them torn open or blown in half or tangled in barbed wire, there were pieces of bodies inside other bodies . . . It was horrible. But there was one man left standing, his head wrapped in a dirty bandage, and you looked at him and just knew he was looking for anyone still alive. In a far corner of the painting, directly opposite where he stood, there was this hand reaching up through the bodies, like whoever it belonged to was scrabbling to the top, trying to be found. I used to wonder what she was trying to tell me with those two pictures. About the time I turned twelve, after her second suicide attempt, I finally figured it out. Love isn't a smiling bride who holds a colorful bouquet and gazes lovingly at her husband; it's a corpse-littered battlefield where the walking wounded have to keep searching for survivors or die themselves."

He reached over to brush a strand of hair from her face and—

—pulled the curtain closed behind him.

He turned to face his family.

Denise lay on one of the metal tables with drains, her body covered by a sheet that had been turned down to expose her head, neck, and shoulders. He stared down at her pale skin, tracing the crescent-shaped scars on her shoulders with his gaze. He'd always wondered how she'd gotten those scars—had even joked that her shoulders looked as if she'd once worn a bra with straps made out of piano wire.

She'd never told him how she'd gotten those scars, or any of the others.

He'd counted them once—or, rather, *tried* to; he'd gotten up to eight when she rolled over, opened her eyes, and realized what he was doing. She'd made him sleep on the couch that night, and he'd never brought up the subject again.

"There was so much about you I didn't know," he whispered to the corpse.

Next to her sat a smaller table, something that reminded him of a hotel room service cart, and on top of that cart was a small plastic black bag with a zipper running directly down the center.

He turned away from his dead wife's face, unable to look at it, and touched the black bag.

After a moment, he remembered to breathe.

His fingers grasped the zipper.

Breathing means in *and* out, *pal; in and out.*

He slowly pulled the zipper downward—it stuck only once—until his daughter was revealed to him.

"Oh, God . . ."

They had left her open. He stared into the hollow chasm of

her center and found himself marveling at the intricate architecture of her spine; then gently, with great tenderness, he lifted her from the bag, feeling the cold, raw, exposed area on her back where the flesh had been removed. He examined her and saw that the same had been done to sections of her legs, the flesh removed with precision, along with cartilage and tendons, as well. He glimpsed bone through what tissue remained and forced himself not to look at it. He brought her closer. The harsh overhead lights gleamed off something rolling back and forth deep within her: a small puddle of dark liquid. Bobbing from side to side in the liquid was a laminated blue strip with numbers on it.

It wasn't until he held her tiny body against his chest that his heart shattered once and for all and he was overwhelmed at the strength of his love for her, this small, cold, dead thing who hadn't lived long enough to receive her name, who'd fought so hard to stay alive these past six months, and who'd been forced out into the hospital-bright sterility of a waiting death.

Something expanded in his chest and snaked its way up to his throat, trapping him in its grip and pressing in with its thumbs . . . oh . . . so . . . slowly.

The first breath to escape him hissed out, dry and desert-lonely; the second emerged as more of a splutter, speckling his chin with saliva; but it was the third breath that undid him: a tight, wet groan that strained the cords in his neck and squeezed his throat to intensify the building pressure in his head until his eyes began leaking; then the groan turned into a soft, nearly inaudible, steady wail of pain and loss and sorrow and, *oh*, *God*, so much regret. He pulled in a soggy, ragged breath as he opened one of her small hands and wrapped her fragile fingers around one of his own, then turned toward his dead wife, an unsteady smile trespassing on his face.

"She's so *tiny*," he whispered. "We need to be careful. Oh, hon, she's so delicate . . . I, uh . . . here." And with his free hand he reached under the sheet and grasped Denise's arm, pulling it out and pressing her hand against his heart, holding it there with his own as he'd done so many times while they lay sleeping together. "There, there." He cradled their wondrous child against him, rocking ever so gently from side to side.

The tears were coming by rote now, unnoticed by him. He lifted Denise's hands from his chest (should her body have begun decomposing this much already?) and tenderly placed it against the baby's cheek. "There you go, hon, there's your mommy, it's all right now, everything's all right, shhh, yes, there you go. We love you, we do, yes, we do."

He bent over and nuzzled his face against the slope of Denise's neck, rolling it back and forth the way she liked for him to do when they cuddled, then lifted his head and softly, lovingly, for the last time in his life, kissed her lips.

Pulling in another strained and soaked breath, he slipped her hand away from his chest and put her arm back under the sheet. He began to cover her face, then saw a small smear of blood, no wider than a piece of sewing thread, that started at her jaw and dipped down into her shoulder.

He realized that his nose was bleeding—it always bled whenever he was seriously upset like this—but whereas it usually embarrassed him, tonight he didn't care.

He reached into his back pocket and removed his handkerchief, then began wiping away the blood he'd left on her. "I'm so sorry," he croaked. "I didn't mean t-to be so s-s-selfish and cruel. Please f-forgive me." Then the sheet came up and fell over her face and she was gone.

He shuffled over to the room-service cart, pushed open the black bag, and began to place his daughter back inside. The overhead lights gleamed off her center again and Robert was suddenly far too aware of how empty he felt, that it shouldn't be this way and . . .

And he couldn't leave here without . . . without doing *something* . . .

He kissed his daughter's fingers and unwrapped them from his own.

He started when he heard the doors swish open.

"Mr. Londrigan? Is everything all right?"

"Yeah," Robert said. "Y-yes, fine. I just need another minute, please."

He waited another silent moment that lasted five eternities until he heard Dr. Steinman leave again (the lingering shadow spilling across the floor from the other side of the curtain had to be a trick of the light; surely the man wouldn't eavesdrop on such a private moment), then kissed his daughter's forehead that was as big as his palm, pulling her nearer to his face—

—and then the air became heavy once again, just as it had in the park earlier; a feeling of density in the atmosphere that seeped into his core and made everything seem to move in slow motion, an underwater ballet, murky and shadowed, and once more there was the sensation of standing outside of himself—

—and once more he sensed the presence of a crippling want—

—and once again there was the sound of three whistled notes in his ears—

—but now his daughter flexed her small hand ever so slightly, her fingers curling of their own accord, grasping a small section of his wrists as she smiled and gurgled playfully and moved her impossibly round, crescent-shaped head from side to side. He listened to the noises she made, and could hear the multitones of Chinese, the impossible Russian vowels, the guttural Basque, and he swore that none of those sounds would ever be extincted from her.

Outside the curtain, he could see Steinman's shadow growing longer—when had the doctor come back through the doors?—but he didn't care.

Denise sat up, the sheet dropping down to bunch around her discolored hips. She pushed out her rotting arms and wrapped them around his waist.

"We did it, Robby," she said. "We remade ourselves through her."

He turned and kissed her long and passionately as their daughter scrabbled toward Mommy's breast. Robert pulled away and Denise took their daughter in her arms and held the tiny face up to her nipple. Their daughter sucked hungrily.

"What am I supposed to do without you?" asked Robert.

"Don't leave us here, not stuck inside some dark drawer or in a plastic bag . . ."

"No . . ."

"You'll have to take us with you . . ."

"I want that, I want that more than anything . . ."

"I always loved you, Robby, even when you were being selfish, even when you were being cruel . . ."

"Oh, God, hon . . ."

"Because I knew that you didn't mean to be that way, it wasn't really you, that you'd punish yourself later . . ."

"So lonely, it's been so lonely and it's only going to get worse. . . ."

The baby finished its meal. Denise handed her back to Robert. He looked into the chasm and saw the mother's milk mixing with the dark puddle of liquid where the blue laminated strip bobbed, then a heavy globule of blood from his nose dripped down, landing in the center of the puddle where it divided and became two, then four, the process continuing until the last visible trace was gone and all their fluids were one.

The lengthening shadow outside the curtain moved, becoming smaller as its owner approached.

"Take us with you," whispered Denise, "inside you, for always, forever and ever . . ."

Robert, now back inside himself and able to command the movements of his limbs, lifted their daughter toward his face, turning her on her side like a cup, and she giggled as his mouth closed around her chasm flap. He tilted her and drank deeply, feeling the resonance of his family thrumming within his core as it slid a cool, smooth, quenching path down his throat.

"I'll wait for the touch of your hand, my love, and then everything will be the way we always wanted it to be . . ."

"I love you . . ."

"I'll wait for you in your secret place, remember? Where the mountain opens up . . ."

"The mountain . . ." he whispered, some part of his mind hinting at the importance of those words as some distant image of a happy childhood memory tried to turn on the lights and wipe the sleep from its eyes.

Denise disappeared under her sheet, and their daughter into her bag.

Robert wiped his mouth, licked clean the tip of his finger, then stood staring down at what parts of his reflection were visible in the shiny surface of the metal table with the drains.

He heard the curtain being pulled back, sensed the presence of the other man with him.

His face looked so fragmented in the shiny surface of the table.

As did Steinman's face. Fragmented.

Sectioned.

A jigsaw puzzle of flesh and bone, almost . . . split . . .

Before he could look up, a very strong hand grabbed the hair on the back of his head.

"Listen up, Willy," said the voice. " 'Did I say all? No! One was lame, And could not dance the whole of the way; And in after years, if you would blame His sadness, he was used to say, "It's dull in our town since my playmates left!" ' "

Robert's face was slammed down against the hard, cold, unyielding surface of the table. Sparks exploded behind his eyes and pain washed over him.

The hand pulled his head back up.

"So tell me, Willy—what further proof do you need?"

"W-what . . . what you're talking about . . ." Robert spluttered through the blood and pain.

"Is this proof enough? Do you despair of your humanity *now?*"

He face was slammed into the table once again. He thought he heard bones crack. His legs started to give out. His body was wrenched sideways and slammed ass-first onto the cold floor.

"Still with me, Willy?"

"*Unghhh . . .*"

His head was jerked back, then to the side. A hand appeared before his eyes, holding a photograph . . . no, not just one, several.

"Look closely, Willy, go on, *look at them!*"

The first photograph was of an infant whose large, malformed head was the shape of a quarter-moon or water balloon, lined with bright red-blue veins that threatened to burst through its all-too-thin flesh. Its face seemed so small attached to the monstrosity around it. Its mouth was open in a cry of pain and fear that was reflected in its eyes.

"My sister, Willy. Do you despair yet?"

The hand holding the photographs snapped to the side, discarding the top photograph and giving Robert a clear view of the next one.

The child had only one eye socket, directly in the center of its forehead where two eyes struggled to stay in place. Its face had no nose; instead, there was a proboscislike appendage that looked like an uncircumcised penis growing from the center of its shrunken forehead.

"My little brother, Willy. Do you despair yet?"

The rest of the photographs were snapped before his face with great speed; Robert had no time to absorb specifics; there were only too-large eyes that weren't where they were supposed to be, heads that were too large or too small or not round enough, faces that were incomplete or that contained an extra nose, eye, or—in one picture—an additional mouth on one cheek, positioned so that it would chew side to side instead of up and down; there were bloated bodies, twisted limbs, scaly clefts that obscured other features.

"My family, Willy. My brothers and sisters. Do they frighten you? Sicken you? Do you wonder where we live, or how? Do you wish us love and acceptance? Would you love us if we asked it of you? Do you despair yet? Do you require further proof?"

Robert was yanked back to his feet and spun around, his face pressed back against the surface of the metal table.

"Answer me, damn you."

Split-Face's reflection crept onto the surface of the metal table. "Do you despair?"

"Y-yes . . ."

"Does this prove to you the indifference of heaven, or do you need more convincing?"

"I . . . I . . ."

Split-Face continued to press down hard against Robert's skull. "Feel that, Willy? Do you feel them inside your head?" There was a new presence within his brain, blossoming outward, an ice bird spreading its wings to cool the searing panic he felt running rampant within him; the ice wings were frozen blue water, dotted in ripples, and were melting ever so slowly near the tips, the blue-rippled droplets at first a sprinkle, then a stream cascading easily through his brain, down his spine, and into his chest, cleansing him, expanding something within his body and consciousness alike; he felt the presence of other minds, other hearts, other . . . others. "I'm putting some of them there, Willy, to keep you company, to remind you, to show you things, to teach you. Take good care of them, Willy, remember them well, or you'll be sorry."

A growling, angry, disgusted, semihuman noise; then Robert's head was slammed once more against the metal table. Blood from his nose swirled into the drain nearest his face.

"They think they're wearing masks, Willy. I tell them the story of the Masks and they listen, and they believe. Do you know the story of the Masks? Did *she* ever tell you?"

Robert hadn't time to answer before a fist struck the base of his neck; his last conscious sensation was of feeling something in his face shatter and fly down his throat; his last conscious thought was, *Do we have a secret, you and I?*—then all was blinding pain followed by merciful darkness.

Later, when he awakened, Denise, silent and dead, was still there.

But their daughter was gone.

Chapter Two

His face was hidden behind a mask.

Robert opened his eyes and pulled in a deep breath through his nose.

Big mistake.

Pain lanced up into his skull.

"Breathe through your mouth, Mr. Londrigan," said a voice.

"Dr. Steinman?" Christ, even talking hurt like hell.

"Talk only if you have to. Trust me on that one."

Reaching up to touch the mass of medical tape covering his nose, Robert allowed his hands to follow the layers of tape that spread out from the center of his face. There was an odd, T-shaped metal brace or splint covering his nose and a small part of his forehead, the medical tape holding it firmly in place.

Steinman's hands pulled Robert's away. "Here." A cup of water and two pink pills were handed to him. "A Demerol cocktail, on the house."

Robert took the painkillers and gulped down the water—another mistake; the movement of his throat muscles seemed to send all vibration right up to his nose. He handed the cup back to Steinman, then lay back on the pillows. After a few moments of shallow mouth-breathing, he slowly opened his eyes and saw Steinman standing beside the bed.

"It'll be fine if you just don't mess with it for about a week."

Steinman gently reached out and touched the splint in the center of Robert's face. "I wasn't going to use anything to hold it in place after setting it, but looking at the X ray I thought it could be a bit iffy if you moved too much. Amazingly, you *don't* have a concussion, but your nose is going to need some minor reconstructive surgery once it heals. A section of bone broke through the side and had to be stitched. You ever see *Chinatown*? Remember that scar on Jack Nicholson's nose?"

"Uh-huh . . ."

"Yours could hold its own against that. So don't mess with my work, okay? Your nose was broken in two different places but at least the breaks were clean. Pills starting to kick in yet?"

"Feel a little shiny, if that's what you mean."

"Shiny. Nice description." Steinman leaned closer. "There's a detective waiting outside to talk to you. I promised him I'd let him know as soon as you were awake."

"Did you see . . . see who . . . ?"

Steinman bit his lower lip and shook his head. "No. I was letting the guys back in. All I saw were swinging doors and a blur at the other end of the hall. I'm so sorry." He reached down and grasped Robert's hand, squeezing it with all the familiarity and affection of a lifelong friend. "Is there anyone I can call for you?"

"I don't . . . uh . . . What time is it?"

"About two-fifteen in the dismal A.M." Steinman rubbed his eyes. "Sorry. I guess I don't have to tell you what a long night it's been."

"When was your shift supposed to end?"

"Not until six-thirty," Steinman replied, looking at his watch. "You want me to call someone for you?"

"Yeah, you could give Denise a call and tell her—" A moment, a breath, a blink, something crumbling inside: "Oh."

Then: "*Oh, God . . .*" as it all came flooding back in clear, unblinking detail.

Steinman raised the upper portion of the bed and held a large wad of cotton under the holes in the cast so the snot and blood from Robert's nose could drain easily; with his free arm he simply held Robert, who wept for a few minutes, jerking occasionally until the pills began to take fuller effect.

Steinman helped Robert arrange and clean himself up a bit. "Want me to send the detective in?"

"I suppose, yeah."

Steinman started out of the room, but stopped when Robert called his name.

"Yes, Mr. Londrigan?"

"I just . . . uh . . . I wanted to let you know that I r-really appreciate all you tried to—"

Steinman held up his hand, palm out, silencing him. "Don't *even*, okay? Oh, one more thing—don't be surprised if the hospital's attorney contacts you in the next few days."

"You suing me?"

"Hardly. For the record, I, personally, am not all *that* well off."

"Huh?"

Steinman tried to smile; the smile looked tired and drained. "I don't even know why I brought that up. I'm sorry, I'm tired as hell." He stared at Robert a moment longer, his face a prism of sorrow, confusion, and deep respect. "Most men wouldn't have made it through all this, you know?"

"Who says I have?"

"Yeah, well . . ." And with that, the good doctor was gone.

Robert lay there unmoving, staring up at the white-tiled ceiling, thinking about what Split-Face had said: " '*Did I say all? No! One was lame, And could not dance the whole of the way; And in after years, if you would blame His sadness, he was used to say— "It's dull in our town since my playmates left!"* ' "

Why did that seem so familiar?

He seemed to recall his mother reading those words to him once, when he was a child of eight and stuck in bed with the mumps.

He concentrated on those words, trying desperately to find

something to connect them to the memory of his mother reading to him, and almost had it when the door opened and the detective came into the room.

The man more resembled a former professional boxer than a cop; everything about him, while not squat, was particularly square and tight and low to the ground. His thick, wavy hair was almost completely white—prematurely so, Robert guessed—and looked somewhat distinguished in a favorite-uncle kind of way. He sported a dense mustache, also near totally white, that made him resemble the actor who used to play the original Captain Kangaroo on the old children's show; it wasn't until he got closer and the numerous small pale scars on his face became evident that the fanciful comparison bit the big one.

The detective found a metal stool and wheeled it over near Robert's bed. While the caricature of the police detective led one to expect his appearance to be baggy-eyed and rumpled, this boxer of a cop was surprisingly neat; from his perfectly knotted tie to his smooth slacks and fashionable overcoat, he was extremely presentable, with wide, gray, alert eyes that would not, for the moment, meet Robert's gaze.

The oddest thing about him, though, the most notably disparate element of his appearance, was his hands; they should have been wide and heavy, as befitting a beefy fellow like this; instead they were thin and delicate, an artist's or a pianist's hands, with long, almost feminine fingers. They looked almost like Denise's hands.

The thought made Robert chuckle painfully; here he was, in a room with Dirty Harry who had the hands of a housewife who soaked her fingers in Palmolive.

"It's my hands, isn't it?" asked the detective in a rumbling voice that sounded as if he'd once gargled with Jack Daniels three times a day. "I know, they look weird attached to this body, but I didn't have any choice in the matter." Still not meeting Robert's gaze, he reached into his jacket and pulled out his ID: Detective William Emerson, Cedar Hill Police Department. He put his ID back into his pocket, removed a small notebook from another pocket, and flipped through until he found the page he was looking for; then—as if something had just dawned on him—he became very still.

After a moment, he reached over and took hold of one of Robert's hands, squeezing it.

"Goddammit, Mr. Londrigan," he said, finally meeting Robert's gaze. "*God. Damn. It.* I am so sorry about your wife and kid. It's a terrible thing. A tragedy. I . . . I don't know what to say to you so you'll know just how awful I feel for you." He looked like he was going to burst into tears. "I just can't imagine how . . . I mean, *what* . . . I mean . . . goddammit. God. Damn. It."

"Thank you," croaked Robert, releasing Emerson's hand.

The detective produced a handkerchief from yet another pocket, blew his nose, then got back to the business at hand. "I'm not going to be long here, Mr. Londrigan—partly because there's only so much I can ask, mostly because you look like the painkillers are gonna knock you for a loop any second now. I've talked to the nurses and Dr. Steinman and the morgue attendants and a bunch of other people and think I've got most of the information. What I need to know from you is, did you get a good look at the guy's face?"

"Not really. He was wearing a Halloween mask."

"Oh, joy. Can you describe the mask?"

Robert did, in as much detail as he could recall. As he spoke, it seemed to him there was something else he ought to be telling the detective . . . something about . . . pictures? He couldn't remember.

Emerson finished writing it down, then looked up with his melancholy puppy eyes and asked, "This may sound stupid, but did you ever see this guy before he attacked you in the morgue?"

"Yes. I saw him in Dell Memorial Park earlier this evening—I mean, yesterday evening, last night—"

"I understand. Did anything happen that might have made

him angry with you? Anything that he might think needed to be avenged?"

"I said hi, complimented his mask, and he told me to go fuck myself."

"Is that all? Nothing else was said, there was no other exchange between the two of you?"

"I . . ." Robert's throat felt tight and dry. "Could I bother you to hand me that cup of water, please?"

"Oh, jeez, I'm sorry," said Emerson. "Didn't occur to me that those painkillers're probably making you dry as a bone." He held the cup while Robert took a few sips through the straw. "You good to go, then?"

Robert nodded his head. "You're very kind."

Emerson took his seat on the metal stool. "So tell me, was there anything else said between the two of you?"

"Yes. He kept calling me 'Willy' for some reason—both at the park and when he attacked me in the morgue. He also said something else, something that I'm sure was a quotation of some sort."

"Can you remember it? Doesn't have to be word for word."

As best he could remember them, Robert repeated the words to Emerson, who copied them into his notebook, then sat back, ran a delicate hand through his thick white hair, and said, "Huh."

Robert tried to sit up. "What is it?"

"I've either heard this or read it somewhere before."

"I thought the same thing."

"Could be it's a line from a famous song or poem or something like that. Huh." Emerson closed his notebook.

"Can I ask you a question, Detective?"

"You bet."

"Why did he steal my daughter's body?" Robert's voice cracked on the last three words. Bill Emerson reached up and squeezed his shoulder.

"My guess, Mr. Londrigan, is that it's some sort of sick Halloween fraternity prank. Pledges have been know to pull shit like this in order to get in. That's the assumption I'm going on for the moment." He looked at his watch. "In a couple of hours, after the sun's up, officers with search warrants are gonna start sweeping through every frat house, kitchen, and dorm room at OSU *and* Denison University. A pledge who'd do something like this isn't exactly in danger of becoming a member of MENSA; he's probably got the thing—uh, excuse me—your daughter's body—stashed in a freezer nearby so he can produce it quickly when his potential frat brothers demand evidence. I just hope we find your daughter fast before word of the searches gets out. Course, once we find out who it was last night that wore this mask you described . . . well, I don't think it's going to be long before we have your assailant and you daughter. Meantime, you try and rest."

Despite the throbbing pain it brought, Robert shook his head. A single tear slid down his cheek. "Not here," he whispered. It was almost like a prayer.

Emerson leaned closer. "I beg your pardon?"

Robert blinked, then focused his gaze on the detective as best he could. Right now this beefy man with the sad eyes and white hair and disparate hands was the only friend he had and like it or not, Robert had to trust him. "I don't want to stay here, Detective. My wife died here. My daughter's body was stolen from this place. Dr. Steinman said I don't have a concussion, so I'd like to go home but I'm in no shape to drive a car and I don't want to call my sister or anyone else to come get me because I don't think I could stand all their tears and embraces and wringing hands and I don't mean to bother or annoy you but you seem like a very decent man so I was just wondering if—"

Emerson gestured for Robert to stop talking. "I'll tell the doctor I'm driving you home. My pleasure. Be right back." He started out the door, paused, then turned back and said: "This has got nothing to do with anything, and maybe isn't the most considerate or sensitive thing to say to you right now, but you seem like you could use a few moments' distraction and maybe this'll be dumb enough to take your mind off your grief for a second or two, but . . . I heard a couple of orderlies talking before I came in here and . . . did you know that two nurses with scissors can make an unconscious man naked in eleven seconds? Isn't that the most useless piece of information you've heard this week?"

Robert smiled at Emerson, even though it hurt like hell; a genuine, grateful smile. "Thank you for that."

"I suggest you try not to sneeze whilst I run my errand. Could be uncomfortable."

Chapter Three

It was well after three A.M. by the time Bill Emerson's car pulled up in front of the house, and Robert made no move to open the passenger door; instead he sat there, quite still and more than a little buzzed on the painkillers, staring out the window at the front door of the structure that he now could no longer think of as home.

After a few more moments of silence, Bill Emerson cleared his throat and said, "I got the right address, didn't I?"

"Huh? Oh, yeah . . . sure. This's where I live."

"You okay to walk on your own? I could give you some help if you—"

"No, no, thank you. I think I'll be able to . . ." The thought collapsed inward and he fell silent once again. He pressed his hands into his lap. The steps to the front door looked so far away. The house looked so empty. The night could not possibly have been any blacker.

"You know what I was thinking about on the way over here?" he finally said.

Emerson said nothing; he seemed content to sit and listen.

"I was thinking about all the pictures of Denise that I *don't* have." Robert turned his head toward the detective. "From the first day I met her, Denise had this thing about having her picture taken. I had to beg her to have a photograph taken of the two of us at our wedding, can you imagine that? Christ, I can remember times when we'd be at a party or some social function the station was having, and she'd spot someone with a camera and practically *run* from the room. One time I tried to sneak up on her and snap a picture with an old Instamatic . . . I swear, I think if she'd had a gun in her hand, she would have shot me. I have never in my life met someone so violently opposed to having her picture taken.

"Last Thanksgiving, we went over to her mother's house and I figured while I was there, I'd dig around and find some pictures of Denise—hell, I mean, she and her mother didn't much get along, but the woman *had* to have some pictures of her own daughter, right?" Robert shook his head. "Not a goddamn one. In fact, aside from one picture of her own wedding, the woman had no photographs whatsoever in her home; not on the mantel, on any of the little tables that were next to the sofa or chairs, none. What the hell kind of family has no photographs of their kids? A child's growing up, it happens so quickly, most parents have tons and tons of pictures, y'know? To mark each moment before it's gone forever. Not Denise's mother. I suppose Denise got her objection to photographs from the woman. And I was thinking that I'm pissed as hell at both of them right now because all I have to remember what my wife looked like is the one—count it, *one*—photo she allowed to be taken at our wedding . . . that, and the picture on her driver's license. Those have to last me the rest of my life.

"Guess I'm . . . I'm feeling a little sorry for myself."

"I think you might be entitled to it, all things considered."

Robert smiled at Emerson. "You have pictures of your wife?"

"Yes. And she's got lots of pictures of me."

"That's really great." Robert looked once more at the front door of his house, then opened the car door and started to get out.

"Don't forget these," said Emerson, handing him a white paper bag from the hospital pharmacy.

"Oh, right. Thanks." Robert took the bag and shook the detective's hand. "I really appreciate the lift."

Emerson shook his head. "I just wish there was more I could do for you, Mr. Londrigan. I mean, what with . . . goddammit, you know? God. Damn. It."

Robert nodded his agreement, then closed the door, turned, and made his way slowly up the steps. He tucked the bag of prescriptions into his jacket pocket, his breath misting into the frosty October air as he fumbled the key to the front door into the lock, then turned and waved at Bill Emerson, who returned the gesture and slowly drove away.

Robert stood there in the cold blackness and looked around; no neighbors were pulling back their curtains to see his return, and that suited him just fine. While many of the people—the ones he'd bothered getting to know, anyway—were good folks, he had no desire to hear anyone tell him how sorry they were for his loss.

He stretched slightly, touched the metal splint taped to his nose, and started to turn the key—

—the front door *clicked* open about a quarter of an inch.

He stood staring at it, wondering if some industrious burglar had seen what happened earlier, had seen the ambulance and his frenzied exit and taken advantage of an Opportunity when it presented itself.

(Vulture Culture.)

Or if . . . yes, that had to be it—he remembered slamming the door closed behind him as he ran out earlier (right?), but right now he could not for the life of him remember *locking* it.

Good thing this was a safe neighborhood. This was not the first time he'd left the house and forgotten to lock the door behind him; when that happened in the past, he'd returned to find the place just as he'd left it. There was no reason to think this time would be any different . . . at least as far as the stuff inside was concerned.

And even if it were, even if he found the place emptied of all its valuables, he didn't care right now; he just wanted a warm bath and a change of clothes and then to sleep for a few hundred thousand years.

Upon entering, he closed the door behind him and made sure this time to lock the damn thing, engaging the two dead bolts as well, then stumbled through the living room and went straight into the kitchen to make himself a cup of chamomile tea.

The house did not close in on him as he'd expected. There was silence, yes, but it was not the morbid, anxious silence that descends on a house after a recent death; this was, if anything, an anticipatory silence, a hold-your-breath-someone's-coming silence, vigilant and expectant.

Robert found it unnerving.

Somewhere in the basement, one of the cats—he couldn't tell if it was Tasha or The Winnie—released a low, mournful yowl, then fell silent. *Poor things*, he thought; *they know that something's wrong but don't know what they should do about it*.

He suddenly wished they'd come up here to keep him company, and damn his allergies. He wanted to feel the warmth of affectionate life against his hand. He turned on the overhead kitchen lights, called their names, waited, and when neither one emerged he called for them again.

Nothing.

Maybe they were mad at him for what he'd said earlier about causing him to take all the allergy pills.

He wished they'd come up; he wanted to apologize to them. Maybe a can of salmon would be sufficient to demonstrate his remorse. He considered going down to fetch them, but the idea of turning on the lights and seeing Denise's perpetually messy work area and all of the unfinished *matryoshka* dolls was more than he could handle right now, knowing, as he did, that whatever work of hers had been unfinished earlier this evening would remain unfinished forever, and it would be up to him to box it up and store it away somewhere.

(*All of us, someday . . .*)

He could neither look at nor think about it now; for the time being, the cats would have to make do with his having called for them.

He sat down at the kitchen table and watched the steam from the tea create dreamscape shapes in the air. For one second the steam formed Denise's profile, and suddenly he was seized by panic because he couldn't recall the details of her face, so he took out his wallet and opened it to the sole photograph it contained: their wedding. God, she'd been so beautiful. Her gaze held everything for him: promise, possibility, passion. Robert found himself remembering every past nuance about the moment the picture was taken; the scent of her perfume, the slant of light, the bead of sweat that ran down his spine, the aroma of the flowers on the altar, the way she held his hand and squeezed it—not one long squeeze but a series of them, as if in rhythm with her heart, now his as well: squeeze (*I, Denise, take thee, Robert, to be my wedded husband*), release, squeeze (*. . . to love and to cherish till death . . .*), release, the two of them exchanging themselves with every pulse, every breath, each willingly bestowing something to the other until, at the moment the photograph was taken, they were no longer Robert and Denise but a one beyond oneness. This day; this time; this breath; this love: immortal.

Only now it wasn't; now it was simply another What Should Have Been.

Christ, but he'd squandered so much time that could have been spent enriching her life.

"Aw . . . *shit*," he whispered, closing the wallet and dropping it onto the table.

He wiped his eyes, then sipped at his tea. It was too hot, so he carried the mug over to the sink and added some cold water. He then took another one of the painkillers Steinman had prescribed for him. That's when one of the cats staged a sneak attack.

Well, not *attack*, exactly, not in the usual sense of the word: The Winnie, the biggest of the two, came trundling up to him, sat her overwide furry black butt directly on his left foot, and meowed. Loudly.

Robert reached down and stroked the back of her neck; The Winnie, obviously pleased by this rare show of affection from him, let fly with her small-chainsaw purr and arched her back.

She's probably wondering where Denise is, Robert thought.

He called for Tasha again and was answered by her faint Don't-bug-me-I'm-tired squeak from the bottom of the basement stairs.

"Ah, hell, you two," Robert said. "I'm sorry about what I said earlier." He grabbed the bag of cat food from the pantry and filled their bowls to overflowing, then gave them fresh water, a saucer of milk each, then cracked open a can of salmon and divided it evenly between two small plates that he set next to their regular food bowls.

The Winnie approached the feast he'd laid out with caution, sniffed at the food, then looked up at him with wide eyes: *Who are you and what have you done with the man who lives here?*

Then she proceeded to eat—somewhat sloppily, as was her fashion.

Knowing that the salmon on Tasha's side didn't stand a chance if she didn't get up here to eat it (The Winnie assumed that all food was intended for her and her alone), Robert went to the basement door and pulled it open wide, calling for Tasha—

—and saw that the lights down in Denise's work area were on.

He stared for a moment, wondering how he could have missed that; when he'd come in here the kitchen was dark, so there should have been at least a small slash of light coming from behind the basement door. He would have noticed that, even under these circumstances; over the years, both he and Denise had trained themselves to turn off a light whenever they left a room, often doing so without even being aware of it.

He moved down onto the first basement stair, cringing at the deep groan it made under his weight. Four years they'd lived here and still the creaky stairs gave him the willies.

He took the stairs one at a time, slowly stooping over as he descended in order to (hopefully) get a better look before he had to go all the way down there.

He did not want to be here, not right now; he did not want to go all the way into the basement but couldn't say why; he knew only that something in the back of his mind was warning him to take that bath and follow it with the hundred-thousand-year nap.

The smart thing to do was turn around and go back to the kitchen.

So, naturally, he kept descending.

Tasha cried out again, sounding almost in pain, so Robert took the stairs two at a time until he was standing in the basement.

He called for Tasha again, who exploded from behind the washing machine and flew up the stairs without so much as a hello. Robert shook his head—man, but was he getting loopy from the painkiller!—and started over to turn off the lights.

Then paused to look at Denise's work area.

Her cluttered, messy, always-in-the-middle-of-finishing-something work area.

All of the major items were in place, the table and hutch and cubby shelves, the chair and lamp, the small filing cabinet that served as an end table where she used to set her sketching pads or drinking glass, but what slapped a vise clamp on his spirit were the other items: the opened sketching pads, the drawings and Polaroids taped to the hutch, the pencils strewn about, the tubes of acrylic paint, the brushes lying on the edge of the table, ready to clatter to the floor if someone didn't move them and quick, and, most of all, the new set of *matryoshka* dolls with blank surfaces waiting for their faces.

Everything about it whispered of permanent incompleteness, of a life cut short and a future that no longer existed; a haunted house waiting for the ghost to arrive; a cold emptiness; the echo of an incomplete sentence.

He decided to leave the lights on, just as she had, undoubtedly because she'd been too upset about the broadcast and the story of the baby and his not bothering to call and warn her about it.

He decided to leave the lights on as a reminder to himself of all the thoughtless little cruelties he'd inflicted on her over the years in the name of Advancing His Career.

He went back up and retrieved his now-lukewarm tea. It was only as he was stumbling back toward the kitchen table that he realized there was a light coming from the living room.

The living room that had been in darkness when he'd passed through it fifteen minutes ago.

He moved toward the doorway and peeked around the edge.

There was a small fire burning in the fireplace.

Panic moved into his core, making itself right at home: *Oh, God, why didn't you ask Emerson to come inside for some coffee or something, you fucking idiot? Split-Face had to have followed you from the park—how the hell else would he have known you were at the hospital?*

He very slowly, very quietly, moved back into the kitchen, set the mug of tea on the counter, and pulled open the cutlery drawer, wincing at the way it groaned. He removed the largest knife he could find.

Exhaling a breath he wasn't aware he'd been holding, he moved back toward the living room. The fire popped loudly, then hissed and sizzled. The scent of burning wood burned his nostrils.

The flames cast malformed, dancing shadows across the floor and up onto the walls, giving the room a sense of permanent disproportion, of an inanimate thing suddenly given sentience and trying to shape itself into something other than what it had been.

Keeping his back pressed against the wall and wishing that he owned a gun, Robert moved left, toward the fireplace and the sofa—which had been moved, turned around so that if one were to sit on it one would face the fireplace and not the other, smaller sofa that sat six feet across from it to form a makeshift conversation pit.

He wondered if it had been moved earlier, while he was still at the hospital.

He wondered why, if this had been done during the few minutes he'd been in the basement, he hadn't heard anything—unless he was a helluva lot more wasted than he'd thought.

Then he wondered if Split-Face was waiting for him, curled up so he couldn't be seen until Robert was right on top of him, curled up all warm and cozy in front of the fire, smugly satisfied with this most recent violation.

Robert slid along the wall, his breath coming out in ragged, painful bursts. God Almighty, what did he think he was doing? He was in no shape for a physical confrontation, even if he *was* armed.

One of the cats yowled again, much louder this time, anxious and angry (more likely than not it was Tasha, defending her food against The Winnie), and the sound—commensurate to some cheap scare tactic from a low-budget horror movie—startled him, causing him to almost drop the knife; as it was he caught it by the business end of the blade and felt it slice one of his fingers.

Gripping the handle with as much strength as he could muster, he moved onward, closer to the sofa and sizzling fire, crackling like the sound of delicate bones snapping, and now—*breathe, c'mon, that's it*—he was facing the side of the sofa, and so moved forward, closer to it, ready to surprise Split-Face's beauty sleep, closer, only three feet away now, the dancing shadow-fire making the room twist and ripple, and now he was only two feet away, readying himself to leap on top of the son of a bitch if he had to, and then he caught a glance of firelight creating glissandos over skin and—

—unbelieving of the sight before him, Robert dropped the knife.

Stood staring at the Impossibility that lay so peaceful before him.

And slowly raised both hands to cover his mouth before any sound could escape; he didn't fear crying out, didn't even fear a hysterical scream: He feared that he might laugh at the perverse absurdity of it all, and that frightened him more than anything else in the world could have at this moment because he knew if he allowed himself to start laughing he'd never stop.

His daughter lay there, still naked, still open in the center, looking for all the world like a newborn in peaceful slumber while Mommy and Daddy watched over her.

He sat down at the end opposite where she lay and stared at her.

She was dirty, covered in places with thick patches of drying mud. Split-Face must have dropped her. Robert hoped it hadn't hurt too much.

Cruising on autopilot, he moved through the house, Just in Case, checking all the rooms to make sure Split-Face wasn't hiding somewhere in the house, then checking to make certain all the doors and windows were securely locked, arming the electronic security system, and, Just in Case he'd overlooked any hiding places Split-Face might have found, retrieving an old baseball bat from the hall closet.

He picked up the knife from the floor and placed it on the arm of the sofa, in easy reaching distance, Just in Case.

He looked down upon the still figure of his daughter and smiled.

In the glow of the fire, her head didn't appear nearly as large as it did at the hospital; it looked almost, in fact, like a normal newborn's head.

He reached out to touch her, pulled back his hand, then reached out again, his palm less than an inch from her tiny face.

He called her Emily, the name he and Denise had chosen. He said silly things to her, jokey things that one might say to a newborn in order to get it to grin. His own voice sounded unfamiliar to him, the voice of a man who had not spoken to anyone in a very long time. "We have all sorts of things for your nursery," he said. "Wait until you see it. There's a shelf full of books with fairy tales and stories about Curious George. You'll like George, silly monkey that he is."

Only then did he dare touch her.

Her flesh was both cold from death and slightly warm from the fire.

He ran his hand slowly, lovingly, over her entire body, noting but not really letting it register that all of the areas that had been stripped of flesh and other tissues were now restored.

He scooted closer and leaned down, staring into the chasm of her center.

Something that looked like a pinkish spider's web filled the area just underneath her ribs, and Robert snaked two fingers inside to clear it away, whatever it was.

The web felt moist, warm, organic.

He traced along its pattern until his fingers encountered something semisolid in the middle.

Something equally moist as the web.

Something with . . . veins and . . . valves.

He pressed down against the tiny, impossible heart with his bleeding finger and felt his blood seep onto its surface.

For a moment, the world was frozen.

Then he felt it; softly, almost imperceptible at first, but he felt it, nonetheless.

Her tiny impossible heart shuddered, then began to beat.

Once.

Then nothing.

Twice more.

Then nothing.

He waited patiently, a parent sitting next to his child's sickbed, but her heart did not beat again.

Maybe she needed to be warmer, maybe that was it.

He removed his hand from inside the chasm and carried her upstairs to the bathroom. He washed her with warm, soapy water in the sink. Her eyes were shut tight, but he remembered how they were the color of her mother's. He compared her fingernails to his own and thought he saw a similarity in shape. He turned her on her side, emptying water from her autopsy chasm, then began to pat her dry with one of the new, heavy, thirsty towels Denise had recently purchased.

He was patting her dry inside when he felt her impossible heart start to beat again. He didn't care how this was happening, he only knew that he was being given a second chance and would not squander it.

He tried pressing closed the flaps of the chasm but they would not fuse together, no matter how much he wished them to. But that was all right, he would love her anyway.

He wrapped her in a fresh, clean-smelling hand towel, then stood with her in front of the bathroom mirror, thinking that he most definitely looked like the father of a newborn baby; not dead, as some part of him believed she still was, just sleeping, little Sleeping Emily, sleeping like babies do all the time.

He carried her downstairs and sat by the fire. His index finger followed the delicate profile of her face. His finger looked grotesque to him and he hoped she wasn't too scared by the feel of it. Some of her skin peeled away at the gentlest of his touch, and he remembered that she had been born too soon, before the thicker skin needed to survive in the world could fully develop; and, besides, they'd taken away a lot of her skin earlier, hadn't they? To help others. Taken it away just like most of her internal organs. To help others. That was all right, she'd pull through and they'd be just fine, the two of them.

He sat there holding her until the fire began to die away, allowing the still-dark night to seep in and absorb parts of the room. He never once thought to eat, or drink something, or get some rest. He just sat there, holding her, rocking back and forth and singing songs and occasionally slipping his finger in against her heart and convincing it to give a few more beats.

He decided then to do something Denise had asked him to do for their child when it was born; not possessing the most appealing of singing voices, Robert had promised Denise that he'd dig out his old flute from his high school orchestra days and practice some soothing tunes to play for the baby when it woke up at night and needed soothing. He gently laid Emily back down on the sofa, placing soft pillows on either side of her so she wouldn't roll off, then went back to the hall closet and rummaged for a few minutes until he found his flute case.

Back on the sofa, he tried out the instrument for the first time in almost twenty years. It sounded surprisingly good. After several headache-inducing notes wherein he got the feel of the thing back, he played for Emily his best selection, the one that had won him an award at a competition in eleventh grade: "Promenade" from Mussorgsky's *Pictures at an Exhibition*. She seemed to enjoy it, and Robert was pleased to discover that he could still deliver a pretty good rendition of it after all these years.

Toward the end, though, his hands began to tremble uncontrollably and he could no longer play or keep hold of the flute. He placed it back in its case, then touched Emily, one trembling hand on her shoulder, the other against her soft, cool, chubby cheek. He brushed her lips with his thumb, then leaned over and kissed her forehead, her perfect-baby forehead. He wanted this to last forever but knew that was selfish.

His hand still touching Emily's cold cheek, Robert suddenly thought of something his sister, Lynn, had talked about on a night last September when the two of them had gone out for their twice-monthly dinner date. Lynn, a biology teacher at Cedar Hill High School, was expressing her concern over the health of Denise's mother when, not missing a beat, she'd segued onto the subject of death. Robert listened to her much more intently than he'd wanted and now, looking down at Emily, he found himself thinking about death in terms of simple biology. Death wasn't instantaneous, the cells went down one by one; it took a while before everything was finished. If a person wanted to, he could snatch a bunch of cells hours after somebody'd checked out and grow them in cultures. Death was a fundamental function; its mechanisms operated with the same attention to detail, the same conditions for the advantage of organisms, the same genetic information for guidance through the stages, that most people equated with the physical act of living. Now, here with his daughter, Robert couldn't help wondering: If it was such an intricate, integrated physiological process—at least in the primary, local stages—then how did you explain the permanent vanishing of consciousness? What happened to it? Did it just screech to a halt, become lost in humus, what? Nature *did not* work that way; it tended to find perpetual uses for its more elaborate systems. Maybe all that crap from the seventies about "all of us, together, make up God" was true; maybe human consciousness was somehow severed at the filaments of its attachment and then absorbed back into the membrane of its origin. Maybe that was all reincarnation was: the severed consciousness of a single cell that did not die but rather vanished totally into its own progeny. Maybe it was more than that—

—maybe he should stop this before it got out of hand. He should call the police, call Bill Emerson and tell him there was no need to search for Emily, she was right here with her father where she belonged, but then they would come and take her away from him again and he refused to lose her twice in the same night.

No, let them look for her and wonder what happened.

Dead was dead, gone was gone, and nothing you or a single cell or its progeny could do was going to change it.

He stroked her cheek and whispered, "Shhh, there, there, time to rest now. You can sleep here, you can stay at home where you belong. Daddy'll watch over you. Always."

He wrapped her in the crisp white towel and held her a little while longer before doing what he knew must be done.

From the closet he took his heavy winter coat, for it was so very cold out there.

From the basement he took a shovel and one of Denise's garden spades.

From an upstairs closet he took a large shoe box that once held his new winter boots.

From the cutlery drawer he took an ice pick, Just in Case.

Finally, from the sofa, he took his daughter, placed her gently inside the shoe box—it was a perfect fit, all snug and comfy— and carried her outside, into the backyard and her mother's garden; it, too, was slumbering, and it seemed appropriate that Emily rest here, in a place where beauty bloomed in spring and summer, faded elegantly in autumn, and froze motionless under winter ice, gathering its strength to emerge with even more loveliness and grandeur than you remembered.

The garden was surrounded by a circle of flagstones. Robert chose the largest of these, the one facing directly east. Emily would like it here, would like the feel of the sun warming her every morning. Yes, this was a splendid spot.

Checking the neighbors' windows on either side of the fenced-in yard, Robert knelt down and overturned the flagstone. The soil underneath was brown and moist and friable. He used the garden spade to loosen an area big enough for the shoe box, and was surprised to discover he needn't have bothered bringing the shovel; the spade was more than enough to dig a hole a foot long and fifteen inches deep. He knelt back and wiped the sweat from his face. He squinted his eyes as he looked up toward the sky and saw the first faint hint of sunlight creeping to life.

He lifted the shoe box, kissed its lid, then lowered it gently into the hole. He shoveled the dirt back in with his hands, patting it down, giving Emily a good, strong blanket of earth. He moved the flagstone back into place, stood, and scuffed more soil around it.

He looked down at Emily's unmarked grave and thought he really should say something.

All he could think of was part of a poem Denise had written shortly after finding out she was pregnant; she'd planned to read it to Emily every night in place of a prayer.

"May the night be your friend, and may dreams rock you gently; may you never know hunger, and may you love with a full heart; may the bright, smiling moon light your way, until the wind sets you free . . ."

He couldn't recall the rest of it.

He blew her a kiss. He went back inside and locked the door behind him. He went upstairs and washed what he could of his face without disturbing the tape and metal splint protecting Dr. Steinman's handiwork. He thought about shaving, but who did he have to look good for now? He took off his clothes and turned on the bath taps, watching like a man hypnotized as the warm water crept slowly up the sides of the tub. He stretched. He saw a small mummified spider floating on the surface of the water. He cupped the water underneath the body in his hands, lifted the spider, tossed it into the sink. He lowered himself into the warm, warm water like a convalescing invalid and laid his head back. He closed his eyes, folding his hands against his stomach. He waited until the water had risen almost to his neck, then used his left foot to turn off the taps. He snuggled down into the water and its soothing ripples as if it were a living liquid quilt. Soon he drifted off into a half sleep. He dreamed that he was living in a great wilderness and watched over many, many children. Denise was there, and so was Emily. The children adored both of them. The children laughed often, for they no longer wore masks to conceal their true faces, no longer dressed to hide their true forms, and though some might think them grotesque, Robert saw them as beautiful. He comforted them, taught them, loved them with all his heart, and was loved by them in return. He stood upon a tall tree stump playing "Promenade" on his flute; then, once the piece was finished, he spread his arms wide as gold-flecked sunlight fell like strands of silk through the trees' thick leaves. They emerged from the wilderness, from the shadows, from the place where the mountain opened, and surrounded him. They touched him lovingly. They were so beautiful. They all looked so happy. They called him Father.

It was such a pretty picture. . . .

Part Two
Parlor Tricks and Cocteau Prayers

"I see nobody on the road," said Alice.
"I only wish *I* had such eyes," the King remarked in
a fretful tone. "To be able to see Nobody! And at that
distance, too! Why, it's all *I* can do to see real people,
by this light!"

—*Lewis Carroll*, Through the Looking Glass

"The most terrible thing of all is happy love, for then
there is fear in everything."

—*Cosima Wagner*

"Once I saw a woman, and I
beheld all her children not yet born.
And a woman looked upon my face and
she knew all my forefathers, dead before
she was born."

—*Kahlil Gibran*, Sand and Foam

Chapter One

It was an old movie theater full of winos and thugs and snoring bums and it stank horribly and was overcrowded and overheated and usually showed lousy movies, but Robert didn't care, especially tonight, especially after the last couple of days, and especially because he would not, *could* not sleep in that house.

The house.

Formerly known as home in a previous lifetime.

Robert looked down at his hands and thought, *I buried her, with these hands I dug up the earth and buried her. Jesus!*

He hadn't been able to sleep for more than an hour since that night—was it only three days ago? It seemed further in the past, somehow, something that he'd been carrying around like a filthy little secret for most of his life. He'd taken to ordering from pizza and Chinese places that delivered, and had even gone so far as to move the coffeemaker and all the fixings into the living room, along with a gallon of bottled water, just so he wouldn't have to go into the kitchen where his gaze inevitably found the back-door window and, beyond it, the site of his daughter's grave.

More than once, he tried to convince himself that it hadn't actually happened, but then he'd catch sight of the shovel and garden spade that he'd dropped inside by the back door, see the small clumps of soil that littered the floor around them, and know for certain that he hadn't imagined it in some kind of grief-induced hysteria.

When he was finally able to bring himself to toss the shovel and garden spade down the basement stairs (making it easier to pretend they weren't in the house at all, and since he didn't have them, he *couldn't have* done what he thought he'd done), a phone call from Bill Emerson brought him back to reality.

"Mr. Londrigan? I was just calling to see how you were holding up."

"Well as can be expected, I guess."

"I was afraid of that. I'm sorry."

"Thanks."

Emerson had cleared his throat and shuffled through some papers. "I just wanted to let you know that we haven't made much progress on the theft of your daughter's body. The searches at the frat houses didn't turn up much—well, we busted about half a dozen students for possession of pot but I don't imagine you much give a shit about that—"

Robert had laughed.

"What is it?" asked Emerson.

"Nothing. You know, I like you, Detective. You have this way of saying exactly what's on your mind the second it occurs to you."

"My wife complains about that all the time. Says I need to learn to either shut up or filter my comments. She never has friends over when I'm home. Should I take that personally?"

Again, Robert laughed. "Listen, Detective—"

"Bill, please."

"Okay, Bill . . . listen. I, uh . . . I don't need for you to keep me posted about this." He almost, *almost* told Emerson then about what had happened; how much trouble could he be in? Emerson knew from driving him home that he'd been out of it that night, that his actions would have been those of a man under a great deal of emotional stress, the detective would understand, Robert was certain of that, just as he was sure that, if it came down to it, Emerson would testify to Robert's state of mind if any charges were filed against him.

The moment passed, and Robert kept it to himself.

"I *have* to keep you posted, Mr. Londrigan—"

"Robert, please."

"Okay, Robert. It's departmental protocol—them's the rules. I gotta keep you posted on any and all progress or lack thereof. Sorry."

Robert found his gaze wandering toward the darkened kitchen and the back door window, but he snapped his head around so he wouldn't give into the compulsion. "I understand. But . . . it's just a *thing*, you know? Flesh, bone, tissue . . . it's just something that would have contained her, given her something to walk around in. It's not really my daughter."

"The bastard still broke the law. He still did something obscene to you and the memory of your family. I don't much care for that sort of thing."

That sort of thing.

Robert wondered how Emerson would react to the sort of thing he himself had done.

He wondered how long it would be before someone found out, before a stray cat or raccoon or some other animal started digging around in the garden (Denise had complained enough about that over the years) and happened upon something buried down there and, hmm, what's this? Think I'll dig in with my claws and find out and—hey! This tears pretty easy and—wow, something's *in there*, so why don't I just give it a little yank with my teeth and—

—stop it!

Gary A. Braunbeck

He pressed his hands against his eyes for a few moments, his body wilting into the lumpy, damp, torn cushions of the theater seat as he tried to follow the dialogue sputtering from a sound system that was probably considered state-of-the-art when Nixon was in office but now was so miserably outdated and badly maintained that what emerged from the speakers was the auditory equivalent of a Rorschach test: a multilayered, hissing, buzzing, popping, thrumming hubbub from which you had to decide for yourself what words you heard and string them together into a sentence, those sentences into dialogue; and that dialogue—combined with the all too frequently blurry images on the tattered screen—into something that resembled a plot.

That was if you cared enough to pay it any attention.

Which Robert did not.

Especially tonight.

Right now he was trying to stop the pile driver pounding in his temples and behind his broken nose, which no amount of painkillers had been able to ease. It wasn't the pain he was trying to stifle so much as its maddening rhythm, for with each damned beat came the words *They're dead*.

Those words hung in his mind like drenched shirts on a clothesline being whipped by the wind, lashing around, then snapping loudly with the tempo of his blood.

They're dead . . . They're dead . . . They're—

—and there it was on the screen right before his eyes, grainy but clear enough: a shaky tracking shot of him walking toward Denise's garden, a shoe box cuddled against his chest—

—*stop it!*—

—not him, not him at all up there, no shoe box or shovel or garden spade, just some young boy pressing his hands against a glass partition, looking at a newborn baby on the other side . . .

He groaned, then leaned back his head and tried to take a deep breath only to find that his nostrils were clogged with snot and pressure. He yanked a handkerchief from his back pocket and readied to Sound the Foghorn (Denise's expression, she'd always kidded him about thinking his nose was a tad too big) when he saw the first speckle of blood drip onto the cloth.

Clenching his jaw, Robert waited for the sound system to screech again, then blew his nose.

So much blood came out that for a moment he thought he was hemorrhaging. The center of the handkerchief was at once soaked through and his palms felt hot and sticky and there was a sudden, almost overpowering taste of copper.

Clutching the sopped handkerchief against his nose, he lurched out of the seat and made his way up the aisle. Someone whose breathing problems made them sound like a twittering bird every time they exhaled suddenly coughed. Robert was almost to the lobby when he tripped over the Breather's outstretched legs. He stumbled, stopped himself from falling by gripping the back of a nearby seat, then looked at the Breather and said, "I'm sorry, I was—"

The rest of it died in his throat when the guy raised his head.

He breathed through his mouth because his face had no nose, and only one eye socket directly in the center of his forehead where two bright blue eyes struggled to stay in place. Above his eye was a rounded lump of pinkish white scar tissue, and it took Robert a moment but then he recalled the proboscislike appendage that had been there in the photograph.

My brothers and sisters, Willy. Do you despair yet?

Robert stumbled backward, half leaning against, half sitting on the arm of a seat behind him, wanting desperately to look away from the face before him but compelled by something unseen to keep his gaze steady and unblinking.

The guy struggled to his feet. Despite the off-center hump on his back that caused him to stoop and lean slightly to the left, he still towered over Robert; he had to be six seven, six eight, at least.

Robert pushed his hands out in front of him. "N-no . . ." There was no doubt in his mind that he was facing the child from the second picture Split-Face had shown him, now grown into full, frightening, impossible adulthood.

"Ian," said the guy, slapping his massive hands against his chest. "Ian." He had no upper teeth, and only a few in the bottom of his mouth; as he said his name again, smiling like someone who'd just found an old, lost friend, his too-large tongue lolled out the side of his mouth, creating a steady, thick stream of drool that trickled onto his shirt and sheened his chin. Noticing this, he reached into one of his own pockets and produced a handkerchief, which he used to wipe away the saliva.

It was something in the way he pulled out the handkerchief and opened it by snapping his wrist and letting it unfurl; the movement was obviously a well-practiced one, something he'd been taught to do so that he wouldn't repulse anyone if he had an Incident in public.

He seemed so . . . *proud* of himself for remembering to do this. In the flickering light of the movie screen, his smile seemed so hard-won that Robert couldn't feel afraid, not now; there was nothing threatening or grotesque or pathetic or even sad about the guy: he was just happy to see Robert.

"Why?" whispered Robert.

He slapped his chest again. "Ian. Me Ian."

Robert pulled in a breath; a fresh wave of blood from his nose began to backwash down his throat, so he leaned forward and blew once more into his handkerchief, rendering it useless.

Ian produced another, fresh handkerchief from his pocket and handed it to Robert, taking the bloody one from his hand. "Here. Ian got lots."

Robert nodded his thanks, blew once again—this time producing much less blood—but when he looked up, Ian was gone.

He jumped to his feet and looked around the theater with the urgency of someone who'd just lost track of a child in a crowd, but there was no sign of the giant.

What the hell just happened? he thought.

An unnerving thought came to him: *He was following me.*

Then, what was rapidly becoming his mantra: *Stop it!*

He continued on up the aisle and out into the lobby, making a beeline for the men's room.

He was just passing the popcorn stand, remembering a time when the Midland used to serve real butter on its popcorn, when a familiar voice said, "Tell me again how you're doing fine."

Lynn, his sister, came up to him, smacked him once on the arm, then began pushing him toward the front doors.

"How did you know where—?"

"Because," snapped Lynn, "whenever you get stressed out or depressed or start feeling cornered, you always go back to your old college haunts. That's how they catch tigers in the wild, you know? They always return to a place of remembered happiness. *You* go either to Ye Old Mill in Utica for ice cream or Devito's Bookstore downtown or here. I used to hate your being so predictable. Now I'm glad. I—*don't you dare* pull away from me like that! It won't do any good."

They were outside now, heading toward the parking lot, the physical state of the world creating a visual counterpart to Robert's feelings.

The first snow had fallen early—in this case, November 1, two nights ago—and it had been an impressive debut for the season. A half foot of now old and crusty snow covered the ground. The last thirty hours had brought nothing more than dry cold, so the snow had merely aged and turned the color of damp ash (too much like Denise's face that last night), mottled now by candy wrappers, discarded disposable diapers, empty cigarette packs, broken liquor bottles, and used condoms. The layer of snow now whispering from the night sky was a fresh coat of paint, a whitewash that hid the ugliness and despair of the tainted world underneath.

A drunken voice, enraged, thick with mucus and pain, called out from somewhere.

Another voice, this one farther away and much fainter, sang, "*Ian . . . Me Ian . . .*"

Gary A. Braunbeck

In the distance, its echo hovering like the death rattle from the throat of a terminal cancer patient, a window shattered.

Robert shuddered as he tramped through the slush and ice and new snow, his gaze darting around as he remembered how terrific this section of town used to be when he was younger, when the Midland Theater was *the* place to see the latest flicks on the weekend and the shops and restaurants surrounding it were always full of laughing couples or groups of friends out having another great Friday night while they were still young enough to enjoy it.

That was before the change took place and left those memories in ruins. Robert supposed every city had an area like this, one that was once clean and popular and exciting until one factory too many decided to close its doors and move elsewhere, leaving only confusion and anger and poverty in its wake. Eventually those who used to be proud to live here, who had helped create the glory of the past, became too frustrated and too poor and woke one morning to find themselves dubbed "white trash" by those who still had jobs and some semblance of a dream. Ignorance, violence, and defeatism lived here now, within the decaying, condemned buildings, scuttling through dank, waste-stinking alleyways, hiding behind rusted garbage cans, ready to pounce on any of the odd, damaged people who wandered these streets where assault, robbery, drugs, even murder and rape were commonplace enough to be considered the norm, all of it somehow invisible to those who lived on the other side of the East Main Street Bridge.

"You always did have a knack for finding such charming, out-of-the-way places," said Lynn, pulling him along with more immediacy. "I used to think there wasn't anyplace that couldn't be made beautiful by snow. Guess this shows me, huh?"

"It used to be nice," said Robert. "You're too young to remember it in its heyday, but this used to be the greatest place. I was . . . I was just hoping to catch a glimpse of its ghost, that's all."

86

Lynn's husband, Danny, was standing next to their Toyota. His shoulders slumped with relief when he saw them.

"Keys," said Lynn.

For a moment Robert thought she was talking to Danny, but then her hand reached into his own left jacket pocket and snatched out his car keys, which she tossed to her husband while pushing Robert toward the Toyota.

"Hold on," he protested, somewhat more weakly than he would have liked. "I'm perfectly capable of driving myself—"

"Oh, shut up," snapped his sister. "You're in no shape to do much of anything right now—or haven't you noticed that your shnoz is doing a Niagara Falls? On top of that, you're shaking."

"Haven't eaten since lunch," he muttered, remembering the limp, leftover, room-temperature pizza he'd nibbled on right out of the box because he didn't want to put it in the refrigerator because that would have meant going into the kitchen, and in the kitchen was the back door, and in the back door was a window, and through the window there was a view of the yard, and in the yard was Denise's garden, and in Denise's garden there was a flagstone, and under that flagstone . . .

"Lunch *yesterday*, I'm willing to bet," said Lynn. By now they were in the car. Lynn blew a kiss to Danny as he drove away in Robert's Audi.

Robert cleared his throat. "I, uh . . . I don't—I wasn't planning on going back home—um, to the house—tonight." He winced at the touch of petulance that had entered his voice. He couldn't get the taste of copper out of his mouth.

"Good," said Lynn. "I'd hate to think we tidied up the guest room for nothing." She put on her seat belt, then fastened Robert's, then started the car. "I've got half a nerve to punch your lights out—disappearing the night before your wife's funeral and trying to lose yourself in this shitty section of town." She shook her head as she drove away from the Midland. "Did you see that the lobby has piss stains on the carpeting? Place doesn't exactly scream 'Good, clean family fun.' Danny wanted to bring his gun along when I told him where we were going. It's goddamn *dangerous* down here, Bobby! I don't need you acting like some character out of a Eugene O'Neil play, you hear me? The iceman probably wouldn't cometh to these parts, anyway. *Christ*, you gave us a scare. Eric was in tears, afraid that he'd never see his uncle again." Her right hand like a stone from a slingshot crossed the distance between them and struck him hard in the shoulder. "You deserved that for making Eric worry. Kid's only four years old."

Cringing from the pain—damn, she had a wicked punch!—Robert leaned against the door. "You discipline your students like this?"

"Even for teenaged hormone-slaves, they're mature beyond their years compared to the way you've acted."

"I just had to . . . to get out and be by myself for a while, all right? There's just been so much to deal with. Too many people, too many flowers, too many phone calls . . ."

"God forbid that anyone care enough to check on you."

"I've had nothing *but* people checking on me for the last three days! From the station, at the funeral home—"

"So what? Did it ever occur to you that maybe all these people are keeping tabs on you because they were worried you might do something stupid like wander off and not tell anyone? Of course not—that would make sense."

"You sound like an *older* sister now. I remember when you were little, you always followed me around like some lost puppy, you always wanted to do everything I did—'My big brother Bobby's the bestest!'—remember that?"

"Pardon me if I don't feel much like waxing nostalgic with you." She sighed disgustedly as she took the on-ramp to the freeway. "Damn it, Bobby! You're the only brother I've got. I know you thought I was a pain in the ass when we were kids— and to tell you the truth, when I started getting older I thought you were some kind of freakazoid—but I love you. I love you, and I can't stand to see you push everyone away so you can go through this alone. You had to handle enough stuff on your own when Mom and Dad were still alive—"

"Do we have to bring that up now?"

"*Yes!*" She hit the steering wheel with her fist, once, just as a siren screamed to life and flashing lights appeared in the rear-view mirror. Robert's entire body tensed as the police cruiser closed the distance between them while Lynn was trying to de-cided whether or not the cops were after her for speeding or some other moving violation. Robert could picture Emerson stepping out of the cruiser and walking up to the car, hand on his holstered gun: *Went by your house just to see how you were doing and when you didn't answer the front door I went around back. There was this big, ugly raccoon digging up your garden, so I shooed it away and damn if there wasn't this box the thing had dug up and—well, being a detective and all, professional Nosey Parker, I looked inside . . . and you have the right to remain silent . . .*

The cruiser overtook, then passed them, its siren singing Me *Iaaaaannnnn . . . Me Iaaaaannnnn . . .*

Robert was so relieved he was surprised he didn't wet his pants.

"Bobby?"

He blinked, exhaled a breath he wasn't aware he'd been hold-ing, and said, "Wh-what?"

"Are you listening to me?"

"About half. Sorry."

"Look, I never told you how much it meant to me that you protected me from what was going on with Dad when he was still drinking. I had no idea how bad things were at the house. You always managed to diffuse things—or clean up the mess afterward—before I was exposed to it."

"You were only a kid."

"We were all only kids once—except maybe for you." She laughed sadly. "Sometimes I think you were *born* thirty-nine years old."

Robert pulled Ian's handkerchief away from his nose (*How*

many others like him are out there? Are they all following me? God, do they know what I did with Emily?) and saw that it was stained with blood, but not as badly as the first one. He couldn't say the same for his shirt, which looked as if he'd come out on the losing end of a particularly vicious street fight.

Denise used to worry so about the way his nose bled when he was stressed.

Denise.

She worried about so much.

As if reading his thoughts, Lynn glanced at him, her eyes brimming with unshed tears, and tried to smile. "She always used to say how it felt like she was training you after you got married. 'He's coming along very nicely,' she'd say. 'I expect he'll be ready for unveiling any day now.' God, Bobby, she was really funny. Like Noel Coward, you know? A real dry wit."

"I know," whispered Robert, his chest tightening. "I used to have to bite my tongue damn near in two to keep from laughing—I didn't want to let her know she'd gotten me with one of her jokes or zingers and . . ." He stopped, convinced that he finally felt tears coming. He hadn't been able to cry for Denise and Emily since the night they'd died.

. . . nothing.

"I never told her how funny she was, Lynn. I never told her how she always made me smile, even when I didn't feel like it."

Lynn, crying freely, asked, "Why not?"

"I don't know. I don't know why I never told her a lot of things. I don't know why I reacted so coldly when she told me she was pregnant, or why I was so selfish toward the end, or why I can't for the life of me find it in myself to cry for her and the baby—no, wait, scratch that last one." He turned to face his sister. "I realize that a person in mourning is supposed to go through all that Kübler-Ross crap, the five stages, anger, denial, bargaining, cha-cha-cha . . . but for the last couple of days I've had this nagging feeling in my gut that the reason I haven't cried, the reason I can't really grieve for her is that my memories of her have been . . . increasingly more vivid. There's this . . . *notion* with me all the time, and even though it's connected with my memories of her, it's like it isn't *my* notion. Is this making sense? Don't answer that, I know it sounds like I'm babbling. Listen—you know those stories about how some people have fillings in their teeth that pick up radio signals, so they hear voices in their head because of it? I feel like there's something in me that's picked up on a signal of some kind, a thought or an idea that Denise left behind, only it's not complete, understand? It's in pieces, scattered all over the house, or at the places we used to go together, sometimes in the pages of one of her favorite books, and every so often I get this feeling that something I can't see is . . . is trying to come together, to fully form itself, and I'm supposed to help it gather up its missing pieces until it's whole. *Then* I'll know what she's trying to tell me, then . . . then . . ." He parted his hands before him and shook his head, unable to make it any clearer.

"God, Bobby, I miss her so much already," choked Lynn. "And I feel so *lousy* for you. I wish I could . . . I don't know . . ."

"Me too," he said, taking hold of her hand.

So why do I feel like I'm being haunted by a ghost of someone else's making?

Then they were in front of the house and Danny was thanking the baby-sitter and there was the still-sniffling Eric, who came running up to the car and threw his arms around Uncle Bobby's legs, then looked up at Robert with the most heartrending expression of worry ever worn on a four-year-old's face; then, as everyone made their way inside, the wind came whipping by and the wet shirts hanging on the clothesline in Robert's brain started snapping again: *They're dead. . . . They're dead. . . . They're . . .*

Chapter Two

The "guest room," as Lynn euphemistically called it, was actually a storage space at the end of the upstairs hall that contained, among other things, a small sofa bed. Several things had been gathered up and crammed into a closet whose door was being held closed (barely) by a bulky antique sewing machine.

One wall was almost completely hidden by a long row of tall bookshelves overflowing with knickknacks, photographs both framed and loose, statuettes, and, of course, books: Updike, Brontë, Stephen King, Vonnegut, William Peter Blatty, Jane Austen, Carson McCullers, Russell Banks, Madeleine L'Engle, Dave Berry, on and on, the collection so varied that "eclectic" didn't even begin to describe it. Denise's own tastes in books, movies, and music had been the same way.

Robert sat down on the edge of the sofa bed and examined the shelves while Lynn taped the metal splint back into place over his nose (she'd insisted on cleaning him up as soon as they were through the door; both of them had been shocked at how swollen and discolored Robert's nose was, not to mention the size of the cut on the side).

"All finished," said Lynn, smoothing down the last strip of medical adhesive tape.

Robert was staring at the doll on one of the shelves. "Where'd you get that?"

"Get what?" said Lynn, looking to where he pointed. "Oh, the nesting doll?"

"*Matryoshka* doll," Robert corrected. "Denise was zealous about calling them by their proper name. Is that one of the set Mom used to have?"

"No. Denise made it for me—and I got the same lecture about

its proper name. It was my birthday present from her last year. I remember she felt bad because she gave it to me two weeks late." Lynn took it off the shelf, then joined her brother on the sofa bed. "This one holds three more inside. Denise did a great, great job."

She offered the doll to Robert, who was stunned to see the degree to which his wife (*late wife*, he reminded himself) had perfectly, almost eerily, captured Lynn's face.

He took the pear-sized and -shaped doll from his sister, examining it more closely. Denise had not only conveyed the basics of Lynn's face—any sketch artist worth their carbon base could easily have done as much—but had gone much deeper, capturing the subtleties of her features, as well; the way the corners of her eyes scrinched up when she was smiling inside and didn't want anyone to know it, the mischievous pout of her mouth when she was bursting to share good news with someone and there wasn't anyone around, the sharpness of her cheekbones that looked almost regal when she chose to accent them with just a hint of rouge—all these details leapt out at him, impressive and mystifying, their craftsmanship nothing short of exquisite.

He'd never really thought she was—had been—*this* gifted.

"God, I hope you thanked her about a million times."

"What do you *think?* Open it."

He did, finding an equally sublime depiction of Danny on the doll inside, then a brightly innocent but very much *alive* likeness of Eric on the doll within that. The last *matryoshka* was that of an infant, newly born and wrapped in a soft blue blanket.

"You don't have another kid—or is there something you're not telling me?"

"Not yet," said Lynn, beaming. "But Danny and I have been trying for a few weeks. Denise knew how much I wanted another child, so she gave me one—at least, with the doll. She told me that the Russian mystics believed that the *matryoshka* had certain powers, that if a person believed enough in the scene the dolls portrayed when they were taken apart and set side by side, then it would come true. I guess a lot of old-country matchmakers used to make *matryoshka* dolls for the women of their village who were trying to find a husband and start their own family. I even read that someone once made a set of them for Princess Alix of Hesse-Darmstadt that showed her marrying Nicholas II and having several children." She held the last doll close to her, a wistful look on her face. "Wouldn't it be nice if that legend was true? That these dolls would cause Danny and me to have another child, a girl this time like Denise painted? We decided if that happens, we'll name our daughter after Denise."

"She'd like that. Romantic and slightly sentimental and a touch bittersweet. She loved that sort of thing."

Lynn put down the doll and embraced him tightly. "I'm sorry that I talked about Danny and me wanting another baby. I know how hard you and Denise tried, and then to have some . . . some *fucker* steal the body like that . . . I was being selfish, I wasn't thinking. Forgive me?"

"Nothing to forgive." Robert returned her brace with equal affection, his mind flipping through its memory pages until it came upon Denise's cramped work area in the basement, and he saw her there as she must have looked when working, alone for countless silent hours, concentrating with almost superhuman intensity as she layered detail upon detail until the face of each doll seemed to be alive, her back aching from the lumps in the old swivel chair that she was forever refusing to replace as above her, neatly aligned on the shelves of a hutch unit she'd bought for twelve dollars at a yard sale two years ago, other *matryoshka* dolls watched over her, giving silent thanks for her having brought them into existence.

Turning the doll over, he saw that she had signed the bottom—her handwriting was always so lovely—with her calligraphy pen. He remembered when she'd taken the calligraphy class at the community center, how excited she'd been, because it meant that she no longer had to buy pretty-picture Hallmark cards, she could make her own. "I think it makes it more special, don't you?" she'd said. "Doing the card by hand—and I can use different colors of ink. They'll be *gorgeous* . . . if I don't screw up." And her calligraphy had been smooth and elegant—as was her name written on the bottom of the first doll. Until the day he died, Robert would recognize her handwriting and calligraphy work on sight, even though he'd never really told her how terrific she'd gotten at it. He never told her how terrific she'd been at a lot of things.

He wondered—Mr. Clueless—why she'd never painted a set of dolls for him. Had he been *that* apathetic about her chosen hobby? Did his apathy cross her mind during those long, silent hours of painting detail upon detail, causing her to wonder if anything she did held real value or possessed a meaning beyond the visual pleasure of looking at the finished product?

I'm sorry, hon, God, I'm so sorry . . . forgive me . . . forgive me . . .

Lynn pulled away, patted his shoulder, and—after reassembling the dolls—announced it was time to go downstairs and get a decent, tasty, home-cooked meal into him.

He didn't argue.

It would be good to feel something warm inside.

In sleep he surrendered to the chill timelessness that always accompanies the suppression of grief. The place in his heart where once existed the love for Denise was silently, stealthily replaced by a lonely ache that filled every crevice of his body.

He awakened to look down upon his sleeping self. He saw a man isolated, apart; ineffective and meaningless. A blink, a sigh, a shiver, and he was lying in the bed once again, reunited with his flesh.

He stared at the ceiling, feeling overwhelmed and invaded, as if another Self, a sad, broken thing that had lain dormant for so long, impatient and inaccessible, was insinuating itself into his flesh, forcing out the man he'd always thought himself to be. Pale moonlight like a beam from a projector shone through the window, alighting on the full-length mirror leaning against one of the walls.

In this bed, he was alone.

But not so in the mirror's reflection.

Denise, her wide gray eyes radiant, was lying next to him there.

The mirror's reflection was repeated in the glass of the window behind him and that reflection, in turn, was repeated in the mirror, back and forth, one into the other, a hundred Roberts, a hundred Denises, reflected one within the other within the other into infinity.

He concentrated on the reflection in the mirror, wondering if he should chance touching her—the Self in the mirror did the same things he did, their movements and gestures synchronized like two Olympic swimmers; if he were to make that Self caress her, would he himself feel the warmth of her lips, the smoothness of her skin, the ordered, necessary, unavoidable erotic truth that was her body? He'd always felt that way. Every time he saw her, every time they kissed, every time he caught a scent of her perfume that entered a room just before she did, he was amazed at the rush of emotions within him. Being with her wasn't like having a fantasy come true before he was ready for it; it was like having a fantasy come true before he'd even had the fantasy.

In the mirror, he put his arm around her, and they began to drift off to sleep—

—*They're dead . . . They're dead . . . They're . . .*

Robert sat up and turned on the small bedside (or was it *sofaside?*) lamp, his body soaked in sweat.

He shuddered, then looked at the mirror.

The black-eyed, bandaged-nosed reflection of him-Now and him-Alone stared back.

Damn it, why did this have to happen again? The first time

he'd had a hallucination—or flashback, or waking dream, or whatever in the hell you wanted to call it—was the night after he buried Emily in the backyard. He spent the remainder of that night sleeping—scratch that, *trying* to sleep—at a nearby motel, but any bed was too big without Denise next to him, so he decided he would not spend the next night in the house, either, or the night after that, or any night, if he could help it. The first step in that plan had been to spend the night in a seat at the Midland Theater, but then his nose had—

—"Ah, hell."

He leaned forward, rubbed his eyes, and looked at the time. Three forty-seven A.M.

He hated the idea of taking another sedative on top of the Demerol—from such mistakes were junkies and corpses made— but he had to get some sleep. The funeral was in seven hours and he didn't want to show up looking dead himself.

Fifteen minutes later, after taking half a tablet of his pre-scribed sedative and turning the mirror around so that it faced the wall, he was more awake than ever. He thought about going downstairs to watch television but was afraid his moving around would waken Lynn and she'd panic and go into her mother-hen routine—

—that wasn't fair to her. She was only doing what she thought necessary, coming after him and all of that. Who'd have thought *she'd* turn out to be the responsible one?

Okay, then: read something.

Denise had gotten him into the habit of reading at bedtime, claiming that it gave the mind focus and therefore made it easier to relax and fall asleep. It also—depending on what you chose to read—helped to unconsciously bolster your literacy level. This last claim of hers, which had seemed absurd to him at the time, gained some respectability later on when Gene MacIntyre, the news director at Channel 7, complimented Robert on his "solid copy."

"I've always preferred the Edward R. Murrow, no-bullshit style of television reporting," MacIntyre had said. "Most reporters hand in copy that's too concerned with grabbing the viewers' attention and holding it—no wonder broadcast journalism has degenerated into overbaked sensationalism. I don't know what you've been doing to sharpen your writing, Bob, but it's working like nobody's business. Your last few pieces have been models of clarity and structure. I like that right down to the ground."

His copy wouldn't have looked so good had not Denise coaxed him into reading more.

And he'd been arrogant enough to think that all of his recent success was his sole doing.

He pulled himself out of bed and stood in front of the bookshelves, searching for a book with the kind of title that would have piqued Denise's interest.

He thought of the bookshelves back at the house that held her favorite books; bittersweet, melancholy, even tragic novels like *The Lonely Passion of Judith Hearne*, *Georgy Girl*, *The Heart is a Lonely Hunter*, *Other Bells For Us to Ring*, *The Small Rain*, *The Dean's Watch*, tales filled with alienation and regret and longing. He once asked her (more out of idle curiosity than genuine interest) why she was drawn to novels that were so sad.

"Because there are only two things that really count," she said. "People you love, and sadness; everything else traces back to them, eventually."

He found himself staring into the eyes of Lynn's *matryoshka* counterpart.

People you love, and sadness.

People you love, and—

—a few inches away from the *matryoshka* doll was a book that seemed out of place. Where the rest of the books on this shelf—in alphabetical order, no less, pure Lynn—were thick, hardcover novels, this was something a child would make in a preschool art class: two pieces of heavy, colored construction paper on which someone had used a three-hole punch so that covers and pages both could be bound with sections of fuzzy green yarn tied into bows. Judging from the way both upper and lower portions of it jutted out at an angle, it had been hastily crammed between the other books even though there was no room for it.

It was obviously something Eric had made at preschool and Robert carefully worked it out of its tight place between Peter Straub and Kurt Vonnegut, not applying too much pressure because he didn't want to tear the "covers."

He took the "book" and sat down on the bed, then read the title on the cover.

Siempre's Magic Mask.

The title flowed across the cover in elegant calligraphy.

In Denise's handwriting.

She must have helped Eric with his little project, of course, that had—

(*I tell them the story of the Masks and they listen, and they believe. Do you know the story of the Masks? Did she ever tell you?*)

—to be it.

He took a deep breath, steadied his hand, and opened to the first page.

The first thing that took him by surprise was that there were no pictures; didn't every child who made a storybook stuff it full of pictures?

The second thing was the printing itself; with the spelling corrected here and there (again, in Denise's handwriting), the text appeared to have been written by an older child, perhaps even a teenager whose skills with a pen left a lot to be desired. Robert could sympathize; his own handwriting was just a notch above scribbling.

But, still . . . who would have printed this for Eric? Not Lynn or Danny, both of them had impeccably neat handwriting.

You're wandering.

He blinked, rubbed his eyes, and read the story:

Once Upon a Time, in a place closer to here than you think, lived an old man who, the grown-ups said, used to guard the great palace that could be seen from the village square. The children all knew that the palace was old and abandoned and falling to ruin. None were allowed anywhere near its rusted gates.

But that did not stop them from gathering in the square some nights before the supper hour and staring at the great structure. Through the mists of evening, up there on the brooding mountaintop, crouching like some dying beast of myth, its teeth and strength crumbling to putrefaction, alone and sputtering toward death as its jaundiced eyes beheld the march of passing years, the sad, deserted palace drowsed as the children watched and wondered and whispered among themselves of the mysterious memories it hoarded of its glorious days of splendor.

A score or more of mangy, scarred, stinking gray monkeys, vicious and violent beyond all bearing, scuttled up and down the decrepit walls, holdovers (or so said the grown-ups) from the last stockade of animals kept at the palace for the amusement of the Prince.

But always, just before the supper hour, the monkeys disappeared behind the decaying walls, and from then until well after dawn no life stirred; no serpents slithered from under rocks, no vultures swooped down to feast on the bloated remains of other animals, for there were no other animals; even the monkeys made no further movement or sounds. It was as if the cheerlessness of the place, formless during the day, became a ghost who haunted the ruins when the moon rose in the sky, one so fearsome that even the wildest and most dangerous of creatures dared not cross its path or make any sound to attract its attention.

And that is how it came to be known as the Specter's Palace.

Well, imagine if you can how excited the children were to discover that there lived, right here in their very own village, someone who once worked within the palace!

"Do not bother him," said their parents. "Hazlitt is a very old and very sick man. His last days on the earth should not be burdened by children troubling him for stories."

The children did as they were told, leaving Hazlitt to his errands in the village and never knocking upon his door, but one night, on the eve of the Harvest Moon, Hazlitt seated himself on the rim of the great stone fountain in the square and waited for the children to gather. As they did, he smiled a wily smile at them and said, "Fetch your mothers and fathers so they, too, might hear what I've to say, and be quick about it."

When the entire village was at last gathered round the old guard, Hazlitt cleared his throat (which caused him no small amount of pain, for he was to die on this night and knew these were his final hours), took a sip of cool water from the fountain, greeted the village warmly, then looked toward the Specter's Palace and said: "Listen. A vast quiet enfolds that deserted shrine, and the wind blows a fetid stench. Is that the hint of an echo from behind its walls?

"In his day the Prince was absolute, ruling over a population of six million souls. Countless grandiose titles blazed upon his colorful banner. One, blazed from the sheer fantasy that often accompanies boredom, was, 'Lord of the Sun, the Moon, the Earth, All Continents Submerged Under the Sea and Those Who Live, Have Lived, or Ever Will Live there.'

"One could hardly be more inclusive.

"During this year in which my story takes place, the palace was beginning to show neglect, for the Prince was an invalid chained to his couch by obesity and stiffened, scabrous limbs, as well as supreme and all-consuming ennui. The entire concern of his ministers was focused on the notion that constant entertainment alone would keep him contented—as well as their heads on their shoulders, for whenever the Prince grew too bored his disposition darkened, and nothing short of a good, bloody display of torture—followed by decapitation—would cheer his spirits. If the subject of this torture was also a young virgin—it mattered not whether it was a girl or boy—who had first been beaten and repeatedly defiled before his eyes, all the better for his mood. And if the virgin's entire family were summarily tortured and killed alongside their child, well, that was a good day, indeed. Since all of the Prince's ministers had families—among them virginal children—his total contentment was their sole purpose in life.

"But all of their efforts failed. Hundreds of weirdly painted, gilded, and otherwise bizarrely caparisoned elephants were prodded into mortal combat, but their slow and bloody deaths failed to produce so much as a smirk on his face; dancing girls who fell out of step were whipped to crimson ribbons for diversion, their flailed flesh stitched into a cloak that was draped about his massive shoulders, but their hideous shrieks for mercy were met only by his yawns; two of his wives were publicly poisoned, but the Prince did not allow even the ghost of a smile to cross his face when one of the women, wracked with convulsions, beat out her brains against the marble dais where he reclined.

" 'What are we to do?' cried one of the ministers in a private meeting later that night. 'His Majesty seems more bored and disagreeable that ever.'

" 'Pray,' answered another minister.

"Their prayers were seemingly answered the following day, for a lone traveler stopped to rest outside the palace and told one of the guards—myself, I can tell you now—about a circus that was at that moment visiting his home, and of the amazing, happy, wondrous entertainment its performers gave to the people. I thanked this traveler and ran at once to the ministers with the news. A dispatch was immediately sent to the traveler's village summoning the performers to the palace.

"The arrival of the circus at the palace was a miracle of timing, for that very morn the Prince had roared that countless forms of unspeakable horror would be loosed upon all under his rule unless he was immediately and successfully amused. To emphasize this, he grabbed a newborn child from its mother's arms and threatened to impale it from anus to throat upon a severed elephant tusk—gleefully laughing at its agonized cries—if his wishes were not met right this very moment! Oh, how the Prince delighted in the suffering of all children!

"I sounded my trumpet—thus saving that child's life. If I will be remembered for no other thing, I will be remembered for saving that child—as long as you, yourselves, care to pass along this tale.

"The leaves of the tall bejeweled screen used to separate the Prince from the rest of the room were flung open wide, and a thundering basso voice cried out: 'Your Most Resplendent, Wise, Holy, and Powerful Majesty! For your entertainment, a display of such artistry and wit even the angels would be moved!'

"Among the many performers hastened before the Prince was a Harlequin, known only as 'Siempre.' His renown in other parts of the world was unequaled. From that day on, it was Siempre who the Prince called upon at all hours to amuse him.

"Eventually the circus moved on, but Siempre, rewarded with fabulous wealth by the Prince and deep respect from all who lived in the kingdom, remained. And for many years Siempre performed for the Prince, who greatly admired the Harlequin's abilities as a clown, dancer, and spinner of countless tales. None had ever made the Prince laugh so often or so loudly.

"But though he often laughed, the Prince seldom smiled,

for much of his character remained brutal and savage, as is so often the case with pampered and arrogant princes who are given absolute power at an early age. The Prince began to notice the way his subjects gazed upon Siempre whenever the Harlequin walked through the palace or visited the villages. No one had ever looked upon the Prince with such awe and affection.

"The Prince became jealous that Siempre's popularity was far surpassing his own. One minister suggested that, if used properly, Siempre might be useful in restoring the Prince's standing in the eyes of his subjects. This idea held great appeal to the obese ruler, who summoned Siempre to his chamber one night and said, 'I wish to learn of your comedic ways so that I too might make my subjects smile. I was, for so long, unkind to them, and I wish to reward their loyalty. Teach me your craft.'

"In truth, the Prince's motives were far less noble; he was no longer the center of his subjects' lives and attention and thoughts, and wanted for them to admire only him. Upon the whims of such selfishness have nations crumbled into the sea.

"Siempre, who was sworn to protect the secrets of his craft, told the Prince in respectful tones that he was honorbound not to reveal the mysteries of his art. Though the Prince at first raged at this, he came to accept Siempre's will.

" 'Then make me a mask such as yours. If I cannot possess your secrets, I will at least sport a like countenance. That will show my people that I am, indeed, a changed man.'

"Alas, Siempre could not grant the Prince even this small request, for the mask of every clown—Pulcinella, Pantalone, or Harlequin—is as individual to them as a man's character. If one were to look closely at the Harlequin, one would see that the contours differ greatly from mask to mask, each one adhering to the structure and movements of the face that wears it: the two faces, it is said, become one, and if the practitioner is truly worthy of his art, the mask turns to skin so that a third face emerges from within the two, the True Face: the one the practitioner had before his parents were born.

"Such was the case with Siempre, who explained all of this to the Prince in soft, compassionate, respectful tones. 'If it please Your Majesty,' said the Harlequin, 'I shall make it my foremost purpose to speak well of you throughout the kingdom, so that your subjects will know your grand heart is no longer blackened by the blood lust and twisted sickmindedness that so permeated your youth.'

"The Prince said nothing for the longest time; then he smiled: a thin, savage, mad smile. He said to the Harlequin, 'That would please me greatly.'

"Lies can fall as sweetly as petals from a rose when they come from the lips of one such as the Prince.

"Dismissing Siempre, the Prince turned to his ministers and cried, 'I shall have his face for my own!'

"And so began the plot against the man who had brought so much joy into the Prince's life, and so much peace to the kingdom.

"For years the Prince lay in wait for the perfect moment, and chose the Festival of Royal Birth to bring his hideous scheme to fruition.

"A sacrifice of a goat was performed on a ceremonial slab high on the west tower of the palace. After the ceremony, Siempre began his dance, depicting, at first, an old man shambling toward Death, his life devoid of happiness or purpose, when suddenly he sees a young maiden walking in a garden. Cupid appears, draws back his bow, and pierces the old man with Love. Suddenly very still, the old man suddenly becomes a swift and eager youth who showers the

Gary A. Braunbeck

maiden with gifts and poetry, among them a sleek black leopard and majestic golden owl.

"Siempre did not know that the Prince had paid the zookeeper handsomely to train these animals against him. When the appointed time came for these animals to make their entrance, the leopard crept in, the owl riding upon the nape of its neck, held there by a special harness the zookeeper had fashioned.

"Upon seeing this, Siempre realized that the Prince meant him harm. He turned toward the divan where the Prince, who was now so grossly immense it took no fewer than five attendants—myself among them—to turn him in his bed, sat smiling a smile so perverted that the Harlequin knew at once the ruler was mad.

" 'I beg of Your Majesty, do not do this. The answers that lie behind this mask are of a nature so vast and prevailing that no man can live with the knowledge.'

" 'Beg all you want, clown,' snarled the Prince, 'but there lives in this land none who has ever denied me . . . and lived.'

"Siempre looked around, saw the guards with their swords and spears at the ready, then folded his hands as if to utter a prayer. 'Will Your Majesty allow me to entertain the court with one last story?'

" 'If you must,' replied the Prince.

" 'You are too kind,' replied the Harlequin. Clearing his throat—and never once taking his gaze from the Prince's face, Siempre told his last story:

" 'Once upon a time, in a kingdom very much like this one, there lived a young man of considerable wealth and power. While visiting the village one day he happened upon a small shop that sold antiquities. Among the items in this shop was an ancient Egyptian vase, thousands of years old. The young man took the vase from the shop and returned to his home where he put forth much effort to break the seal that held close the vase so he might get to the treasures he was certain were hidden within. Try as he did, he could not pry the lid from it. Finally, in a fit of youthful, impatient rage, he smashed the vase on the floor. Inside was only one object: a single, perfect red rose from five thousand years ago. For a moment the boy inhaled the scent of the rose and was overwhelmed by its heady, intoxicating nature . . . but then, of course, he felt cheated, for he was certain the vase had contained jewels of great value. Still, he admitted to himself, the rose gave off a wondrous scent, unlike any other flower he'd ever smelled before. He decided to give the rose to his mother, but when he looked down at his feet he saw that the rose had crumbled into dust. Many, many years later, when the young boy was an old man lying on his deathbed, a priest asked him to confess his greatest sin, and the old man whispered, "I am ashamed that I did not recognize the priceless treasure the old rose gave to me." And so he died, his final words remaining forever a mystery to those who were present to hear them.'

"The Prince—confused and unmoved by the Harlequin's story—produced from the pocket of his robe a flute and blew three long, shrill notes into the air. Leopard and owl as one leaped upon Siempre and with talon and claw tore his mask and face from his skull. The Harlequin fell to the floor, screaming, hands covering the raw, seeping red meat where once the base of his One True Face had been. Blood soaked his costume through. The people of the court and kingdom stood shocked and silent.

"The chief minister carried the soft, pliant, dripping mask-face up to the Prince and placed it in his trembling hands.

"Then, to the horror of all present, Siempre rose to his feet and pulled his hands away from his skull. His eyes had remained firmly embedded in their sockets and stared at the Prince not with hatred, but pity.

" 'Wear it well,' he croaked in a ragged voice that held all the sorrowful rot of the deepest, dankest crypt, 'for you shall not wear it long. It is the beginnings of my One True Face, not yours, and no craftsman, alchemist, or magician can make it so.'

"The Prince laughed at this and snapped his fingers. Guards fell on Siempre—I was one of them, I am ashamed to say—dousing him in oil and setting him aflame. He ran laughing through the palace and through the gates, disappearing into the mountains.

" 'Now,' said the Prince to his subjects, 'I shall be the one who gives laughter to your hearts and to whom you show such affection and awe.' He lifted the warm, seeping mask-face high above his head, allowing a few thick globules of Siempre's blood to spatter on his flesh, then quickly and firmly draped the Harlequin's face over his own.

"The Prince began to twirl and shuffle, as if in the beginnings of a Harlequin's Dance, and strange sounds came from deep inside him; but, at last, he became very still, a statue, something carved from stone. The sounds from deep within him—sometimes lunatic tunes, sometimes words that appeared to be answers to questions no one else could hear being asked—took on a musical, contented quality as the power of the trance became greater.

"Then something . . . happened.

"They say if you stand atop the west tower during the time that once was known as the Festival of Royal Birth—the time you now call the Night of the Harvest Moon—you can still hear the echo of the terrible, anguished scream that exploded from the Prince at the moment Siempre's severed mask-face came into contact with his flesh. It is, they say, a prolonged shriek of unparalleled horror, one that grew so loud and rose so high that its sound encircles the earth forevermore.

"And, if you have the courage to listen closely, somewhere amidst that echo can be heard the last words the Prince ever spoke before collapsing into a cold, dead heap:

" *'Yes, I see them. So many children. Your brothers and sister . . . and I despair. Yes, I despair!'*

"Upon the Prince's death, Siempre's mask-face was thrown into a vat of bubbling clay in hopes the fiery temperature would destroy it. When later the vat was emptied, the Harlequin's mask-face, now forever encased in clay, tumbled out onto the floor.

"A servant whose duty it was to dispose of the mask-face claimed that, as she lifted it from the floor, its still lips suddenly formed a benevolent smile. Terrified, she hurled the mask-face against a wall where it shattered into thirteen pieces. These pieces were then gathered and distributed among only the most trusted of the Prince's guards—myself included. Each of us was given a map of a different continent, then instructed to take our section of the mask-face, journey to our assigned continent, buy a horse of the strongest and noblest lineage, and travel as far as our horses could carry us. When neither we nor our horses could move any farther, we were to dig a hole thirteen feet deep, bury our section of the mask-face, and fill in the hole so that no one would be able to tell it was there.

"Each soldier carried out his duties to the letter.

"Except for one.

"Me.

"I knew in my heart that the palace must be left with some reminder of what the Prince had done to Siempre, so on the night before I was to leave on my journey, I stole into the courtyard in the middle of the night and buried my section there. In the morning I left with the others, so as not to arouse suspicion.

"But that one section of the mask-face remains buried in the ruins of the palace. And every night, when the moon is high and the animals fall silent, know that it is because the Harlequin walks the ruins, searching for the piece of his One True Face that is buried beneath the rubble."

His tale finished, Hazlitt rose, picked up his pack, and wished everyone in the square a good night. It was only as he neared the edge of the village that he turned and saw a young boy following him.

"You would be the orphaned boy, Rael?" asked Hazlitt, for a dream the previous night had told him he would meet this child.

"Yes, sir, that I be."

Gesturing the child closer, Hazlitt reached into his pack and removed a long, thin, shiny object, which he placed into Rael's hands. "This, boy, is the very flute that the Prince often played to signal his guards it was time to begin the torture of one more innocent child. I took it from his fat, disgusting body that day. You take it now, Rael, and learn to play only the most beautiful of tunes upon it. Then, for me, play those tunes as often and as well as you can."

"But the villagers," said Rael, "they might grow tired of my playing."

Hazlitt smiled. "That is why you cannot remain here, boy. Come close, and I'll tell you a secret."

And the old guard told the boy where the thirteen places on this earth were that the pieces of the mask-face were buried. "Each is buried at the base of a mountain, boy, and you'll know these mountains because each of them will open for you if you command them to do so." Hazlitt then told Rael the words he must speak to make the mountains open up. "I'll show you the first," said the old guard, "for it's right there, easily seen from the village square. The rest you will find easily enough on your own.

"Find others such as yourself, Rael, and let your music bring joy into their lives. And if you find the music is not enough, then take them with you into the mountains, to the special world that waits within."

Then, patting the boy's head and pointing him toward the place where the mountain would open up upon his command, Hazlitt wandered off into the night to find a suitable place to die. Whether or not he did die that night, no one ever knew. But he was never seen or heard from again.

As for the orphan boy, Rael, he did as Hazlitt told him, and eventually found all of the opening mountains. He lived a long life, filled with friends and music and many great adventures—perhaps you've even read about some of them. He once played his music for the children in a village called Hamelin. But that is another story for another time; until then, look there, up toward the ruins. See the shuffling, hunched figure making its way over the collapsed walls and piles of stones? Could that be Siempre, still searching? So quiet are the animals. So still. Do you think they have known the treasure of the old rose? Perhaps the Harlequin is not looking for his face, at all; perhaps he searches for dusty petals, or jagged sections of an ancient, smashed vase.

Perhaps he has forgotten what he is searching for.

We can only wonder, and listen to the echo of a sweet, distant music. . . .

At the bottom of the last page, written in the same sloppy, childlike script as the rest of the story, were two sentences: *Did she ever tell you this one, Willy? Hope you decided to stop and smell the Old Rose!*

As soon as Robert finished reading those words, the pages, the covers, the yarn, all of it crumbled to dust in his hands,

Gary A. Braunbeck

drifting through the air and down between his fingers, vanishing before even one particle touched the floor.

This neither shocked nor surprised him, because the only thing he could think at that moment was: *The fucker was here! He was in this house!*

This house where Lynn and Eric and Danny slept.

"Why bring them into this?" he whispered. "They've got nothing to do with—"

—he suddenly doubled over, sobbing loudly, the repressed grief snarling to the surface and joining hands with his fear and growing paranoia, dragging steel hooks against his suddenly pliant soul, shredding him to ribbons. He stumbled backward and collapsed onto the bed, his nose bleeding again as he wrapped his arms around one of the pillows and pulled it close to his chest because he needed to feel something against him, near him, part of him, something other than this pit where his memories felt like cement and every emotion turned into a straight razor that slashed his guts into pulp—

—he shuddered once again, the tears like metal shavings in his eyes as his grief, undammed, gushed through him until his nostrils were clogged and his throat was raw and choked with backwashed blood from his nose—

—oh God, what was he going to do? Who was this crazy fuck who'd broken his nose and stolen the body of his daughter and why did the bastard have to break into Lynn and Danny's house? And there was no way he could explain this to anyone and not sound like he'd gone off the deep end, he had no proof, the book had just *poof*'d away into nothing, and why'd he ever have to look for something to read in the first place? All he wanted was to sleep and he'd almost made it, he'd almost made it to the funeral without letting it get the better of him. Who the hell did he think he was kidding with his "I can't cry for them" crap? There was no *can't* about it. He simply wouldn't allow himself.

Portrait of a Failed Macho Man, undone by a fairy story.

So he lay there, the convulsions becoming progressively less severe, the flow of blood from his nose staunching itself, his sobs turning into soft, pitiful, ragged croaks.

He flopped over onto his back and stared up at the ceiling, wondering for just a moment if there was a beam up there that could take his weight.

Denise would have kicked his ass for thinking something like that.

He listened for the sound of Lynn's footsteps in the hall; he *had* to have wakened her.

Nothing; no sound, no voices, no movement.

He pulled himself into a sitting position, putting his head between his bended knees to ease the rising nausea, the tears still trickling down his numbed cheeks. He considered what he should do next. He decided to pull Danny aside tomorrow and tell him—after all, hadn't Lynn said something about Danny owning a gun? He'd have to tell Bill Emerson about this, as well; if Split-Face was going to start stalking Lynn and her family, Robert wanted something done to stop it *now*. Coming after him was one thing, but *this* . . .

Not within reach of his arm. Split-Face would not harm any of them.

Never.

Sometime later, he lifted his head when the first plaintive morning song of a bird filtered in from beyond the frosted window. Stumbling like a drunkard and wondering why in hell this bird hadn't flown south like it was supposed to, he lurched out of bed and to the window, rolling up the blind.

Outside it was purple gray; dawn just creeping in, night not quite finished with the world yet. A glittering layer of ice-snow enshrouded the yard as a dispirited breeze sloughed its way through the trees.

Unable to find any trace of the bird, he closed his eyes and pressed his head against the damp window glass. The contrast of its icy temperature against his own feverish one jarred him and he pulled away, snapping open his eyes.

Denise stood behind him in the window's reflection; naked, her hair tumbling down over her shoulders, a dark velvet cradle, lying gently against the slope of her breasts. He watched as her arms slipped around him, her fingers twirling patterns into his sparse, matted chest hair, then gliding down, down, her fingertips brushing over his nipples as they swept down, slowly down, teasingly down, pausing playfully as she laid her cheek against his bare shoulder, then rolling her head around so her lips kissed the nape of his neck, then one of her hands reached below his waist with craving and purpose; he arched his back to make it easier for her, not daring to turn around because he knew she'd be gone, only in this amorphous reflection could they be together, so he was content to watch as she kissed his neck and rubbed his stomach and massaged his cock in a way that always drove him into a frenzy—

—watched, but didn't feel any of it.

At all.

God help him, he couldn't feel anything at all.

Lynn was furious when she saw the state of the pillows and sheets later that morning. "Damn it, Bobby!" she snapped at him over breakfast. "Why didn't you wake me up? It wouldn't've been any trouble to get fresh sheets and pillowcases."

"Like to watch people bleed in the middle of the night, do you?"

"Oh, sarcasm, that's good—but then, that's my Big Bestest Brother. Always have to do it alone, don't you?"

"Write a new verse to that song."

She poured him another cup of coffee and placed two more strips of freshly grilled bacon beside his pancakes. "You seemed okay last night. What brought it on? You have bad dreams or something?"

"Or something." He speared a good-sized chunk of pancake

onto his fork and stuffed it into his mouth before she could ask him for more details.

"You should have woke me up," Lynn whispered, sitting down. She glared at him for a long moment, then her features softened as she reached across the table and took hold of his hand. She looked into his eyes and Robert nodded his head. Words would only have diminished what passed between them.

Robert glanced through the morning newspaper Lynn had been reading when he came into the kitchen. It felt good, felt *normal*, to be doing this, sitting at a breakfast table, sipping coffee and flipping through the paper, just like millions of other people were doing at this moment.

He turned the page, folded the paper, then folded it again, then one more time (something that used to drive Denise crazy), and was preparing to read an article about yet more road work on I-70 when he saw the article at the bottom left, next to a used-car lot advertisement: DONOR HEART LOST IN TRANSIT.

The story told him just enough to tell him nothing at all: A donor heart that was Life-Flighted from a central Ohio hospital to the Columbus International Airport appeared to have been lost somewhere en route to Johns Hopkins. All that was known for certain was that the heart—intended for a three-year-old child—was inside its transport container when put aboard the plane, but when opened in the operating room at JH, there was nothing inside but ice and what one source described as ". . . some sort of decayed tissue." The tissue was being analyzed and the three-year-old child—whose name was Heather Wilson— was in guarded condition. The family was still hoping another heart would become available.

No . . . thought Robert, remembering the small heart within his daughter's chest that gave out with the softest of beats when his finger brushed its surface. *No, it couldn't have been hers. It couldn't have been . . . please, no . . .*

"Hey, you."

He looked up at Lynn, blinking at the sight of her face as if emerging from a dream. "Huh? Wh-what?"

"You seemed to have driven off the highway for a minute."

"Uh, yeah . . . I guess I did." A pitiful smile. "Sorry about that."

Finishing up his breakfast—surprised that at least his appetite was getting back to normal—he looked around for his coat and said, "I'm going to head back over to the house and take a shower. Tell Dan thanks for the shirt, I'll return it later this week."

Lynn quickly gathered up the breakfast dishes. "Give me a couple of minutes and I'll come with you. Eric and Danny are both still asleep—Eric slept with us last night. I'll leave Danny a note to let him know we'll meet him at the funeral home. The baby-sitter should get here about—"

"No," said Robert firmly. "I'll be fine—wait, scratch that: I *hate* the thought of having to go back there by myself but—"

"Then just let me—"

"It's something I *have* to do, understand?" He rose from the table and hugged Lynn so tightly he was surprised he didn't crack one of her ribs. "Thanks for fixing up my nose gear again this morning. You've been really great. I never thought when we were kids that you'd grow up to be someone I both love and need so much. But I *have* to face the house, eventually; so unless you and Danny and Eric want to put this place up for sale and move in with me, I'll have to do it by myself."

"But I—"

"Already have two men in your life who depend on you for damn near everything. You don't need to adopt me."

She pulled back, grinned, wiped one of her eyes, then playfully slapped his shoulder. If it weren't for the sadness behind her gaze, she could have passed for happy. "You're right—and don't think it doesn't pain me to admit that." She smoothed

116

down the collar of Danny's borrowed shirt. "But you tell anyone I said that, I'll disown you."

"No, you won't."

"No, I won't—but it sure sounded full of conviction, didn't it?" A tear slipped from her eye; this one, she wiped away with an angry hand. "Don't worry about me, I can't help it. Denise's dying just got me to thinking about things, y'know? How it seems like the two of us were always depending on people who wound up deserting us—not that I'm saying Denise deserted you, right, but her being so suddenly *not there* anymore, it just reminded me of . . . of . . ."

"I understand, Lynn. Really, I do." He was annoyed by the distress in his voice but was damned if he'd let her know it. "And you and I will . . . we'll talk about things, sort through some of that old shit that should've been taken care of long ago. But not now. Later, okay?"

"Promise?"

"Promise."

She stuck out her pinkie. "Pinkie-Swear?"

"You haven't asked me to do that since you were four."

"*Pinkie-Swear?*"

They locked pinkie fingers, twisted them once to the left, then right, then pulled apart. "May I leave now?"

"You may."

"Thanks, Teach." Robert kissed her cheek, grabbed his coat from one of the hooks by the back door, took his keys from the counter where Danny had left them, and left.

He did not notice the crumpled popcorn bag lying in the snow beside the back door; nor did he see the Midland Theater ticket stub he stepped on as he walked toward his car. Had he noticed either of these things, he might have been compelled to turn around; having done so, he would have seen his handkerchief, freshly washed and air-dried (and now embroidered with his initials), hanging from the hook where, in warmer weather, Lynn tied one end of her clothesline.

Chapter Three

Pieces of an incomplete device: a house, a street, a sad and confused man pulling his car into the driveway.

Robert decided the best way to deal with the house was to simply keep moving once he was through the front door, and he did just that.

Straight into the oddly chilly kitchen, never once looking up from the floor, to feed and water the cats, then upstairs to shower, shave, choose a suit from the closet Denise would have liked (not looking for too long at any of her clothes hanging alongside his own), then put on a tie, find his best dress shoes, and back downstairs to give each cat a perfunctory head-scratching before leaving them again to an empty and cheerless house.

Outside, cold light shone down, making the snow sparkle, making things bright enough to guard a little while longer against the trespass of black, meaningless space and time.

This house, filling with a cold breeze wafting from the kitchen; this street, snow-silent and slumbering; this hollow man driving to his wife's funeral as two cats, both mewling for further human contact, watched him leave from their places on the window seat in the living room.

All components of the same device.

Brief, sorrowful, afterthought lives on lonely planet Earth.

She had been moved to the small ersatz chapel in the west wing of the funeral home. Robert saw the dozens of mourners who were milling in that direction and knew he wasn't ready to face things just yet, so he ducked into the cramped "coffee room" just to the right of the main entrance.

Gene MacIntyre was already there.

"I figured you'd probably want to hide out for a few minutes," said the news director, handing Robert a steaming cup of something that looked like tar. "Nice decoration on your nose, there."

Robert said nothing as he took the coffee and sipped; it tasted a hell of a lot better than it looked, a pleasant surprise. Tossing his coat onto the back of a chair, Robert sat on the small sofa while MacIntyre refilled his own cup, then hovered near the door, occasionally craning his head into the hall like some nervous lookout at a bank heist.

"I'm not good at making speeches, Bob, and I'm even worse at expressing sentiment, so what I've got to say I'll say only once, okay?

"I'm fifty-six years old. I am not one of the warm people. I drink more than I should, I like to smoke my cigarettes, I love to gripe, and if I were ever to crack a smile my whole system would more than likely go into cataleptic shock—which'd probably make several people happy. Despite all of this, I can stand here and tell you that I am not a callous grouch who doesn't give a hang about others' feelings. Especially your feelings, and especially right now.

"I buried my own wife seven years ago. Ovarian cancer. I thought for sure I'd die too, or at the very least go crazy. For a while I did—go crazy, that is. Which I suppose is a form of death.

"My point is that you're going to go into that chapel in a few minutes and most of the people in there are going to try and comfort you. It's included with the flowers and coffin. They'll give you a hug or shake your hand or some other type of giving-comfort gesture, and every last jack one of them is going to say something like, 'It's all right' or, 'You'll be fine' or, 'At least she's at rest' or my personal favorite—'The worst is over now.' They don't *mean* to be stupid, it's just the only way they can think of to offer some scrap of comfort to someone who's beyond it right now.

"Take my advice—smile at them if you can and hug them back or shake their hands and then just say thanks. But know this: The worst is not over. Not by a long shot. You haven't even *begun* to experience the worst of this yet. You know, I still walk through the door some nights and expect to hear Jenny's voice or smell her baking that god-awful meat loaf she could never get the hang of. I still only sleep on the right side of the bed and I still keep her pillow on the left.

"I want you to know that I'll do anything I can to help you through this. But don't try to fight the grief, don't tell yourself you can handle it, because you can't—it handles you until it decides it's finished. And it's never finished, not really. That hole in your heart, that empty space, that pain will be with you every moment of every day for the rest of your life. Sure, maybe it won't be as strong as it is right now, but it'll always be there. Always.

"I feel really bad for you, Bob. Because the worst is still coming."

Robert finished his coffee, winced as it hit his stomach, and said, "I knew I could count on you to cheer me up."

MacIntyre lifted his coat from the back of the sofa to reveal a thick brown envelope, which he tossed onto Robert's lap.

"What's this?"

MacIntyre sneered. "The focus group report." It was no secret that MacIntyre, a twenty-four-year veteran of television news, held the whole focus group procedure in utter contempt. Channel 7's news department, thanks to the upcoming departure of anchorman Ken Jeffries, was now suffering the scrutiny of a consulting group, called in by management to reshape the look and substance of the news programs because it was feared Jeffries's leaving would hurt ratings. So the consultants ("Smug little bastards rate just slightly under child molesters and serial killers in my esteem," MacIntyre had once pontificated) had been given carte blanche by management to do whatever they deemed necessary, even if it meant firing on-air personalities and cantankerous news directors. Part of this small-scale Inquisition was to host focus groups—a theoretically average group of viewers who were asked to sit in a room and watch videotapes of certain on-air reporters and make comments.

Those comments, Robert knew—along with the consulting group's review of the pertinent data gathered from those comments—were contained in the envelope MacIntyre had just unceremoniously dumped into his lap.

"Aren't you going to open it?"

"Don't you find this just a little insensitive?"

"I'll add it to my list of sins. You want me to haul out the sackcloth and ashes? We could sit in here and wring our hands and moan and groan, if you'd prefer."

"I'm about to bury my wife, and you hand me an envelope that holds the future of my career inside. Bankers, housewives, tech-heads, pizza-delivery boys, and garbage truck drivers pass judgment on me and that's all she wrote."

"Then I'll kill the suspense. You were a huge hit with everyone. Nine different focus groups, and you were the only on-air talent to get damn near straight tens from everyone. The *only* thing that even came close to a negative comment was some lady who said she thought your nose looked a tad too big for your face."

"She ought to see me now."

"All the information's in there if you want to read what she and everyone else said. I gotta tell you, Bob, I usually put zero faith in focus group results, but . . . you were 'the people's' overwhelming choice to replace Jeffries. Even the lady who thought your nose was a little too big said you'd be the best choice for the job." MacIntyre rubbed his eyes, then sighed. "I really hate to tell you this next part but . . . the consultants got a stiffy when we ran the story about Denise's death and the theft of your daughter's body. A popular reporter loses both his wife and daughter in one tragic sweep. Over two thousand calls have come into the station in the last three days. You should see the sympathy cards, the letters, the flowers. Christ, one lady in Hebron even sent you a basket with fruit and homemade candy, with a little Bible tucked in between the pineapple and bananas."

Robert said, almost absentmindedly: "I'd like to have the fruit and candy. Denise used to make homemade candy."

"Bob?"

He looked up. "H-huh?"

"Can you handle hearing the rest of this?"

"Does it make a difference?"

"The anchor position is yours. That's solid all the way across the board. That part makes me happy because I know you'll do a first-rate job and won't turn into a prima donna like dear old Ken—he's the network's problem now. The part that does not make me happy—and I fought tooth and nail with the consultants and management both over this—is that while you're on personal leave, the six and eleven P.M. broadcasts are going to run short follow-up segments about you; twice a week for the first two weeks, once a week after that until you come back to work. 'This is how our beloved coworker is doing' pieces. Reasons are twofold: One, the consultants don't want the public to forget either what your face looks like or the tragedy you've suffered, and, two, these follow-up pieces are going to be designed to touch the hearts of our viewers and will probably guarantee that the ratings will go through the roof when you return to assume the main anchor position—they've even started planning the publicity campaign for the ten days prior to your return. You lose your wife and kid, and everyone in the news department benefits."

"Vulture Culture," said Robert, seeing the anger and disgust in MacIntyre's eyes and liking the man all the more for it.

"I wouldn't blame you if you told them to sit on a doorknob and spin."

Robert shook his head. "I won't. I'd like to, but I won't. I want the job. Denise wanted it for me, too." He tossed the envelope onto the sofa. "Man, this stinks! My drive, my *obsession* with getting this anchor position . . . I couldn't spare a thought for anything else. Well, I *could have*, but I didn't. And I brushed Denise aside because of it. She didn't mind all that much, you know? She was *used* to being brushed aside by people who claimed to love her, to care about her. I figured it was no big deal. I mean, she understood how important the job was for me, for *us*. I just assumed that once it was all over, once I got the job, she'd still be there, waiting patiently just like she'd waited patiently for everything else throughout our entire marriage, I figured she'd still be around and I could make . . . make it . . . make it up to her. Ah, hell, Gene! *Hell!*" He leaned forward, elbows on knees, and pressed his face into his hands, swallowing hard to ease the throbbing behind his nose and eyes.

MacIntyre sat down next to him and put a nervous hand on Robert's shoulder. "Look, Bob, I really stink at this male-bonding crap but . . . I hope you know how I feel about you, how I felt about Denise. I know my timing here left a lot to be desired, but I just wanted to . . . give you something to look forward to."

Robert gave a short, sharp nod of his head.

"That's what you have to do now, Bob. As soon as you toss that handful of dirt onto her coffin, you have to start giving yourself things to look forward to, little rest stops where you can pull over and climb out of your grief long enough to—oh, hell, I stink at metaphors. Look, there's no crime in still looking forward to things: good music, a tasty meal, a new movie, vacuuming the goddamned carpet, even—"

"Our house has hardwood floors."

"You're missing the point. Remember when I said that you haven't even begun to experience the worst of this? You want to know what the worst part is? Place settings and pronouns, because those are the two things that will forever remind you that she's gone for good. You'll find yourself setting the table for two instead of one because you do that sort of thing on automatic pilot, anyway; and you'll have to learn to replace all the 'us,' 'ours,' and 'we's' with just 'me' and 'mine' and 'my.' You'll be shocked at how often you still talk about yourself as if you were part of a couple—hell, I still do it, and it breaks my heart every time I catch myself because there *is* no 'us' anymore. Be on guard for them, Bob, place settings and pronouns; they'll undo you every time."

Robert patted MacIntyre's arm once, then picked up the envelope. "Your heart was in the right place, Gene. I'm glad you told me about this now and didn't wait until a crew showed up to film my first 'recovery' segment."

"I did what I could, but—"

"It's okay. Denise'd probably get a big kick out of it, once she finished being pissed."

MacIntyre nodded, squeezed Robert's shoulder, then rose to his feet. "We should probably head on out there."

"I know. Can I keep this?"

"Yeah, just don't let anyone else know about it yet. That report won't be officially released until the end of next week."

"You could get canned for leaking this to me, you know that, don't you?"

MacIntyre shrugged. "There are worse things."

"Don't I know it."

And so the two of them—

—*what? You think it's too sad, this picture. But so many of them are.*

The mourners; don't you want to see them? Don't you want to know what they said to him, don't you want to see the tears streaking their cheeks? Their pain is so exquisitely genuine. They all weep for the loss of love? What could prettier or more romantic than that?

I see—the discovery of love. You want me to tell you about love's discovery.

I don't need to. Even now, as he is climbing into the funeral home limousine that will take him to the cemetery, he's telling you about it himself as he remembers, his mind flipping back through its pages,

*disassembling the dolls to line them up side by side so they'll reveal
the truth that is the fruit at the center of the mystery flower.*

He—*the man I once was, who is still within me, and I within him*—
was still cutting his teeth as a television reporter on assignments
of the dreaded "filler" variety—a birthday party for a lion at the
zoo, the opening of a new health food restaurant, other stories
without even *that* much depth.

This assignment promised to be no different from dozens of
others: an exposé on local corporate health programs. He was
to go in with a camera operator and videotape several executives
from an insurance company working out in the vast new exercise
club recently added to the ground floor of their monolithic office
building. He was all set to listen to a bunch of Vice-Presidents-
in-Charge-of-Nothing-in-Particular-and-Doing-a-Damn-fine-Job-
of-It fill the tape with a bunch of self-congratulatory hot air as
they boasted of their "maverick" employee health program, how
they kept the well-being of their staff in mind at all times, hey,
ain't we great, cha-cha-cha.

The health club itself was quite impressive, filled not only
with state-of-the-art exercise equipment but also more basic
things like a pommel horse and parallel bars. From the equipment to the sleek chrome self-serve juice bar, someone had
dropped a pretty penny. Robert couldn't help wondering how
many premium increases were going to result from this but
thought it best to keep that to himself.

He introduced himself to the three interviewees, worked out
which of them would answer what questions (one of the stipu-
lations being that he had to get all three of them—VPs, and all
male, surprise, surprise—on camera), and who would be using
which piece of equipment. Everything went off without a hitch,
the VPs all laughed and sweated and smiled brightly for the
camera, and all of them managed to get in some mention of a
new coverage program the company had recently introduced.

Executroids on Parade. Film at eleven.

He checked with the camera operator, taped some reaction shots, and was getting ready to pack it up and go when a plain-faced woman wearing unfashionably thick-framed glasses and her hair in a tight bun walked by. He glanced at her and she smiled but nothing more passed between them. She went to a far corner, removed her glasses and warm-up jacket, let down her hair, and tied it back in a ponytail, then—after a series of painful-looking stretching routines—sprinted to the parallel bars.

She was perfection.

Swing up, legs straight out, swing in, kick back, spin around, legs corkscrewing, head down, grab the bars, flip-kick out, legs up-apart-over-and-back for a flawless free-floating somersault, pitch to the side and grab the bars, spin, then a fast roll onto a single bar, balancing on one hand, pushing back-and-out-then-off, slow midair pirouette, feet seeking firm purchase, standing erect on a single bar, then a double flip to the floor.

Robert watched, breathless.

She hadn't even broken a sweat, as far as he could see.

"You want me to get this?" asked the camera operator.

"Not yet."

He wanted to share this with as few people as possible.

Several people in the club had stopped what they were doing to watch her; by the time she finished the next set of exercises, every set of eyes in the place would be focused on her.

She sprinted toward the pommel horse where she became, in his eyes, physical poetry.

Soaring through the air, hands down, landing squarely in the center of the thing, balance, legs apart, swinging back and forth, then around and around, each arm lifting just her legs swung underneath it fast as fan blades, one arm up, then down, legs fanning around, then she pushed up in the air, legs above her head, pirouetting with her hands this time, then facing the other direction, legs swinging back-then-front, then higher, always higher, spin, grab, balance, fan, pirouette, flip-kick, her movements growing faster and more precise, soar, spin, legs up, muscles rippling, defying gravity as her body became thought and just hovered in the air, then a blur of motion and she was back on Earth, sprinting toward the parallel bars once more. . . .

Robert stood transfixed.

There should have been music; her grace demanded that the world-Now be filled with something as rich to the ears as her movements were to the eyes.

When he'd first met her gaze as she walked past he felt kind of sorry for her, sorry for this plain-faced ragamuffin woman who wore her hair in a bun and whose glasses made her face look too wide—God, how arrogant and stupid and condescendingly sexist could a man be?

She was power here, poetry and grace and light, up there above it all, stronger than anyone or anything gawking at her from the prison of the ground below and—

—*good God*, thought Robert: *I've got a hard-on!*

He looked down at the bulge in his pants and felt his face turn red. It had been quite a while since he'd felt stirrings like this; even before Amy had broken it off with him, so calculated and coldly, his desire for physical passion had become more of a reflex action than genuine need, something he pulled out of cold storage long enough to make himself believe that what he felt for her was True Love, forcing himself to be affectionate because that's what True Lovers were supposed to do, they were supposed to become engulfed by desire at the merest glance, the subtlest touch, all of it right there on the surface; the blazing, overpowering, erotic intensity of a million sensations teeming at the fingertips, the need so immediate it actually ached, making them painfully aware of the invisible heat between them, savoring the scents of each other's bodies, screaming inside for as long as it took to cross the distance between them and hold each other close—all of this he'd tried to summon with Amy toward the end, but the best he could manage was a halfhearted and never fully stiff erection that she once actually giggled at.

He stared at her as she dismounted the bars and sat cross-legged on the floor by her warm-up jacket, her cheeks flushed and her face sheened in the thinnest layer of perspiration. Robert worked up that much sweat just getting out of bed in the morning.

Several people applauded her. She looked up and tried to smile but was too embarrassed, too shocked that people had actually been paying attention to her.

Robert felt genuinely dizzy.

Without her glasses, her ponytail draped regally over one moist shoulder, there in her leotard and slightly frayed leg-warmers, her face glowing from the strength spent, she seemed ethereal to him. It was no magical movie-transformation, no Cinderellaesque cliché wherein the mousy girl suddenly blossomed into a stunning beauty, no way; at best, with her hair down and no glasses and clothes that clung to her curves instead of sagging around them, this woman would always be plain to those eyes that only saw beauty in three-dimensional terms; she would always be the "nice" girl at parties where everyone else came with a date, the good-natured girl who always arrived and left alone, who would always be touted for her "nice personality," who would always be invited to join in with the beauties because her plainness like a microscope lens only magnified their loveliness, the girl who would always have everyone wondering why she couldn't find a guy. *She's so sweet.*

He knew that, under any other circumstances, he would not have given her a second glance.

And condemned himself a million times over for it.

Because she buried all memories of any woman he'd ever been with, stared at, longed for, or dreamed of. She was the first woman he'd ever seen who possessed true beauty—time's gift of perfect humility.

Why had he never known enough to see this before?

Passion, grace, and fire, here at the scene of a sexist jerk's undoing.

Sometimes the heart is captured and its wings are bound.

Sometimes a fantasy comes true before you've even had it.

Sometimes you see the soul and just fall in love and can't do a damn thing about it.

She gathered up her things, toweled off her face, and headed toward the showers. As she walked across the floor toward him, her gaze was fixed solidly on Robert.

Don't say anything, he prayed. *If you speak to me, I'm in deep.*

"Hi," she said. The peal of bells, that word.

"Hello," said Robert, feeling schoolboy tongue-tied. *Okay, keep going and don't tell me your name; if you tell me your name I'm going to silently add "Londrigan" to it just to see how it sounds.*

She held out a hand. "My name's Denise."

"Robert," he replied, taking hold of her hand and feeling about a billion volts of electricity shoot up his arm. *I can still make a clean getaway if you don't smile. Please don't smile. If you smile, I am good and truly done for.*

She released his hand, stood back, said, "It was nice meeting you, Robert," and walked away.

Robert released a breath, his shoulders slumping, and let his head drop.

That was close.

He picked up his microphone and wound the cord around it, checked his notes one more time, then turned to follow the camera operator outside.

Denise was standing in the doorway.

He froze in his tracks.

And she smiled at him.

Cue the *Dragnet* theme here, and say hello to love's discovery.

Chapter Four

The snow had begun falling again, lightly, but seemed heavier because of the sharp, steady wind blowing in from the east. The cemetery looked almost pristine, a newly completed ice sculpture.

The mourners clustered together near the head of the grave, their backs to the wind. Looking at them with their hair and coats flowing forward, Robert couldn't shake the feeling that all of them were fighting against some force, unseen and unknown, that was trying to suck them into the ground. He walked quickly around the grave and the eight or nine floral arrangements positioned at the head, noticing as he did that someone had thought to send irises—Denise's favorite flower. He took a place next to Lynn, who, like most of the people assembled here, had her hands shoved deep into her coat pockets and was staring at the ground—not into the open grave, mind you, but somewhere just to the right where a bit of soil could still be seen through the snow. A few people, MacIntyre included, folded their arms across their chests and watched the sour sky, blinking against the new snowflakes that fluttered down and clung stubbornly to their eyelashes. Everyone stood in postures that seemed more distracted than grieving. Robert looked around at all the faces, all of their friends, none of whom would meet his gaze. Had they already wrung dry their grief? God. He felt as if he'd stepped into the fifth reel of some impenetrably enigmatic foreign art film, one of those profoundly ponderous black and white meditation pieces where no one speaks for minutes on end and then, just when your patience is stretched to the max, some minor character no one has given a second thought to steps into camera range and starts paraphrasing Camus or Borges while the trees melt behind them: a head-on collision between Cocteau and Dali. Even the minister looked surreal, his face something that was hastily painted on a *matryoshka* doll, his pear-shaped body standing at the head of the grave with a Bible clutched in one shaking blue-cold hand, squinting as he read the passage committing Denise's mortal remains to the earth. Completing the requisite benediction, he signaled the men from the funeral home to lower the coffin into the ground. It hissed hydraulically into the cold, dark, open maw of the grave. Robert had to fight the urge to turn away. He didn't want it to end like this, not with distracted *matryoshka* mourners and surreal Cocteau prayers and sour snow on an ice-knife wind. Even his own hand looked like some fuzzy image on a movie screen as it scooped up the symbolic handful of frozen death-dirt and tossed it down onto the lid of the coffin. The pear-shaped minister stalked over, misting some words of comfort, then grimly wobbled away. Most of the mourners stopped to say something. Robert nodded slightly and returned their embraces or handshakes as he tried to smile, then thanked them, catching a peripheral glance of a sad-eyed MacIntyre offering him a terse two-finger wave before heading on, and then, quite suddenly, Robert found himself standing alone at the head of the grave.

A few feet away, dusted with snow, sat the mound of earth that would be shoveled in on top of the coffin. The handle of a shovel protruded from the side of the mound. Robert jammed his hands into his coat pockets to make sure he'd brought along the workman's gloves.

Part of the arrangement with the funeral home and cemetery management (one that had cost him a lot of time, energy spent arguing with people, not to mention a hefty chunk of cash) was that Robert himself would be the one to fill her grave with dirt. He didn't want any overweight, foul-tempered, cigar-chomping union droid on a noisy earthmover to seal Denise's remains into the bowels of the planet. Only he would do that, and screw the physical pain that would result from the labor; it seemed the last decent thing he could do for her.

He heard approaching footsteps that sounded too heavy to be either Lynn or Danny. He didn't bother turning around.

A few moments later, Bill Emerson joined him at the grave.

"Hello, Mr. Lond—uh, Robert."

"Detective," Robert said. Then: "I mean, Bill."

"Sure was a lovely service, I thought."

"Were you at the funeral home?"

"Yes."

"I didn't see you."

Emerson shrugged. "I can blend into the woodwork pretty well. It's a gift I try to use for the forces of good."

Robert grinned. "I appreciate your coming."

"It's not a completely altruistic gesture. I had this notion that maybe Mr. Mask was going to show up at the funeral and find a way to make himself known to you. But I didn't see anyone who set off my yo-yo alarm—and my yo-yo alarm hasn't failed me yet." He looked at the grave and coughed. "It's just such a terrible thing, you know? I don't know how you're able to deal with it. I mean . . . God. Damn. It."

Robert said nothing.

Emerson pulled his notebook from his jacket pocket and flipped it open to a previously marked page. "Okay, besides paying my respects and offering such overwhelming comfort to you, I found out something I thought you might be interested in."

"Oh?" Robert turned away from the grave.

"Yeah. You remember telling me that the guy who assaulted you said something about a lame kid who couldn't dance and missed his playmates?"

"Yes."

"It's a line from a poem. Robert Browning's 'The Pied Piper of Hamelin.'" He then quoted the passage word for word. "And what he said to you earlier that night in the park? 'So, Willy, let you and me be wipers of scores out with all men.' That's from the poem, too. You said he kept calling you Willy, right?"

"Right."

"As far as I can interpret it—scholar of English literature that I am—the narrator of the poem is telling the story to some guy named Willy. I was left with the impression that the narrator is the little lame boy who's telling the story as an adult. But then I voted for Walter Mondale back in the day. I guess I'm trying to find out if that particular poem has any special meaning for you."

Robert felt suddenly chilled to his marrow. "Oh, God . . ."

"What is it?"

He shook his head, disgusted with himself. "I don't know why I couldn't remember this before, but . . ." He snarled a soft, derisive laugh. "It was Denise's favorite poem."

"You're certain about that?"

"Yes. Doesn't that stink on ice? All the little details about the things she loved that I could never bother myself to remember, and now I have instant recall."

Emerson said nothing for a moment, then—after consulting his notes—asked, "How many people besides yourself might have known that was her favorite poem?"

"I have no idea." A pause, then: "You think it's someone who knows us?"

"It'd explain his knowing the poem was her favorite. My guess is he figured you'd remember that, eventually."

"Why?"

Emerson shrugged. "Only he can answer that one. I could spit out a half dozen theories, but odds are they'd only upset you and probably turn out to be wrong, anyway." Emerson replaced the notebook in his pocket. "I've intruded long enough. I'll call you in a couple of days, just to update on any progress and—oh, damn, almost forgot: I got a plateful of homemade brownies that my wife made. She wanted me to give them to you with our sympathies. You want 'em?"

Robert—still slightly reeling—blinked a couple of times, then said, "Uh . . . yes, yes, thank you very much. See that couple over there by the Toyota? That's my sister, Lynn, and her husband. If you'd give them to her, she'll put them in her car and take them back over to her house. Please tell your wife I said thanks a million."

"You ain't tasted them yet," said Emerson, shoving his hands into his pockets and starting to walk away. "I'm just kidding—I had one on the way over here . . . hope you don't mind. They're yummy as all get out."

"Bill?"

"Yes?"

"I think whoever took my daughter's body is following me. I think they might have broken into my sister's house sometime yesterday."

Emerson became all business. "Did you see something? Hear something? Was anything taken or any threatening notes left?"

"No, nothing like that," lied Robert. "I thought, *maybe* I saw someone hanging around the house last night—I stayed at their place. I just . . . I have this feeling that he's following me, y'know?"

"I'd have to agree with that."

"And I think he followed me to my sister's last night. I don't know if he's going to try and hurt them or not—"

Emerson shook his head. "I don't think so. I think he's just trying to rattle you, and what better way to do it than make you think he's after your sister and her family? Don't worry, I won't dismiss anything. I'll make sure a cruiser does several extra drive-bys over the next few nights. If I can do anything more, I will. In the meantime . . . does your brother-in-law own a gun?"

"Yeah, a Bulldog .44. I had a chance to talk with him a little before the funeral. He keeps it in a drawer in the bedside table. Has a trigger lock. He wears the key around his neck, next to his St. Christopher medal."

Emerson looked over at Danny and Lynn. "I'll have a word

with him, reassure him that I don't think they've got anything to worry about. It's you he's interested in."

"I'd appreciate anything you could do to make him feel better. By the way, my sister doesn't know. I'd like to keep it that way. If anyone tells her, I think it ought to be her husband."

"Your wish is my command."

Before Robert even had a chance to register his being alone at the grave again, Lynn was by his side.

"A detective bearing brownies. Now I've seen everything."

"He's one of the good guys, Lynn."

"I figured. He's got such a . . . I don't know . . . *kind* way about him."

Robert looked over his shoulder and saw Emerson talking with Danny. The detective seemed to be going on about how yummy his wife's brownies were. Danny finally surrendered and tried one. From the look on his face, they *were* yummy as all get out. Then Emerson's face became serious and Danny was all at attention.

"So what's next, Bobby?"

"I don't know." He faced her. "You don't think it's morbid, do you? I mean, my insisting on being the one who buries her?"

"No," whispered Lynn, her eyes growing wide with respect. "I think it's an incredibly loving thing to do. Don't ask me to explain it, but it seems like it should . . . *secure* your place by her side, you know? You were together in life, always there for each other, and now you're going to do this one last thing for her so she'll know that, when your time comes, you want to be by her side forever." She leaned up on tiptoe and kissed his cheek. "I think this will make her very happy and proud."

Robert squeezed her hand, then kissed her cheek. "Do you have any idea what Denise's favorite poem was?"

" 'The Pied Piper of Hamelin.' Sure. Why do you ask?"

"No reason." He felt deeply, totally ashamed. "Listen, would you mind if I took a little walk, just for a few minutes? I just need a few minutes to myself to get ready for this." He glanced at the mound of soil. "I can't start just yet."

"Danny and I will wait in the car. Take as long as you need—and don't forget that Danny brought a shovel along. If it gets to be too much for you, he'll help."

"Danny is sometimes too nice for his own good."

Lynn smiled. "Please don't tell him that."

Robert grinned but it felt phony. "I won't be too long." Then he started up a nearby hill.

After stumbling down the other side of the hill and walking across an ice- and snow-sheened path, he came to a small incline that led him to a plat filled with various statues: cherubs, squatting gargoyles that guarded the entrances of family crypts, marble animals at rest, and one piece in particular that commanded his attention: a stone sculpture of an angel standing at the less-accessible north entrance. He wiped a few stray tears from his eyes and looked up at the face of the angel. If ever a sculptor had captured an expression of grief so purely, he'd not seen it. In its face was everything from anguish and rage to acceptance and peace. He saw in that face the way all mourners were meant to be; diminished, yes; brokenhearted and scared, certainly; but if you looked at the face long enough you saw a certain, enviable measure of tranquillity that hinted at actualization, a look suggesting that all the conflicting emotions associated with death eventually coalesced to warm a sorrowing heart with the knowledge that, though it seemed to take forever, life was over in a second but that was all right, because there would be someone waiting for you at the end to make Act IV a little easier. Though Robert had often laughed at that sort of psychobabbling sentimentality, he found himself now hoping that some of it might be true.

He turned away from the statue and wiped his eyes, then stood watching his breath mist into the cold air.

A moment later he saw her coming down the hill toward him. He ground his teeth and bit back on his anger, telling himself that Lynn only followed him out of concern and he shouldn't be too unpleasant with her—

—except that, as she grew closer, he saw it wasn't Lynn.

He couldn't recall seeing this woman among the mourners either here or at the funeral home, but something about her seemed familiar.

Reaching the bottom of the hill, leaving a perfect trail of footprints in the snow behind her, she paused, looking around, then smiled when she spotted him. Recognition blossomed over her face as she came toward him with a determined and—considering the snow and ice—surprisingly steady stride. She wore dark sunglasses and a wide-brimmed hat with a dark veil that was, at the moment, lowered. Coat, skirt, shoes, gloves—everything she wore was black, reminding Robert of some movie star from the forties or fifties who dressed this way so she wouldn't be recognized in public. It was almost comical.

She removed something from her pocket that looked like a sheet of paper, and Robert had the most absurd thought: *She wants an autograph.*

Though he'd had his share of awkward run-ins with fans, Robert prided himself at being adept at handling these situations. Denise, despite her irritation at her and Robert's being interrupted whenever they went out to dinner or a movie or just shopping on the weekend, always complimented him on how tactful and courteous he was with them. He graciously accepted her praise but never told her about those times when various women (and, in a couple of cases, younger men) would slip him a motel room key or croon promises of sweaty, grunting, screaming ecstasy were he to "clear a few hours" to spend in their company.

If this woman coming toward him now turned out to be a fan seeking an autograph, Robert thought it very likely he'd knock her teeth down her throat. How dare she or anyone invade his privacy at a time like this?

She was only a few yards away.

He couldn't shake the notion that he knew her from somewhere. Maybe she was one of the new interns at the station.

There was a great deal of anger in the way she moved toward him, and Robert suddenly found himself thinking of John Lennon outside the Dakota in New York and poor, young Rebecca Shaeffer answering her door, how both of them had looked into the face of their assassin before the bullets turned them into a police statistic—

—the woman's hand snapped up toward his face and the sharp gleam of light off blue steel momentarily blinded him as he heard the unmistakable *click!* of a hammer being cocked—

—and before the first round split his skull in half he remembered a snippet from a Wall of Voodoo song, something about how the singer had wept when Lennon died yet envied his assailant when he visited the shrine—

—but when he looked again he saw that the gleam came from a silver cigarette lighter she held in her hand, and the click had been the sound it made as she struck up the flame.

Robert had unconsciously taken out a cigarette and placed it between his lips. When had he bought a fresh pack? And why? He'd promised Denise he was going to quit.

He leaned toward the flame and lighted his smoke. "Thank you. I don't know what I was thinking . . . didn't bring a lighter or even any matches with me."

She folded back her veil and removed her sunglasses, then her hat.

Robert was so shocked to see her again that he let the cigarette drop from his lips into the snow where it sputtered, hissed, and died. "*Amy?*"

Her version of a smile—something between a snarl and a smirk—appeared on her face. "I'm glad you can still recognize me."

Her strawberry-blond hair was shorter now than it had been when she and Robert were together, but aside from that—and her having lost a little weight—she still looked the same; same placid face covered with creamy, wrinkle-free flesh; same perfectly shaped lips; the same heavy eyebrows that she always spent at least ten minutes plucking and shaping every morning; and the same haughty, distant, almost condescending glint in her light green eyes. Robert remembered that glint well, its chilly, unspoken "I deserve better than you but you'll do for now" that had been the last thing he saw as she packed up what few belongings of hers she'd agreed to bring to his apartment and walked out the door without so much as a "See you around" or a backward glance. Though their relationship hadn't been ideal—especially toward the end, his having lost all genuine passion for her—it was nonetheless the only thing Robert had had in his life besides his job at Channel 7. When Amy Wilder had walked out of his life, it shattered him, poisoned his hopes of ever falling in love again (or at all), and left him in that dark, cynical no-man's land where it was simple to lapse into the easy promiscuity of the failed romantic. How odd that the heart makes no sound at all when it cracks.

But then came the day some months later when he found himself in the newly built health club of an insurance company, watching Denise sprint toward the parallel bars, and all the Amy-hurt had simply vanished.

"I know we didn't part under the best of circumstances, dear Robert, but don't I at least rate a hug?"

"Of course." He embraced her. For a moment, she did not move—such was her way, calculated to make you want her returned embrace even more—then slowly, lifelessly, put her arms around him for just a moment before pulling away and smoothing down her coat. It was like hugging a department store mannequin, only without the overpowering affection.

"You haven't really changed a bit," he said.

"I'm sorry for your loss." Flat, toneless. "I hope you know that."

"I appreciate your—" No. He wouldn't do this. Not with her. "Why are you here, Amy?"

"Ah, there's my dear Robert, always getting to the point. At least where we were concerned." She held out the piece of paper that he'd seen in her hand. "I came to give you this."

It was an envelope with his name written across the front in Denise's handwriting. The T at the end glistened as if the ink was still wet—Denise had always used either her calligraphy pen or an old-fashioned fountain pen for all her cards and correspondence, claiming that they gave her letters an old-world quality that she hoped made them special.

She had used a fountain pen for this.

He brushed his thumb across his name and watched unbelieving as the T smeared almost to the far side of the envelope's face.

The ink was still wet.

But that couldn't be. This *was* Denise's handwriting—God knew he'd seen it enough in the last eight hours alone to be able to recognize it—yet the ink was still fresh, as if the letter had been penned only a few minutes ago and no blotter handy.

"Remember that article she once told you about, the 'extinction' piece? She never got around to telling you about the part of it that dealt with the two types of time, *did she*, dear Robert? No, of course not. The ancient Greeks believed in two kinds of time, dear Robert: *chronos* and *kairos*. *Kairos* is not measurable. In *kairos*, you simply *are*, from the moment of your birth on. You *are*, wholly and positively. *Kairos* is especially strong in children, because they haven't learned to understand, let alone accept, concepts such as time and age and death. In children, *kairos* can break through *chronos*: when they're playing safely, drawing a picture for Mommy or Daddy, taking the first taste of the first ice cream cone of summer, when they sing along to songs in a Disney cartoon, there is only *kairos*. As long as a child thinks it's immortal, it is. Think of every living child as being the burning bush that Moses saw, surrounded by the flames of *chronos*, but untouched by the fire. In *chronos* you're nothing more than a set of records, fingerprints, your Social Security number, you're always watching the clock, aware of time passing—but in *kairos*, you are *dear Robert* and only dear Robert."

He was only half listening to her, his confusion replaced by a terrible fear, flavored with a pinch of anger. "What the hell is this, Amy?"

"I think you should read that right away," was her only reply.

He snapped up his head and glared at her. "I asked you a question!"

"And I answered it."

"Goddammit, you didn't! All you said was simply what you *wanted* to say instead of answering me."

Her smile grew wider and more lifeless. "Ah, *that* old chestnut. One of our greatest hits, wasn't it? 'That's a response but it's not an answer.'"

Robert bit down on his reply, still trying to catch his breath from the shock of seeing his late wife's handwriting yet again. Breathing steadily to slow the pile-driver pounding of his heart, he fumbled with the envelope until he had it opened, cursed his shaking hands as they unfolded the single sheet of stationery inside, and read: *Send me a picture of the daughter we never had, the bright little girl with chubby pink cheeks and wistful smile and wide gray eyes that say,* I used to feel lonely but it's all better now. . . .

"Where the *fuck* did you get—" The rest of it died in his throat when he looked up.

Amy was gone.

He looked around for some sign of her but she was nowhere to be seen—and there was no way he could have missed her in that black Joan Crawford outfit, not against all this snow.

Her footprints.

They came down the hill, crossed the plat alongside his own, and stopped directly in front of him.

Poof. No more Amy.

Someone began whistling "How Much Is That Doggy in the Window?"

The chubby basset hound came romping out from the trees that surrounded most of the north entrance, barked three times, and ran toward him, covering the distance by diving in and out of the snow in its path like a dolphin moving through water.

Robert stuffed the note from Denise into his pocket as the dog came closer.

"Suzy . . ." he whispered.

There was no mistaking that torn left ear, or the limp that favored her right side because her back left leg, which never properly healed, had been broken when Robert was six.

The eyes, thought Robert. *Look at her eyes.*

A moment later the dog was upon him, all paws and excited scratching against his legs—*pick me up, pick me up!*—then a cold nose against his cheek and a warm, sloppy, happy tongue all over his face as she squirmed and barked and kissed him, her tail wagging nonstop.

He knelt down in the snow, cupped the dog's head in his hands, and looked at its eyes.

The right one clear, the left slightly obscured by a milky white cataract.

Suzy, the only dog he'd ever owned as a child.

"Well, hello, you," said Robert.

"Hello yourself, asshole," replied the dog.

Robert was on his feet immediately, staring down in disbelief.

Then came the cackling laughter from somewhere to the left. "You should see *your* face! Bo-Bo the Dog-Faced Boy looked more intelligent." One of the squatting gargoyles guarding a nearby crypt leaped down to the ground. "Old ventriloquist gag a magician once taught me, I couldn't resist. But I was right—she's happy to see you."

Split-Face waved at Robert—*We have a secret, you and I . . .*

"How's it going, Willy? Nice nose decoration you've got there. Do you despair yet?"

Ignoring Suzy's insistent pawing against him, Robert fisted his hands, ready to defend himself.

"Take it easy, Willy, I'm not going to hurt you. In fact, I sort of wanted to apologize for our last couple of encounters."

"You broke into my sister's house!"

"Guilty as charged, but you shouldn't let that get in the way of our beautiful friendship." He was only a few yards away now, and Robert clearly saw that Split-Face wore no mask.

There was very little soft tissue on the upper portions of his face, and what flesh there was had become hardened to the point it more resembled scales on a lizard's back; in places this scale-like flesh was semitranslucent, allowing Robert to see the red and blue veins that spiderwebbed the areas where most people had cheeks. Split-Face had no nose, only two tear-shaped caves through which he breathed, both of which seemed to leak constantly. His left eye was a good quarter inch lower on his face than his right, and he had no ears to speak of, just bits of dangling flesh on either side of his head. Though his jaws were intact, he possessed almost no chin; the flesh under his lower lip had only the smallest of rounded bone fragment beneath it, the rest simply blended into his neck like melted candle wax, creating a thick, disturbing wattle that pulsed with every leaking from his nose caves.

The worst part, though, was the overall shape of his face and head; his skull seemed to have been wrenched apart with a crowbar, then pieced back together by someone with no knowledge whatsoever of human anatomy; there were lumps where none should have been, craters where there should have been lumps, and one section, beneath his too-low left eye, where the cracked and yellowed bone was actually exposed to the elements, Robert caught a glimpse of something metal and realized there was a rusty pin holding those two small sections of his faceplate together.

"What in God's name happened to you?"

"Tragic shaving accident when I was very young," replied Split-Face. "I don't like to dwell on it." Pointing at his face, he said, "What about this? Does this make you despair, Willy?" Not waiting for an answer, he wiped the sleeve of his coat across his caves. "Hey, at least this cold weather keeps them running. Most times they're blocked and I have to breathe through my mouth. That dries up my throat and makes it hard for me to swallow. I also get hoarse and cough a lot. But I guess I don't have to tell you what that's like, do I?"

"Leave my sister and her family alone."

Split-Face shrugged. "I have no interest in them, Willy, I just wanted to rattle your cage and let you know that I can find you any time I want."

The questions came out of Robert in a rapid, deadly cadence: "What the hell do you want with me? What happened to the woman who was just here? Where did the note come from?"

Split-Face held up his hands. "Whoa there, Willy! One at a time."

Suzy plopped her butt down in the snow, looked up at Robert, and whined.

"Where did *she* come from?" asked Robert, kneeling down and petting his childhood dog. "I thought she was dead."

"Why? Because you woke up one morning and she was gone and your dad was passed out in the wreckage of the living room?"

Robert nodded. "I always figured Dad must've gotten mad and accidentally killed her. He's the one who broke her leg, you know?"

"I know," whispered Split-Face, his voice filled with genuine compassion.

"He was always kicking her out of his way whenever he'd get on one of his mean drunks—and most of his drunks where mean. Oh, he felt like hell about it afterward—he even bought her a new doghouse—but I'll never forget the way she screamed when he kicked her that night. I was out on the back porch and I *heard* the bone snap. Poor little thing." He scratched the top of Suzy's head. She licked his hand and moved closer to him. Then something occurred to him: "Jesus! It's been over thirty years since she disappeared. She should be dead."

"Don't say 'should' here in *kairos*, Willy. It's strong in animals, too. Why do you think actors never want to do scenes with children or dogs? *Kairos* is so strong in them that you can't look at anyone who exists in boring old *chronos*."

Robert pulled Suzy close to him, hugging her. She wiggled and wagged in delight.

"Right now, Willy, I'm pulling a couple of old parlor tricks—and I *abhor* parlor tricks, for the record. Right now we're frozen in *kairos*—otherwise known as the 'Once Upon a Time' world. I can do almost anything I want or need to do here—mark the 'almost.' So, if you're worried about your sister and her family, as of right now, here in our 'Once Upon a Time' world, it never happened. Oh, *you'll* remember the story, the book, the way it crumbled into dust, but if you ask Danny or Detective Emerson about it, neither one of them will have any memory of you saying a damned thing about it to them." He snapped his fingers. "One parlor trick, nothing up my sleeve, free of charge."

"I don't believe you."

Split-Face sighed. "There's a shocker. Why don't you ask Danny or Emerson about it, then? Just make sure you take note of the odd way they'll look at you and the 'there, there' tone in their voice afterward."

"Why did you steal my daughter's body?"

"Because if I hadn't, you would have killed her."

"She was already dead."

Split-Face laughed. "Oh, Willy, Willy, Willy—haven't you caught on yet? There's *chronos*-dead and then there's *kairos*-dead. Had I left her there in the morgue, you would have buried her today along with your wife and *then* she would have been good and truly dead and there would be no hope left for any of us."

"*Any* of us?" Robert closed his eyes and hugged Suzy once again, wanting to never let go again.

Someone giggled. Robert opened his eyes.

Gary A. Braunbeck

He was surrounded by children. Some were deformed, just as they'd been in the photographs Split-Face had shown him, others had obviously been injured or maimed, while others appeared to be quite normal—at least physically. One look in their eyes told him that even the normal-looking ones had experienced something awful that haunted them still.

"Puppy dog!" cried Ian, who suddenly came dancing around from behind the crypt. He was twirling a baton and wearing a jester's belled hat. He pointed at Suzy and sang out, "Pup-pee dog! Pup-pee dog!" while the bells on his hat jingled and jangled and the children pointed at him and laughed and giggled.

Most wore modern-day clothing but some were dressed in rags, with "shoes" that were made from sections of animal hide and fur wrapped around their feet and tied to their ankles with sections of rope. All of them were transfixed by One-Eyed Ian's jester dance.

"Did you know that we're very near one of the thirteen places on this earth where the mountains open up?" said Split-Face. "They usually don't come out en masse like this to see someone, so you damned well better appreciate it." He reached into a pocket of his coat and pulled out a shiny flute. "I think it's time you and I were properly introduced," he said, holding out his hand for Robert to shake. "My name is Rael."

"Rael," repeated Robert, shaking his hand.

Ian continued dancing his comical jester's dance, but now some of the children were joining in and singing—"Ring around the rosy, Pocket full of posies, ashes, ashes, all fall *down!*"—then it was on their backs in the snow, arms and legs fanning to create snow angels, kicking up snow clouds that drifted around them like fog, making their figures more and more ghostlike.

"We are the 'us' I was talking about," said Rael. "We need her back or we'll . . ." He lowered his voice so the others wouldn't hear. "We'll be forced back into *chronos*, and it'll kill most of us."

"I don't understand."

"I'll alert the media. Look, Willy, do you think burying your daughter in Denise's garden was your idea? *I* put that in your head at the hospital."

"Why?"

"Because, whether you want to believe it or not, there are worlds within worlds that you walk through every day. There are levels of existence that you *chronos*-dwellers are never aware of, and one of those worlds, one of those levels, is *home*; home is a living thing. Not just a house and yard, but *home*. Home remembers all your hopes, your dreams and plans, and it can point you in the right direction when you lose the way back to your heart—and you lost your way a long time ago, Willy."

"Pup-pee dog!" sang Ian, jingle-jangling through the snow clouds and laughing ghosts.

"*Home* will bring her back, Willy. I just needed to make sure neither of you strayed too far from there."

"Why?"

"You're starting to sound like a stuck record. 'Why, why, why?' Write a new verse to that song, will you?"

"Answer me!"

"I can't."

"Because . . . ?"

"*Because I'm not allowed to, all right?* You'll understand why soon enough—providing you don't fuck things up."

The children were clapping and dancing in the midst of their Festival of Swirling Snow. Some now carried banners that flapped in the wind, others had large bottles of water cradled in bamboo baskets, a few held leather harnesses with sleigh bells above their heads, jingling and jangling along with Ian as they twirled by, and one carried a well-used bodhran, using his thumbs to strike the surface of the goat-skin drum. Suzy ran into the celebration, barking happily. Robert wished she had stayed.

"Go home, Willy, so you can find what should be waiting there."

"I have to bury my wife."

Rael smiled. "There's that *chronos* mentality again. Okay, fine, you gotta bury your wife. So go on, then, head on up that hill and do what a man's gotta do."

Robert rubbed his eyes, said, "I still don't know what happened to—" But when he looked up again, he was alone, with only one set of footprints—his own—to ground him in the world-Now.

He crossed the plat and started his climb back up the hill, but with every step his body began to scream its discomfort; his back, legs, and particularly his shoulders, arms, and hands throbbed with pain and pressure.

He saw Danny and Lynn standing near the grave. When they spotted him, Danny came over, put his around Robert, and said, "Man, I don't know where you found the energy to take a walk after that. I'm whipped. We'd better get going; everyone'll be over at the house waiting for us. We told them around one-thirty, right?"

Lynn was beside him, then, taking his arm in hers and leading him to the car, past Denise's grave, now filled with earth, its smoothed surface being covered by a whisper of snow.

Chapter Five

The post-funeral gathering (Robert couldn't bring himself to think of it as a *reception*) was held at Lynn's and Danny's and was—if the term was at all applicable—as pleasant a gathering as one could have expected under the circumstances. There was food and coffee and various rolls, cakes, and desserts (Mrs. Emerson's brownies turned out to be, in Robert's opinion, even yummier than all get out), as well as hugs and tears, handshakes and warm embraces and soft words of comfort ("If you need anything, just call, anytime"; "I'll be around if you need to talk";

"We'll all keep you in our prayers."); when it started to seem as if everyone there would never leave, Robert made some remark about being tired and the place cleared out in minutes.

He was sitting alone in the kitchen when Danny came in carrying a tray filled with empty glasses and dishes. "Boy, those folks sure ate a lot."

"Death tends to give you an appetite," replied Robert.

Danny, setting the dishes carefully onto the counter by the sink, looked at Robert and said, "Is that a kind of joke?"

"Kind of."

"Just checking."

Robert smiled. He liked Danny an awful lot. If ever there was a man more dedicated to making a good home for his family, Robert had not met him.

(If you're worried about your sister and her family, as of right now, here in our "Once Upon a Time" world, it never happened.)

"So," said Danny, "how's your back and shoulders doing?"

"Mostly it's my arms and hands. I'm surprised I can unbend my fingers."

"Tell me about it. And I still got chores to do around here later. Lynn likes her house in order."

"That was some pretty hard work, wasn't it?" asked Robert, trying very hard not to think about the fact that they were having a conversation about something that had not happened.

At least, according to Rael, in this sad-assed place called *chronos*-world.

"Yeah," said Danny, "but it felt like the right thing to do, you know? Hell, I gotta tell you, Rob, that I didn't think you'd have it in you to do something like that but, man, I had a hard time keeping up with you."

"Coming from someone who's worked construction for the last ten years, I'll consider that a compliment."

"I mean it. I figured a guy like you—y'know, who works a lot at desks and computers—I figured you'd be sort of a softie when it came to manual labor but—*whew!*—was I wrong!"

So, here they were, discussing their labors at the grave. And if they were talking about something that had never happened as if it *had* happened, then did it take such an Einsteinian leap of the imagination to believe that something like the break-in, which had happened, now hadn't?

(If you ask Danny or Detective Emerson about it, neither one of them will have any memory of you saying a damned thing about it to them . . .)

"You okay?" asked Danny.

"Wh-what? Oh, sorry—drifted off the highway there for a minute. Yeah, I'm okay. Well, no, not really, but . . ." Robert sighed. "Please tell me you know what I'm trying to say so I can stop trying to say it."

"I'm with you, pal."

"That helps, Danny. Thank you."

"No problem. You want a beer, or maybe some Irish Creme? I got a bottle stashed away for special occasions."

"Thanks, but no—I'm driving, remember?"

Danny's shoulders slumped in disappointment. "Shit. I mean, I was hoping you'd stay here tonight. I know Eric'd love it, and we'd love to have you."

"I appreciate it, but I already told Lynn I have to start getting used to the house being empty, you know? And I can't think of a better time to do it, can you?"

"Guess not." Danny started rinsing off the dishes in the sink, then stopped abruptly when something occurred to him. "Ah, hell, I almost forgot—an old friend of yours stopped by but you were off someplace—anyway, she said she couldn't stay but she left her business card." He dried his hands, then took the card from his shirt pocket and gave it to Robert.

Amelia Wilder Modeling Agency
For When The Picture Has To Be Pretty

Robert stared at the card, read the phone number below the caption, then absentmindedly turned it over. Written on the back, in handwriting eerily similar to Denise's, was: *May 21, 1978. Not such a pretty picture.*

Something else in the darkness of Robert's memory stirred but did not awaken. That date. There was something about that date. He'd been in high school then, readying to graduate like all the other seniors, and something had happened . . . but what?

He glanced up at Danny—who was rinsing the rest of the dishes—then slipped the card into his pocket next to the note Amy had given him at the cemetery.

He thought about everything Rael had said to him about time and home and losing the way back to his heart, and decided that he had to do something to prove to himself that either the world as he knew it was shifting into something unrecognizable or that he was suffering some kind of mental breakdown.

Just move the angle of the camera a little to the left of normal before snapping the picture, and when the photo is developed there is nothing in it that you know as real.

There are worlds within worlds that you walk through every day.

There was only one thing he could do to find the answer.

He was only a few blocks away from the house when he suddenly craved a cigarette. He checked the pack in his coat pocket and discovered that he was out, so he took the next side street and pulled into the first convenience market he found.

He decided to buy three cans of pink salmon (two for the cats, one for himself) and a quart of buttermilk. For some reason, the cats liked buttermilk rather than regular milk for a treat. He was almost ready to check out when he suddenly had the overwhelming desire to bake some cookies, of all things, so he picked up another quart of buttermilk, some eggs, flour, chocolate chips (for some reason, they just *had* to be chocolate chip cookies). Then, while standing at the counter and waiting as the clerk found a carton of his brand and then began scanning the purchases into the register, he heard a voice cry out, "*Robert? Robert Londrigan?*" There was a combination of surprise, sadness, shock, and glee in the voice. Robert turned around, saw the woman coming through the door toward him, and said, "Debra? Debra Jamison?"

"*Robert!*" she cried again, throwing her arms around him and squeezing. "My God, how long has it been? Seven, eight years?"

"Closer to ten, I think."

He had dated Debra for a little less than a year before she broke it off. Two months later, he'd met Amy Wilder while covering a local beauty pageant.

Debra. Always so anxious to please everyone else that she often forgot to take care of her own needs and wound up resenting everyone because she was so unhappy. Robert had tried to make her see that, to understand that the more she put others' feelings first and her own second, she would always feel alone and unappreciated because most people were selfish and it never occurred to them to thank anyone for the little kindnesses, the brief acts of thoughtfulness or compassion they received. She tried to change, he had to give her credit for that, but Debra Jamison would always be the type of person whose need to feel kind outweighed everything else, even her own peace of mind.

She smiled at him and touched his cheek. "I heard all about what happened to you on the news. Oh, Robert, I'm so sorry for everything. Was she wonderful? I'll bet she was wonderful."

"She was a gift," said Robert. "And I didn't appreciate that as much as I should have."

Debra came very close to touching his nose splint, then quickly withdrew her hand. "You look tired."

"The funeral was earlier today."

"Boy, the years don't treat us well sometimes, do they?"

"They seem to have been generous to you. My God, you haven't changed a bit."

It wasn't just something nice to say to a lover you haven't seen in a decade, nor was it his way of trying to keep the conversation pleasant; Debra Jamison had not changed one bit since the last time he'd seen her: same curly, light brown hair (which had, it seemed, the exact same amount of gray in it that had been there ten years ago), same freckles, same pouty lips . . . and, like Amy Wilder, a face that was oddly free of age's wrinkles. Sure, maybe some of this might be the result of hair coloring or plastic surgery, but Robert could sense, somehow, that there had been no cosmetic tune-ups done here.

It was as if both Amy and Debra had simply been frozen in time . . . or at least, made somehow immune to its ravages.

"You look . . . wonderful," he whispered to her.

She grinned and kissed his cheek. "You always knew the right thing to say to make my day."

"I . . . uh, look, Debra, it's great to see you again, but I've had kind of a long day and—"

She held up her hand. "Say no more. Are you in the book?"

"No, the number's unlisted . . . but here." He took out his pen and scrawled his number down on the back of his receipt and gave it to her. "Please call me sometime?" Why he asked this of her he didn't know; their breakup had been quiet but nonetheless painful . . . still, he'd always considered her a friend. Or maybe he was just being courteous and trying to get the hell away from this reminder of his life before Denise.

"I *will* see you again, Robert," said Debra, then, excusing herself, scurried down the aisle to find whatever it was she had come in here for.

Robert put his bag of goodies in the backseat of his car and drove out of the parking lot, casting one quick glance back to see if he could get another look at Debra. Unable to spot her, he turned his attention back to the road and the rest of the trip home.

Had he been able to see Debra as he drove away, he would have noticed a certain blankness cover her features as she watched him leave. It looked as if something not unlike the soul had been quickly and quietly removed from within her. Her eyes emptied of their sparkle, and her face became unnaturally still. If it weren't for the movement of her breathing and the blinking of her eyes, she could easily have been mistaken for a mannequin.

Chapter Six

Robert almost tripped over the package when he unlocked the front door—it was already getting dark and he'd forgotten to leave the porch light on. Cursing under his breath, he picked it up and shoved it inside the bag of groceries, then let himself inside.

The first thing that registered was how cold the house had become while he was gone. Checking his watch, Robert estimated he'd been gone six, perhaps seven hours. He could have sworn that the furnace was running when he'd left, but even if that weren't the case, the place should not have been *this* cold.

He set the bag down on a table in the living room and checked the thermostat. The furnace was on. He could feel the heat coming through a nearby vent in the floor.

He picked up the bag, went into the kitchen, turned on the lights—

—and saw the pieces of broken glass on the floor.

Someone had smashed in one of the lower windowpanes in the back door.

Later, Robert would think it odd that he hadn't panicked at that moment; it was almost as if he'd been expecting something like this.

He was very calm, at least at the beginning. He carefully set the sack of groceries on the kitchen counter, buttoned his coat against the breeze flowing in from the broken window, and walked slowly toward the door—noting as he did that there were small clumps of water and dirty snow forming a trail across the kitchen tile. It wasn't surprising that some of the snow hadn't melted, not with the kitchen being this cold, and that's when his mind became two separate entities for a little while; he could almost imagine two small cartoon versions of himself—one dressed in white, with angel's wings, sitting on his left shoulder, while the other, adorned in garish red and holding a pitchfork, sat on his right.

The thing to do, said Angel-Left, *is turn around, leave, and call Bill Emerson.*

Nah, said Devil-Right, *you want to know, so keep going, go 'head, take a look.*

The thing to do was leave.

So, naturally, he kept going.

The screen door had been propped open with one of the larger stones from Denise's garden. The cracked remains of a small clay flowerpot lay next to the stone.

See there? said Devil-Right. *They propped open the back door, then covered their fist with the flowerpot to break the glass.*

Which is exactly why we should leave, said Angel-Left, more out of duty than any real conviction or hope that anyone was going to listen.

Robert blinked—*poof!* the cartoon versions of himself were gone.

He flipped the second of two light switches by the back door. The first switch turned on the lights in the kitchen; the second turned on not only the back porch light, but also a set of three lights that were installed in the ground around the periphery of the garden. He remembered the afternoon Denise and he had installed the lights, how happy they'd been when the things actually worked, because neither of them was exactly gifted in the home improvement department. But they'd done it Denise's way—following the enclosed instructions to the letter, even when it seemed to Robert that some of the steps were superfluous—and, three hours and forty-five minutes after opening the box, success!

Denise had been smug—proud of him for being such a "good little helper," but smug, nonetheless.

"Now if I get the urge to plant something at ten P.M., I can," she'd said.

"Why would you want to be working in your garden at that hour?"

"You don't have a green thumb. You wouldn't understand."

"I think I have a green enough thumb."

She'd laughed. "Are you kidding? I've seen rhododendrons commit suicide rather than have you tend to them."

Robert's gaze lifted to the three low beams of light that shone into her garden. *Those ought to be brighter*, he thought. *I gotta remember to get new bulbs.*

He reached down and gripped the doorknob.

Locked.

Huh.

He turned and looked at the cats, both of whom were on the counter where they knew they weren't allowed, investigating the bag of groceries.

"Why would someone break into a house and then lock the door behind them?"

The cats stopped what they were doing and looked at him: *You don't actually think we're capable of answering that, do you?*

It seemed to him that the cats should have been skittish as hell, still; someone had broken in not too long ago.

So they either had nerves of steel or didn't have the brains God gave a toenail.

Robert shook his head and looked back outside.

His hand reached over to flip the second switch again.

Then froze.

He narrowed his eyes and leaned forward. "What the—"

His eyes then grew very wide very quickly. He unlocked the back door, flung it open, kicked aside the flowerpot, and stormed into the backyard. Halfway between the house and the garden, he turned for another look at the stone holding open the screen door.

"Oh, shit . . ."

It was the same flagstone he'd used to cover Emily's grave.

He sprinted the rest of the way to the garden, falling on his knees and skidding the last two feet through snow and scattered clumps of dirt.

Reaching over to the nearest garden light, he turned the fixture toward him, then down.

Though its beam was weak, the light was strong enough to show him what he needed to know.

Emily's grave had been violated. All around the hole were clumps of dirt mixed with snow and mulch.

Robert leaned back and covered his mouth with one of his hands.

Easy, pal, easy . . .

Taking a couple of deep breaths, he steadied himself, adjusted the light so it pointed directly into the opened grave, then got down on hands and knees for a closer look.

Something wasn't right. The earth at the top of the grave was scattered all around, but down about three, four inches, it looked almost as if the soil had been—

—*no. Don't go there.*

He looked again.

Blinked, rubbed his eyes, looked again.

About four inches down the direction of the earth . . . changed. Where the top three inches or so was scattered about just as it would have been if someone had dug it *up*, everything below had the bowed shape of soil that had been dug in from underneath—like that groundhog's nest he'd discovered a few months after they'd first moved here.

He thrust his arms down into the hole, pulling out the earth with his hands until he gripped the shoe box.

157

Even before he pulled it fully to the surface, Robert's hands found the large hole in the lid.

"No animal," he whispered to himself. "No animal did this."

He pulled the box out of the grave, then brushed the earth from its lid.

And saw the hole.

Only a small portion of the tear seemed to be bent outward; the rest of it was pulled down inside the box.

He gripped the edge of the lid but did not lift it.

His mouth was suddenly dry and his stomach was churning and damned if he didn't feel like his bowels were going to give out—he always reacted this way when he was frightened, everything went right down into his gut—

—and if he didn't open the lid he wouldn't have to know. As long as the lid was closed it could go either way; if he decided her body was still in there, then it was and that was that: Bury it again, replace the stone, mop up the glass and snow and puddles in the house and fix the window, and then everything could be just like it was.

Removing the lid would destroy any possibility.

The smart thing to do was leave it alone.

So he removed the lid and saw the dirt covering the soft white towel in which he'd wrapped her.

He brushed that dirt aside, then took a corner of the towel between his thumb and forefinger to pull it back—

—and realized that it had *already* been pulled back.

He set down the box.

Swallowed once. Very hard.

Then turned his gaze toward the house.

He saw his own footprints very clearly in the snow.

Why hadn't he noticed the others before?

Because they're so small, came the answer, though whether from Devil-Right or Angel-Left he couldn't tell and didn't care.

Just outside the small circle of rocks that marked the garden's edge, small indentations in the snow formed a trail that led to the back porch.

Go home, Willy, so you can find what should be waiting there.

Robert turned the nearest garden light out toward the yard, careful to point its beam downward.

He began to crawl alongside the indentations—which, now that he looked closer, he saw were a series of small handprints that were followed by a pair of smooth skids.

She was crawling, pulling knees and feet behind her.

A few feet along, the handprints disappeared, replaced by the footprints of bare feet belonging to a child of perhaps one or two years of age.

The closer Robert got to the house, the larger the second set of footprints became.

Here, they looked to have been made by a child of three; closer still, a child of five or six.

The last two footprints—these on the two small steps leading onto the back porch—belonged to a child at least eight years old.

From the porch on, there were no prints, just clumps of snow and earth or puddles where the snow had begun to melt or had already melted.

Over the threshold, across the kitchen floor, then a sharp left—

—into the basement.

Go home, Willy, so you can find—

—both cats were now at the edge of the counter, craning for a look.

"What the hell is it with you two?" said Robert, reaching over to scratch the top of Tasha's head and hopefully restore some sense of normalcy to his core. "You act like this is no big—"

The top of Tasha's head was damp.

Ditto The Winnie's.

Damp and cold.

Ice-cold.

Or recently melted snow cold.

He pulled his hand away and wiped it on his coat.

"Getting friendly with burglars now, are you?"

The cats paid him little mind.

He looked down into the basement.

Something wasn't right. The shadows cast by the light fell at angles different from those he remembered when he was here this morning.

He stepped onto the first stair.

The shadows slanted right instead of left. Denise's work area was on the right and that was the light he'd left on.

Someone had turned it off. Now the only light came from the bulb that hung over the washer/dryer area; that's why the shadows looked wrong.

There was a sudden *thunk!* from the basement, followed by a hiss, then a series of progressively softer *whump-whump-whumps* as the washer went into its spin cycle.

This was too much. Someone breaks into the house, locks the door behind them, pets the cats, then does the fucking laundry?

Robert ran down the stairs. The first thing that registered was the absence of the shovel and garden spade he'd thrown down the stairs three nights ago. He made his way over to the washer, watching it vibrate, then—out of curiosity—touched the door of the dryer.

It was warm. Inside was a load of clothes that had only finished drying a few minutes ago.

He crossed to a set of shelves left of the washer, took down his toolbox, and removed a hammer, then stormed over to Denise's side of the basement. He kicked over a few boxes along the way to make sure the intruder wasn't hiding behind them, checked the dark corners around the water heater and furnace, and was reaching up to turn on Denise's light when he became aware of his heart beating furiously in his chest. He could feel it in his temples.

How long he stood that way—one arm at his side, gripping

the hammer, the other lifted in the air, fingers gripping the thin chain of the light—he couldn't say. He was only aware of time passing. The washer finished its spin cycle and fell into silence. Robert remained still, listening to the faint, irregular drip of water as condensation fell from the pipes. He could hear his own breathing. He wet his lips, then admitted to himself that he was scared. He squeezed the wooden handle of the hammer for reassurance. No good; he was still petrified.

Then came a sound from somewhere behind him.

A soft sound.

But close.

Every muscle in his body seemed to come unwound all at once; his skin broke out in gooseflesh and his breath suddenly caught in his throat. Whirling around, he yanked so hard on the light cord that it snapped off between his fingers, but the light came on and Robert was able to see—a moment before it rolled off the table and clattered lightly onto the floor—what had made the sound.

One of Denise's detail brushes—a thin, camel-hair number—had fallen out of the rack.

Robert knelt down to pick it up (that's what he told himself, anyway; the truth was it was either kneel or allow his knees to buckle from the sudden relief) and saw the small spatters of red that it had left on the floor. The hair of the brush was still wet with paint.

He rose slowly, and was about to lay the brush back on the table when he saw that, except for a plain brown box in the center of the table and about half a dozen brushes soaking in a jar of cleaning fluid, Denise's work area, her fiercely guarded corner of privacy, had been stripped clean.

She had once yelled at him for having come into this area while she wasn't at home. He couldn't remember what he'd been looking for—undoubtedly something he could have found elsewhere in the house—but whatever it was, he'd figured that it wouldn't bother her.

She'd gone ballistic when she found out, screaming that he'd violated a part of her.

He never forgot her rage, nor the hurt on her face and in her voice.

But mostly he never forgot her rage.

That rage was now his. Rael—or whoever had gone through the trouble to stage this parlor trick from hell—had come down here and sheared away all traces of Denise's work, probably stuffing everything into that goddamned box—

Robert slammed the hammer onto the table and ripped the lid off the box, hoping that he could remember how she'd had everything arranged. He thought he might be able to reconstruct it well enough if he—

—his hand froze inside the box.

No pencils, no paint tubes, no sketch pads or Exacto-knife.

He carefully removed the two *matryoshka* dolls and set them side by side on the table, then turned on the small jeweler's lamp whose neck jutted out from the side of the hutch.

He needn't have bothered; even with a minimum of light he would have recognized Denise's face on the largest doll—roughly the size of a pineapple, his own on the smaller, this one no bigger than an average gourd.

They were just as wondrous as the ones she'd made for Lynn—no, scratch that: if anything, these were even *more* stunning and exquisite. Viewing the painstaking details through the magnifying lens of the jeweler's lamp revealed that much.

The subtle upward sweep of her thin eyelashes, the tongue-in-cheek melancholy of his own grin, the arc of shadow at the corners of both their eyes, shadows that seemed comfortably indigenous and did not alter their shape or position when either doll was turned this way or that, into or out of the light.

Denise was dressed in a *sarafan* and kerchief, both tinted in gold. She looked like a wandering princess separated from her family; Anastasia among the ruins.

She had worn a similar costume two years ago at Halloween

when she insisted they both get dressed up to give out the candy. It had been an odd request but he'd gone along with her whim, having—despite the self-conscious feelings at the start—a great deal of fun.

He couldn't remember what costume he'd worn that night. Too bad; it seemed important, somehow.

The Denise doll's kerchief even had the same small stain near its center, the result of his having tripped with a tray of treats, baptizing her in a shower of not-quite-dried candied apples. God, how they'd laughed about that.

He lifted the top off the Denise doll and removed the smaller *matryoshka* from inside it, then removed the one inside that.

He looked at the faces on the other two dolls and felt his knees start to give. He pulled up Denise's chair and fell into it.

From left to right, the dolls portrayed Denise, Amy Wilder, and Debra Jamison; Denise in her Halloween costume from two years ago; Amy as she had looked at the cemetery this morning, right down to the color and style of her coat and the Joan Crawford hat with its veil pulled back; and Debra as she had been only a couple of hours ago. The faces might as well have been photographs they were so precise.

He picked up the Debra doll and shook it; it felt and sounded as if there were two, possibly three other dolls inside it. Try as he did—for the better part of three minutes, grunting with effort—he could not get the two sections of the doll separated so he could see the others hiding within. He thought about getting a screwdriver and forcing it open, but then his attention wandered to the *matryoshka* that bore his own likeness.

Unlike the other dolls, this one did not have a groove encircling its center; there was no way to separate the top half from the bottom.

He shook the Robert doll.

Paused.

Then shook it twice more.

It was hollow.

He set it back down on the table and wiped his eyes, wondering if Denise, like her mother with her pictures of the wedding and battlefield, had been trying to tell him something with this doll. Perhaps she'd made it one night while he was at work, one of the many nights she was alone here while he was out fighting the good fight in order to advance his career. Maybe she'd been hurt, or lonely, or frightened, or disappointed, and had created this hollow *matryoshka* out of anger toward him. Maybe that's why she'd made it hollow—her way of letting him know she thought he was turning into some kind of shallow, self-centered—

—*speaking of self-centered, how typical to take something like this and make it all about* you.

He set the doll down next to the others and swung the jeweler's lamp over to see if there was something in the small details that he'd overlooked.

"Oh, God . . ."

The doll was dressed in the exact same clothes he'd worn to the funeral—the same clothes he was wearing now; not only that, but in its left hand it clutched a piece of paper—

—he moved the magnifying lens closer—

—and could just make out the words *Send me a picture of the daughter . . .*

In Denise's handwriting.

"Rael," he whispered, then: "*Rael!*"

He jumped to his feet, hands fisted in rage, and screamed, "*Rael! Goddammit!* If you're in this house and can hear me, then *say something! Right now!* If you were telling me the truth and I don't have to be afraid of you, then show yourself."

He yelled so loudly that the cats leaped from the counter and ran in fur-shedding, scitter-claw panic to their secret hiding places.

"Now, Rael! If you're in this house, then show me *your goddamned ugly fucking face right now!*"

He grabbed up the hammer and started for the stairs but was stopped by the echo of laughter.

A child's laughter.

He took the steps three at a time, bolted through all the rooms and turned on the lights, then, finding no one hiding down here, ran upstairs, kicking open every door as he came to it, flipping on the lights, and searching each room as thoroughly as his panic and anger would allow.

By the time he came to the bedroom he'd shared with Denise, the child's laughter had been joined by that of other children, one of them even singing, "Olly, olly, oxen-free!"

Then the pitter-patter of little feet rushing down the stairs.

Robert chased the sound, his eyes darting from side to side at even the smallest hint of a shadow where he didn't remember one being, and very nearly fell over his own feet at the top of the stairs; grabbing the banister, he steadied his balance and quickly descended, hitting bottom as three more sounds simultaneously invaded his world: the scrape of something metal being dragged across the concrete floor of the basement, one child's laughter becoming weeping, and the screen door banging shut.

He entered the kitchen and saw that someone had unpacked the groceries and laid out everything he'd need in order to bake cookies, including the ingredients, the battery-operated mixer, a mixing bowl, and three cookie trays (all of them only a few weeks old, and none of which Denise had lived to use). He flung open the back door and saw that both the flowerpot and flagstone were gone, the garden lights had been set back into their original positions, and the garden was as it had been a little while ago.

The box had been either taken or reburied, because it was nowhere to be seen.

The flagstone was back in its proper place. There was no sign that the garden had ever been disturbed.

Even the footprints were gone, covered now by a fresh whisper of night snow.

He went back inside, locking both the screen door and back door, then quickly did the same to the basement door, slamming the bolt lock solidly in place. He grabbed a kitchen chair and jammed its back underneath the doorknob. Whoever was rearranging things down there couldn't get out unless he *let* them out; the basement windows were too small for even a child to squeeze through.

Now it was just a matter of finding whoever else was in the house with him.

He stood in the center of the middle room, drenched in sweat and gulping air, trying to be as quiet as he could. Blood thundered through his temples and his mouth was desert-dry. A thin, sharp bead of perspiration cut a smooth path directly down the center of his spine. The lights of the house seemed so much brighter and richer than they had before, streaming all around him to coat his surroundings in bright liquid, gathering in a shiny skin on the backs of his hands.

Too bright; everything was too bright, painfully bright, reminding him of the lights in the hospital—not only from the night Denise had died, but all those nights he'd spent in the hospital throughout his childhood, always a sickly child, and clumsy, or healing from a beating given to him by his father when the man was drunk, injuries he and his mother always lied about by calling him clumsy.

He closed his eyes and tried to summon up memories of early childhood that had no connection to pain or confusion or terror and could not do it; before Lynn's birth when he was nine, those three had been his only constant companions. Even after that night Dad had hit him so hard Robert's spleen ruptured and he spent three weeks in the hospital recovering from the surgery ("He took just about the worst tumble off his bike that I've ever seen a child take," his mother told the doctor in the emergency room, both of them knowing damned well that she was lying and there wasn't a thing to be done about it), he would come awake in the middle of the night and see the slash of corridor light creeping in under the door and hold his breath, convinced that Dad would come and hit him again, or call him names like "sissy-boy" or "weakling" or "mistake." Those names had hurt worse than any fist, because whenever Dad was drunk and called him those names—and worse ones—Robert knew for certain that his father didn't love him, maybe even wished he'd never been born.

Still, there was something poking at the edge of his memory about that three-week stay in the hospital. He'd been in the children's wing, that much he could remember, and when he was able to get up and take short walks through the corridor, one of the nurses—he couldn't remember her name, just that she was large and gray-haired and always smiled like those Christmas-card drawings of Mrs. Santa Claus—would take him on the elevator and they'd go up and look at all the newborn babies through the glass. That had been nice—

—and it was *that* part of the memory that nagged at him suddenly; it seemed ridiculous as hell to be focusing on something so distant when there was a very real possibility in the here-and-now that he was in a house with definitely one and maybe even more intruders . . . but, still . . . there it was: an image of him standing there, eight years old and hooked up to a portable IV that he wheeled around like some toy wagon, his face and hands pressed against the glass, making goofy, puffin-face expressions at the babies who were either always crying or asleep.

The glass was cool, so cool; he'd liked that. Nurse Claus had said it was because of his infection and fever, how the cool glass seemed even cooler because he was still sick. When he asked about the other baby room, the one he could see through the swinging doors, Nurse Claus told him that was the isolation ward, where they put the "real sick" babies so they could get better.

Gary A. Braunbeck

Nurse Claus—that's what he'd called her, and she'd laughed when he explained why, then kissed the top of his head and told him he had quite the imagination and was such a good boy.

A good boy.

Babies behind glass.

He blinked the nagging memory back into the shadows, then opened his eyes to the still too bright lights and the oncoming migraine of which they warned.

He started at the farthest room upstairs, turning off all the unneeded lights room by room until, at last, he was back in the kitchen, staring at the chair jammed against the basement door.

He yanked the chair from under the doorknob, gripped the bolt lock, and took a deep breath, making sure that he still had the hammer—he did; sometime during the last five minutes he'd slipped it into his coat pocket, though he was damned if he could remember doing it.

At the same moment he disengaged the lock, the music started.

"Oh, I don't know what to make
Of this life I'm leading . . ."

He walked into the living room, toward the entertainment center where the lights of the receiver and CD player glowed like the headlights of a car about to crash into a frozen deer.

"A child ever searching to belong
I've got one foot in history and the other in the future
Something's got to give before too long . . ."

John Nitzinger's "One Foot in History," the first song he and Denise had ever danced to . . . and he'd waited until the night he proposed before daring to show her that he was a rotten dancer. He remembered how surprised he'd been that she owned the album—back in the days when vinyl was the only game in town—and how she'd just sat there smiling at him as he raved on about Nitzinger and Bloodrock, the band John Nitzinger had written several songs for. "Two of the greatest seventies rock acts that 'classic rock' FM radio has forgotten about!"

She kissed him when he finished going on about it, and asked him what his favorite song from the album had been. He told her, and she carefully cued the record and asked him to dance with her.

"I'm a lousy dancer," he'd said.

"I know, but it'll be so much more romantic if we're dancing when you ask."

"Ask what?"

"You *were* planning to ask me to marry you, weren't you?"

"Uh . . ."

She slipped one hand around his waist, the other cupped the back of his head. "Mr. Eloquence, and you're all mine."

"There's loneliness for sale
And the people here are all buying
All been dipping in the till
Now the whole damn world is dying . . ."

Robert reached out and turned off the stereo. No one but Denise had ever known how much that song meant to him, all the lonely hours he'd spent listening to it when he was in high school, headphones practically fused to his skull to drown out the sound of Dad's shouting, listening to Nitzinger's melancholy growl of a voice grow ever sadder with each verse yet still, seemingly with gritted teeth, admit that there might be some hope, and seventeen-year-old Robert Londrigan would lose himself in the music because there was no love in his life, no romance yet, definitely no hope . . . and he so wanted there to be. Any one or all three, just . . . *something more.*

Only Denise had ever known about that.

Whoever had programmed the CD player had not picked this song at random.

He tore the hammer from his pocket, strode back into the kitchen, and opened the basement door.

"Olly, olly, oxen-free," he whispered, and started down.

To his left, the dryer was now running, busy fluffing the load of laundry from the washing machine. The clothes that had previously been in the dryer were now neatly folded and stacked inside their wicker basket, ready to be put away.

To his right, the Debra Jamison *matryoshka* doll had been taken apart and a fourth doll now sat beside it.

As Robert approached Denise's work area, his gaze locked on her filing cabinet to the right of her table. It had been moved, unlocked, and both drawers pulled open. The key was still in the lock.

Denise kept that key hidden down here, and would never tell him where.

It was a privacy thing, and he respected that.

He closed his eyes and took a deep breath.

One thing at a time, pal; one thing at a time.

Okay; first the filing cabinet.

Two files had been pulled out and were lying atop the others. Robert's intention was to simply put them back inside, then close and lock the drawers. He had sworn to Denise that he'd never invade her privacy again, and he intended to keep that promise, even now. After that, he would get the hell out of here, call Bill Emerson and tell the detective everything that had happened up until now, and deal with the consequences as they fell on his head.

He grabbed up the files.

A photograph fell out of the topmost, thickest file.

Robert picked up the photo, fully intending to simply slip it back inside the file, but sometimes the eyes will unconsciously commit acts the mind wishes it had the nerve to do.

He saw the photograph.

My brothers and sisters, Willy. Do you despair?

The child had only one eye socket, directly in the center of its forehead where two eyes struggled to stay in place. Its face had no nose; instead, there was a proboscislike appendage that looked like an uncircumcised penis growing from the center of its shrunken forehead.

Me Ian.

He was holding the same photograph that Rael had shown to him in the morgue.

He sat down and opened the file. The first thing he saw was a neatly typed sheet of paper with a paper clip in the upper-right corner.

Ian Henry Akerman, age 3 weeks, 2 days, 11 hours
CYCLOPIA
Head: microchephaly
Eyes: a single eye with a diamond shaped orbital cavity present in the middle of the face where the nose is usually located. Eyes are in the same orbit with a single optic nerve. Eyelids are so short as to be functionally absent.
Ears: low set and malpositioned.
Nose: cylindrical-shaped appendage covered by skin and located above the eye on the lower part of the forehead. There is no nasal cavity or philtrum.
Mouth: triangular with small upper cleft lip and cleft palate.
Skeletal: polydactyl and talipes equinovarus
CNS: holoprosencephaly, spina bifida, encephalocele and acrania.
Other Findings: missing facial bones, hypoplasia of the adrenals, congenital heart disease.
Treatment: none.
Prognosis: patient will not survive more than 24 hours.

At the very bottom of the page, Denise had written: *You sure showed them, didn't you, Ian?*

Gary A. Braunbeck

Switiching to automatic pilot, Robert slid the photograph of Ian as an infant back under the paper clip and turned to the next case description.

Marie Alice Simpkins, age 9 years, 6 months
MUCOPOLYSACCHARIDOSIS (Scheie's Syndrome)

Broad mouth, hazy corneas, clawed hands, scaly skin.

He flipped through the cases and photographs—Jenny, four, progeria; Ralphie, two, gangliosidosis; Michael, five, kernicterus; Theresa, eleven, lipogranulomatosis; Humberto, twelve, nuerofibromatosis—and saw the misshapen heads, the too-big mouths, the skin that looked more amphibian or reptilian than human, the stumpy arms and legs, the willowy feet or hands, the elongated necks, and his heart began to break for these children—not just the ones who were deformed, but the all of them: Albert, six, beaten with an iron, blinded in left eye, deafened in left ear; Kylie, three, sexually assaulted with cucumber, burned with cigarettes; Jerry, five, left hand crushed with hammer; Laurie, two, Down's syndrome, face held under scalding water . . . the list of afflictions and atrocities went on and on, a gallery of violence and brutality that sometimes existed only on the genetic level as the children were maimed by their own cell structure before they were even born, and at other times had the horror inflicted on them by parents or other so-called loved ones who hadn't the guts to deal with their own shortcomings or disappointments or broken dreams and so chose the coward's therapy—abusing those who could not defend themselves.

And at the bottom of each page Denise had written some comment: *You'll be able to play an instrument if you want to, Jerry! Your skin is looking so much better now, Laurie; you'll be an absolute heartbreaker! Ornery as ever, Humberto—I love it!*

The thing that became clear to Robert as he read through the file was that, in every instance, either the child should not have survived beyond a few hours after being born, or there was no hope of healing the physical and emotional wounds.

Yet there was something in Denise's comments that led him to believe—to *know* with a certainty most dare not hope for—that each of these children had survived; not only survived, but somehow, through some sort of near-miraculous intervention, begun to heal, to shake off the effects of their abuse or undergo treatment that, if not outright *curing* them of their affliction, at least allowed them to live on and become a functioning adult, one who knew love and acceptance and friendship and home.

He laid this first file on the table and looked at the second, so used now to the sensation of tears running down his cheeks that it seemed to him they had always been there, a part of his flesh that only now was coming to full life. He wiped his eyes as best he could and looked at the cover of the other file. There only thing written on it was a date: July 10, 1969.

Three days before the child Robert had once turned nine years old.

He'd been in the hospital then, had been there, in fact, for almost two weeks recovering from the splenectomy. He recalled the way his father had finally come to visit him on his birthday, bearing gifts and kisses and tears and apologies. It seemed like someone else's past now. Robert preferred to think of it that way most of the time.

He opened the file.

And it was at this moment that his undoing began in earnest.

It contained only one yellowed newspaper clipping and blue-smudged carbon copies of three statements given to police investigators.

He began with the newspaper clipping:

CEDAR HILL, OHIO,
NEWBORN FOUND IN HOSPITAL BATHROOM
IN CRITICAL CONDITION

A newborn found abandoned in a rest room at Cedar Hill Memorial Hospital was still listed in critical condition this morning as the search for its mother and/or father continued.

A nurse from the neonatal unit discovered the baby about 2:45 yesterday morning, said police Sgt. Raymond Vecchio.

The exact age of the 3-pound baby girl has yet to be determined. Hospital officials refused comment on rumors that the infant had been physically abused prior to its abandonment.

The newborn is being kept in the neonatal intensive care unit. Doctors would not speculate on the baby's prognosis.

Robert was suddenly eight years old again, standing outside the glass with Nurse Claus and looking at the newborns, then catching sight of the other doors, the other glass wall where the "sick" babies were kept. Jesus H. Christ-on-the-Cross, he'd been there at the same time as this poor child!

And again some nagging memory, still hiding in half shadows and haze, whispered secrets to him from its safe, clean, unlighted place.

He put the clipping aside and read the first statement. Some of the words were smudged and hard to make out, forcing him to squint, and by the time he finished reading the last of the three statements he would be in the grips of an oncoming migraine, but for the moment there was something compelling him to read on; it seemed important. Vital. *Absolutely necessary*.

He began reading:

Alice Rutledge, July 16

I've been a pediatrics nurse for going on . . . oh, I guess it's close enough to twenty years now to call it. I don't usually work the graveyard shift, understand, but Tammy Cramer's car developed another one of its problems and she couldn't make it in—she lives way out past Hebron—so she called and asked me if I'd switch with her. You know—

I'd take her midnight-to-nine and she'd get in the next morning for my nine-to-six. We all keep telling that girl she ought to get rid of that lemon she drives, but the poor girl just can't afford it, what with two kids and her husband gettin' laid off from the plant and everything. Anyway, I'd just finished making the rounds, I guess it was two-thirty or a bit after, and I stopped into the rest room to wash up on account of one of the patients—that little boy who calls me "Nurse Claus"—all the gals up here got a real kick out of that; it's sort of a new nickname for me now. Anyway, he'd woke up from a real bad nightmare about his daddy and I was trying to get him back to sleep when all of a sudden he throws up, real violent, right? It's a terrible thing to see a child vomit like that. Poor boy just had his spleen bust on him and it ain't good for a child who's recovering from that kind of trauma to be vomiting like that. Okay, so me and Janet, we get him all cleaned up and settled down and I call Dr. Waggoner and he tells me it's okay to give this poor little guy his pain medication a little early, so I did, and he fell asleep but now I've got dried vomit on my uniform and such. So I go into the rest room to clean up as best I can. I spent five minutes or so scrubbing off my hands and uniform and I was just about to head on back to the nurses' station when I see this bunch of stained towels all heaped together under one of the sinks. Well, we can't have that in a public rest room, especially up here where all the kids are. I figured that someone had maybe overloaded their laundry cart or something but even as I leaned down and pulled the mess out I knew that wasn't right—I mean, it was a lot heavier than it ought to have been. I started to pick it up to toss it in the laundry hamper and it . . . it moved. I almost dropped it, it scared me so bad. So I laid it on the counter by the sink and I unwrapped it and . . . oh, dear, I'm sorry, I don't mean to turn on the waterworks like this but . . . good Lord. That baby wasn't more than ten, twelve hours old. Its umbilical cord was still attached. It makes me sad, it makes me sick. It wasn't enough of a burden that the poor little thing had to be born looking like it did, but then to have someone do something like . . . that . . . to it . . . it makes me sick and sad. Right down to the ground.

Not allowing himself to think about it too much, Robert exhaled and moved on to the next statement:

Janet Tyler, July 16

Until the day I die I'll never forget the look on Alice's face when she came running out of that rest room. I followed her back inside—and let me tell you, one thing I never do unless there's a damned good reason is leave that station unattended—and she shows me this heap of dirty, bloody towels with a baby inside. I have to be honest with you . . . at first I wasn't sure it was a baby, I thought maybe it was some kind of animal . . . course, I only saw part of its face until Alice opens the towels and there's its body. I couldn't look at it for too long—not because it turned my stomach or anything like that, understand—it was just too damned sad—and I say this to you as one who's seen more than her share of retarded and deformed children. I don't mind saying that there's no pit in hell deep enough or hot enough for the person who cut up that baby like that. We called Dr. Cummins—he was the Attending that night—and he came up and called Security. No one passed the nurses' station that I saw. Dr. Cummins examined the baby, then stitched it up and gave it something to help it sleep. We put it in the IC unit up here and pulled a nurse from the ER to keep an eye on it. The odd thing is, Alice kept going on about how that baby was just born and . . . and I'm not trying to cast doubt on Alice's abilities as a pediatrics nurse—hell, no, the woman helped train me!—but

I've been at it for about eight years and would like to think I can tell the difference between a baby right out of the chute and one that's a bit older. I'll swear on a stack of Bibles that that baby she found was at least six days old. Do you guys have any idea who took it? I'd sure as hell like to know how they managed to get past us and the security guard.

The last statement was as brief as it was unnerving:

Regina Bautista, MD, July 16
   Dr. Cummins made a mistake, that's all. Perfectly understandable, under the circumstances—the lateness of the hour, the condition the child was in, all the confusion with Security and police, the nurses being shorthanded that night. Perfectly understandable. I examined the baby later that morning—I think it was around ten-thirty—and I found an infant that was at least two weeks old. It was as alert as possible, considering the medication it was on, and its eyes were surprisingly alert for a child . . . of its condition. In fact, its eyes tracked extremely well. Its umbilical cord had dropped off and its navel was almost fully healed.

The onslaught of the migraine was nearly instantaneous. Robert put the file in his lap, pulled out the bottle of painkillers, and popped one into his mouth. It took three tries, but he at last managed to swallow it.

He couldn't remember if he'd taken one earlier or not.

Leaning back in the chair, he closed his eyes and tried to absorb everything he'd just read and seen.

As the man I once was sits there still as death, we need to talk about madness.

It's probably wrong to assume that madness is something born on a note of epiphany; sanity rarely ends amidst a glorious, cataclysmic, earth-shattering moment of Götterdämmerung; no: when a human mind can no longer maintain a wakeful, staring, unrelenting grasp on reason, when it begins to buckle, when it's been confronted with too much horror, or grief, or confusion, or pressure, or fear, or a quietly crystalized combination of all five, sanity slowly grinds to a halt in a series of sputtering little agonies, flaking away in bits and pieces, flotsam of a refugee column casting off sad little remnants— a hope here, a fond memory there—on a road of defeat as a deeper and deeper darkness falls. And perhaps this is why so many madmen are found laughing in locked cells; at some point the only thing left them is their sense of humor, and it all becomes rather funny.

Sitting there with his eyes closed, almost—not quite, but almost unaware of it, the man I once was laughed. Very softly. Just for a moment.

Because something in his mind had just sputtered.

Shhh, quiet now; he's opening his eyes.

From the kitchen came the busy noises of dishes and bowls being moved, an egg being cracked open, then the electric buzz-whirrrrrr of the mixer starting up and getting down to the serious business of making cookies.

Robert knew he should run upstairs and catch Rael, or whoever it was, in the act—he wanted to do this, more than anything else, run up there and grab them and confront them, tell them to get the hell out of his life and his head and give back to him the safe, dull, consensual reality that he'd known for most of his life, at least until these last several days—but the center of his chest was heavy and, as it was that night in the park when all this began, everywhere in his body there was sudden, extravagant pain, more pain than he thought he could ever endure without succumbing to death or unconsciousness, rendering his limbs all but useless, and his vision was blurred, and his throat was tight, and he almost no longer cared. Let them have at it.

He dropped the files onto the table and saw that the new *matryoshka* had been set with its back to him. He reached out, with great effort, his arms like lead weights, and began to turn it around.

There was another sound, then: crinkling.

The new doll was sitting on paper.

A package.

The package, to be exact, the same one Robert had nearly tripped over before coming inside.

He moved the doll aside and read his name and address written in an almost childlike scrawl on the brown wrapping paper. The return address was his own, as well.

The buzz-*whirrrrrr* of the mixer stopped for a moment while the three metal cookie trays were separated and the first bag of chocolate chips opened.

Robert watched as his hand dug its fingers into the brown package paper.

The buzz-*whirrrrr* of the mixer started again just as Robert's fingers tore into the paper and ripped a clean, straight path right down the center.

He watched and listened, fascinated by the whole thing; image and soundtrack to some art-house foreign film: *The Mixing Hand Rips. Wild Matryoshkas. The Seventh Chip. Pelle the Cookie.* All starring Max von Sydow as Happy Guy. Dubbed and letterboxed for the cinema purists.

As he watched the movie play out before him—hand tearing, package coming apart, sounds of cookies being made—Robert began to feel shiny again—no less weighed down, but the pain was receding. Pill must be kicking in.

He decided that the movie must be some kind of black comedy, because there was a certain absurdist humor to it. A Rube Goldberg short-subject. So he allowed himself to laugh once again. He thought it was a pity that von Sydow was always cast as the brooding, worried, depressed so-and-so. Hell, the guy did a Woody Allen movie, didn't he, and when he's finally cast in a comedy, what kind of part does he get? A depressed, suicidal artist. No wonder he turned around and did that Stephen King movie; he probably needed something light.

That struck Robert as funny, so he laughed again.

The cookie soundtrack droned comfortably on as the package revealed its contents: *Rockin' '78: The Cedar Hill High School Yearbook*.

"Aw, isn't that nice?" Robert said to no one in particular. "The year I graduated." He looked at the three *matryoshka* dolls facing him. "See, Dad had finally gone into AA that year because he'd gotten laid off in February and we were all afraid that his drinking might get a lot worse. I guess he did, too, what with no job to waste his boozing time anymore . . . so we didn't have a lot of what you'd call your 'disposable income,' right? I *wanted* to get a copy of the yearbook but we couldn't afford it so I never did. And *now* . . . somebody sweet has gotten one for me." He leaned forward and smiled at the dolls. "Want to take a look inside? Have a stroll down memory lane? Oh, let's!" He flipped open the oversized hardcover to a page at random. "The drama club! The spring play that year was *Spoon River Anthology*—you know, two and a half hours of dead people coming out of their graves long enough to read their own epitaphs. Big hit with the teens, major chuckle-fest. Oooh—says here that the musical that year was *Finian's Rainbow!*" He leaned even closer toward the dolls and whispered, "So, how *are* things in Glockamora? And will you all return there some fine day?"

(Take a breath and get a fuckin' grip, pal!)

"And here," he said, ignoring the voice in his head, "is a photo of the sexiest little bunch of cheerleaders this side of a *Playboy* Pay-Per-View special, the Cedar Hill Wildcats Cat-ettes. I always sort of liked their short skirts, gave you just enough of a glimpse of the Promised Land to make you watch only them in hopes of seeing more . . . but then I was seventeen and constantly horny and had never had sex with anyone who wasn't my right hand, so I think I'm entitled to wax nostalgic about my long-lost teenaged raging hormones. But I see I'm embarrassing you ladies, so let's move on—ah! The senior pictures! We didn't have the money for me to get any taken, so I won't be in here but that's no great loss to Posterity—I had hair like the fifth Bee Gee. Let's see." He flipped randomly back and forth through the photos. "Here's Vanessa Tartar—who, oddly enough, didn't like seafood. I was the only person who thought that was funny. And John Wade, the living Howdy-Doody. Yeah, yeah, and here's Rick Rush—great name, if I'd had a name like that I could've been a star. Rick played football. Betcha can't guess what his specialty was? Hah! This is Kim Luther—I had sort of a crush on her but she never knew it, and Molly May, and—oh, we're leaving someone out." He reached out and turned the fourth *matryoshka* doll around, not surprised to find that some its still-wet paint came off on his fingers. Wiping his fingers off on his coat, he looked up at the fourth doll at the same time he turned to the next page of senior photographs—

—and found himself looking at the same face on both page and doll.

Cathy Pope.

It wasn't by accident that he saw her face in the yearbook; there were only five photos on this page, all of them three times the size of the other senior pictures. Cathy was the only girl on the page, and whoever had done the layout had put her picture right in the center.

The caption at the top of the page read: IN MEMORIAM.

Below Cathy's photo was a quote, and a set of dates: *I don't want to try to be like anyone else; I just want to be the best Cathy I can be! 1961–1978.*

He looked from the photo to the likeness on the doll.

They were an exact match. Her sparkling brown eyes, the long, thick, dark hair that tumbled about her shoulders like a velvet cradle, the little splotch of freckles on her nose that she'd said she hated but that Robert knew she hoped made her look

181

cute. In both doll and photo, her seventeen-year-old bloom shone strong and radiant.

Robert's throat muscles were suddenly about two times too big for his neck to contain. "Oh, Cathy . . ."

They'd met in November of '78 at a recruitment session for the audiovisual club. Robert had been interested in doing something on-camera while Cathy had wanted to get involved behind the scenes, maybe producing a talk show or something like that. He'd been drawn to her shy sweetness and the way she seemed to think everything he said was funny. It was the first time in his almost eighteen years of inhabiting this planet that Robert had actually felt attractive. He remembered their first few dates, the way it had taken him a while to get used to her dry wit, how his whole body seemed to vibrate whenever she'd hold his hands. "I'm sorry my fingers are so bony," she'd say, but he didn't mind, not one little bit. She was the first girl he'd ever made out with, the first whose breast he'd ever touched, the first he'd ever cried in front of during a bad date shortly after his dad had gone into AA. She had listened to him as he talked about how bad he felt for his mom and how he worried about his little sister. He told her about how his spleen came to be ruptured, the weeks in the hospital, and how he had bad dreams that Dad might fall off the wagon and do something like that to Lynn.

"What about you?" she'd asked, putting her smooth, warm hand on the back of his neck as they sat in the front seat of her father's '75 Mustang. "Don't you worry about what all that's done to you?"

"Not really," he said. It was the truth. "I mean, I've been the only thing that stands between him and Mom and Lynn for so long that . . . I just don't think about how it affects me. That doesn't seem so important."

"Well it is to *me*, you goof! I don't like to think of you being in pain."

He'd almost laughed at that but managed to swallow it back

at the last minute. " 'In pain.' You make it sound romantic."

"Nothing romantic about it. I don't see anything romantic about having your youth ruined."

Always, she'd been that way, one of the most compassionate people he'd ever known. And she never seemed to get angry with people who let her down. Once, when a couple of her friends had canceled movie plans with her at the last minute (and he knew how much she'd been looking forward to going out with her girlfriends), Robert asked her why she wasn't mad.

"What good would it do? Getting mad just saps all the energy you could use doing something positive. Sure, they stood me up, but now I've got a whole evening to do with whatever I want. I could read, listen to music, go window-shopping—"

"Or you could hang up and come get me and we could spend the evening together."

"Took you long enough. See ya in twenty minutes!"

By January they were officially a Couple. It was in March, after a particularly long and steamy make-out session. They were sitting next to each other on the couch in her parents' den (her parents had always been cool about not bothering them when they were alone at her house), still fully clothed but definitely seriously mussed. She was snuggled against him, her cheek against his chest while her hands drew small, indecipherable patterns on his shoulder. It was warm and close and intimate and he'd wanted for it to never end.

"Listen to me," she whispered, "because I'm only going to say this once—and you'd better not laugh if you know what's good for you."

"Okay."

"Okay. I'm crazy about you, Robert Londrigan. Since we've been going out I've never been happier or felt sexier or looked so forward to each morning because it means another day that I get to see you. Get that smug grin off your face."

"I'm not smug."

"You look like Bo-Bo the Dog-Faced Boy. Stop it."

"Let me think about something depressing." A beat. "Sorry, can't seem to find anything right at the moment."

"Shh." Her finger against his lips. "*Listen*. Dad said you could drive his new car when we go to the prom."

"The *Caddy*?"

"You're not being quiet—do you want to hear this or not?"

He mimed locking his mouth and tossing away the key.

"I've already found my dress—and no, you can't see it. I . . . I love you, and I think you love me, so I feel okay telling you this next part." She sat back and faced him. "I'm a virgin, okay? It's not that I haven't had the chance to be with a guy . . . in that way, I've just never met one who I cared enough about to . . ." She sighed, looked down, shook her head, then stared directly into his eyes. "I love you, Robert, and here's what I'd like to happen: after the prom and the parties, I'd like for us to drive out to Buckeye Lake to my parents' summer cabin, and I'd like us to spend the night together in the same bed, and I'd like for us to make love like two people who love each other are supposed to, all right?"

He touched her cheek. "I love you, too, Cathy."

"You'd better."

Then she gave him one of the ten greatest kisses in recorded history.

Two months later, on the way back from visiting her grandmother in Columbus with her parents, a drunk in a pickup truck crossed the center line on I-70 doing eighty-eight miles an hour and hit them head-on. Everyone—except the drunk, who would later blow his brains out while out on bond—was killed instantly. From what Robert was able to find out from Cathy's friends at school, there wasn't enough left of her for an open-casket funeral.

That was the first time Robert thought it amazing that the human heart made no sound when it cracked. It had almost killed him, losing her.

He reached into his coat pocket and pulled out the card Amy

Wilder had given to Danny, then turned it over and once again read the words on the back: *May 21, 1978. Not such a pretty picture.*

May 21, 1978. The day Cathy and her parents had been killed.

No wonder he hadn't wanted to remember why the date seemed familiar. It had taken the better part of three years for him to recover from her death—not that they weren't other girls after her; he'd turned into a regular hound dog after graduation, and once he got to college people often joked that he was constitutionally required to bed down with a new woman every four days. He'd drunk a lot during those three years—too much, in fact. But it seemed the best way to distance himself from the ache Cathy had left. Boozing and screwing, screwing and boozing, with a little school thrown in for good measure.

Sometime in the middle of his sophomore year he woke up with a hangover in the bed of a woman at least fifteen years older and whose name he couldn't remember and realized that he was going to wind up in a detox ward if he didn't stop. It amazed him then—and still did—that he hadn't caught anything worse than a mondo case of crabs from his reckless behavior. That morning, waking in the older woman's bed and realizing he not only couldn't remember her name but had no idea where they'd even *met*, he suddenly felt like a living literary cliché, a character cut from a first-draft Fitzgerald. Some might see a certain tragic romance in his actions those three years after Cathy's death; Robert thought he was just being an asshole.

He spent a very, very long time and much effort trying to expunge the memory of those times from his universe. It also meant expunging Cathy's memory.

He had been shockingly successful.

Until this night, in the basement of the house he'd once shared with Denise, he had not thought of Cathy Pope, even briefly, in at least ten years.

He didn't feel shiny anymore.

Dear God, had he ever really taken time to know *any* woman? Even those with whom he was involved only for a little while? Would it have been that much trouble, was it too much to ask that he pay a little more attention, that he participate in a conversation without trying to find a way to make himself or his dreams its subject? Had he really destroyed that element of genuine character that erased ego and machismo from a man's nature and allowed him to be vulnerable and wholly *himself* when he was with a woman who cared about him?

What the hell had happened to the fine man that the awkward boy had once imagined himself becoming?

"Where'd you go?" whispered Robert.

I should have turned out to be a better person—a better man— than this.

He had the memories of so many dismissed women to prove that.

He threw the yearbook across the basement, smiling at the loud *smack!* it made when it slammed against the side of the water heater.

Above, the mixer droned on, buzz-*whirrrrrrrrrrrrrrrrr*.

"Turn that damned thing off, will you?" he yelled.

As if in response, the stereo started playing again—only this time they'd found the record album and were playing that much louder than the CD; the cracks, hisses, and pops in the twenty-odd-year-old vinyl were, in places, almost louder than the music itself.

"Oh, I guess progress will provide for its children
Even though their eyes won't see the sky
I'll remember sparrows, but by then they'll never miss them
It's sad enough to make a grown man cry."

"Oh, no," whispered Robert, knowing what was about to happen.

Like it had every time he'd tried to play it for the last five

Join the Leisure Horror Book Club and

GET 2 FREE BOOKS NOW—
An $11.98 value!

┌─ Yes! I want to subscribe to ─
the Leisure Horror Book Club.

Please send me my **2 FREE BOOKS**. I have enclosed $2.00 for shipping/handling. Each month I'll receive the two newest Leisure Horror selections to preview for 10 days. If I decide to keep them, I will pay the Special Members Only discounted price of just $4.25 each, a total of $8.50, plus $2.00 shipping/handling. This is a **SAVINGS OF AT LEAST $3.48** off the bookstore price. There is no minimum number of books I must buy and I may cancel the program at any time. In any case, the **2 FREE BOOKS** are mine to keep.

— *Not available in Canada.* —

NAME: _____

ADDRESS: _____

CITY: _____ **STATE:** _____

COUNTRY: _____ **ZIP:** _____

TELEPHONE: _____

E-MAIL: _____

SIGNATURE: _____

years or so, the record stuck at this point: "... cry"—*snick!*— "... cry"—*snick!*—"... cry"—*snick!*—"... cry"—*snick!*

He stumbled up the stairs and into the kitchen. He could smell the first batch of cookies baking in the oven. Someone had torn up a couple of cardboard boxes and duct-taped them over the broken window in the back door. The kitchen and house were getting warm again. The mixer had been placed on its stand and the next bowl of batter, placed firmly on the rotating plastic dais that was part of the mixing unit, spun round and round as the metal beaters churned.

Once more, something inside Robert's mind sputtered, just a little.

So he laughed, just a little.

He headed toward the front door, unlocked and opened it, then turned to the house and called out to whoever or whatever was there to hear, "I'm going out for some cigarettes, honey. Be right back."

Upstairs, the toilet flushed and a child giggled.

Robert staggered out the door, closing it behind him but forgetting to lock it.

A minute after he rounded the corner of his street, the dead bolt on the front door locked into place.

Chapter Seven

He walked around for maybe forty minutes before the cold and snow started getting to him, so he ducked into a bus-stop kiosk and sat on the cold metal bench. At least he was out of the snow and wind.

He felt the firmness of the cell phone in his pocket and knew all he had to do was call Lynn and Danny and ask them to come get him.

And what would you tell them? That you decided to surrender the house to a bunch of ghosts that use the toilet and have a thing for Nitzinger songs and chocolate chip cookies?

He fumbled a cigarette into his mouth and smoked it in about two minutes.

He was just lighting a second smoke when the last bus of the night on this route pulled in. He didn't look at any of the disembarking passengers—like him, they were too tired and too cold for social graces. It wasn't until he looked up to wave the driver on—*just sitting here, not waiting for you*—that he caught sight of the lone passenger sitting near the back of the bus.

Brown eyes sparkling, dark hair still a velvet cradle, and her seventeen-year-old bloom as strong and radiant as ever, Cathy Pope blew him a kiss, smiled, then waved as the bus pulled away.

Part Three
Remain in Light

"The individual has a host of shadows, all of which resemble him and for the moment have an equal claim to authenticity."

—*Kierkegaard*, Repetition

"So I'll drive out to some big, flat ranch, strip down to the pink to let my skin breathe, and I'll dance for lightning, I'll dance for rain, I shall dance for pleasure, I shall dance for pain, I'll scream out at the emptiness until my lungs bleed and try for the volume that will make the fossils stir deep in the desiccated earth and rise to the surface, hard skeletal denizens of a long-dried ocean swimming through layers of rock, wreaking a tectonic tsunami that will shock the city from its flatland coma."

—*Lucy A. Snyder*, "Permian Basin Blues"

"The only abnormality is the incapacity to love."

—*Anaïs Nin*

Chapter One

Once upon a time, at Denise's request, Robert attended a performance of Shakespeare's *As You Like It* in Schiller Park. They had been dating for just over five months and this was to be the first time he'd ever seen her onstage. She had spoken often enough about her love of the theater, recounting various experiences—some humorous, others rather terrifying—that she'd had both on the stage and behind the scenes, but she'd not invited him to see her act until tonight.

As he sat down that warm July on the sloping green hillside that faced the stage, he couldn't have been any more nervous if he were in the production himself.

The production was pleasant enough, if a tad on the long side. The director had decided to set the show during Colonial times. Denise, according to the cast list in the program, was playing the role of Betsy Ross. Which actual Shakespearean character Betsy Ross was replacing Robert couldn't tell, not being familiar with the Bard's works.

At some point near the end of the first act, one of the leads made a reference to ". . . our dearest Betsy," then pointed toward a stoop-shouldered old woman sitting on a tree stump at the far left side of the stage.

It wasn't just because of the makeup, the spirit gum and gray wig and whatever else she had used to give herself the appearance of age; this was no would-be starlet employing every possible artificial trapping, conveying the essence of old-womanhood through crafty affectation; Denise *was* old. Through some kind of sorcery he hadn't the capacity to comprehend, she had aged fifty years since disappearing to the backstage area two hours ago. No one was *this* good. She was an old woman, one who had nearly been broken by the storms but had managed to persevere, despite all the chaos around her. You could see it in the way she lifted her head, slowly, with hard-earned dignity, an old woman who didn't snap to attention for anyone but made them stand waiting while she decided whether or not they were worth her time; you could tell it in the way she sat with her legs pressed together at the knees, defiant, regal, and strong; you knew it by the subtle, nearly imperceptible way her hands trembled when she put down her sewing and let go of the needle—a slight twitch of her index finger, a slow flexing of her thumb, a smooth, liquid unfurling of the muscles beneath her liver-spotted, tissue-paper-thin flesh as she lay her hands palms-down on the surface of the flag on which she had been working; all of these nuances and countless others were there, and not in any one-two-three manner, not some vain actress moving through a directed series of overrehearsed, catalogued movements; here was *an old woman,* not ancient by any means, but old nonetheless—and if he'd doubted that she was the real thing, if he'd had any lingering suspicions that all of it was just part of an intricate (albeit damned effective) illusion, if he'd thought that she'd do something—anything—to break the spell—a small, telltale gesture that said, *See, I'm still your Denise*—all of it went right down the tubes the second she opened her mouth and spoke her one line, because that voice, that weathered, tattered-silk voice that still held the ghost of its bygone youth, that voice of one who'd walked headfirst into life and emerged at the far end a bit worse for the wear but still very much her own person, a voice filled with both wisdom and naivete with just a raspy touch of playfulness around the edges, this voice told him in no uncertain terms that the Denise he knew and loved was not here at all: She had been replaced for this moment in time—completely, totally, incontrovertibly replaced—by an old woman who'd been summoned forth from her grave somewhere in American history.

He was so proud of her he might have burst wide open right there and then had it not been for the audience applauding at the end of the act.

Afterward he found her backstage, packing her makeup into a plastic tackle box. He came up behind her, put a hand on each of her shoulders, spun her around, and kissed her.

"What was *that* for?" she asked, looking around to make sure no one was staring at them.

"That was one of the most phenomenal things I've ever seen! Do you have any idea how incredible you were? My God, if I hadn't known better, I'd've sworn it wasn't you up there. *Everything* you did was right on the money, was . . . was—"

She laughed and playfully smacked his arm. "Take a tranquilizer already! Sheesh. One lousy line."

"But you—"

"Did it well? Thanks. I'm glad you enjoyed the show and—oh, no, you don't. If you want to kiss me again, we have to go somewhere a little more private."

"That's almost coy, coming from you."

"It is? Remind me never to do it again. I'll have to wash my mouth out with vinegar as it is. Coy? Never have I shuddered with more horror."

That's when he knew he was going to ask her to marry him, but decided to wait until they were back at her place. Privacy was very important to her. She thought public displays of affection were inappropriate—her one nod to Puritanism—and had told him often enough that things of an intimate nature should be reserved for intimate places; the least he could do, after having practically attacked her backstage, was wait until they were completely alone before asking the most important question a person can ask and another can answer.

While driving to her side of town he once again complimented her performance, this time less effusively and with not as much drooling.

"Thanks," she said. "I've always liked acting. It gives me a chance to change my face, make it prettier or older, threatening or younger. I long ago gave up any hopes of being cast as the ingenue. I don't 'look' right—at least that's what every director I've ever worked with has told me. You can do everything with makeup to a plain face except make it beautiful, and beautiful's the only thing that counts with a 'stage picture.' Which is a nice way of saying that no one will ever cast me as Juliet, damnit. So I have to be content playing mothers, or grandmothers, or colorful eccentrics, or characters who've got no business being in a Shakespearean piece. *Betsy Ross*, for chrissakes!"

"Do you at least get a lot of good supporting roles?"

"Don't I wish. Oh, sometimes, sure, I get a nice meaty role, but mostly what I get is what you saw tonight—one-line throwaway parts. What most theater people call 'stage dressing.' "

"Is it enough?"

She looked down at the makeup case on her lap and shrugged. "Doesn't matter." A sad silence, then: "You know why I do this? Because I like pretending that I'm different people. Someone other than who and what I am. I get to be all the people I wish I were. Might be. Should have been."

"I think who you are is perfect."

"That's sweet, and is probably going to get you laid in about twenty minutes, but it won't help all that much the next time I spend three hours at an audition to end up with one line.

Look, most of the time I'm perfectly happy with the way I am but, still, sometimes . . .

"So I pretend. And I like to think that I actually bring these people to life for a little while, that I lower, I don't know, certain *walls*, and give them safe passage into this world. I used to have this fantasy when I first started out—*still* have it, sometimes—that these characters I played actually hung around after the show closed, that they really existed, only on a different plane, you know? Like ghosts. And all of them look a little like me. Isn't that a scary thought? Dozens and dozens of ghosts roaming the night out there, touring all their various worlds, and all of them looking a little like me."

He laughed as he reached over to touch her cheek. "How do I know you're not one of them?"

Silence. A thin, wistful smile.

Then: "You don't."

At her apartment he discovered a vinyl copy of Nitzinger's *One Foot in History* and regaled her with his views on unjustifiably overlooked seventies rock acts. She'd smiled and asked him his favorite song on the album, then played it, and they danced, he asked her to marry him, she said yes, then they made slow, moist, satisfying love on her small bed; later, they married and tried to have children but Denise miscarried a few times, Robert became more and more obsessed with his career while she waited for him to notice her again, then she got pregnant once more and this time carried the child for almost seven months before something went wrong and she died and the world that Robert once knew disintegrated and he went a little mad.

As the incident on the bus would soon prove.

For several days after spotting Cathy Pope on the number 19, Robert had taken to riding that particular bus in the evening in hopes of seeing her again. Part of him wanted to believe that the girl was just someone who looked remarkably like his dead high school sweetheart, but another part, the part that was begrudgingly growing to accept concepts such as *chronos* and *kairos* and dead babies that clawed their way out of backyard garden graves, wanted to find her and know for certain that it *was* her; what he would do *then*... well, he'd deal with that question *when* and *if*.

Surprisingly, Robert found that he enjoyed riding the bus. The number 19 stopped at several shopping centers, libraries, and movie theaters along its route. He liked watching as people got on with their purchases, or small pull-carts of groceries (a lot of elderly citizens rode the number 19, especially on Tuesdays and Fridays, according to the driver), or listening to the young couples who were "just starting out" as they discussed their entertainment budget for that night prior to the movie. Somehow, riding the number 19 made him feel more a part of the reality he'd always known and had taken for granted and now wanted desperately to have returned to him.

He delighted in looking out the window and watching the city pass by. He'd never much noticed before, but Cedar Hill, especially between the hours of seven and eleven P.M., was actually a very pretty, homey little city. He wondered why it had taken so long for that to register with him. Denise had known it. She'd liked riding the bus, even after Robert warned her that some of the "bus people" (as he arrogantly referred to them) might be of questionable character.

"Don't you have any faith in human beings at all?" she'd asked him.

He'd had no answer for that.

But for well over a week now—a time blissfully free of any night sounds in the house, new *matryoshka* dolls, meeting up with former lovers, or any contact from Rael—there had been (mostly) nothing but pleasant times for Robert-the-Bus-Rider.

There had also been no sighting of the girl who might or might not have been Cathy Pope. He decided to give it one more night, then to hell with it; if there was no proof, then he could, and *would*, dismiss it.

The stitches in his nose had all completely dissolved, leaving him with, as Dr. Steinman had promised, a very *Chinatown* scar. He chose not to cover it up; he needed to be able to see it, to know that he carried a physical mark from the night Denise had died; he *deserved* to be marked.

He'd done his first official interview for the station and it had aired twice and generated a lot of viewer response. "It's going to work like a charm," MacIntyre later told him. "When you come back to work, if this is any indication, the ratings'll kill the competition."

Somehow that didn't make Robert feel any better.

Nor did his visit to the library.

Try as he did to not think about it, Robert couldn't rid himself of the story about the donor heart that had somehow disappeared in transit. He wondered if other such incidents had occurred, and after two hours at the library's computers and an hour leafing through the various newspapers they carried, he'd discovered that, in the first twelve hours after Denise's death, at least three other donor organs had disappeared on their way to those who needed them; two others had terminally malfunctioned shortly after being transplanted, and not only had one—a liver—malfunctioned, killing the recipient, but the autopsy revealed it to be in a state of decomposition commensurate with a five-day-old corpse; the doctors could offer no explanation for this.

All of these items were far from front-page news, and none of them mentioned from where the donated organs had originated.

The worst part, though, was the last item he discovered: The child who'd been waiting for the donor heart had died two days after the one taken from Emily (Robert was certain of this now) had vanished.

He sat weeping at the computer terminal, whispering apologies to the child's soul and family.

Something in his mind sputtered.

Something in his core crumbled.

And maybe somewhere in there the child's soul tried to tell him that it was all right, it wasn't his fault, shhh, there, there, mister, it's okay.

Maybe.

Then came the incident on the bus.

It was a Wednesday, around eight-fifteen P.M. Robert was returning home from a trip to the hardware store where he'd purchased (better late than never, at least now he had the nerve to face the thing) a new pane of glass to replace the broken one in the back door. He'd also bought a couple of new pipes to replace those under the bathroom sink (something Denise had bugged him about for weeks before . . . before). Until the two young men boarded, there was only Robert, the driver, an elderly couple near the front, and a quiet woman who looked to be around thirty-five years old. The ride had been pleasant, until the Disgusting Duo got on. Dressed in stylishly torn, oversized blue jeans and loose shirts to match, each of them wore baseball caps with the brims turned toward the backs of their heads. One was white, one was black; they took seats in the back of the bus; both talked too loudly and had a decidedly limited vocabulary. The bus driver looked too tired to confront the boys about their loudness and language, the elderly couple held hands and cast concerned looks at one another—*We mustn't do anything to provoke such people*—and the quiet woman sat staring at her lap.

Robert tried to drown out the young men's voices by concentrating on the noise of the bus's wheels and engine, then turning his attention to the conversation of the elderly couple, trying to hear the story the old woman was telling (which he *did* hear but wouldn't register with him until much, much later), but it seemed the two punks in the back were determined to be heard.

They want *trouble*, he thought. *There can't be any other reason for them to act this way.*

"Man, lemme tell you, when that bitch answered the door and I saw how fat she was, my dick went limper than a noodle— an' she knew it. I mean, it wasn't like she was an uggo or nothin' like that, know what I'm sayin'? She mighta been pretty if she wasn't so fuckin' fat. But I figure, what the fuck, you know? Mebbe she don't get a lot of dick 'cause she's a tubby and I tole my friend that I'd go out with her so him and her roommate could have the place to themselves."

"Hey—more cushin' for the pushin'," said the other one.

"I heard that. Man, that bitch's pussy was *sloppy*—y'know, all wet and slick and shit. My cock kept slidin' out so I decide she's gonna suck me good, know what I'm sayin'?"

"Fat bitches give the best head, man, don't they?"

"Like Roto-Rooter! Kept lickin' the jism and moanin' like it tasted so good to her, then she gulps the whole thing in her mouth and groans and I comed real hard and—you know what that cunt did? *Spit it out!* Then has the nerve to get pissed at me 'cause she got a little wad of load on her cheek."

"You fuck her in the ass? Shoulda fucked her in the ass. Far chicks like gettin' it up the poop chute."

"Fuck you! I's afraid I'd have to push my dick through some old crusty shit she didn't get wiped. An' then the fat twat wants me to go down on her! Huh-uh! No way—know what I'm sayin'? Smelled like Alpo between her legs. I'm a class-A Snatch-daddy, know what I mean? I got *stan-dards*, and I ain't gonna be eatin' no sloppy, stank-smellin' pussy."

"Not without one of them things, them—snorkel masks!"

Then both exploded with laughter, bowled over by their mutual wit and whimsy.

Now shut the hell up, thought Robert, noticing the way the elderly couple looked suddenly ashamed to be members of the human race. These two guys had probably ruined what had been a nice evening for them. They looked scared, but more than that they looked . . . sad. As if the behavior of these two jerks was proof positive that they'd lived too long.

"Bastards," whispered Robert under his breath.

The woman sitting across the aisle from him looked out the window, then back down at her folded hands—which were now balled into fists. She gripped the strap of her purse so tightly her knuckles were nearly white. Her shoulders slumped downward as if she were anticipating an oncoming blow from an invisible fist.

"Hey, you ever tongue clit?"

"Shit! All the time, dude. Ladies like that."

"There was this one time when this bitch I's dating—biggest fuckin' whore you ever met, but man, could she fuck! Like her ass was on ball bearings. Anyway, there was this one time I's goin' down on her—you know, she had her legs wrapped real tight around my neck and she was scratchin' my shoulders and *screaming!* 'Eat that pussy, baby! Eat it good!' Bitch was hot. Anyway . . ."

Robert stared at the woman across the aisle from him, the thunder of blood in his temples drowning out the nonstop filth spewing from the back of the bus.

She made a sound, just one sound, but that was all Robert needed.

A short, hard, wet sniff.

She was trying not to cry.

He saw the way she sat, hunched and tense as if afraid of being struck; he noticed the way she was dressed, a nice skirt, a pretty blouse, and a fall/winter coat that was too old to be the current fashion but was in fine condition nonetheless, maybe given to her by a grandmother now long gone, so she took excellent care of it and wore it with pride because it looked nice and brought back warm, affectionate memories of the woman to whom it had once belonged; he watched the way her lower lip quivered and how her eyes stared unblinkingly at her hands, not wanting to get upset like this in public because then people would notice her and she didn't like being noticed, didn't like people sizing her up based on her looks because she'd always thought that you should judge people on the quality of their character, but how could she not get upset at having to sit here and listen to *this?*; then he saw her eyes, soft and gray, and something behind them let down the scrim for a moment and revealed her fully: Alone but not necessary lonely (though a certain permanent melancholy in her features hinted otherwise), a good person, a decent person, a person you could count on to be there for you when you needed a friend, someone who listened not only to what you said but to the unspoken needs between the words, and here she was, probably on her way home from working late at some tedious office job that she did exceptionally well even though her efforts went unappreciated, sitting here and enjoying the ride, relaxing with her thoughts until these two cretins with their dirty-joke-book vocabulary got on, and now she was trying not to cry because maybe, just maybe these creeps reinforced her fear that there was less and less decency in the world, and if that were true, then what the hell hope was there for someone like her who probably saw herself as plain and ordinary even though she was neither, never was, never would be?

" 'Oooh, baby, fuck that big cock in my wet pussy! Fuck it in me hard!' Bitch could talk that *trash*. . . ."

She made a sudden movement, one that surprised even her—you could tell from the shocked expression that crossed her face, because she looked out the window, hoping that her stop might be close but it wasn't and that didn't matter anymore, all that mattered was getting off this bus so she could try to compose herself and forget that she'd once shared space with a couple of misogynistic foulmouthed scumbags who between them didn't have the brains God gave a hangnail, so she reached up to pull the cord and signal the driver to stop, then yanked her hand back before doing so because that might cause people to notice her and Jesus, why did this have to happen? She was just tired and wanted to get home and have a nice dinner, maybe watch a movie she'd taped earlier in the week.

There was no pity in Robert for her; he didn't feel sorry for her, he was angry for her.

Just this once, he thought. *Just this once the world will not be this way within reach of my arm.*

He turned around in his seat and said, "Could you please keep your voices down?"

The two young men stopped talking and looked at him with hollow-point bullets in their eyes.

"You talkin' to us, motherfucker?"

"Yes, I am. I would appreciate it if you'd please keep your voices down."

"Aw, we breakin' your concentration?"

"You're very loud and your language offends me."

"You dissin' us, motherfucker?"

"What do you think you're doing to the rest of us?"

"Free country, free speech. Motherfucker."

Something sputtered in Robert's mind and he laughed. Just once.

"Something funny, motherfucker?"

"Hey, here's a thought," said Robert, peripherally aware of the sound of crinkling paper, "why don't you try something like 'sir' or 'buddy' or 'dude' or even 'asshole' instead of that other word of which you seem so fond?"

"Tellin' us how we should talk now?"

"I'm asking you politely, for the last time, to either watch your language or keep your voices down."

"Suck my cock, you faggot."

"Butt-buddy!"

"Why don't you leave us alone and go back to eyein' that uggo sittin' across from you?"

The woman froze at the word "uggo."

That one hurt, Robert could tell.

"Shut your filthy mouths," he snarled at them.

One of them unbuttoned his coat and reached for something under his shirt. "Why don't I shut your fuckin' mouth, *asshole?*"

"Looks to me like his teeth needs some cappin', know what I'm saying?"

One of them moved to pull a gun from under his shirt.

Robert's mind sputtered.

It wasn't until a minute later, when the bus came to a sudden stop and the driver was running down the aisle shouting something Robert couldn't understand, that he saw what had happened: One of the young men was lying on the floor with a broken arm and a bloody knot on the side of his head, and the other was on his knees trying to pull a large shard of broken glass from his cheek. The shattered remains of the new door pane lay on the floor. Robert was clutching one of the sink pipes in his hand.

The driver skidded to a halt, picked up the gun, and grabbed Robert by the back of his coat.

"That's it for you, pal! Sit your ass down and wait for the cops or I'll—"

"It wasn't his doing, sir," called the elderly man from up front. "I saw the whole thing. Those two young men pulled a gun and threatened him."

"That's exactly right," said the old man's wife. "He was only defending himself." The old woman suddenly looked familiar to Robert—her smile, the sharpness of her nose, the calming hazel of her eyes—but he couldn't quite place where he might have seen her before . . . though it seemed to him that she ought to have been wearing some kind of cap or hat.

Both she and her husband were trying not to smile too obviously. They looked at Robert with quiet approval and tight-grinned admiration: *You're a good boy.*

The bus driver turned toward the woman across the aisle. "Is that right, miss?"

"Yessir . . ." she said, not making eye contact.

"Look, pal," he said, then stopped. "Hey, I know you, don't

I? Yeah, you're that guy on the news, right? Bob Londrigan?"

"Um, yeah . . . yes, I am."

"Huh. Whatta you know. Look, Mr. Londrigan, I gotta call this in. You're gonna have to talk to the cops. I'm sorry."

"Yeah . . . me, too." He looked at the woman across the aisle. "I'm so sorry, miss. It's just that they were so obviously upsetting you and—"

"It's all right," she whispered, still shaking and not making eye contact with him, either.

"No, it isn't. I got all pissed off and self-righteous and whipped out the macho bullshit because I was afraid they were going to ruin your evening and the only thing my behavior succeeded in doing was the same damned thing!" He stepped toward her and, without thinking about it, reached down and took hold of one of her hands. "Please forgive me. You see, I haven't been myself lately. It doesn't matter if you know who I am or not, see, because the thing is . . . the thing is, my wife died about eleven days ago and ever since then all I've been able to think about is how many ways I ruined things for her the way these two idiots ruined the evening for you—I mean, I assumed they were ruining your evening, offending you, and when they called you 'uggo' and I saw the expression on your face I guess I just . . . I guess I just saw the way my wife must have felt all those times I said something cruel to her, or canceled dinner or movie plans at the last minute when she'd been looking forward to them all week, or committed any one of a million little cruelties that chip away at a person's self-esteem or their hope or their belief that if they'll just be patient, their affection will be returned to them in equal measure . . . and I had to do something, understand? I had to prevent it from happening to you because I didn't stop it from happening to her, and I'm sorry, I'm so sorry . . ." He wasn't even aware that he'd begun weeping. "I'm so very, very, very sorry, and I just wanted you to know that, that not everyone's like these two guys, not every man thinks of women in those terms, and I used to, I really did—I mean, it wasn't quite so base or crude as they were being, but I looked on women like that, you know? I mean, I might have shown up with flowers and held doors open for them and taken them to nice restaurants or things like that, but always, somewhere in the back of my mind, I was trying to figure out how to get them into bed and I think now, I really, truly believe, that that made me a lot worse than these two, because at least they're up front about it, at least they're honest enough not to try and put a nice, charming face on it, but *me* . . . I was so damned covert about what I wanted, I was so dishonest and duplicitous that when you get right down to it, I had no more respect for women than they do, I just dressed it up in nicer clothes and practiced it in classier surroundings, and I hate myself for having been that way but I'm not anymore. I hate the man I used to be, understand? I hate him and ever since my wife died I've been . . . I mean—"

"Hey," said the bus driver, "take it easy, Mr. Londrigan, please . . ."

"I can't help thinking now that, ever since she died, I've finally turned into the kind of man who could make her happy, who could return her affection in equal measure, who could listen to her and understand her needs and want to do something about them only to please her, see? Only to please her, not to shut her up about something or make her happy long enough to get what I wanted out of her . . . and I just wanted you to know that I'm sorry those two guys upset you, and I wanted you to know that I'm sorry I behaved the way I did, and I wanted you to know that I think you're a lovely, decent, wonderful person and the man who finally gets you is going to be the luckiest guy in the world because he'll *know* that you're the greatest woman in the world and he'll treat you the way I should've treated her and . . . and *I'm sorry!* I'm sorry for all of it, it shouldn't have happened and I wish I could take it all back, I wish this had never happened . . ."

He expected her to pull her hand back and demand that he get away, but not only did she not do that, she now placed her other hand on top of his own and half smiled. Her expression puzzled him. She looked surprised, slightly overwhelmed, a touch confused, a bit proud—

(*You're such a good boy . . .*)

—and more than a little moved. It took a moment longer before he was able to peg the expression, but then it hit him: She wore the look of a teacher who'd just had a breakthrough with a particularly difficult student.

In the moment before she spoke to him, Robert became aware of several things simultaneously: The two young men on the floor of the bus had stopped moving—not simply given up and slumped into unconsciousness, but *frozen* in place, just like the bird beyond the bus's window, paused in midflight, its wings outstretched, just like the elderly couple at the front, stopped halfway between rising from their seats and standing fully erect, just like the snow trickling down outside halted just before it hit the ground.

Aside from himself, the woman, and the bus driver, the whole world seemed to have been put on pause.

"Oh, *Bobby*," said the woman, "you've finally started to get the idea, haven't you? I mean really, truly get the idea!" She reached out with her other hand, cupped the back of his head, and pulled him close, kissing him on the lips.

Kissing him the way Denise used to, soft and warm and moving her lower lip ever so slightly side to side.

God, how her lips felt exactly like Denise's.

She pulled away, beaming, and looked at the bus driver. "I think he's come a long way, don't you?"

"Hey," said the driver, "he's Willy, and Willy rocks."

Rael reached up and tore off his bus-driver mask. "You passed this test, Willy—and let's all give a listen, shall we? Tell us what he's won, Mr. Announcer. 'Why, for his splendid if slightly misguided efforts, Rael, Willy has won a wish fulfilled!' "

"No," whispered Robert, feeling part of his mind crumble, "please . . . no . . ." He felt dizzy and confused and sick to his stomach; everywhere in his body there was once again the old familiar exquisite pain, and he reached up and rubbed his eyes, trying to slow the beating of his heart, rubbing his eyes hard, harder, as hard as he could, wanting to rid them of the last image burned into them, and when he finished, when he pulled his hand away from his eyes and blinked, the brakes of the bus hissed and there was a slight lurch and—

—and he was back in his seat, holding the hardware store bag containing his purchases, and the old couple was still up front, as was the bus driver—a *different* bus driver—and there was the woman sitting across the aisle from him, and now the bus was stopping to let on two young men dressed in stylishly torn, oversized blue jeans and loose shirts to match, each of them wearing baseball caps with the brims turned toward the backs of their heads. One was white, one was black; they took seats in the back of the bus. Both of them resumed their conversation as the bus pulled away.

"Man, you buggin', you know what I'm sayin'? Buggin' worse'n a can of Raid."

"Like hell I am."

"Like hell you ain't. The thing is, dude, *anything* can happen in *kairos* if you know wha'cher doin'! It's like—okay, y'ever see one of them little kids, right, and they're talking to their 'imaginary' frien'? Just 'cause you can't see that frien' don't mean it ain't there, know what I'm sayin'? But if you, like, don' got no idea how to use *kairos*, you could make yourself crazy in a New York minute. 'Specially if someone done went and *gave* you that ability and you either don' know it or know it but don' know what the hell to do with it. Like handin' a two-year-old the remote control to reality."

"I hear ya."

"Thas cool—so don't you go tryin' to tell me I don't shit about it, got me?"

"Or what? You'll sic one of your 'imaginary' friends on my ass?"

"You got that right."

Robert turned in his seat. "What did you say?"

The two young men looked at him. "I'm sorry," said one of them. "If we was talkin' too loud, I apologize." There was no threat in his voice; the apology was genuine.

"*Kairos*," said Robert. "What were you saying about *kairos?*"

The two young men looked at one another: *Don't know what he's on, but maybe if we ask nice he'll give us some.*

"I'm sorry, man," said the other, "but we wasn't talkin' about . . . What'd you call it? *Karo?* Isn't that some kind of pancake syrup?"

Robert gritted his teeth. "What were you saying to your friend when the two of you got on a few moments ago?"

"We was just arguin' over what to get on our pizza. This is kind've a guys' night out, y'know? Get away from the girl-friends." They smiled at him, then, with much quieter voices, went back to their conversation.

Robert looked around, near frantic, and checked the world outside the window; snow falling like it was supposed to, birds flying in strict accordance with all known laws of physics, people walking along just as free and straight as you please, everything fine here in *chronos* world, call your travel agent for more information on our *kairos* package.

Robert's mind sputtered, and he laughed, just once, very quietly.

The woman across the aisle looked at him and smiled.

She was not the same woman as before.

"Have we ever met?" he asked her.

"No, I don't think so," she said. "But I watch you on the news all the time. I was very sorry about your wife and baby."

"Th-thank you. Oh, here's my stop." He reached up and pulled the cord.

It wasn't his stop but that didn't matter; all that mattered was getting the fuck off this *Twilight Zone* express before Rod Serling got on.

Robert disembarked about six blocks from his house.

As he made his way home he took care to touch as many things as possible to make sure, to be absolutely certain, that this was the world he knew and that everything in it was real, was solid—buildings, mailboxes, store windows, streetlight posts, anything at all (he even found himself stamping on the ground a few times to clear away the snow and make sure the sidewalk was still under his feet); he didn't just *look* at people as they went past him, he studied them with an intensity that was probably a little frightening from the receiving end, but he had to study them in this way, you see, because at any second any one of them might turn around and call him Willy and tear away the mask . . . but none did. There was one instance, though, when a little girl and her parents passed Robert while he was crossing the street. The parents, both normal enough looking, in their mid-to-late thirties, typical citizens of Generica, walked on either side of their daughter, each holding one of her hands, each with that tired, vacant, glassy, it's-been-too-long-a-day stare. The girl looked to be around eleven or twelve, most of her face hidden either under a heavy winter cap or behind a thick wool scarf. Only her eyes were visible. Robert could feel her stare even before he passed the family.

No, it wasn't his imagination—she was staring at him, unblinkingly and intensely. He stared back at her as they moved passed each other, then, once across the street, turned to see if she was—

—yes, there she was, walking along with her parents, but her head turned so that she could watch him until either he or she moved out of visible range. Robert remained where he was, tracking her until the family reached a corner and began to turn. That's when the little girl pulled her hands from her parents' grips, turned fully around to face Robert, and waved at him—

—the kind of wave that, between friends, says, *We have a secret, you and I.*

Then she pulled down her scarf so her mouth could be seen and mouthed the words *You're a good boy.*

Robert ran the last two and a half blocks to his house.

Chapter Two

In the basement, on Denise's worktable, two dolls had been removed from inside the Cathy Pope *matryoshka*: One depicted the young woman Robert saw on the bus (that is, if he'd actually taken the bus, if he'd actually seen her, if the two young men and elderly couple and bus driver had actually been part of the world and not something he hallucinated, then yes, this was an excellent reproduction of her features), the other wore the face of the little girl who would not stop staring at him.

After finding these, Robert didn't even bother to search the house for whoever had painted them.

He did, however, search through the liquor cabinet, and by the time NOVA began on the local PBS station he wasn't *exactly* drunk, mind you, but any sort of movement beyond shifting his weight in the chair was not something he cared to attempt.

So there he sat, a bottle of Bailey's Irish Creme on one side, a plate of homemade cookies on the other (he was amazed that the cookies had lasted this long; he must remember to ask for the recipe if he ever found who baked them).

He'd had no intention of watching the program—he'd just been flipping around with the remote in hopes of finding some rerun of a mindless sitcom (*Where's* Laverne & Shirley *or* Hogan's Heroes *or* Green Acres *when you need them?* he thought. *Nick at Nite, why hast thou forsaken me?*) when he came upon the promo—" 'Mysteries of Regeneration,' on the next NOVA"—and something hiding in the back of his brain whispered, *Watch this*, and he obeyed.

The program began with a rather graphic depiction of a lizard's tail being separated from its body, then—with the aid of time-lapse photography—showed how the lizard was able to grow it back. After that, it was on to a lab where Kirlian photography was used to illustrate something called "The Phantom Leaf Effect." There was a shot of an ordinary maple leaf, then the same maple leaf was placed in darkness so its golden aura could be photographed. Robert found it kind of eerie, the way the black screen suddenly began to fill with a bright gold outline of the leaf, but then it got really weird because one of the scientists performing the experiment tore away one-third of the leaf and placed it back under the lens of the camera: Once again the screen went black, but this time when the leaf's aura was shown, it was missing one-third of its original form.

"Now, watch closely," intoned the narrator's voice, "and you will witness one of the true great mysteries of modern science."

Robert, half fractured out of his skull, sat staring at the television screen for what seemed a month and was just starting to drift off when, very slowly, part of the aura began to move, bleeding outward like the thinnest trail of spilled gold ink, and within a few moments the shifting section of the aura perfectly formed the missing portion of the leaf. Then the screen split in two and the original photograph of the whole leaf's aura appeared next to this one.

They were identical.

"Holy shit," he whispered to himself, then wondered what would happen if they photographed the lizard's tail; would its aura bleed outward to form the rest of the lizard?

The scientists were getting ready to do just that when he passed out.

Chapter Three

In the dream their bathroom was lit by the glow of half a dozen candles as Denise reclined in the warm, soapy water and Robert bathed her; one of their favorite methods of foreplay . . . once upon a time.

But tonight, in this dream, uniquely in this dream alone, he felt not only the sensations that rippled through his own dream-body, but those experienced by Denise's, as well.

"I want to tell you something," he whispered to her. The water seeping from the cloth in his hands massaged her with warmth, easing the strain. "I know, now, that I was meant to be here for you. Shhh—don't say anything, just listen. It used to be, when I told someone the story of my life, it would stop there. But since I've met you . . ." She closed her eyes and Robert kissed her wet hair and placed another warm, soaked cloth over her face. "Since I've known you, I have told you the story of my life, and you've asked to hear it again . . . and I find, now, that when I tell it over, it's no longer my story. It's *ours*, and I will protect that with sword and shield." The diamond droplets of water trickled down her cheek, glided over her chin, slipped down her neck, and slid a moist path between her breasts; then his hand was there, the soapy washcloth rubbing gentle circular patterns, moist and creamy, lilac-scented, and she stretched, arching her back, sighing as the washcloth dropped away and his lips began trailing down her neck, pausing at her shoulder, then to the slope of her breast, then he delicately cupped one breast in his hand, his thumb stroking her nipple until it became firm. His lips covered her nipple, drawing it into his mouth meekly yet hungrily, and she closed her eyes all the tighter, hearing a low growl rise from deep in her throat, emerging as a sigh, and the slowly drifting lights behind her closed lids separated, shimmering in rhythm with the spasms below her waist, becoming thousands of bright pinpoints that seemed to surge from somewhere in her center as she reached out and clutched the back of his head, guiding his wonderful lips to her other breast, feeling him take the nipple in his mouth as the fire and lights intensified within both of them, caressing her, moving her, rocking her, tickling, rolling, arching her toward him, and she felt the softness of the bed beneath, the satiny brush of the sheets against her back as he continued kissing her everywhere and endlessly, licking her, a bite here, a nibble there, probing her with his fingers, cupping her breasts in his hands and tonguing her nipples in slow, wet, maddening circular patterns. There was a thin beam of moonlight slipping in under the window blinds; each hair on his body was isolated by that light like bluish gossamer, a wrapping. He ran his fingers up her arms and the little hairs there sprang to attention, then he touched her eyes with his fingertips; they were like pads, responsive to her every pore. Her eyelids fluttered beneath his touch and she drew her own fingers down his cheeks to the bone of his jaw, then down his neck, leaning forward and kissing his lips. Her mouth felt larger than human to him, able to protect his own in its clasp. His tongue beat against her lips and opened them and soon their saliva was mixing, then his mouth was crawling down her body and she lay back, opening her vagina for him. Soon, her murmurs seemed to fill the room. She arched her back slightly as her knees bent around the small curve at the back of his head, pressing it slowly downward. They twined around each other as if their limbs had lost their natural form. A moment later he lifted his head from between her wet heat and moved up her belly to her breasts again, at first teasing her nipples, then sucking them deep into his hungry mouth, trailing his lips across her shoulders, his breath moist and warm against the side of her neck, his cock rigid and hot, his entry smooth and painless, the two of them rocking together, pumping slick and steady as he plunged into her over and over again, and it was good, it was great, it was heaven, and Denise grabbed hold of his shoulders and rolled him onto his back, straddling his hips, locking her ankles under the backs of his knees as her own pushed out and down, her ass rolling back and forth across his groin, pushing him deeper inside her as his hand grabbed one of her breasts and his mouth encircled the areola, slurping and sucking and biting as he thrust himself upward with more force, ramming his erection deeper, deeper, and deeper still, and she threw back her head and arched her back, her nails digging into his chest, and then came the sounds, low, throaty growls, grunts and sighs and strangled screams as their rhythm grew faster, harder, frenzied, bedsprings squeaking as she groaned instead and drove herself down, pushing his cock in so much deeper it was starting to hurt but she didn't care, she wanted him to bury it in her up to her throat so she tangled her fingers in his sweat-matted hair, God, he felt so good, so thick and solid, pulsing, throbbing, sliding wet and steamy into her slick sex as she reached over and pulled a silk scarf from the headboard and fashioned it into a blindfold that she tied around his head, something she'd never done before, burying his gaze in darkness as she doubled her efforts, grinding down with all her strength; he arched his back and groaned, she threw back her head once again and squealed, then moaned, then screamed, her juice-soaked thighs sliding against his own, then he was sitting up again, burying his blindfolded face between her breasts, his tongue searching for, then lapping at her nipples, biting them, hard, harder, and she loved it, it was incredible, and now they were moving side to side as well as up and down, the chaotic motion setting fire to her body as she pulled up and slammed back down on him, tossing her head to the side, and now he was shuddering beneath her because he wasn't in control now and never had been, it was all her, and it was good, so good as she bucked and thrashed and wiggled, driving herself down hard, squealing and howling and screaming,

"God, yes, do it . . . do it, Bobby . . . *shoot it* in me, in me, in me *Now! Yes! God, Yes!*"—

—and Robert suddenly had the feeling they weren't alone in the room—

—*Jesus, is Rael hiding in here somewhere, watching us?*—

—then realized it wasn't the room . . . he felt as if they were no longer alone in *the bed*—

—*She doesn't . . . she doesn't feel right, something's different, something's wrong*—

—suddenly unable to open his eyes, he gripped her hips in the blackness and began to explore her body with his hands—

—the hips weren't as wide as he remembered them being and she didn't smell the same way she used to after they'd been at it and were both sweating up a storm—he could detect his own smell in there, his sweat and semen, but his own smells weren't mixing with hers like they should have been—

—*this isn't her*—

—craziness, it *had* to be her, so he kept exploring her form with his hands, and this time when he went to her breasts, breasts that had been just as he remembered them, they, too, had changed; they were smaller, more delicate, not the breasts of a woman but those of a girl maybe twelve or thirteen years old who'd only just really begun to come into her own physically—

—*wake up, pal, c'mon, just open your eyes and that'll be it*—

—Christ, he hadn't had a wet dream in over fifteen years, and now that he was finally having another one it had to be about a *little girl* . . . great, terrific, wonderful, just slap on the cuffs and call him "Short Eyes" and let everybody on the whole cell block do the Jailhouse Rock on his ass—

—*open your eyes, c'mon*—

—he released his grip on her body and tried to force himself to roll over on his side—that's how he always woke himself up from a dream he wanted to get out of, just roll over and—*bam!*—wide awake and safe, thanks so much—

Gary A. Braunbeck

—but he couldn't roll over because of the weight on top of him, and even though it wasn't that *much* weight, it was still enough to hold him down, so now his hands thrashed about frantically and he felt the blindfold enshrouding his head, worked his hands back to find the knot, but he couldn't untie it so instead gripped the damn thing and *yanked* it downward—

—no dream, this was no dream, because he was seeing everything in color and he *never* dreamed in color and besides he could see the moonlight from the window glinting off his watch and he *never* slept with his watch on, and he could also feel that damn spring that made that lump in the middle of the mattress that always got him at some point during the night if he wasn't careful and *what the hell was he doing in the bed, anyway?* he'd passed out in the chair in front of the television and oh God oh God oh God, he was going to come, he could feel the pressure building, could feel his wetness, her wetness, and he shouted something, gibberish, as his arm shot out and turned on the lamp on the bedside table—

—the first thing he saw was her face, so young, so red with passion's efforts, so covered in sweat as she grunted, thrusting herself down onto his cock that was ready to explode—

—the next thing he saw was her tender, twelve-year-old body with its breasts that were only now starting to fully bud—

—and the last thing he saw, just before he came inside her, was the long, pinkish white autopsy scar that ran directly down the center of her torso—

—"Oh, God! *Emily!*" he screamed, horrified, feeling himself shoot inside her—

—then she threw herself forward and—with a hand that was missing one of its fingers—grabbed the lamp from the table and smashed it against the side of his head.

Chapter Four

Like some cartoon cliché where a character gets bonked on the head by a falling anvil, the first thing Robert saw upon opening his eyes was stars; they surrounded him, some dim and distant, others so close he thought he could actually *feel* their light touching him. They flickered and snapped and filled his nostrils with the scent of burning wood and kerosene.

He blinked—Christ, it *did* feel like an anvil had been dropped on his head—then opened his eyes a little wider.

The stars flickered once again, throwing sparks as tongues of fire swirled around and around like small tornadoes, while others reached upward, forming inverse tears of flame.

Torches.

He was surrounded by burning torches.

He attempted to lift his head but the pain was tremendous. Someone nearby whispered, in a child's voice, "Shhh, c'mon, easy there—here, take this—" And a small woman, a very *tiny* woman, bone-thin, whose facial features resembled those of a bird, slipped a couple of tablets into his mouth and then held a canteen filled with grape juice to his lips. Robert swallowed the pills, then laid his head back and waited. When the pain began to recede, he reached up to touch the side of his skull and found that part of his head had been heavily bandaged.

"Had us going there for a little while, Willy," said Rael. "Personally I thought you were going to *Big Sleep* on us but Ian, he kept waking you up to make sure you didn't slip away—though I'm guessing you don't much remember that, do you?"

"No . . ."

"Doesn't matter. Just be sure you thank him later. Ian was *very* worried."

Gary A. Braunbeck

Finally able to fully open his eyes, Robert sat up and discovered that he was in some kind of underground chamber—maybe an abandoned mine or (the thought caused him to shudder) underneath a cemetery.

"Nice to have you with us, Willy."

"Uh-huh."

"Feel a little bit like you're both here and *not* here, right?"

"Yeah . . ."

"That's normal, under the circumstances. Anyway, welcome to Chiaroscuro—also known as Desolation Row and the Ant Farm. I'm kind of wishy-washy on which name I like best."

The walls of the chamber soared upward at either hand like the sides of a ravine. As he looked up, it seemed to Robert they would never meet in the darkness overhead.

He was lying at the crossroad of several different paths, all strewn with random stones and loose piles of scree. Illuminated by the light from the dozens, possibly hundreds, of torches, he saw that these paths became narrow and steep, the rocks growing fewer but larger, stacked one on top of the other. In the distance he could make out something that looked like a chaotic staircase of massive, wedge-shaped boulders. This was evidently the anteroom of some vast, silent, ancient chamber.

Ahead, he could see a bluish radiance, haloing some kind of rock formation. On a small plateau, under an overhang of white calcite that curved gracefully upward like a snowdrift hollowed by the wind, stood a cluster of meticulously carved stones, each roughly the size and shape of a woman, arms outstretched, holding something whose shape he could not quite discern. Their bodies were complete but all of them lacked faces.

He turned slowly around, looking upward, and felt his breath catch in his throat.

Crisscrossing above his head like strands of a web was an intricate network of handmade bridges, some constructed from disparate sections of metal, others made from rope and planks of wood. Below these bridges was a catwalk, also made from wood, that seemed to encircle the entire chamber. Lighted torches and battery-operated lanterns hung from the surrounding walls, and every ten or fifteen feet there would be a rope ladder, some leading down, some leading up.

And everywhere above there were hollowed spaces that looked like small tombs, each of them lit from within and tenanted by children. Robert could hear music coming from some of the chambers, laughter from others. Some of the chambers were cut off from the others by means of curtains that had been nailed into place somehow. The more he stared, awestruck, the more apparent the ingenuity that had gone into constructing this place. The curtains were not nailed into position as he'd first thought; expandable shower curtain rods had been used in each doorway, so that if the tenants desired privacy, they had only to slide their particular curtain closed. Some used quilts, others blankets.

"How . . . how many of you are there?" he asked.

"Enough to keep my hands full, Willy," replied Rael. "These catacombs go on for miles, and where one series of chambers ends, there are passageways to others just like this. *Thirteen* other places like this, to be exact. Each one near—"

"Where the mountain opens up?"

"So you *do* pay attention. Cool beans. There's an underground spring not too far from here—the cleanest water you've ever tasted. I could offer to give you a tour but you don't look to me like you're up for much sight-seeing at the moment. In fact, you kind of look like a sick walrus trying to climb over a rock, so I'd lie still if I were you."

Robert coughed. "Can I ask you something?"

"I'd be surprised if you *weren't* full of questions, the way I've been fucking with you—sure, ask away."

He gestured to the living quarters surrounding them. "I know the music probably comes from battery-operated cassette and CD players, but I *swear* it looks like a couple of the . . . rooms are watching televisions. How is that possible?"

"They're watching videotapes on VCRs, actually—though we have managed to lay hands on a few DVD players. You see, we don't get cable here, and a satellite dish might eventually draw someone's attention. To answer your question, though—portable generators, most of which we've stolen, I'm ashamed to say, along with a lot of other things, but we're not here to discuss the problems I might be having with my conscience. I might be able to do a little sleight-of-hand with time, *kairos*-wise, but I can't summon electricity from thin air. Most of the 'rooms' as you call them are also equipped with portable air filters. A lot of the kids have breathing problems—asthma, allergies, things like that—and the atmosphere in here lately has been making those conditions worse. But we do what we can to make life as good as it can be."

Robert stared at him. "Can I ask you another question?"

"Ask me anything you want, Willy."

He looked at the flute dangling from Rael's belt, remembered the story he'd read that night at Lynn's house, and said: "Are you the Pied Piper of Hamelin?"

Rael shrugged, then smiled. "You know, I've come to rue that day I told old Bob Browning that story. I could have told it to Shakespeare, or Blake, Milton, Poe, even Dickens, for that matter . . . but, no, I have to go and shoot off my mouth in front of Mr. Romance . . . but, yes, I am. Of not only Hamelin, but Dresden, Auschwitz, and all the Third Reich's other vacation spot outlets, Vietnam, the orphanages—'orphanages,' that's a fuckin' laugh—the *dying rooms* in Romania, and the mountains of China . . . Let's see, where else? Cambodia, Kosovo, El Salvador, Rwanda . . . you name a place where children were forced to take part in the fun and frolic of humanity's compassion at its most benevolent, and odds are I've paid a visit there. Like Jerry and the Dead say, I can't tell you what a long, strange trip it's been. And it still ain't over. Sometimes I wonder if it ever will be. Now let *me* ask *you* a question, Willy. Pay attention, there may be a test on this material later.

"Do you despair yet?"

"I think maybe I do."

"Do you know why?"

"No, not really."

Rael considered that for a moment, then gave a short nod of his head. "That'll do. Not quite the response I was hoping for, but I can work with it. For now."

"Where are we?"

Rael made a *tsk-tsk*-ing sound with his tongue. "I could tell you, but then I'd have to kill you." He laughed. "Sorry—I've always wanted to say that to someone. I—oh, get that look off your face! No one here is going to hurt you—in fact, it's kind of our goal to protect you from here on. Did I mention that I was sorry about that business in the hospital? I was in a bit of a panic and . . . to tell you the truth, I was angry that she chose you."

"Who? Denise?"

"That's just the name you know her by, but, yes, Denise."

"What name do you know her by?"

Rael shrugged. "That's just it—I've never known her real name, so I took to calling her Persephone." He gestured outward at their surroundings. "It was a little joke between us, but the nickname stuck."

This was already too much for him to keep up with, so Robert blinked, sat up a little more, and returned to his original question. "You still haven't told me where we are."

"Noticed that, did you? Must be those legendary reporter's instincts. Okay, here's the thing, Willy. I could tell you exactly, *precisely* where we are, right down to the latitude and longitude with zero error margin, but what reason do I have to trust you'll keep it a secret? How do I know that you wouldn't leave here and come back with an army of police and social service droids and a bunch of sad-ass misguided missionaries from Save the Children? Don't bother answering that, because we both know I have no reason to trust you on that point. If what you really want to know is, am I going to keep you here? then the answer is: for a few hours or so, then I'm going to let you leave, *unharmed*. But before I do that, it's important that you and I get better acquainted." He looked to his left and grinned. "But that can wait a bit longer. Dinner hath arrived."

Ian emerged from one of the chambers, carrying the little bird-woman in his arms; she held a paper plate containing potato chips, pieces of diced fruit, and a cheeseburger.

"It's Ian's birthday today," whispered Rael. "It's been quite a while since we've had to celebrate a birthday here, so we're having a bit of a picnic in his honor. Ian likes cheeseburgers."

"Cheeeeese-boogies!" shouted Ian, laughing. He knelt down beside Robert and gently placed the bird-woman on the ground. She took a few shy steps toward Robert, smiled at him, then offered the plate. Robert accepted the food and thanked her. She shrugged, blushing, and began to turn away.

"Wait a moment," said Robert. "Please?"

The little bird-woman turned back to face him. She looked absolutely terrified.

"It's okay," said Rael.

The bird-woman hunched her tiny shoulders and took one step forward.

Robert stared at her for a moment. "I . . . I know who you are."

Denise's file: Andrea Walsh, age twenty-two. Virchow-Seckel syndrome.

"You're *Andrea*, aren't you?"

She smiled again—as much as her cleft palate would allow, anyway—and nodded her head, blushing even more. The veins in her hairless head, already so close to the surface they looked like red and blue strands of webbing, stood out in a way that Robert would once have thought grotesque but now found sweet and endearing.

"He knows your name, Andrea," said Rael. "Isn't that nice?"

She ran back to Ian, smiling again at Robert before hiding her face in the crook of Ian's massive arm.

"Andrea's a little shy," said Rael. "But she's getting a lot better." He looked at affectionately. "Hell, who knows—we might even get her to talk above a whisper someday."

Andrea looked at Rael, made a *shoo*-ing gesture with her hands, looked at Robert, then giggled and hid her face again.

"Cheeeeese-boogie!" said Ian, pointing at Robert's plate. "Ian make cheeeeese-boogie!"

"Thank you, Ian," said Robert, and bit into it.

It was delicious.

"You make a mean cheeseburger, Ian."

"Ian cook good."

"Yes, you do."

Ian reached into the pocket of his coat and produced a cold can of Coke, which he popped open and gave to Robert. "Get firsty!"

"Yes," said Robert, taking a sip. "Cheese-boogies make me firsty."

Ian grinned, his two eyes glittering in their single, diamond-shaped socket.

But his skin looked so pale and sweaty.

"Is he all right?" Robert asked Rael.

"Why don't you ask him, Willy? He's still here, you know."

Robert looked back at Ian. "I apologize for that, Ian. It was rude."

"Today Ian's birfday. Ian . . ." He rolled his eyes upward as he counted to himself. "I forty."

"Wow. Happy birthday. I wish I had a gift to—" He caught a glimpse of his watch, unhooked the metal clasp, and offered it. "Here you go, Ian. Happy fortieth birthday!"

"Oooooh, pretty!" Ian took the watch and held it in front of his face, watching in wonder as its gold and silver band reflected the light. "So pretty."

Gary A. Braunbeck

Andrea pulled her face out of his arm and stared at the watch in openmouthed wonder.

Robert took another bite of the cheeseburger, then washed it down. "Ian?"

"Uh-huh?"

"Do you feel okay?"

Ian grimaced, then shook his head. "Ian hurt." He pointed at his throat, then his chest.

Robert looked at Rael.

"Ian has throat cancer," Rael said. "He's been in remission for almost as long as you've been alive, but it's recently begun spreading to his lungs."

Robert's heart broke for the one-eyed giant. "No wonder—look at this place! Even with your goddamn air filters, you can't expect someone to survive down here and—"

"And this place has nothing to do with his physical problems, Willy! If it weren't for this place—the only home he's known outside of the Dumpster we found him in—Ian wouldn't have lived more than a few miserable hours, if that long. *This place*, Willy, protects him. It protects all of us . . . or at least it did, until *chronos* began to creep in, bit by bit. Ian's forty, *now*, and Andrea is *now* twenty-six, but there are children here who've been around longer than half the fucking *trees* outside. We didn't have to worry about man-made shit like time and 'then' and 'now' until 'recently,' thanks to you. Get it through your thick skull once and for all, that *here*, Willy, right smack dab in the center of *kairos*, we don't age as long as we *stay* here. Ian, Andrea, myself, and a few others had to leave in order to track you down and, as a result, we absorbed a bit more *chronos* out there than I'd planned on, and ever since we came back it's been spreading through the place like a virus. Until a couple of weeks ago we had no need to filter the air because the breathing problems had been healed; until he found you in that movie theater, Ian's remission was permanent; until she helped bake those cookies for you, Andrea's pneumonia was just a distant

224

memory. But once *chronos* infects you, it gains momentum like you wouldn't believe—and we contracted more of it than I can heal on my own. Now, with your help, we might—mark that word, pal, *might*—be able to reverse the effects. I don't know exactly how long we've got before the damage is irreversible— my guess is a week, maybe two—but we don't stand a chance in hell if you don't help us."

"Why me? How am I so important to all of this?"

"Because you can bring her back to us. She loves you, and she's been preparing you for her return—after all, you think she's dead and that just ain't the way it is. Can't very well expect her to come a-knocking on your door, all smiles and caresses and grave-dirt smoochies, can you?"

"So she's . . . she's alive?"

Rael shook his head and snorted in disgust. "Don't ask stupid questions, I'm just starting to like you. Yes, *Robert*, your wife is still alive."

"H-how is that . . . possible?"

"Aye, there's the rub." Rael rubbed the back of his neck, then looked down at his feet and sighed. When he lifted his head again, there were tears in his eyes, though his voice retained its quiet rage. "You know, Willy, I wasn't always the devilishly handsome, charming, debonair GQ cover model you see before you now. There was a time when I didn't look any different, really, than any one of a million faceless faces you pass on the street every day. I was a foundling. Never knew who my parents were or why they dumped me on the steps of the little church in the village. I was born in Europe, somewhere—it's been so long that I've forgotten the name of the village and even if I could remember it, it doesn't matter a damn because the place no longer exists—that's one of the drawbacks to being immortal: You not only get to experience the joy of watching everyone you know grow old and die, but eventually any place you live will crumble to dust and be forgotten."

"Sounds lonely."

Gary A. Braunbeck

Rael glared at him. "I'm gonna give you the benefit of the doubt and assume there's genuine sympathy in there someplace. You want to hear the rest of this or not?"

Robert stared into Rael's gaze, tracing the path of a single, angry tear as it crept along the rim of his left eye to the corner where it hung on for dear life, and remembered a line from a Gerald Kersh story he'd read in college that had always stayed with him: . . . *there are men whom one hates until a certain moment when one sees, through a chink in their armor, the writhing of something nailed down and in torment.*

"I didn't mean to sound sarcastic, Rael. I apologize."

Rael sniffed and wiped his eyes on the sleeve of his coat. "Yeah, well . . . anyway, I spent the first ten years or so of my life in that village, living in a small basement-room of the church. The vicar was a kindly gent, very Old Testament, though, made me read from the Bible for three hours every night. But he gave me a home and helped educate me and fed me well and let me play with the other children in the village. It was a life, good enough. Then one evening an old man named Hazlitt told us the story about the prince and a clown and the clown's mask, gave me this flute, then sent me out into the world.

"I don't know how long it was before I realized that, once I accepted this flute and left the village, I wasn't aging like I was supposed to. Don't get me wrong, I got older, but it worked out to something like a week's worth of aging for every year—I don't know, it might've been less than that; math was never one of my strong suits.

"I'm going to skip ahead several hundred years, if you don't mind—I mean, I *could* tell you about all the places I traveled and the people I met and how I began to assemble the children who live with me and the way we mapped out the catacombs that link the thirteen places where the mountains open up, but it'd take forever and bore the piss out of you and wouldn't make all that much difference anyway." He reached into his coat pocket and took out a half-empty bottle of scotch, unscrewed the cap, and pulled down a couple of deep swallows. Wiping his mouth on his sleeve, he looked at Robert and offered the bottle. "Where are my manners? Want a snort?"

"No, thank you. I'd like to keep what's left of my wits about me."

Rael smiled. "It's good you make jokes at a time like this. Have to teach me how to do it sometime." He took another drink, capped the bottle, and slipped it back into his pocket. "Okay, so here I am later on, looking maybe nineteen or twenty even though I'd been walking around for the better part of six hundred years. Lotta sight-seeing and odd jobs, only gotten laid a few dozen times—can you imagine what it's like to go for sixty-five years at a stretch before any nookie comes your way? Does wonders for your wrist strength but not a lot for your self-esteem. But I digress.

"By this time I was fully aware that there was something not quite right about myself but I'd given up trying to figure out what it might be. The thing that bothered me most about the time before I started working at the Bathelt's farm was that I almost never dreamed when I slept—and I didn't sleep all that often. Still don't. But back then, on those rare occasions when I *did* dream, it was always about what the old vicar in the village had taught me about the angels, and that's something I need to share with you.

"You see, not all angels are these ethereal, white-robed, wondrous, golden-winged refugees from a beauty contest that you're always seeing depicted in books and movies—oh, no. Many of them—and I'm talking about the ones who sit by God's side and have His favor and love and respect and are the first to get tickets for the WWF Summer Slam—the *good guys, capiche*? A lot of them are so hideous in their appearance that they make Lovecraft's Great Old Ones look like *Playboy* centerfolds. We're talkin' class-A uggos here, tentacles and dripping teeth and putrescent flesh all dark and oily with larval eruptions that drip phosphorescent goo. All clear on that? Good."

He took the flute from his belt and blew three notes, each one successively louder and purer.

"Story time," he said to Robert, then called out: "I said *it's story time!*"

His voice echoed through the chambers with near-deafening volume.

A moment later, the children erupted from their rooms with squeals of laughter and anticipation, scurrying down the ladders, running across the catwalk, dashing over the bridges. When Robert looked up at them he thought for a moment that this cavern perhaps opened somewhere near the top, because he was again seeing stars—some so far away they were mere pinpoints of light—but as he watched, the more he became aware that these distant stars too were moving, circling around other catwalks, traversing higher bridges, descending other ladders, or being lowered in their wheelchairs on wood-and-steel elevator platforms that were operated through a massive and ingeniously constructed system of chains, pulleys, winches, and counterweights, all coming toward him, not stars at all but yet more torches and lanterns being carried by children whose rooms were hundreds of feet above those he first saw.

It was incredible. He'd thought there might be only a few dozen children living here, maybe a hundred, but now saw that their numbers were legion; there had to be at least a thousand children, maybe even more. He craned back to try and pull all the shadow-children into his vision but was overwhelmed with dizziness and vertigo.

There were just too many of them.

"Don't freak out on me, Willy, not now."

"Dear God, Rael—*how many are you?*"

"I lost count somewhere around 1973—both the year and the number. That math aptitude thing again. Plus, I was pissed about Nixon and the whole Watergate freak show, but we don't need to go into that."

The children continued to descend from above until the chamber was packed; never before had Robert seen so many in one place. He attempted to stand once, and before the pain and dizziness got the better of him and he dropped onto his ass again, he looked around at the sea of surrounding faces and realized he couldn't see where the crowd ended.

Throughout the rest of his time at Chiaroscuro, Robert would come to divide the children into three categories: the Deformed—faces and bodies like those he had seen in Denise's files; the Damaged—children who were recovering from physical abuse so severe he couldn't even begin to imagine the pain and terror they'd been through; and the Lost—children who were neither deformed nor outwardly damaged, but whose eyes betrayed they'd seen and experienced things no child should ever have to witness or endure.

Suffer the little children who come unto me, he thought.

But they all seemed happy.

Rael looked around as if doing a head count, then closed his eyes and lifted up his arms, silencing their whispers and giggles.

He remained like that for a moment.

"What is it?" Robert asked.

"*Shhh!*" was Rael's reply. A few more moments passed wherein he remained frozen like that; then he lowered his arms, shuddered, and opened his eyes. "Just seeing if everyone was accounted for. We're all in our places with bright smiling faces. Except for one, of course."

"Denise."

"Or Persephone, or whatever in the hell her name really is." Rael walked through the children, climbed the staircase of wedge-shaped boulders, crossed one of the bridges, and stood above them all on the plateau that held the carved female figures.

"I suppose," he said in a pretty good Basil-Rathbone-as-

Sherlock-Holmes imitation, "you're wondering why I called you all here."

The children laughed for a moment, then fell quickly silent once more. Ian sat down next to Robert and affectionately draped one of his massive arms around Robert's shoulder. Andrea climbed over onto Robert's lap. He held her tenderly.

The quiet was nearly absolute.

Rael parted his hands. "Say it with me, everyone."

The children as one responded: "Once upon a time . . ."

And Rael began the story.

Chapter Five

". . . when a stranger was not someone to be feared, when a man walking a long and lonely road could stop at a house where he saw a light burning in the window and find himself welcomed there with no questions or suspicion, when a good meal and warm bed were still treasured as gifts, there lived a farmer named Hans Bathelt, a stocky man of good character, an American of German descent, whose parents had come to the United States shortly before the outbreak of World War Two. Hans was a decent and God-fearing man, and took as his wife a woman named Lillian.

"Throughout the mountain community where they lived, it was well known that Lillian was a granny-woman, a midwife, a healer skilled in the use of herbs and magick spells: a white witch. It didn't matter to Hans what people called her, for he knew his Lilly's powers were a gift from God and therefore holy.

"Still, there were some who feared her, who whispered among themselves that Hans had fallen victim to one of her spells and so could not see her magic for the devil's work that it was. But no one ever said this to Hans.

"For many years Lillian cared for the people on the mountain, sometimes traveling for many hours on horseback throughout the night to relieve a young girl of fever with the magick of pennyroyal and clove, or with the power of rosemary, magnolia, and goldenseal mend the leg of man who had been injured while working his fields, or cure a newborn of colic with a pinch of asafetida and basil, or heal an old widow of melancholy merely by brewing a tea with ground linden flower. Those who received her help were always grateful, and quick to defend her to those who swore her powers were evil. Then came the day that the preacher fell ill and lay close to death. Prayer did not help, nor did the medicines that were brought back from the city a hundred miles away. At last, with hope dwindling, everyone agreed it best to send for Lillian.

"Standing at the preacher's bedside, Lillian mixed a potion from her stock of roots and herbs, then lighted her candles, drew her sigils upon the wall, and uttered her prayers as she spooned the potion into the preacher's mouth.

"Come the dawn the preacher was healed and decreed that Lillian's powers were, indeed, sent from Heaven Above. Everyone praised her openly, but in secret there were still those who believed her to be a handmaiden of Lucifer. One man made the mistake of saying this in front of Hans, who quickly struck down the man and warned him, 'Never say such foul things of my Lilly!'

" 'You cannot see her for what she truly is, Hans Bathelt,' snarled this man, wiping the blood from his mouth, 'for she has bewitched you as surely as Christ shed His blood for our sins.'

"Hans said nothing to this accusation; instead, he walked away, vowing never to speak with this man again. But who among us could hear such a thing and not wonder, if even for a moment, if it was true? Hans tried to forget what he had heard but could not. Lillian sensed that something was wrong and asked her husband what was troubling him.

" 'They say that you are in league with Lucifer,' he told her, 'and that I cannot see this because you have placed me under your evil spell.'

"Lillian laughed, then took her husband's hand in hers and placed it upon her belly. 'My dear husband,' she said. 'Would the Good Lord have finally granted our prayers for a child if I were a servant of the devil?'

"So overjoyed was Hans that his Lilly had at last, after so many years of trying and so many disappointments, conceived a child that he immediately forgot the ugly rumors and dedicated himself to her care.

"Lillian was very careful throughout her expectant months not to tempt fate or do anything that would cause people to question her spiritual allegiance; she never admired her swelling figure in a mirror; she never touched a horse; she would not allow her photograph to be taken, nor did she spin any wool; she never removed her wedding ring, even though her swollen fingers caused her much discomfort; she did not eat any fish, nor tubers of any kind; never once did she cross a stream of running water or, most important, walk through a cemetery.

"Hans too paid close mind to his duties; he never referred to the child as 'it,' only 'her,' because they both wished for a baby girl; he never ate a potato after sunset, nor did he spit in the house or allow a black snake to cross his path. Both he and Lillian were careful never to make clothing for the child until after the seventh month of Lillian's pregnancy, and asked all their friends who wished to make a gift of clothing to do the same, as well as wait until after the child was born for making any caps or bonnets for it so that it would not be born with an enlarged head.

"The next spring Lillian bore Hans a daughter, who was born with a caul that her mother at once dried and preserved so that the child could burn it upon reaching her thirteenth birthday and fully accept her magickal powers. They named her Joanna, a name chosen by Hans from the Bible, and a lovelier, healthier, happier newborn you never did see! People—even those who secretly believed Lillian to be evil—came from all over the mountain to see the child, and all were moved by her innocence. The preacher baptized Joanna in the Lord's house a fortnight later, and the community resumed its everyday existence, miles away from the crowded, dirty, dangerous city. Hans and Lillian made their home a good and loving place for their child, a clean place, and happy.

"But as Joanna grew it became apparent to everyone on the mountain that she not only possessed her mother's gift for healing and other forms of magick, but was gifted with Divining, as well. As she grew, Joanna claimed to be able to speak with the spirits of the dead, to project her soul from outside her body during sleep, to hear the approach of a storm days away, to smell an evil or unkind thought, and communicate with beings from other realms, legendary creatures such as Hoopsticks and Stark-Eye; the Lovers of Black Hand Gorge; the Burning Man; and, most unsettling to all, she once claimed to have spoken to Ol' Scratch himself.

" 'I spit right in the Devil's eye,' she said, 'and told him that he wasn't wanted here!'

"The people of the mountain loved her; those who didn't love her feared her.

"Joanna grew into young womanhood, and on her thirteenth birthday took her dried caul out to the graveyard and there burned it. From that night on, it was Joanna whom the mountain folk called upon for healing and magick. Lillian took pride in her daughter's achievement and abilities that now far surpassed her own, and eventually became Joanna's assistant, a position she was more than happy to assume.

"One day a stranger wandered onto the Bathelt Farm and asked if he might spend the night in their barn, for he was weary from his travels and wished shelter on this winter's night.

" 'You'll not sleep with animals on my farm,' said Hans, opening wide his door. 'But you are welcome to spend the night in our house. We have a spare room in the attic. It's small, but comfortable.'

"The stranger thanked Hans and entered his house. Lillian insisted on fixing the stranger a meal to warm his belly after so cold a journey, and he gladly accepted. After finishing his meal—and what a feast it seemed to him, what with how little he'd had to eat recently—the stranger asked if there were any chores he might perform for the family to repay their kindness. Hans thought about this, then told the stranger that, in the morning, he could help repair a broken plow so it would be ready for next planting season.

"The stranger did as he promised the next morning, rising before anyone else in the house. By the time Hans was awake and seated at the breakfast table, the stranger had repaired not only the plow, but a hole in roof of the barn and a loose board on the Bathelt's front step, and had stacked enough wood and brought in enough coal so that Hans would not have to trouble himself with those tasks for the remainder of the winter.

" 'Do you have a name?' asked Hans.

" 'Yessir,' replied the stranger. 'I am called Rael.'

" 'Well, Rael, may I ask you a question?'

" 'As you wish, sir.'

" 'Do you have anywhere to go, any family waiting for your return?'

" 'No, sir,' replied Rael. 'I was a foundling. I have no family nor home such as yours to speak of.'

"This was not quite the truth, as all of you know, for Rael *did* have a home, here in Tabernacle, with many of you, and was journeying forth to find more of your brothers and sisters to bring back with him; but for some reason that he couldn't name, he *had* to find the Bathelt farm and stay there for a while.

"And that is how he came to be the family's handyman.

"Rael lived with them for several months, and a more loving family beyond these walls he never found. But during the months he lived with them, Joanna began to take midnight walks that she would not allow anyone to accompany her on. This worried Hans and Lilly deeply, even though Joanna was always sleeping in her bed the next morning.

"Then, one morning, Joanna's bed was empty. She hadn't come back from her midnight walk. Both Hans and Rael set out to look for her, but before they were too far away from the farm Rael convinced Hans to go back and stay with Lilly. 'This is no time to leave her alone,' Rael said to him. 'Don't worry, my friend—I will find Joanna for you.'

"Hans went back to stay with his wife and Rael continued his search alone. It's hard to say how long he wandered through the snow and thick forests looking for the young woman he'd come to think of as his sister; a few days, at least, possibly a week. He lived off what little food he had packed to take with him, and when that ran out, he used Hans's rifle to shoot whatever small forest creature was foolish enough to show itself.

"Eventually, he found a sign of Joanna: her footprints in the snow. Rael pulled his cap over his ears, gave his gloves a tug, slung his rifle by its strap over his shoulder, and began the long trudge uphill along the path made by Joanna's footprints. As he ascended, the trees became shorter and more twisted, looking in patches as if they had been seared by fire from overhead. The stench of burnt wood hung heavy in the air. For a while he could see patches of gray sky above but soon the trees were not much higher than his head, briary Scotch pine and dwarfed and gnarled spruce, and when he looked down he could no longer see Joanna's footprints, for by then the snow had begun falling heavily again, erasing not only Joanna's footprint's but Rael's own behind him. Still, he went on, confident that he would not get lost because he had walked this way many times before with Hans when the two went hunting; besides, it seemed to him that if Joanna had climbed this far up the mountain, she must have done so for a reason, so Rael concluded that she must have kept going.

"He continued his climb. It became more difficult, for once

he was out of the trees the way became rougher, steeper, winding around huge boulders and skirting short but dangerous drops. The new snow on the old, hardened snow below made his footing much less sure. Several times he slipped and almost fell, and once saved himself from tumbling off a difficult ledge only by grabbing hold of some old roots that jutted from a jagged outcropping in the wall of the mountain. The wind was high, whipping the snow against him in wet sheets, plastering his hat and coat and face. He could not see more than a dozen feet in front of him and then only when the wind momentarily hitched and shifted direction, blowing the snow from behind him. His progress was slow, but he knew from previous journeys that he didn't have much farther to go. Soon he reached the crown, where the path abruptly steepened for the last hundred feet before leveling off at the top. Despite the cold and the icy wind, Rael was sweating underneath his coat, but he forced himself to make the rest of the climb, scrambling inch by inch to the top where he came to rest on a table-sized ring of flat stone. He could see nothing that he could reach out and touch. The snow had covered his entire body and had turned all except the red sun of his sweating face as white as the whirling white space that surrounded him. If there had been another human face near that high flat tabletop of stone that lay only a few steps away from the edge of the mountain, he would have seen it, but there was none. He pulled his snow-frozen coat tight around him and waited for the whiteness to dim. The wind died down for a few blessed moments, and Rael was able to see that, if Joanna had come this far during the last snowstorm, she would not have been able to see that only a few steps beyond this point the mountain disappeared under your feet and dropped off into a seemingly bottomless abyss of stone, ice, and snow.

"He sat there for a few more minutes on the altar of stone and wept for her loss. How was he ever going to be able to tell Hans and Lilly about this? How was he going to be able to live with himself after breaking their hearts with news of his failure?

He lay back on the flat stone and closed his eyes—and it was then that he felt the presence of . . . of *something* all around him, something ancient and powerful, and wondered if Joanna's talk of Hoopsticks and Stark-Eye and all the other creatures of myth was more than just a young girl's flights of fancy. Though he never doubted her magickal abilities, Rael often thought her talk of leaving her body and speaking with the dead and all of it was just wishful thinking, maybe even a sign of madness. But now, in this place above all places, he could *feel* the lingering essence of something that was beyond his understanding, something that had walked the Earth even longer than he, something that would cause his mind to crumble if he were to ever face it . . . and yet there was a sense that if he *were* to face it, he might somehow recognize it, and it him.

"But intermingled with this essence that charged the air like the electric blast of a vanished lightning bolt he felt something of Joanna, and hoped beyond hope that she was alive, after all, that she hadn't stepped off into the abyss a few steps beyond the stone altar. It was this hope alone that enabled him to pull himself up from the stone, turn coldly around, and begin the descent.

"When he finally reached the Bathelt farm he was weak and sick and feverish and hungry and frozen nearly to the bone. He collapsed in the snow a few feet away from their front step. How long he lay there before Hans came out for more firewood he did not know, but he was aware of Hans crying out his name, of Lilly's tears falling upon his cheek . . . and of Joanna's healing hands on his face and chest.

"He was delirious for days, aware only of Hans's voice and Lilly's tears and Joanna's potions, prayers, and hands. *I don't wish to die, not now*, he thought. *There are children waiting for my return*.

"Darkness and light became one and the same for him, his flesh a fiery prison, his bones the edge of razors twisting inside his muscles. But Joanna ministered well, and within the week

237

he was better: weak, still slightly feverish, some of his limbs frostbitten, his mind a whorl of confusion, but alive.

"He awoke one night and realized that he was lying on his attic bed that had been moved down here in front of the fire. He stared for a while into the crackling flames and remembered the seared treetops he had encountered on his way up the mountain. Then a hand gently touched his cheek and he turned to see Joanna's luminous face smiling down at him.

" 'I am so very glad that you found your way back, Rael. I thank you for your efforts, but the truth is, I was never lost.'

" 'I'm just happy . . . happy to see you're safe,' he whispered. His throat was swollen and raw with pain. Joanna held a cup to his lips and he sipped at the healing tea she had brewed for him. When at last his throat felt better, he took hold of her hand and asked, 'Where were you?'

" 'If I answer you, Rael, then you must promise me that you'll not tell Mother or Father. I wish to tell them in my own way, in my own time.'

" 'I promise,' he whispered.

"Joanna then leaned forward and kissed his forehead. 'Very well—but remember, we have a secret, you and I.'

" 'I'll remember.'

" 'Good.' She looked around to make sure that they were alone—both Hans and Lilly were known to rise during the night for a drink of water—then moved closer to Rael and said, 'I have taken a husband, and he has taken me. We declared our love before God by the stone altar at the mountain's top. Don't speak, Rael, just listen.

" 'My husband is none other than the Burning Man, whose name I now know: Siempre. Oh, my Rael, my sweet Rael, how I love him! I cannot tell you how thrilling it was to leave here on my midnight walks, knowing that he waited for me at the end. He has wooed me for many months now. I first saw him in a vision, where he called my name and held out his hand, whispering, "Come to me, my love." The night I did not return from my walk was the night we were married. So cold, it was, that night, but the heat from his body protected me from the wind and snow. And after he accepted me and I him, he touched a hand to the frozen stone altar and the ice and snow melted away, leaving the flattened stone as warm as this bed in which you now rest.

" 'We lay down together on the stone and joined our bodies as husband and wife; afterward, as I rested in the safety of his arms, he kissed my cheek and asked, 'I'd like to tell you a favorite story of mine. Would you like to hear it?'

" 'Oh, yes, my love,' I said. 'Say to me, tell me anything you wish!'

" 'He kissed two of his fingers, then placed them against my lips and said: 'Listen:

" ' "On the morning of the eighth day after Creation, God called for Raziel, the Angel of Mysteries, to bring his quill. Raziel listened as God spoke, and wrote down in a book all that he was told. It was a daunting task and took many, many years to complete. This book, the *Sefer Raziel*, contained all celestial and earthly knowledge. It was from this book that the angels were to instruct the children of men. To assist him in this, Raziel called upon the Grigori, an order of High Angels whose understanding of the Mysteries was said to nearly equal his own. Their ranks, it has been said, were drawn from the Intelligences, Sephiroth, Archons, and Hayyoth. Raziel chose them carefully, for such was the nature of knowledge in this book that only the most judicious of his brethren could be trusted with its dispensation. And their *names*, given to them by the Four Angels of Judgment, their glorious names!—Crown, Wisdom, Splendour, Beauty, Foundation, Kingdom, Strength, Victory, Understanding, Mercy, and thousands more that would sear a human tongue were it to try and speak all of them.

" ' "They were to help Raziel in bestowing Knowledge upon mankind—but only certain knowledge, for some of what was contained in the *Sefer Raziel* was Forbidden to the human race. On this point God was most clear and firm.

" ' "Raziel descended from Heaven and gave the book to Adam, who looked upon the pages and was greatly confused; though most of the passages were easily understood, some of the writings contained within—the Forbidden Knowledge—were indecipherable to him, as they were intended to be. One of the Grigori, the angel Gash, out of innocent curiosity, peered over Adam's shoulder as he read through the book and discovered that a portion of the Forbidden Knowledge was of so secret a nature that not even they, the Grigori—among the holiest and most trustworthy of angels—could interpret the language and sigils used by Raziel. When they confronted the Angel of Mysteries about this, Raziel said to them, 'Only God and the Four Angels of Judgment know the meaning behind those passages. It is not up to us to question Their reasons.'

" ' "The Grigori were most displeased with this answer and so, envious that they had not been made privy to this most secret-within-secret Knowledge, stole the book from Adam and cast it out into the sea. Vowing to further avenge this insult, they bestowed upon the human race as much of the Forbidden Knowledge as they themselves knew: the casting and resolving of enchantments, the knowledge of the clouds, the science of the constellations, how to make knives and swords and devise ornaments, tinctures for the beautifying of women, the course of the moon, the signs of the sun, how to fashion the weapons of war, the angel Penemue instructed mankind in the art of writing while others busied themselves with teaching children the bitter and the sweet and, as a result, cursing many of them with a childhood lost to Bad Wisdom.

" ' "When the time came to return to Heaven and answer for their actions, many of the Grigori refused to leave the Earth; the gift of Forbidden Knowledge had made the human race much more attractive to them, and many had taken human women as lovers. Raziel, his heart broken by their words and deeds, returned to Heaven with those few Grigori who were willing to accept punishment for what they had done.

" ' "God looked upon these Fallen Angels who stood before Him and—after conferring with the Four Angels of Judgment— decreed that they should be banished to the north side of the Third Heaven—the place called Hell—for a thousand years, where they might contemplate their sins in darkness and loneliness; once their penance was paid, they would be welcomed back into His kingdom with open arms and much rejoicing. This was a small price to pay, and the Returning Grigori gladly accepted their punishment.

" ' "Those Fallen Angels who chose to remain behind kept most of their angelic powers but were stripped of their immortality, and the children born of their couplings with human women were monsters, hideous, filthy, and deformed giants— the Rephaim.

" ' "Looking upon the unspeakable foulness of their offspring, the Fallen Angels realized the depth of their wrongdoing and begged for admission back into Heaven. God refused them. Disgraced and filled with regret, the Grigori decided to imprison the Rephaim in the deepest bowels of the Earth and cast a spell of Eternal Sleep so that these creatures might never succumb to the temptation to intermingle their seeds with those of the human race. The Rephaim, though horrible in countenance, were merely children at heart, and wept with fear and confusion when told of the fate that awaited them. So sad was their keening, so anguished and lonely and helpless, that God was moved to mercy and—unknown to the Fallen Angels—allowed these children to multiply so that their offspring might carry through the ages the tale of how the Grigori fell.

" ' "God sent one thousand human women into the depths of the Earth to mate with the Rephaim. Out of necessity, for no human could look upon the Rephaim without going mad with fear and revulsion, these women were blind.

" ' "The children born of this second coupling too were giants, though less terrifying in appearance. The Greeks called them Cyclops, the Iroquois named them *Ga-oh*, in India they whisper of the *Maruts*, the Aztecs told the tale of *Catcitepulz*, the Japanese wrote of *Emma-hoo* and the underground world of *Jigoku* . . . All of these myths and more sprang forth from the Second Fallen Births.

" ' "Most of these children died along with their mothers during birth, but three survived, and the True Angelic Essence was strong within them. To these three was given the sacred task of recounting for the rest of time how the Angels fell. Their hearts were good and pure, as was their magick, but they also possessed the gifts of conscience and immortality.

" ' "They journeyed to the surface of the Earth and there, with tears in their eyes, said farewell to one another and parted.

" ' "These Three have been called by many names, but the ones that come closest to those given them by God can be found in the *Popul Vuh* of Quiché Maya: the Sorcerer of Fatal Laughter; the Sorcerer of Night, Unkempt; and the Black Sorcerer. Down through the ages, though they grew weary and lonely and heartsick, they performed their duty well and without complaint. The Rephaim passed away, as did the earthbound Grigori who spawned them, and soon only These Three remained, giants walking the Earth, neither fully human nor wholly angelic, the two essences in constant conflict, their home nowhere.

" ' "Then came a day when God looked down and knew the time had come for them to rest. 'My good and loyal servants,' He said to them. 'I see that you grow tired, and that your hearts ache from the loneliness inflicted on you by your task. The time has come for you to sleep. Such dreams I have prepared for you as part of your reward for serving me so very well! But before you lay down your weary heads, to prove my gratitude, I will grant you one request.'

" ' " 'We have, in our journeys, seen much pain and suffering and despair,' they replied. 'Though we are so very weary, our task is not yet complete. We wish to comfort and to heal this race for whom the Forbidden Knowledge is more burden than blessing.'

" ' " 'This cannot be,' said God, 'for what is Known can never be made Unknown. The suffering you see is the price of their Knowing.'

" ' " 'Then we wish to leave behind descendants of our own,' they replied, 'so that they might remember us and our task to the world of men. Perhaps, in remembering, they might find an answer to the Mystery of Suffering where we could not.'

" ' " 'So it is granted,' God said, deeply moved by their concern for the world of men. He sent down from Heaven the angel Shekinah, sometimes known as Matrona, who is the Female manifestation of God, who sits enthroned above a cherub under the Tree of Life, and whose splendor is 65,000 times greater than that of the sun.

" ' "Shekinah coupled with These Three, and from this Final Birthing emerged the Hallowers, a race of beings who were equal parts angel and human, the two essences in complete harmony, who possessed all worldly and celestial wisdom, and who were able to move freely between the Earth of men and the Kingdom of God: *chronos* and *kairos*.

" ' "The Hallowers were given full responsibility for the world of men. Some called them ghosts, some called them spirits, others named them *demuourgos*. Most of mankind called them, simply, guardian angels. 'Over every blade of grass and sleeping child stands an angel whispering, "*Grow*." '

" 'Promise me, my love, that you will pass this story on to our child.' "

"Joanna was silent for a moment, then took Rael's hand and placed it on her body. 'Do you feel it, my sweet Rael? I carry in my womb a child!'

"Rael felt her swollen belly, sensed the life growing within, and asked, 'How long have I been ill? How long have I been gripped by this fever?'

" 'You returned to us nine evenings ago,' replied Joanna.

Gary A. Braunbeck

"Rael knew this was impossible, for he could feel the child move inside Joanna. *Nine days?*

" 'How long ago did you . . . lie with your husband?'

" 'A fortnight.'

"Rael shook his head in disbelief. 'That cannot be! You feel as if you're at least five months along!'

" 'Siempre is a man of many mysteries, dear Rael. Our love is a miracle, so why do you find it so hard to believe that our child could be even more miraculous?'

" 'Because it goes against Nature.'

" 'Then you and I have nothing more to talk about,' snapped Joanna, rising from her chair and leaving Rael alone by the fire."

Rael paused in his narrative, examined the sea of faces beneath him, then smiled and said, "Do you want to know the rest?"

The children as one shouted yes, yes, yes, please.

"Then close your eyes," said Rael, lifting his arms high, then bringing them slowly back down. "That's it, shhh, there you go, close your eyes and be very quiet . . . quiet . . . there you go . . ."

Within moments every child in the chamber was asleep. Taking care to be as quiet as possible, Rael climbed back down and rejoined Robert, Ian, and Andrea.

Robert said, "What's happening to—"

Rael held a finger to his lips and shook his head, then made a gesture to Ian, who helped Robert to his feet and began to lead him farther down the chamber's path. Rael and Andrea both grabbed a torch and followed.

When they were far enough away that the echo of their voices would not disturb the children, Robert asked, "What's going on?"

"Right now, they are all dreaming their own ending to the story," said Rael. "It's the way it has to be until Persephone— excuse me, *Denise*—is back with us. The actual ending of the story hasn't happened yet, but what *does* remain of it is a bit too grim for them. They'll take it a lot better if she's the one who tells them." He looked at Robert's slightly unsteady walk. "You okay to go on? I could have Ian carry you or we could grab one of the extra wheelchairs."

"I think I'm okay to walk if . . . Could we not go so fast, please?" His head was still throbbing and all the painkillers had managed to do was make him woozy.

"You're the guest."

They slowed their pace. Andrea moved forward a little and took hold of Robert's hand.

"Think you've made a conquest, Willy."

Robert looked at Andrea and smiled. She blushed in response.

"Okay," said Rael. "You need to hear the rest of this."

Robert noticed that the path they were walking had begun to slope downward. "Where are we going?"

"You'll see soon enough. Got your flashlight, Ian?"

"Uh-huh!"

"Good. Don't turn it on until I tell you, okay?"

" 'Kay."

"How's your throwing arm today?"

Ian laughed. "No-hitter! Ian frow no-hitter!" His voice was raw and scratchy; Robert could almost see the tortured throat muscles shredding apart as Ian spoke.

Rael squeezed Ian's shoulder affectionately. "Cool beans." He moved up next to Robert and Andrea. "Ian's sort of my unofficial second-in-command down here. He not only does most of the cooking, but makes and mends all our clothing. Boy's a wonder with a needle and thread, aren't you, Ian?"

"Ian sew real good!"

Rael smiled. "Okay, Willy, think you can handle the rest of this?"

"Like I have a choice."

Rael nodded. "True. I was just trying to be a considerate host. Oh, well . . . here goes.

"It didn't take long before everyone on the mountain knew of Joanna's pregnancy—and man, let me tell you, talk about fickle public opinion! Those folks who'd been Lillian's defenders began to have their doubts about the nature of her power, what with her daughter claiming to have played 'Hide the Salami' with some creature out of myth, and those who had all along claimed that Lillian was in league with the devil . . . more and more folks started paying closer attention to what they had to say. Not a fun time around the Bathelt house, trust me.

"The odd thing was, at no time during all of this did Hans ever once think *I* was the one who'd gotten Joanna pregnant— or if he did, he never said anything about it. Either way, it only served to reinforce for me what a decent man he was. Hell, if I'd've been in his place, the first person I would've accused would have been my live-in handyman. No, Hans was convinced that his daughter had been raped by some madman-hermit who lived somewhere higher up on the mountain. He even managed to organize a search party with what few friends he had—me included—but we never found anything. I knew we wouldn't. Hans got real quiet after that, started living more and more inside himself. He also took to drinking this rotgut moonshine some guy who lived farther down the road brewed up in a still he kept behind an outhouse. The more Hans drank, the quieter he got. Wouldn't even talk to me.

"I knew he was going to blow eventually, and couldn't figure out how to stop it.

"Anyway, as Joanna's pregnancy progressed, it became evident that something was terribly *wrong* with the child she was carrying. For one thing, she carried it to term in less than a month— no premature birth, no miscarriage, but *full term*. Add to this all the weird shit that started happening all over the mountain and you can understand why the Bathelts started getting threats. There was a farmer whose prize cow gave birth to a two-headed calf, this leprous moss started growing everywhere, crows started flying through windows, children dreamed of the dead rising from their graves, clouds in the sky assumed the shapes of great beasts, flowers started growing on unmarked graves in the middle of that winter—you couldn't spit and not hit something that wasn't thought to be a portent of doom.

"Joanna went into labor on the coldest night of the winter, and it was an agonizing birth. Lilly had to do everything herself because none of the women on the mountain would come to help—but the preacher was there, I gotta give the old fart credit for that. He did what he could—which mostly was to keep Hans occupied so he wouldn't interfere with the birth. So the preacher sat out there with me and Hans and watched the man pour that rotgut down his throat. There was no other way to keep Hans quiet and in one place.

"A little after two A.M. that night Joanna screamed. It was an awful, ragged, horrified sound that I hope I never hear twice. All of us jumped up and ran into the bedroom. Lillian was sitting in the rocking chair holding this bloodied towel and cooing to it. I don't think she realized how much she was sobbing. Joanna was curled up on the bed, covering her eyes with her hands, muttering to herself, and . . . laughing, very, very quietly.

"The preacher and Hans just stood there—I think both of them knew that something was wrong with the baby, but neither one of them wanted to see what. I started over toward Lilly and saw something on the edge of the bed. It was the caul she'd removed from the baby's face. Understand, a caul is supposed to be a good sign, right? It means that the child has special powers and will grow up to do wondrous things. None of this made sense to me.

"So there I am, finally, standing over Lillian and the baby. I cleared my throat and whispered her name but Lilly didn't even know I was in the room. So after a minute or so I reached down and pulled aside the towel and saw Joanna's baby.

"I've seen a lot of awful things in my life, Willy—plagues, wars, famines, attempted genocides, you name it—but I have *never* seen a child *that* horribly deformed. It had two arms, two legs, a torso and head, nose, lips, eyes . . . but everything was *wrong*, you know? One eye was a lot higher than the other, it had a huge facial cleft, its skin was gray and looked like it had scales, its hands . . . no. You don't want the details, just take my word for it. It was not something that could ever pass for human. But at least it was dead, I could tell that much.

"I had to turn away, and that was one of the worst mistakes of my life because both Hans and the preacher knew then that the child was a monstrosity. The preacher was the first to come over, and the man damn near passed out from the sight. He managed to compose himself, though, and made the sign of the cross over the baby and began to whisper prayer after prayer . . . Then Hans came over and elbowed both of us out of the way.

"He looked at the baby, shuddered, then covered his mouth with his hand and sobbed. Just once. There was enough misery in that one sob for a dozen men, and I wanted to touch him, to put an arm around him and say how sorry I was—the man was my friend, after all—but everything about him warned you to stay the fuck away. He shuddered a little more, closed his eyes, then pulled his hand from his mouth and stood up straight. You could have heard air molecules collide in that room, it was so quiet.

"I expected him to explode, to scream and lash out and destroy anyone or anything he could get his hands on, but he didn't; he simply reached down and took the baby from Lilly's arms, covered it with the towel, and laid it on the edge of the bed. He leaned over and kissed Joanna's cheek, then touched Lilly's face, then walked out of the bedroom. The preacher and I looked at one another—I think each of us was hoping the other one would know what to do.

"Joanna was very still on the bed. I had to listen hard in order to make sure she was breathing—she was. But Lilly . . . Lilly was still rocking back and forth and cooing and weeping and stroking the empty space between her arms where she'd been holding the baby. 'Poor little thing,' she said, over and over, all the while touching empty air as if she will still holding the thing.

"Hans came back into the bedroom. He was carrying his shotgun—an ugly piece of work, I think it's called an over-and-under: two barrels, a twelve-gauge and a twenty-gauge, one on top of the other. He tossed this empty wool sack onto the floor and looked at me. 'Put it inside,' was all he said. I took one look at his eyes and . . . the Hans I'd known was gone, so I did what he said. He told me to put on my coat and follow him. As we were about to go out the door he turned toward the preacher and said, 'Take care of them, see that they want for nothing.' Then we left.

"We walked through the snow and wind until we came to the edge of a ravine. Hans stuck the business end of the gun in my back and told me to remove the child's body and lay it on this tree stump nearby, then he pointed the gun right at my head and said, 'The Bible says that the children of the serpent must be dealt with as you would deal with the serpent himself—"Let no limb rest near the other, lest the serpent rise again." He reached into his coat pocket and pulled something out, then tossed it down at my feet.

"It was a hatchet.

"I shook my head and started to say something. Hans emptied both barrels into a tree trunk five feet to my left and damn near brought the whole thing down on my head, then loaded fresh rounds and held the gun on me. ' "Let no limb rest near the other," ' he said again. I gotta tell you, Willy, if the world would have ended right at that moment, I think I would've cheered.

"I bent over and picked up the hatchet. I planted my feet solidly in the snow so I could keep my balance. I looked at Hans and he nodded. I had no choice, you know? The thing was dead, anyway, right?

"I pulled in probably the deepest breath I've ever taken and raised the hatchet so far over my head I could hear the bones in my shoulder start to crack. I waited a couple of seconds, hoping that Hans would come to his senses, and when that didn't happen I raised the hatchet a little higher and swung it down with everything I had and the rest of it happened so fast

I couldn't react in time, because the *very second* I started to bring the hatchet down I heard this wheezing sound that I thought maybe was Hans but then I saw the baby's chest rise and fall and realized that it was pulling in its first breath of life and then I saw the hatchet swinging down and tried to stop it but there was so much momentum and it was so cold and I was freezing and I knew I should jerk my arm to the side but it wouldn't do what I told it to and then I see that baby has opened its eyes and is looking at me and the hatchet and I screamed and then there was the awful *chunk!* sound and the baby's head rolled off the tree stump and hit the snow and its eyes were looking up at me and its mouth was moving and all I could think was, *It wants to know why*, but by then I'm pretty out of it . . .

"I zoned out big time, Willy. I did as Hans told me, I chopped off its arms and legs, then cut each of those limbs in half, then put all the pieces back into the sack—except for the head. I buried that at the foot of the tree stump. Then Hans and I started walking all over the mountain. Every forty-five minutes or so we'd stop and I'd bury another piece of the baby, then we'd move on. It must have been close to five-thirty in the morning before I buried the last section of the body. I turned around and looked at Hans. He nodded his head and smiled at me and said, 'I'm sorry, Rael. I'm sorry that I was blind to the true nature of my Lilly's powers—did you see it? A monster born from Satan's loins if ever there was one. But I cannot bring myself to harm Lilly or Joanna . . . perhaps they were bewitched, as well. I still love them, but I cannot face them ever again. I cannot face anyone ever again.' Then he shoved the barrels of the gun against his face and blew his head off.

"I buried him where he dropped. I took his gun and reloaded it and started walking back to the altar of stone at the top of the mountain. I don't know how long it took me to get there— I'd stop every once in a while and sit against a tree and sleep for a little bit, then wake up and move on. The night turned into day, then into night again. When I reached the top of the mountain I saw a man sitting on the stone altar. His flesh was blackened, charred, smoldering. He looked at me and said, 'So you know?'

" 'I know,' I whispered. 'You are Siempre, the clown Hazlitt spoke of. And you are a Hallower. That's why the prince died when he put your mask on his face: He saw all that you have seen.'

"Siempre nodded, then stared down at the ground. 'I'm dying, Rael,' he said. 'So I need you to sit with me and listen to what I have to say.' "

Rael stopped, wiped his eyes, then removed the bottle of scotch and pulled down two deep swallows before offering the bottle to Robert. "You want a snort *now*?"

"Yes." Robert took three deep drinks from the bottle before handing it back. "*You're* a Hallower, aren't you?"

"I found out that night. Siempre told me. He told me so many things. Suddenly I started to realize why I'd lived as long as I had. You see, when Shekinah mated with the Sorcerer of Fatal Laughter; the Sorcerer of Night, Unkempt; and the Black Sorcerer in order to give birth to the Hallowers, there was a slight glitch, a little codicil that God wrote into the plan. It seems He wanted the Hallowers to fit in with the human race better than our ancestors had, and so arranged that the knowledge of our true nature—our 'angelness,' if that's even a word—would be slow in returning to us. Think of it in terms of an amnesiac regaining bits and pieces of their memory over a long period of time: searching for stars in a constellation or trying to make sense out of a series of dots on a page; trace the pattern of the stars, connect the dots—*boom!*—'I remember now!'

"That's how it's *supposed* to happen, and for most Hallowers that's how it does happen. But with some it's"—he snapped his fingers—"instantaneous, a repressed memory that suddenly snarls, full-blown, to the surface. That's how it happened with Mozart and van Gogh and Mark Twain: One second they're just guys, going along doing their guy thing, and the next—

whammo!—it all comes back to them and their souls scream for release, so they compose a *Thirty-ninth Symphony* or paint a *Starry Night* or write *Letters from the Earth*. Stuff like that. Then in an instant—poof! The memory is gone and they think of themselves as being merely mortal again and so live a normal life span and die."

"Did Siempre tell you why this happens? You said Hallowers were supposed to be immortal."

"We are—*supposed to be*, that is. I mean, when Siempre gave me the examples of van Gogh and Twain and Wolfgang Amadeus, the first thing that went through my mind was, 'They're all dead.' How is that possible? How could someone *forget* that kind of knowledge once it came back to them?" Rael shrugged. "So I asked Siempre. I looked him in the eyes and said, 'Why is this happening? How is it possible that you're about to *die*?'

"He looked at me and gave this sad-assed smile and said, 'Something has gone wrong between us and our Creator. Please don't ask me what, because I *don't know*. I can only tell you that we, who are supposed to be eternal, are dying away. After I am gone, you will be the only one left and it should not have been that way.'

" 'What do you mean by that?'

" 'The child who was born tonight, she, too, was a Hallower. Had she lived, she was to be your wife. I had hoped that the two of you would be the ones who would continue our race . . . but that cannot be. Not now.'

"I sat with him until he died, and then I buried him at the base of the altar, and then I decided that I'd had enough. What the fuck good was it, me being the last of my kind? What could I do to stop the despair and horror and loneliness that humanity inflicts on itself? So I sat there and thought of snipers in clock towers centering passersby in rifle scopes and the last sad whimper from the throats of crippled old men left bound and starving and neglected in putrescent beds and terrified two-year-olds methodically tortured to death by remorseless parents while neighbors who *knew* ignored the agonized shrieks, and I wondered if God's love was measurable only through the enjoyment He seemed to take in the suffering of the innocent, but then I remembered *Starry Night* and *The Heart is a Lonely Hunter* and ' . . . it was then that I carried you,' and tenderness . . . but it didn't do me a damn bit of good, and you know why? Because I knew then that physical evil and moral goodness would be forever intertwined like the strands of a double helix encoded into the DNA of the universe. Man was supposedly created to know wrong from right, to feel outrage at everything monstrous and evil, yet the scheme of creation itself was monstrous; the rule of life was get through the door and take that smack on the backside from the doctor's hand so you can be set adrift in a charnel-house cosmos packed from end to end with imploding stars and bloodstains inside chalk outlines. And what then? A crap shoot: If you did manage to survive the agony of being born, there was always the chance you'd die from a fatal disease, or be killed by a drunk driver, or crushed by a falling building during an earthquake, or drowned by your mother after she strapped you in good and tight and shoved the car into a lake, or you might be skinned alive or raped or tortured or beaten to a pulp or strangled or decapitated just for the fun of it, the thrill of it, the hell of it—'*So, whatta you wanna do tonight, Angie? Jeez, I dunno, Marty, whatta you wanna do?*'

"I thought about all the savagery I'd seen during my time on Earth. Good God—the human brain can detect one unit of mercaptan amid fifty billion units of air; the eye possesses tens of millions of electrical connections that could process two million simultaneous messages, yet can still focus on the light from a single photon; the nervous system is a wonder, capable of miraculous things, yet more often than not every fiber of an individual's being is geared toward destruction. So what chance did I have to end the despair I saw all around me? Matter is nothing more than energy that's been brought to a screeching halt, and the human body is only matter, and the fundamental tendency of matter is toward total disorganization, a final state of utter randomness from which the cosmos is never gonna recover, becoming more and more unthreaded with the passing of each moment while humanity flings itself headlong and uncaring into the void, recklessly scattering itself, impatient for the death of everything. So what if I *did* stay around and try to protect my brothers and sisters before the world could trap them in its jaws? Somewhere out there was a son of a bitch who *would* get his hands on a child before I could save him, and this son of a bitch would drag him into basements or alleyways and split him open or burn him or twist his most sensitive parts with handyman's tools until the child screamed enough to get his torturers excited, and then . . . and then it would go on and on and on, a race sinking further into the pit of depravity, all the while forgetting that they possessed the ability to write music or formulate equations to explain the universe or cure diseases, create new languages and geometries and engines that power crafts to explore space. But it seemed the only reason humanity bothered siring children was so it could have something to mutilate and terrify and starve.

"So why should I even fuckin' *bother*, Willy?" Rael shrugged. "To hell with it, I thought. If God has decided to give us the finger, then a big 'Fuck you, too' to the Almighty. So I shoved the business end of Hans's gun under my chin and let fly . . . but only one barrel discharged and the angle was bad. I don't know what the hell happened—maybe my hands jerked at the last second before the gun went off, maybe the recoil kicked in before the rounds fully hit home—who knows? I remember the tremendous pressure, and the fire that seared my bones, and the instant of pain followed by numbness, and I remember that I *saw* pieces of my face scatter outward, blasted and bloody. Then it was just darkness and I felt happy.

"I have no idea how long I lay there before regaining consciousness. I only know that when I opened the one eye that was still in my head and saw where I was, I thought, 'Shit—I'm still alive!' I tried to move, tried to get my hands to grip the shotgun again so I could properly finish what I'd started, but it was too far away from me.

"And it was *moving*.

"It took a few seconds before I could see what was happening, but then a bit of sunlight started filtering down and I saw the tiny hand gripping the barrel, pulling the gun over to the edge of the mountain and shoving it over the side. I thought I was hallucinating, but then I felt another tiny hand touch my cheek.

"I lay there and watched the various parts of the baby girl come back from their graves and reassemble themselves, and then she crawled around, gathering up all the sections of my face she could find, and she began putting me back together."

Robert closed his eyes for a moment and thought of the scars on Denise's body and how she never wanted to talk about how she'd gotten them.

"She couldn't find all of my pieces," Rael continued, "but she did come across a couple of frozen animals and used small sections of their flesh and skeletons to construct the rest of my face as best she could. She moved very slowly. She was still in a lot of pain, she was still bleeding, but she was alive." Rael pointed toward his face. "You think this looks bad now? You should've seen what I looked like after she finished up with me that morning. But over the years, she's done more work on me. I might even end up with my old face back, who knows?

"When she finished and I was able to stand again, I picked her up and wrapped her in the wool sack that Hans had given to me, then turned and ran down until I was off that mountain for good. She was weak and sick and I was panicked as hell because I didn't know what to do to make her better, so I stole the first car I could find and drove until the thing ran out of gas. After that, I carried her through the back streets and alleys of the city until I found a hospital, then I snuck in through the delivery doors of the morgue in the basement and used the service elevator to take her up to the pediatrics floor. I left her in the rest room there. From the look on your face, I'm guessing you can fill in most of the rest."

Robert, stunned, could only nod.

"I kept track of how she was doing through newspapers and television, and when it was obvious that the doctors had done all they could for her, I snuck back in one night and took her out of there. It was time for her to come home and grow into the woman who would be my wife. But as she grew—and she grew quickly—it was obvious she didn't feel the kind of love for me that a woman should feel toward the man who's going to be her husband. We continued to gather more children and bring them here, and all of them came to think of her as their mother. But me—I was relegated to the role of favorite uncle because she had chosen *you* to be her husband." Rael stepped closer to Robert. "There's something I've always wondered about, Willy: What the hell did you do to make her love you this much? You were—what? Eight years old when the two of you were in the hospital?"

"I was almost nine."

Rael considered that for a moment. "What did you do?"

"I don't know—I mean, if I saw her or anything like that, I don't remember. I was pretty sick for a long time. I know that Nurse Claus—that was a nickname I gave this nurse on the floor—anyway, she would take me up to see all the newborns, and she showed me the doors to the ICU where the sickest babies were kept . . ." He shook his head. "I was in the hospital at the same time as Denise, but I swear to you, Rael, I *swear* I don't remember what I could have done to . . ." He parted his hands in front of him and shrugged. "I wish I knew. You don't know *how much* I wish that."

"I believe you, Willy," said Rael, gently taking Robert's arm and leading him farther along the path.

"Will you tell me something, Rael?"

"If I can."

"If it was so important that she be here with you and the

children, why did you bring her back to the house the night you took her from the morgue?"

"Because she needed to be held by you in the home she had come to love. That was the only thing that could get the process started again."

"The process?"

"Of remaking herself. You see, Willy, the thing is, I couldn't figure out for the longest time why it was that she and I didn't die. Then one night we got to talking and I remembered something Siempre had told me about the beings we were descended from. I am a descendant of the Sorcerer of Night, Unkempt. Denise is descended from Siempre, who was a direct descendant of the Sorcerer of Fatal Laughter. Neither of us ever knew the names of the Rephaim from whom the Three Sorcerers were descended because, being Rephaim, they died nameless. But the fallen angels whose original seeding eventually led to our births, those names we know very well.

"I am a descendant of the Archon Pronoia, Denise is a descendant of the Archon Pthahil. They were the angels who assisted God in creating Adam. Pthahil sculpted Adam's body from several handfuls of earth. Pronoia supplied the nerve tissue. Then God showed them how to give the body life. So we carry with us the knowledge and ability to make Man, and it was that power, that sentient race memory, if you will, that was awakened within us by some kind of survival instinct and forced to the surface at the moment when we should have died. We can create and heal but we can't unmake anything—including ourselves."

They stopped at the base of a short stone staircase that led to another curtained living chamber. Rael led Robert up the steps and into the chamber, then asked Ian and Andrea to wait outside.

"See anything familiar, Willy?"

The chamber was perhaps fifteen feet wide and ten feet deep. Another curtained entryway stood opposite where Robert and the others had entered. Between the two doorways was an antique four-poster bed, the kind Denise had always wanted, a heavy oriental rug on the floor, a writing table, a chair, an old record player, a piece of furniture covered with a blanket, and a shelf filled with books. But what drew Robert's attention at once was the painting that hung on the wall above the bed; it depicted a battlefield covered in bodies and parts of bodies, but there was one man left standing, searching for anyone who might still be alive, not seeing the single hand reaching up from below the gore and death in hopes of being found.

"This was . . . this belonged to her mother."

"So you actually *saw* her mother?"

"Yes. Denise was devastated when the woman died—I mean, they didn't exactly get along, but they still loved each other . . . I guess . . ."

Rael walked over to the painting and examined it. "I always thought this thing was morbid as hell, but she liked it." He turned back toward Robert. "How long were the two of you married before you met her mother?"

"About a year and a half."

"That never struck you as odd?"

Robert shrugged. "I knew there were a lot of issues between them ever since her father had died, so I never pushed it too much."

"But you *did* push it a little, once in a while?"

"Of course I did! She was my wife and I wanted to meet her mother."

"One more question, Willy, then we can get on with the rest of this: After you finally met her mother, did you ever see Denise in bare feet again?"

Robert had to think about that one for a moment. "I don't know, really. I mean, she always wore socks to bed, even in summer—her feet chilled easily. But I can't . . ." He shook his head. "I can't answer that one, Rael. Christ! You'd think a husband would notice something like that about his wife, wouldn't you?"

Rael said nothing. Outside the chamber, Ian and Andrea were softly singing the Beach Boys' "In My Room," and doing a surprisingly good job with the harmony.

Robert listened. There was something so eloquently innocent in the way their voices blended; just a couple of children having fun, quietly singing a favorite song to pass the time until something else came along for them to enjoy. He walked over and pulled back the curtain, watching the way Ian held Andrea on his lap and stroked her hair, how Andrea traced patterns on Ian's hand with her fingertip, the gentle manner in which Ian leaned down at one point and kissed the top of her head, then held her close, rocking back and forth as they continued singing. There was nothing sad or lonely about their embrace; it was, quite simply, a moment of untainted grace. Robert smiled at them and hoped that, in this whispered-song communion, they felt happiness, purpose, family, and home.

"They really love each other, don't they?"

"Ian and Andrea love everyone, they can't help it. It's not in their nature to hate or be cruel."

"Ian looks so sick . . ."

"Worry if you want but it'll do no good. Neither will pity, so spare us those, thanks so much."

Robert let the curtain drop back into place and faced Rael. "So you and Denise held all of this together?"

"Either of us can do it alone for a while, if necessary, but it eventually puts a strain on our abilities. Fully maintaining this place in *kairos* takes our *combined* abilities. She has powers that I don't and vice versa. Teamwork, Willy, that's what has to be restored to save us."

Robert reached up and touched the bandage on the side of his heat. It felt damp. When he pulled away his hand, there was blood on his fingertips. The memory of how he'd gotten the wound—something he'd been trying not to think about—came

Gary A. Braunbeck

snarling back to the surface, full-blown, and he shuddered with revulsion.

"Let me guess," said Rael. "You just flashed back on that little roll in zee hay you had earlier, right?"

"Yes . . ."

Rael stood over by the piece of furniture covered by the tarp and took a corner of it in his hand. "Why do you think she did that, Willy?"

"Guess maybe I was supposed to think the whole thing had been a dream. I guess I scared her when I woke up and she panicked." He wiped the blood on his jacket and started to look at his watch, then remembered giving it to Ian. "How long have I been here, anyway?"

"That depends."

"On . . . ?"

"On whether you're talking about *chronos* or *kairos*. You're talking *kairos*, then you've been here about"—he snapped his fingers—"that long. If you mean how long according to the passage of time *out there*, my guess is you've been in your coma about three days."

Robert started. "What the hell are you talking about?"

Rael shook his head and grinned. "Oh, come on, Willy—you don't think I'd be stupid enough to *physically* bring you here without her, do you? Remember earlier, when I asked you if you felt like you were both here and not? Well, right now, as we speak, you're lying in *chronos* in the intensive care unit at Cedar Hill Memorial. Lynn tried calling you for a day and a half and when you didn't answer, she checked all of your old college hangouts, then called the station to see if you were there. Not being someone who intrudes on a person when he wants privacy, she gave you a little more time, tried calling again, and *this* time when you didn't answer, she hopped in her car and drove over to the house and used that extra set of keys you gave her to let herself in. She found you upstairs. She's one cool cookie, your sister—didn't freak out, didn't lose her composure and panic,

260

knew exactly how to check your vital signs when she called for the ambulance. You could learn a thing or two from her about keeping your act together."

It took a moment for Robert to absorb all of this. He looked down at his jacket, slacks, and shoes, then said, "Then how can I be dressed like this?"

"Because whenever you think of yourself, you think of yourself as appearing like this to the world—designer jacket, tailored shirt, nice pants and shoes, the whole nine yards. Appearances are very important to you, Willy, though I doubt you've ever admitted that to yourself."

"But my head, the cut—"

"The last thing you remember. If your bedmate had cleaned your clock by choking you until you passed out, you'd be standing here with a sore throat and bruises on your neck but you'd still be dressed like that."

"Then my *watch*, how could I give it to Ian if—"

"*Knock it off, will you?*" shouted Rael. "Jesus H! What is this, the first round of 'Find the Fallacy'? You want to piss away more of your life asking me questions in hopes of discovering some flaw in the logic, go ahead. I can answer every one of 'em, Willy—I may choose *not* to, but you'll only find that out if we continue. You want to know about the fucking watch, fine. It will not be among your personal items either at the hospital or at home when you get there. You *determined* that when you made the conscious decision to give it to Ian. Quantum physicists call it something like 'the observer effect' and have got equations and statistics and black-box experiments galore to back up their theories, but what it actually boils down to is this: There are places throughout the universe where the corners of the finite and infinite aren't quite squared, so it's easy for a small determination to slip through the cracks and alter even smaller details of consensual reality; when that happens people start throwing around terms like 'phenomena' or 'mass hallucination' or 'miracles.' I've always preferred 'parlor trick' because *anyone* who can free their mind from thinking only in three-dimensional terms can affect the structure of the physical world, be it rewinding and reconstructing a chosen moment in time or just doing a bit of conjuring. You ever see that old television series *Bewitched*? I loved that show; Samantha Stevens *rocked!* Her being a witch had *nothing* to do with her powers—she didn't think in only three dimensions, she *knew* the cosmos was just a work-in-progress, so it was child's play for her to do that sexy nose-wiggle and drop a three-hundred-pound elephant in the middle of the living room. And poor Darren! If ever there was a more accurate depiction of humankind's inability to wrap its mind around a force greater than the time clock, I ain't seen it. But I digress." He snapped back his arm and tore the tarpaulin from the piece of furniture—

—which was not furniture at all but a body that sat propped against the wall of the chamber with its arms and legs akimbo, looking for all the world like a marionette whose strings had been cut away in middance.

Robert immediately recognized the young woman from the bus who'd been so hurt by the foulmouthed punks' graphic descriptions of their sex lives.

Her eyes were open and staring. At first Robert feared she was dead, but then saw the slow, almost imperceptible rise and fall of her chest as she breathed.

"Is she all right?"

Rael shrugged. "Far as I know. Once we got her back here, she wasn't too talkative." He gestured for Robert to come closer. "Before you ask, no, I didn't come across her; she found me. The whole thing on the bus was her design. Ever seen her before—before the incident on the bus, I mean?"

Robert shook his head and tried to swallow but found he couldn't work up much saliva.

Rael sighed. "I was afraid of that."

Kneeling down in front of her, Robert reached out and touched her cheek; she wasn't exactly cold, but the warmth of flowing-blood life was quickly becoming a distant memory.

"Who is she?" he asked, pulling away his hand.

Then Rael grabbed hold of Robert's forearm and pushed it forward again, pressing Robert's hand against the young woman's face. His fingers barely brushed the surface of her skin before her eyes fell through their sockets and into the back of her skull.

There was no blood.

Then in a series of soft, dry sounds, the young woman's entire head began collapsing inward, her flesh crumbling and flaking away, becoming dust as her face sank back, split in half, then began dissolving.

Robert was so shaken by the sight that he lost his balance and fell forward and shoved his hand through her hollowed chest cavity. He tried to pull himself from the shell of desiccating skin and brittle bone but only managed to sink his arm in up to the elbow. A moment later, before he could release the scream rising up in him, Rael clamped a hand over his mouth and yanked Robert free of the body.

Hyperventilating against Rael's hand, Robert stared in wide-eyed horror as the rest of the young woman collapsed inward, revealing nothing within, and quickly turned to a pile of dust that joined with the earthen floor to become the dirt of bad memories.

"Take it easy, Willy, easy, there you go . . . I'm going to take my hand away now, okay, so you follow your sister's example and keep yourself under control, all right? I don't want you flipping out and scaring Ian and Andrea, okay?"

Robert gave two short, sharp nods of his head.

Rael took his hand away. Robert collapsed onto the floor, landed painfully on his ass, and pulled his knees up against his chest, wrapping his arms around them and rocking back and forth. Rael squatted down next to him and waved a hand in front of his face.

"Don't space out on me, Willy, not now." He snapped his

fingers, startling Robert, who stared into Rael's eyes and started to cry.

Rael called for Ian and Andrea to come in. Andrea saw Robert crying on the floor and ran over to him, throwing her arms around his neck and kissing his cheek and whispering, "Don't be sad, don't be sad," over and over. Robert let go of his knees and embraced her as he would his own child and wept into her shoulder.

"Aw," said Ian, kneeling down beside them and putting one of his massive hands on Robert's back. "It okay," he said. "It okay."

Robert pulled one arm from around Andrea and took hold of Ian's hand, holding it against his side and squeezing as tightly as he could. He did not wish to let go of either of them.

After a few moments, Rael clapped his hands loudly together and said, "Okay, enough. This gets any more warm and fuzzy I'll lose my lunch. Come on, everybody, on your feet! That's it, up we go. Good." He opened the second set of curtains in the chamber to reveal a pair of large oak doors, each with a massive iron handle, each engraved with countless mysterious symbols and misshapen faces and ownerless hands reaching outward.

"Ready to throw your no-hitter, Ian?"

"Ian all set!" He coughed, wincing at the pain. "Ow," he said, pressing a hand against his chest.

Robert saw the pain on Ian's face and almost started crying all over again.

"Hey, Willy."

"*What?*"

"Do you know why you despair?"

He looked into Ian's face as the giant tried to look brave, like it didn't hurt all that much, then at Andrea's small, fragile form next to him as she stroked his hand, and tried to imagine what kind of a life they'd had before Chiaroscuro.

To his amazement and horror, he could.

He reached out and gripped Ian's hand again, then pulled Andrea close to him. "Yes, Rael, I think I do."

"Outstanding." Rael grabbed the door handles and pushed. The two massive doors opened outward with an ancient groan into a darkness so deep that the blackest shadow would have been a white-hot sun. "Let's go, Willy. Time for you to meet the folks."

With Ian and Andrea beside him, Robert moved forward and through the doors into the darkness. Once the four of them were outside the chamber, Rael turned and closed the doors behind them. "Do not move an inch, Willy, got that? The ledge we're on is maybe, *maybe* twenty-five inches deep. You could take one baby step forward, but you'd never finish the second one."

"Right here's good for me, thanks."

Rael laughed. "Ah, that dry wit of yours. I'm surprised Denise didn't smack the shit out of you every chance she got. Ian?"

"Uh-huh?"

"Turn on your flashlight before Willy's eyes get too accustomed to this blackness."

It was a large industrial-model flashlight, and its light cast a wide- and bright-enough beam that Robert could make out his companions from midtorso up; in Andrea's case, he could clearly see her neck and head, but still felt her hand in his and that was comfort enough.

Narrowing his eyes against the glare of the light, Robert turned toward Rael and asked, "Where is this place?"

Rael said nothing in response, and after a moment didn't need to.

Somewhere outside the circle of light there was a space deeper than deadest sea, currented now only with dust and pebbles deep-laid in granaries of silence where time was stored, cached, and frozen. It was an ancient place, beyond the measurement of age, whose mass and depth diminished the human form to less than a particle of memory in the nucleus of a dying cell. No wind entered this place, no soft breeze blew through, yet there was something out there, a *presence*, still and slumbering, whose slow intake of breath caused everything—the ledge, the walls, the bones beneath the skin, the atmosphere itself—to thrum.

Robert had never felt more meaningless in his life than he did at this moment.

"The folks," he whispered.

Rael put his hand on Robert's shoulder. "Here, in this place, sleeps the Sorcerer of Night, Unkempt. The Sorcerer of Fatal Laughter and the Black Sorcerer sleep in places like this at opposite ends of the world. If you were to mark the three places on a world map and then join them with a single unbroken line, they would form a perfect triangle."

Robert began to slowly shake his head, whispering, "No, no, no, no . . ."

"You need to see this, Robert. It's important that you believe." Rael looked at Ian and said, "Time for the windup and pitch, Ian. Make a great one, okay?"

" 'Kay," said Ian, stepping to the side and pulling back his arm once, twice, then lifting up one of his legs as he shifted his weight for the throw and then the flashlight was airborn and twirling, its light creating dizzying strobe patterns as it rose above their heads and then began to fall down, down, down, and yet farther down.

"Keep your eyes on the light, Willy. You'll only catch a glimpse of part of him, but that's all you'll need."

Robert found himself staring into the center of the falling light, catching glimpses of rock formations and stalactites and fissures in stone, and almost turned away for fear of what he sensed he might see, but then the flashlight bounced off a cluster of stones somewhere and spun sideways—

—and for a moment that threatened to sear his mind forever he saw it, he stared down on part of the slumbering form of the Sorcerer of Night, Unkempt, and seeing a section of its face he screamed within himself as he'd never before screamed. No nightmare, no Titan from storybooks, no grief, no euphoria, no imagined childhood bogeyman could have prepared him for facing something this sacred, for sacred it must have been, as anything so mythic and extreme and unimaginable must be sacred. It was both terrifying and compelling, a thing beyond All Things, a being above All Beings, beyond love and bliss or their sum, beyond grief and violence or their total, beyond grace and prayer or their cumulative effects on the psyche, beyond even the place in humankind's unconscious where the monstrous and depraved joined hands with the majestic and beautiful to begin the dance that ended with physical evil and moral goodness forever intertwined like the strands of a double helix encoded into the DNA of the universe, and, finally, beyond the capability of Robert's mind to comprehend and catalogue its hideous grandeur. He tried to force himself to close his eyes, to blank every detail of the sight from his memory and lock it away and bury it so he'd never have to look at it again, but he could not look away.

"Watch the light, Willy," said Rael, applying the subtlest pressure against Robert's back, easing him toward the edge. "Just watch the light, watch it and believe and understand that you can never again be a part of the world you once knew . . . watch the light . . . and bring her back to us . . . Bye-bye, Willy . . ."

"Bye-bye," echoed Ian and Andrea as the light beckoned him.

Back and forth, glimmering first in his left eye, then his right, a pendulum of brightness, back and forth, back and forth, and then, with a final push, he was over the side and flying through space, flying toward the light as—

(*I thought I saw . . .*)

—it rose up to meet him, glittering off the flesh of the ancient thing beneath, swinging, closing in on him, closer, closer, ever closer, until it seemed that—

(*. . . a response in the . . .*)

—he and the light and the slumbering Sorcerer were one, and here he would sleep until the world he knew had passed away and a newer, better place waited for—

(. . . *left pupil—yes! There, did you* . . .)

—all the Ians and Andreas and Raels and the countless nameless others, and then he would awaken and take their hands and they would follow him from the shadows of this place into the light the light and remain there in the—

(. . . *see that?*)

—light, the light, the light. . . .

Chapter Six

. . . from Dr. Steinman's penlight shone into his right eye, then his left, and at last Robert blinked and pulled in a deep breath, feeling the slick pressure of the tube in his nose running all the way down into his stomach.

Steinman made a last check of Robert's pupils with his penlight, then clicked it off and slipped it back into his pocket. "Nice of you to join us," he said, taking Robert's pulse.

Robert tried to speak but found that his throat tissue had been replaced with sandpaper. He glanced to Steinman's left and saw the IV stand that held at least three clear plastic bags, two of which were emptying into him, one that was filling with semi-dark liquid from his stomach.

"Here," said Steinman, picking up a cup of crushed ice and holding it to Robert's lips. "Don't swallow, all right, just let the ice lie in your mouth and melt."

It took Robert three more helpings to empty the cup and allow the blissfully cool chips to coat his throat enough to summon a whisper, but when at last he was able to dredge up a semblance of his voice, he touched Steinman's hand and said, ". . . ong?"

"What was that?"

"How . . . long . . . ?"

"Close enough to five days to call it. Do me a favor, look at my finger, that's right. Now follow it with your eyes—no, don't move your head, okay? Just your eyes. There you go . . . now over here . . . now back, one more time, there you go. Good." He looked over his shoulder at someone Robert couldn't see and said, "His tracking is fine, pupils equal and reactive." He looked at Robert again. "Now, squeeze my hand. Very good. Now with your left, squeeze. Excellent." He went to the foot of the bed and pulled back the sheet, then removed a tongue depressor from his pocket and ran it up the inside of Robert's left foot. "Can you feel that?"

"Tickles . . ."

"It's supposed to. What about your right foot, feel that?"

"No . . ."

"That's because I didn't do anything. How about now?"

"Tickles."

He put the sheet back, then stood next to Robert. "Can you tell me your name?"

". . . gotta be . . . kidding . . ."

"Yes, I'm famous throughout the medical community for my Noel Coward–like wit. *Do you know your name?*"

". . . . Londrigan." He swallowed painfully. "Robert Londrigan."

"Do you know what day it is?

"Do you know what year it is?"

Robert answered that one correctly.

"Know what day it is?"

"Not really."

"It's Tuesday. Do you know where you are?"

"Making a cameo in the new *Alien Autopsy* sequel?"

"He's fine," said Steinman, patting Robert's shoulder, then checking the dressing on the head wound. "We gotta stop meeting like this or people are going to talk."

Steinman was then pushed gently aside by a puffy-eyed Lynn, who looked at her brother's face and said, "Oh, *Bobby*. I was so

Gary A. Braunbeck

scared." She touched his cheek. "You know who I am, right?"

Robert looked at Steinman. "I've never seen this woman before in my life."

Both Lynn and Steinman blanched slightly.

"Oh, lighten up!" said Robert.

"*Bobby . . . ?*"

"Yes, *Lynn?*"

She smacked his arm. Kind of hard. *Ouch.*

"Oh, I'll just *bet* you think that's funny. Laugh it up, Uncle Chuckles—you're not the one who tried getting in touch with your sorry ass for two days and then found you unconscious with all that blood on the bed. I—why the fu—why are you smiling?"

"I love you, sis."

"I love you, too, but right now if we were alone in this room I'd pinch your oxygen tube just to watch you turn blue for a second."

"No, you wouldn't."

"No, I wouldn't . . . but I'd sure *think* about it."

Robert reached through the bed railing and took hold of his sister's hand. "Thank you," he said, his voice cracking slightly on the second word. "If you hadn't found me, I'd probably be dead right now."

"Like that hadn't occurred to me?"

"How long have you been here?"

Lynn sniffed, pulled her hand away, and took a tissue from her purse to wipe her eyes. "A little while."

"She's left here only twice since you were brought in," said Steinman. "And even then her husband and little boy had to come and physically remove her from the room."

Lynn shot Steinman an irritated glance. "Are you still here?"

"Looks like."

"Now, now," said Robert.

Steinman laughed, made a notation on Robert's chart, then gave further instructions to the nurse before turning to leave. "You can have liquids for the rest of the day, Jell-O and tea or coffee for breakfast. We'll start you on solids at lunch tomorrow."

"How much longer will you need to keep him?" asked Lynn.

"At least forty-eight hours. Try to get home and get some sleep tonight, Lynn. The nurses'll make sure he behaves himself."

"I promise. Thanks, Doctor."

"Hey, it's why they pay me the big bucks." He looked at Robert. "When your head gets to hurting—and trust me, it will—press the call button next to your hand and they'll bring you something."

"A Demerol cocktail?"

"The best in town." Steinman left.

Lynn pulled a chair up beside the head of the bed and sat down. "You look like shit."

"I can't tell you how much that lifts my spirits."

She laughed a little. "Come on, Bobby—between that scar on your nose and the bandage on your head, you almost don't look like the same person. Which reminds me—" She looked around for something, spotted a magazine lying on the windowsill, and picked it up. "Gene MacIntyre stopped by last night with this. He wanted me to tell you how sorry he was that you didn't get any warning about it, but even he didn't know they were going to do this until the magazine came out." She held out the new issue of *Columbus Monthly*; there, on the cover, full-bleed and in less than flattering color, was a photograph of Robert. "You're famous—at least in the tristate area. When did they take this picture?"

"That's a publicity shot the station had taken last year." Robert took the magazine from Lynn and read the caption over his head: WHEN NEWSCASTERS BECOME THE NEWS: THE STORY OF ONE CENTRAL OHIO TELEVISION REPORTER'S PERSONAL TRAGEDY.

"Ah, fuck me with a fiddlestick!" snarled Robert, throwing it down.

Lynn immediately picked up the magazine and opened it to a dog-eared page. "But it's a really nice story, Bobby, not at all sensationalistic or pandering. The people who wrote this have a lot of sympathy for you. They even talked to a bunch of Columbus and Cincinnati television reporters and asked them how they'd react in the same situation. You ought to read it." She offered the magazine to her brother once more; when he didn't take it, she folded it open to the story and laid it on the bedside table. "Well, I'll leave it here anyway, in case you change your mind later."

Robert gave it an irritated glance. "Thanks. Maybe later."

Lynn shifted her position in the chair, then cleared her throat and removed a handkerchief from her purse. "This is going to sound strange, but you left this at the house the night before the funeral. I found it outside the next day. I guess you dropped it when you left."

"And you're giving it to me now because . . . ?"

"Because all the time you were unconscious, I kept holding it and praying. I just thought that if I could touch something of yours, then it was like you were still with me, okay? And don't you dare laugh at me about that. Here."

Robert took the handkerchief. It was neatly folded to display his meticulously embroidered initials. He remembered when he'd had the nosebleed in the movie theater and had given this to Ian in exchange for a clean one. Ian must have washed it and then—

(*Boy's a wonder with a needle and thread, aren't you, Ian?*)

—stitched his initials into it as a gift.

(*Ian sew good.*)

For several moments neither of them said anything, then Robert placed the handkerchief on his lap, reached out, and took hold of Lynn's hand again. "You look tired."

"Yeah, well . . ."

"Why don't you go home? I'll be fine."

"Do you want me to go?"

"Not really, no. I hate hospitals."

"After what happened to you the last time you were here, that doesn't surprise—oh, shit!"

"What?"

"I promised Bill Emerson I'd let him know the minute you were awake. That's what he said when he stopped by here yesterday—'The minute he's awake. It's very important.'"

"Did he say what it's about?"

Lynn smiled. "Yeah. It looks like they caught the guy who attacked you."

Robert could feel the color drain from his face. "Wh-what?"

"I know! Isn't that great?" She picked up the phone from the bedside table, took a card from her wallet, and dialed the number written on the back. "Yes, hi, is Bill Emerson in? Lynn Connor, Robert Londrigan's sister." She smiled while she waited for Emerson to come to the phone. "Detective? Hi, this is—okay, right, sorry—*Bill*. Yes. Uh-huh, about twenty minutes ago. I know, I know, I'm sorry, I was just so happy that he—of course." She wrinkled her brow at something Emerson said. "I don't know, I'll ask." Covering the mouthpiece, she leaned forward and said, "He wants to know if you'd like him to bring some of his wife's brownies. She made a fresh batch just for you."

Robert shrugged. "Sure, yes, that would be . . . fine?"

"He said yes, thank you very much—and he said to tell your wife that it was very sweet of her to do that, he really appreciates it."

"My interpreter," whispered Robert to himself, then lay there quietly as Lynn finished her conversation with Emerson, all the while feeling his stomach tighten at the prospect of perhaps having to lie to the detective again. He didn't want to. He liked Emerson.

Lynn hung up and poured some fresh ice chips. "Here you go."

"How'd you know?"

She shrugged. Robert accepted the chips and relished the expansive coolness as it spread through his mouth, trickled down his throat, then spread its beautiful ice wings through his center.

"He'll be here in about forty minutes."

"Maybe you *should* go home."

"And miss this? No way, big bro. I want to see the bastard who stole my niece's body and then attacked you twice."

"Twice?"

Lynn stared at him for a moment. "Well, yes. I mean, he was the one who broke into the house and hit you with the lamp, wasn't he?"

"I . . . I couldn't say for certain. I just came awake and . . . and . . ."

Lynn squeezed his hand. "Don't worry about it, Bobby. Bill said he didn't think you would've gotten a look at him this second time."

"How the hell can he even make the *assumption* that—"

"The police found something. I don't know what, exactly—I sure as hell didn't see anything besides you and the lamp at the house—but Bill says they've got something that might prove this guy's the one they're looking for."

Robert closed his eyes and thought about Ian and Andrea and Rael and all the children he'd seen at Chiaroscuro. *Did you do this?* he wondered. *Is this guy another one of your parlor tricks, Rael?*

"Bobby?"

Startled by Lynn's voice, Robert snapped open his eyes. "What?"

"Sorry. You've had your eyes closed for a little while and I was worried that—"

"Still here. My head hurts like a son of a bitch, but I'm still here."

"Want me to get the nurse to give you a shot?"

"Not yet. I—how much longer until Bill gets here?"

Lynn checked her watch. "Any time now."

"I was out for over *half an hour?*"

"That's why I got worried—I mean, at first I figured you were tired, you know, and a little nap probably wouldn't hurt too much, but then I got to wondering if letting you sleep this soon after you just woke up was a good idea, so . . . I got worried."

"Jesus . . . I—no, don't call the nurse, I don't want a shot until this business with Bill is over. I want to be rid of this. You know?"

"I know." She leaned in and kissed his cheek, then stroked what hair of his wasn't hidden under the bandages. "I don't know how you've held up, Bobby, I really don't."

"I don't think I have."

"Yeah, but you never did give yourself credit for being as strong as you are."

"I got nothing on you, sis."

"I am woman, hear my roar."

Robert grinned. "Do you have any idea how many times you played that damn record when you were a kid? I used to hear it in my sleep and wake up screaming."

"I got on your nerves a lot, didn't I?"

He shrugged. "You were the little sister. It was your job to get on my nerves. What are you doing about your classes?"

"Why do you think God made substitute teachers? This close to Thanksgiving and Christmas, it was easy to get a sub. Stop worrying about me, okay?" She kissed his cheek again, then sat holding his hand in loving silence.

Robert began to drift off again but the throbbing inside his skull kept him from succumbing to sleep; but even if he had fallen asleep, Emerson's noisy entrance would have wakened him.

The detective came in pushing a television/VCR unit on a squeaky-wheeled cart. "Sorry, but this was the only one they could find for me. Sounds like nails across a chalkboard, doesn't it?" He positioned the unit at the foot of Robert's bed, unwound the cord, and plugged it in. "Oh, here you go." He reached into the large shoulder bag he was carrying and removed a fat plastic bag filled with brownies. "I'll have you know she put *pecans* in this batch," he said, pronouncing it *pee-cans*. "She never puts pecans in them when she bakes 'em for me, claims it binds me up." He looked at Lynn. "Sorry. Probably more information than you needed, huh?"

Lynn was trying not to laugh. "That's okay."

"Yeah, well . . ." He turned to Robert. "No way I'm leaving here without a few of those, just so you know—and yes, they *do* bind me up but they're just so tasty I don't care." He readied the VCR, inserted a precued tape, then took off his coat and pulled the other chair in the room up next to the side of the bed. "So, how're you doing?"

Robert held up the bag of brownies. "I can't eat anything solid yet."

Both Lynn and Emerson reached for the bag at the same time. Lynn got there first.

"I'll hang on to these," she said; then, to Emerson: "And she's right not to give you *pee-cans* if they bind you up."

"I'm a cop, I could arrest you."

She looked at Robert. "Do something—I'm being hassled by The Man."

"You took my brownies. You're on your own."

Emerson grinned, then busied himself for a few moments taking several items from his shoulder bag, a few of which he placed on Robert's tray table, others he either kept in the bag and placed on the floor near his chair. "Hey, the damnedest thing happened to me a couple days ago. I got a job offer from a local advertising agency. Guess what they want me for?" He held up his too-delicate hands and wiggled the fingers. "A *hand model*. Can you believe it?"

"Well, they *are* very nice hands," said Lynn. "They look better than mine. Wanna trade?"

"I know," replied Emerson. "They want to use 'em in jewelry ads. Pay's real nice, to boot. My wife, she keeps making jokes about me becoming the supermodel of hands."

"Are you going to do it?" asked Robert.

"Oh, heck yes! I already submitted a written request for permission from the department. Don't think they'll turn me down on it—you know, good PR and all that. Besides, there're so many cops that moonlight anyway and *don't* report it that they wouldn't dare say no to one who goes through all the right channels."

"And if they said no you'd do it anyway and live with the slap on the wrist it'd get you?"

"Read my mind." Emerson then fiddled with the remote control to the TV/VCR unit for a second, took a deep breath, and released it slowly; as he breathed out, the aura of good humor that usually surrounded him dimmed slightly. It was now time for Things Serious.

Bill stepped into the background; Detective Emerson moved forward.

"Okay," he said to Robert, his voice a bit more formal, "I'm guessing that your sister told you that we think we caught the guy who attacked you?"

"Yes."

The detective nodded, looked at Lynn, then at the large brown envelope on the tray table. "Miss Connor—"

"If I have to call you Bill and keep you away from pee-cans, then it's Lynn."

The detective smiled. "Sorry, I forgot. Look, Lynn, I don't mean to sound like some old-fogey, sexist fart—I'm not one of those guys who figure that just because a woman's got ovaries she can't handle the nastier aspects of life—but . . . you're a mother, right?"

"Right . . . ?"

Emerson winced slightly, as if what he was about to say next physically stuck in his throat. "The thing is, some of the stuff I have to show your brother is . . . fairly ugly. On the way over here I was trying to figure out how I was going to ease into the more unpleasant aspects of this, but the truth is almost every aspect of this is pretty nasty. It might be doubly so for someone such as yourself—a parent, I mean." The detective huffed in frustration. "Do you know what I'm trying to say here?"

Lynn looked at Robert for a second before answering. "I don't want Robert to go through this alone, Detective. If you show him something that I don't think I can look at, I'll avert my eyes or something, but I won't leave the room, if that's what you're hinting at."

"Okay," said Emerson. He started the tape, waited until an image appeared on the screen, then pushed the pause button.

On the screen was an image of a bland room with sound-proofed walls. A long metal table sat in the center of the room. A man who looked to be somewhere around forty-five sat at the table, dressed only in a tattered overcoat, facing the camera. The shadowy back of a second figure—probably another detective—loomed in the right-hand side of the frame.

"Okay," said Emerson. "What happened was this: Two nights ago, around ten-thirty, we got a call about a body that was discovered along the banks of the Licking River near the Church Street Bridge in Coffin County—"

" 'Coffin County'?" said Lynn.

"An old nickname for the east end of Cedar Hill," replied Emerson. "There used to be a big casket factory there that burned down in 1958, took out a couple of blocks of businesses when it went. The area never recovered. Anyway, this call comes in, and we hightail it over there to find these three kids who'd been playing down by the water, throwing rocks at the rats and such. They're pretty shaken up about the body. They showed us where it was and it was . . . it was fairly gruesome, but doesn't really have any other connection to what happened next, except that it prompted a search of the immediate area, which was no piece of cake. You've been out of it, so you probably don't know that we had quite a shift in the weather around here. What was supposed to be snow turned out to be freezing rain. Made walking along those banks a real picnic, especially for my trick knee.

"About a half mile or so down the bank, one of the officers on the scene spots this inflated inner tube floating in the water. Looks to him like there's some kid riding in it, so he wades out and manages to get hold of the thing and pull it in . . .

"The body of an infant had been strapped into the inner tube and set afloat. The body itself wasn't all that wet, so we figured that it hadn't been in the water for very long. We called for backup and expanded the search area. A couple miles farther along the bank, we came across this old woman who was holding another dead infant. She kind of went nuts when we tried to take it away from her, kept saying stuff about how she was a good mother, how the county shouldn't have taken her Jenny away from her. It was pretty pathetic. We let her hang on to the body for a little bit because that was the only thing that seemed to keep her lucid, and she told us to head on 'over there, the devil's work is done over there.' About a hundred yards away we discovered this plywood and tin lean-to that had been built just underneath the Church Street Bridge. There was no door, just a blanket that was nailed across the top of the thing. The blanket was pinned back so it was easy to get a look inside the place.

"There were about five more inflated inner tubes inside the structure. There was also another dead infant."

"Jesus," whispered Lynn.

Emerson, purposefully not looking at her, continued: "A preliminary search of the structure uncovered several empty bottles of formaldehyde that had been reported stolen from a funeral home near North Tenth Street about a week or so before. We also found two heavy plastic bags that had been stolen from the crematorium out by Hebron—whether or not some of the corpses we found were stolen from the crematorium is something we're still trying to find out. It's a goddamn mess, is what it is." He rubbed his eyes, cracked his knuckles, and then, looking sadder than Robert had ever seen him, went on: "Over the next couple of hours the bodies of seven other infants—all of them strapped into inner tubes that had been set afloat earlier—began washing up on shore between Church Street and where the Licking begins that weird little fork around Heath.

"Just as we're finishing up at the site, the dispatcher radios me about some guy a couple of restaurant employees found sleeping in the Dumpster behind their building. Except for the coat he had on, the guy was naked and babbling on about water and babies in the stream. Don't have to be Einstein to make the connection here." He pointed to the television screen. "He didn't give us any trouble when we came to get him. In fact, he seemed kind of *relieved* that someone had shown up. Like maybe he'd been hoping or praying for it." He stretched his back, then asked Robert: "I'm guessing that you didn't get a good look at his real face the second time, did you?"

"I didn't see anything this last time, Detective," Robert lied.

"I sorta figured." He reached down next to his chair and lifted a plastic evidence bag, Inside the bag was a large rubber Halloween mask that bore an unnerving resemblance to Rael's face. "Is this the mask he was wearing?"

"Oh, God . . . where did you—"

"It was inside the lean-to. He had all sorts of masks and coats and hats and blankets and junk. But I remembered the way you described the mask he was wearing and guessed this was the one. Does it look like it?"

Robert focused on the phrase *look like,* because then what he said next didn't feel so much like a lie. "Yes, it looks very much like it."

Emerson looked at the mask, then set it down. "One of the desk sergeants tells me this mask is of that character Jason from those *Friday the 13th* movies. I guess this is what he's supposed to look like underneath that hockey mask he usually wears."

"How can you be sure that he was the one who . . . who attacked me in my house?"

Emerson reached for one of the brown envelopes on the tray table, opened it, and removed several small plastic evidence bags. Each one contained a wrinkled newspaper clipping, some of them very recent, others browned and brittled with age. The detective sorted through them for a moment, setting a few to the side while laying others in a row. When he was finished, he pointed to the clippings that were on the tray table. "Recognize these?"

Robert gave the clippings a quick scan. "Yeah. Those are all the articles that the *Ally* ran about what happened the night Denise died."

"He had these stuffed into the pocket of that coat you see him wearing there. These other clippings, they're along the same lines, sort of." Emerson sorted through the other stack of articles. " 'Mother Drowns with Four Children in Auto Accident,' here's one about a couple of teenagers and a little kid who drowned when their fishing boat overturned at Buckeye Lake . . . there's a whole bunch like that. They all have two things in common—the victims all drowned, and in every single case, at least one of them was a child. The drowning part I won't even start to get into because, the way he tells it, there's some kind of healing properties in the water that will bring the children back to life . . . Guy's nuttier than a wagon load of pralines, that's all there is to it. No, the thing that's important here is that you lost a baby daughter, and he lost his baby sister when he was a kid."

"So you know who he is?" asked Lynn, pulling a tissue from her purse.

Emerson nodded. "His name is Joseph Alan Connor—"

"*Connor?*" said Lynn and Robert simultaneously.

Emerson nodded. "Hang on, it gets better. When he was around five, he accidentally scalded his baby sister to death while trying to give her a bath in the kitchen sink. His sister's name was Lynn."

Robert blanched. "*Lynn Connor?*"

"Yeah." Emerson looked at Lynn. "I don't say this to scare

you, Ms. Connor, but all things considered, I think it was damned near a miracle that he fixated on your brother and not yourself."

"Oh, *that*'ll help me sleep better tonight."

Emerson looked embarrassed. "I'm sorry. But he's in custody now and, believe me, he's not going anywhere." He shuffled through the papers from which he'd been reading the background information. "Neither of his parents were home at the time of the baby's death—the mother was a barfly and the father was a drunk who, according to the social services reports, frequently beat Joe and may have sexually molested him on more than one occasion. During one beating, Joe suffered a severe skull fracture that left him with minor but permanent brain damage. The parents reported that Joseph had 'fallen' down the basement stairs. My guess is the father shoved him down those stairs, but that could never be proven. Mentally, he'll never be more than seven or eight years old."

Lynn looked at the face on the screen and wiped at one of her eyes. "How old is he?"

"Twenty-six."

"Christ!" said Robert. "He looks *twice* that age."

"Considering the nonstop party his life's been, I'm surprised he looks *that* good." Emerson cleared his throat, stole a mouthful of Robert's ice chips, then continued: "After his sister's death— the scalding incident occurred a year or two after his skull was fractured, so there was never any question that it was an accident—he was removed from his parents' home and placed in the custody of Children's Services. He was shuffled in and out of foster homes for the next ten years; none of the families ever kept him longer than a year. They couldn't deal with his nightmares and mood swings, or with his limited mental capacity. When he turned eighteen, he was released." Emerson sat staring at the photocopied forms he was holding.

"What do you mean, 'released'?" snapped Lynn.

"I mean that once a ward of the state is eighteen, he's given fifty dollars, set up with a job—in Joe's case, he emptied garbage cans at strip malls—and turned loose."

Lynn looked angry now. "Good God—did he even have a place to live when they 'released' him?"

"As far as I know, he didn't."

"Wonderful." Her voice cracked slightly. She turned away for a few moments.

"Bill," whispered Robert, "I still don't see how this led you to connect him to—"

"My guess is that, since your sister's name was Lynn Connor, and she was mentioned in a couple of the earlier articles, he felt that he was supposed to find you. After all, you had both lost baby girls."

Robert shook his head and pointed toward the newspaper clippings. "But the first of these clippings didn't appear in the paper until *after* I was attacked in the morgue."

Emerson nodded. "He spent a lot of time at the Open Shelter. They've got a police-band radio there that's always turned on. That's how he heard what happened. He probably listened to the EMTs and cops talking back and forth and decided to head for the hospital. Once there, it'd just be a matter of listening to the nurses and interns and asking questions in passing." Emerson shrugged. "It was kind of a busy night that night; people are more prone to answer a question than waste their time trying to explain why they *can't* answer something. So he listens and asks around, finds out your wife and little girl have been taken down to the morgue, and sneaks down there. We haven't been able to figure out how he managed to get down there without a card key, or why the hospital security cameras didn't pick him up, but I'm figuring all of that will come out in the wash, so to speak."

"Why would he take Emily's body?"

"I think maybe he managed to convince himself that it was his sister down there, which would explain why he assaulted you. According to his records, he had no past history of violence."

"Can I ask you—"

Emerson waved his hand, silencing Robert. "I need you to listen to him and tell me if his voice is the same one you heard either that night or when you were assaulted in your home."

Emerson depressed the pause button and the tape rolled.

"Where did you find all the babies, Joe?" asked the detective on the tape.

"Lynn tells me where I can find babies that nobody wants. And I always finds them where she says. In alleys, in boxes and trash cans. And I always finds them when it's raining or snowing. She uses the water to talk to me, see? She tells me that Mommy and Daddy didn't really want her so that makes these other babies, these trash can and alley babies, just like her."

His voice was that of an old, old man: ragged, tired, full of brittle sorrow.

On the tape, Joe looked down at his folded hands and began to whisper: " 'Those who see me in the street hurry past me; I am forgotten, O Yaweh, as good as dead in their hearts, something discarded . . .' "

Emerson paused the tape again. "Is that him? Is that his voice?"

"What the hell was that he was saying?"

"Part of Psalm 31. Does that sound like the voice?"

Again Robert focused on *like.* "Yes." Good God, was he condemning this poor man to prison every time he spoke?

He reached for some crushed ice to wash the taste from his mouth.

"That's good enough for me," said Emerson, turning off the tape.

Robert waved a hand. "Not for me."

"I don't understand."

"Okay, so maybe everything you said so far's right, maybe that poor kid made some kind of . . . I don't know, schizophrenic connection with my daughter's death and his sister's, and, sure, everything else might have happened the way you say it did, but how can you conclude that he's the one who—"

Emerson opened the large brown envelope and removed the photographs inside. "These are photographs of the body the kids called about and the seven dead infants that were recovered. Five were girls. None of them were too badly decomposed." He sorted through the pictures, trying not to look at any one of them for too long. "Of the five girls, three of them had autopsy scars that matched those that would have been on your daughter." He laid the three photographs on the tray table. "If one of these bodies is your daughter's, then we have the man who took her."

Robert cast a pleading glance at Lynn, who pulled in a deep breath and came over to his side, taking hold of his hand but not looking at the photographs.

Robert looked.

So small, so delicate, if it weren't for the scars that split them down the center of their chests, these pictures might have been taken while they slept safe and warm in the cribs as Mommy and Daddy stood beaming over them, proud parents, *she's so sweet*. Child, parents, family . . . home.

It doesn't matter, he told himself. *The poor kid's going to be put away no matter what you say or do here, these children are already dead and there's nothing that can be done about that, so why not give Bill the satisfaction of knowing that he's solved the case?*

It was a weak justification, but the only other option was to tell Lynn and Emerson the truth; if he did that . . .

Robert wiped his eyes, pulled in a deep breath, and pointed to one of the photographs. "Th-there. This is . . . is her."

"Are you certain?"

"*Yes.*" God forgive him. Joseph Alan Connor forgive him.

Emerson marked the photo, then quickly cleared them away. Robert leaned into Lynn, who stroked his cheek.

"One last thing," said Emerson, "and then I'll let you get some rest." He produced a final plastic evidence bag. "This is what cinched it. It was in his coat pocket. Is it yours?"

Later, Robert would remember the following minute as having elapsed in slow motion. He would replay it many times for the rest of his life.

Emerson handed him the bag.

He took it and at once recognized the object inside.

Don't bring it close, he thought. *If you don't look at it too closely, then you won't have to accept what it means.*

Then: *Please, no.*

He lifted the bag closer, turned it over and read the delicate inscription on the gold back: *From D to R, in the Second Year of Forever.* Then turned it back around.

"Yes," he croaked, barely able to get the next few words out. "This is my watch. Denise gave it to me on our first anniversary."

Emerson nodded, then reached for the bag. Robert pulled it away.

"I have to hang on to this for a little while longer," said Emerson. "I'm sorry, but—"

Dear God, please, no, don't let it be.

"Bobby," said Lynn, "what's wrong?"

Please, no, no, no, no, no . . .

"I, uh . . ." He handed the evidence bag back to Emerson. "Would one of you mind getting me some more crushed ice? My throat's really starting to bother me."

"Sure thing." Lynn grabbed the pitcher and went out to the nurses' station. Emerson held the door open for her.

As soon as both of them were away from the bed Robert snatched up the pile of photographs and quickly flipped—

(*We got a call about a body that was discovered along the banks of the Licking River . . .*)

—through them, all the while praying he wouldn't find what he was—

(*It was fairly gruesome . . .*)

—looking for.

But he did.

At the bottom of the pile.

He covered his mouth with his hand in order to keep himself from shrieking.

Then his mind sputtered.

There before him, in graphic black and white, was a picture of Ian: naked, alone, and very, very dead.

He shoved the tray table away and fell back against the pillows before Emerson saw what he'd done. The detective came back and quickly assembled everything, slipping the photographs and newspaper clippings back into their respective envelopes, then back into the shoulder bag. It was only as he was removing the tape from the VCR that he noticed Robert's face.

"Jesus, Robert, are you okay?"

Robert couldn't speak, there was too much pressure fanning out from his core. He was aware of the tears forming in his eyes and the way his lungs ached in his chest, but beyond those sensations he had only one thought: *Me Ian. Ian sew Good. Cheese-boooogies!*

Emerson put a hand on Robert's shoulder. "Listen to me, okay? I know it's all horrible, it got to me like you wouldn't believe, but for what it's worth, I don't think he meant to hurt you. I also don't think he killed any of those babies, I think they were already dead when he either found or stole them. He'll be taken care of now, Robert. He's up on the sixth floor here, the psychiatric unit. For observation. There's no way that poor kid's gonna be found competent to stand any kind of trial. They'll keep him here until they find a decent institution that will take him. He'll be okay, he won't be alone anymore, he'll be sent someplace where people will take care of him."

"All those children . . ." choked Robert.

"I know, I know."

Lynn came back into the room, took one look at her brother, and moved Emerson aside.

"Oh, Bobby . . ." She took him in her arms and held him.

Gary A. Braunbeck

Almost blinded by tears and sobbing so hard that his throat ached and his eyeballs throbbed in their sockets, Robert began to wrap his arms around his sister but stopped when something soft brushed against his hand. He turned his head and saw the handkerchief Ian had embroidered for him. He grabbed it in his fist and held it against his chest, silently swearing to the indifference of heaven that he would never, ever be without it for the rest of his days. *Me Ian. Today Ian's birfday. Ian cook good cheese-booooogies!*

"I'm so sorry," he whispered.

"Shhh," said Lynn. "There's nothing to be sorry for."

"So, so sorry . . ."

Bill Emerson stood very still, not wanting to move and perhaps intrude on what was passing between them.

"Shh, it's okay now, Bobby, it's all over, come on, come on . . ."

Robert pulled back and looked at his sister's face and was overwhelmed by the love he felt for her. "I'm sorry," he said once more.

"For *what?*"

The intervals between sobs were getting longer now. "Do you remember when you were six and I used to get you ready for school because Mom and Dad both left for work at three-thirty in the morning?"

"Yes . . . ?"

"Do you remember that one morning when I was in a really bad mood? It was my first year after high school and I didn't have a job yet and college wasn't in the picture because we couldn't afford it? You were all shook-up because you couldn't find something you were supposed to take in for show-and-tell that day, so you asked me to find it for you, then went into the living room to put on your socks and shoes. I was sitting at the kitchen table drinking a cup of tea—I could look up from the table and see you in there, putting together all your school stuff . . . you looked so serious and grown-up already—and I told you to find it yourself, it

288

wasn't my problem, and then you said something like, 'You're just lazy!' . . . I don't know if that's exactly what it was, but then you said, 'I hate you!' and that made me madder than hell . . ."

"Bobby, come on, calm down—"

"And all I wanted to do was scare you a little, that's all, just a little sadistic teenage show of something to remind you that I was your big brother and I was the one in charge so you'd damned well better listen to me, so I grabbed a *fork* off the table and threw it at you. A fork. It couldn't have been a spoon or a plastic cup or a wadded-up dishcloth or something like that, no . . . I had to grab a fork. I remember how you looked up and saw it coming, and then you tried to move out of the way but somehow you managed to jump right into its path. It caught you in the side of your bare foot, your right one, and then you dropped to the floor, screaming. Your face was all red and tight and there was so much pain in your eyes . . . the fork had gouged three little holes in the side of your foot and they were bleeding. I ran into the room and tried to put my arms around you but you kept backing away like you thought I was going to beat you . . . I kept saying, 'I'm sorry, I'm sorry' over and over and you kept crying about how bad it hurt and tried to get away because you were scared of me—"

"Shhh, Bobby, please, this isn't doing you any good—"

"Then I guess the pain got to be too much because you stopped trying to get away from me and pressed your face against my shoulder and said, 'It hurts, Bobby, it hurts, make it stop.' Like I was just your big brother who could make the hurt go away and not the asshole who'd hurt you in the first place. Oh, God . . . it was the first time in my life that I ever saw the pain I caused another person—it wasn't just the physical pain, hon, that was bad enough, I know, but the moment . . . the moment I threw that fork at you I was no longer your big brother who you looked up to and loved, I was just a monster . . ."

"Please stop, Bobby, *please* . . ."

"And I know it wasn't the worst kind of pain a person could experience, but I think it must have been the first of its kind for you. I've tried to forget it over the years, or excuse it by saying that I was just a self-centered teenager, or that things around the house were always pretty tense, or that you were just being a snot, but whatever argument I use, nothing will ever change the fact that I . . . I took away a veil of safety for you, I was always the one you came to when you were scared, and that morning I acted just like Dad on one of his mean drunks. You were *terrified* of me for a few moments, I saw it in your eyes, when I reached out to hug you and you pulled away from me, I saw you realize that you now had no one to turn to when you got scared, that you would never feel safe in the world again because even someone like your big brother, someone who said he loved you, someone who held you when you were a baby and gave you baths in the sink and changed your diapers and read to you and sang lullabies so you would go to sleep—this same loving someone would turn on you and hurt you for no good reason in less time than it took to snap your fingers. Oh, God, Lynn, I've never forgotten that . . . things were never the same between us after that . . ."

Lynn reached down and cupped his face in her hands, lifting his head. "Look at me, Bobby. *I don't remember that.* I swear I don't."

"But you still have those three little scars on the side of your right foot."

She stared at him for a moment, expressionless, then, slowly, her eyes widened. "Is *that* how I got those? Huh. I always wondered."

"I'm sorry."

"It's okay."

"I didn't mean to do it. I didn't mean to ruin anything for you, I never wanted you to be afraid of me."

"I know, shh, c'mon . . ." She gave Emerson a quick look: *Get the nurse to give him his shot, okay?*

The detective slipped quietly out the door.

"Take a deep breath, Bobby, come on." She helped him to lie down, then brushed some hair off his sweat-dampened forehead. "You need to sleep, you're still in a lot of pain . . ."

"I shouldn't have done that, I should have always protected you . . ."

"You did, Bobby, you always protected me."

"No child should ever have to experience something like that, ever . . ."

"Shhh, it's okay it's all over now . . ."

"Not for them . . . never for them . . ."

The nurse came in with Emerson and administered the shot. "Here you go, Mr. Londrigan, this'll help with the pain so you can sleep."

"Do you . . ." whispered Robert.

"What Bobby? Do I what?"

"Do you despair?"

The last thing he saw in his mind's eye before sleep claimed him was Ian's smiling face, admiring his birthday present as if it were the grandest thing on the face of the earth, but then it was replaced by the image in the black and white police photograph and a quick mind-sputter and Robert tried to hang on to what consciousness remained to him, because he knew that when he woke up he could never return to the world that he'd known; it had died on the banks of the Licking River along with the sweet-natured, one-eyed giant who cooked good cheese-boogies and could work wonders with a needle and thread. . . .

Chapter Seven

He awoke sometime after four A.M. to find a small basket of flowers on his tray table. There was an envelope stuck between two of the roses. He tried to sit up, couldn't, but managed to reach out and remove the envelope.

Inside was a note, written in Rael's childlike scrawl:

Ian died soon after you left. We had to get rid of his body because Death acts like a homing beacon to the gathering powers of chronos. It's getting bad here, Willy. One of the kids who was born with HIV woke up with the night sweats and can't stop coughing for very long. I don't know how much longer I can keep everything together on my own. I'm sorry you had to find out about Ian like you did. I had no way of knowing that guy was going to find him and take your watch. Ian really loved you. That watch meant the world to him. He was very happy that you liked his cooking. It was the last thing he said before he went to sleep for the last time. Don't let us down, Willy. Please. P.S.—Andrea says hi.

As soon as he finished reading it, the note crumbled to dust in his hands.

He tried to find more tears for his lost friend but could not.

He spread the embroidered handkerchief over his chest, crossed his arms on top of it, and drifted back to sleep humming "In My Room."

Chapter Eight

The next five days—the last ones the man I once was would ever know—passed quickly. From his hospital bed, Robert made a series of phone calls to his lawyer, his stockbroker, and his bank. It was amazing how quickly the detritus of a life could be gathered up and readied for disbursement.

True to his word, Dr. Steinman kept Robert only forty-eight hours before releasing him.

As Steinman was replacing the large bandage on his head with a smaller one, Robert asked him a very odd question. Steinman stopped what he was doing, wrinkled his brow, and said, "I'm not sure, I'd have to look it up."

"Would you mind terribly? I know it's an odd request, but I can't remember which one it was."

Finishing up his work, Steinman handed Robert two written prescriptions and said, "Don't run off, I'll be back in a couple of minutes."

Robert dressed himself in the clothes Lynn had brought over during one of her vigils while he was in the coma. She remembered to bring his wallet along; there was more than enough money for him to take a cab back to the house and not have to bother his sister for a ride. That was good; he didn't know if he could do what had to be done if he saw her again this soon.

Just as the nurse rolled in the wheelchair that would take him down to the lobby, Steinman came back and said, "The right."

"Which one?"

"The little toe on her right foot. How did she lose it?"

Robert shrugged. "I don't remember." He shook Steinman's hand. "You want to see me when?"

"Two weeks. Call my office and make an appointment some-time in the next few days."

"Will do."

"Mr. Londrigan?"

"Yes?"

"I'm really happy that this is all behind you. Now you can get on with your life."

The nurse helped him into the wheelchair, and then took him down to the lobby that was part of a hospital that was part of town which was part of a state that was part of a country that part of a world to that he no longer belonged.

He would never see Dr. Steinman again.

The cab dropped him at the house. He went inside, removed a couple of envelopes from a wall safe in the room that was once his study, located his overnight bag, then grabbed his car keys and went back out into the world to which he no longer be-longed.

His lawyer had all the necessary paperwork ready. Robert signed the forms, thanked his lawyer for getting everything taken care of so quickly, then took his copies of the paperwork and walked the two blocks to his next appointment.

The stockbroker's office was located on the seventh floor of the building that also housed Robert's bank. Everything that he had requested had been taken care of. Robert signed over the stock certificates, handed them to his broker, who then handed him a thick manilla envelope and a sizeable cashier's check, minus commission and various transaction fees. "It's our policy that you be accompanied out of the building by a security guard. The check's made out to you, but there's fifty thousand dollars in cash in that envelope."

"I'm going downstairs to the bank," said Robert.

The broker shrugged. "Even so, you'll have to be accompanied by security."

The guard stayed with Robert all the way down to the bank,

then stood near the lobby exit while Robert went back into the manager's office.

"I have to say, Mr. Londrigan, that we're sorry to be losing your business."

"I have no idea how long I'll be abroad, and I've always been the type who prefers to have his cash on hand when traveling for any prolonged length of time."

The manager nodded in sympathy. "I envy you—a trip around the world. Not that you don't deserve it; not after all that you've been through—which reminds me: Did you receive our flowers and sympathy card?"

"Yes, it was very considerate of you, thanks."

The manager then began placing a series of multipage forms under Robert's hand for his signature here, here, and here. When that was done, he also handed Robert a thick manilla envelope and a sizeable cashier's check.

"You have the necessary information?" asked Robert.

"Yes, sir. All you need to do is sign the check in the manner detailed on these instructions and I'll take care of the rest."

Robert took the check his broker had handed him less than thirty minutes ago and endorsed it accordingly, then handed it to the manager. "I deeply appreciate your keeping this confidential. I know you had to . . . *sidestep* a few rules to help me do this."

"It's easier when it's a question of *depositing* funds." The manager signed a couple of forms, then slipped them into an envelope along with the check. "Done."

Robert shook the manager's hand. "The deposit won't be credited until Monday, right?"

"You have my word."

"Good. If she found out about this before I left on my trip, she'd slap me silly. I figure once I've left, she's stuck with it." He grinned. "But she'll keep it, don't worry about that. My sister is nothing if not practical."

The security guard not only accompanied him out of the

building, but insisted on walking Robert all the way to his car. Robert thanked him, then stuffed all the various envelopes into his overnight bag, zipped it closed, and drove from downtown to the Cedar Hill Mall, where he made several purchases at various stores before dropping nearly ten grand at the electronics warehouse outlet. After that, he stopped for lunch at the Sparta, where he wrote a letter over his cheeseburger—which, while delicious, wasn't nearly as good as Ian's.

After finishing his lunch (and leaving a tip that was three times the cost of the meal), he put the letter in an envelope, sealed it, then drove over to a nearby travel agency and spent close to three thousand dollars.

Then he drove to the 300 block of Granville Street.

A few minutes later, he stood in front of his parked car looking at an empty lot where his late mother-in-law's house should have been standing. A large sign at the front of the property proclaimed THIS LOT FOR SALE. IDEAL FOR HOME BUILDING. He and Denise had been here last year at Thanksgiving, not long before the woman died. Robert had been given a tour of the house. He'd helped Denise remove her mother's effects after the funeral.

Standing here now, he couldn't for the life of him recall what she'd done with the woman's possessions.

"Can I help you?" came a voice.

Robert blinked, then turned to see an old woman with a small pull-cart of groceries standing a few feet away.

"Do you live around here, ma'am?"

"Yessir. Lived here most of my life."

Robert gestured toward the empty lot. "How long has this been here?"

"This? Oh, Lordy, I guess it's been four, five years since that place burned down. Sure do wish that someone would buy it already. Darned lot's an eyesore, you ask me." The old woman stared at him for a moment, then said, "Hey! I seen you on the television. You're that Londrigan fellow, aren't you?"

"Yes, ma'am."

The old woman took his hand. "I want you to know that my Harold and me, we felt really sad about what happened to your wife and little girl."

"Thank you."

"They ever catch the guy that—"

"A couple days ago."

The old woman nodded sadly. "Well, that's something, anyway. You doing okay?"

"I'm getting there."

She looked at him a moment longer before letting go of his hand. "Well, it was a real pleasure meeting you, Mr. Londrigan."

"Thank you for . . . for saying what you did about my wife and little girl."

The old woman said nothing, only nodded sadly once more— Robert suspected that all her nods looked sad these days, even if she was happy as a clam—then continued pulling her little cart along behind her. He had a momentary impulse to offer her a ride but stopped himself from making the offer when he saw her turn left suddenly and walk toward the steps of an old Victorian-style house where an old man—her Harold, no doubt—came out the front door and, despite her objections, took the cart away and lifted it up onto the porch for her. Robert couldn't help noticing that she didn't object *too* much to his assistance; in fact, she seemed to be hiding a smile. *That's my Harold, always looking out for me.*

He cast one more quick glance at the empty lot, then waved at the old couple, even though neither of them saw him do it. As he drove away it occurred to him that he hadn't asked the old woman's name. He hoped he hadn't come across as rude.

He checked his new watch, bought only a few hours ago; it wasn't quite three-thirty yet. Danny should be alone at the house.

Once there, Robert was both disappointed and relieved to see that Lynn's car was gone; only Danny's rusty pickup truck sat in the driveway.

It'll be easier this way, he told himself.

He grabbed the new overnight bag he'd purchased at the mall and double-checked to make sure everything was inside.

Danny looked at first surprised, then worried when he answered the door and saw Robert standing there.

"Sorry to just show up like this," said Robert, "but I knew you got home around this time on Fridays and I wanted to catch you alone."

Seeing the overnight bag, Danny said: "Decide to come over and do your recuperating here, huh? Good. Lynn was worried about you being alone and Eric'll like having—"

"No, that's not it. We need to talk, okay?"

"Sure, anything wrong? Looks like that guy hit you good." He led Robert into the kitchen where the makings for a ham-and-cheese sandwich were spread over the counter. "You hungry? I'm sorry that Eric and me didn't actually see you at the hospital. We were there but you were still unconscious."

"I know. Thanks for all you guys did, by the way."

"Hey, you're family, y'know?" Danny finished making his sandwich, then poured himself a cold glass of root beer and grabbed a bag of potato chips before joining Robert at the kitchen table. "So, what's up?"

For a moment Robert only stared at his brother-in-law, taking the measure of the man.

"I need you to help me with something."

"Sure thing," Danny said between bites. "You need to move something or have those bathroom pipes finally given out on you? I can come over tonight after work and bring my tools."

"No, nothing like that." Robert placed the overnight bag on the table in front of Danny.

"What's this?"

"A gift," replied Robert, removing the three airline tickets from his coat pocket. "I know that things have been tight for you guys for a while now, and that you were hoping to visit your folks in Oregon over Christmas and New Year's—"

"Not gonna happen," said Danny. "I checked plane ticket prices and, man!" He shook his head in the same sad way as the old woman with the pull-cart of groceries. "Too rich for my blood. I gotta get the roof fixed and it looks like we're gonna have to replace the stove. Even with all the extra work the company's had this year and the overtime, there's no way we could afford to—"

"Danny?"

"Yeah?"

"You're a great guy, you work harder than any man I know, and I've always liked you, but sometimes you talk too much." Robert tossed the plane tickets on top of the overnight bag. "Three first-class tickets to Oregon for the holidays. Inside one of the ticket envelopes you'll find a voucher for a rental car that will be waiting for you. All paid for."

Danny reached out and tentatively picked up the tickets. "You're shittin' me?"

"There's that talking too much thing again."

"Sorry." Danny opened the ticket, read it over, then looked in the other two envelopes, as well. "Damn, Robert . . . I don't know what to say."

"You guys have done a lot for me these last weeks and I just wanted to thank you."

"Yeah, okay, cool . . . but you didn't need to do this! Jesus, I mean, I wasn't even pricing first-class tickets. I can't imagine . . . Man, this must've cost you a pretty penny."

Robert grinned. "I can afford it, believe me."

Danny put down the tickets, wiped his hands on his shirt, then rose from the table and came around and gave Robert an awkward but sincere hug. "Thanks, Robert. This really means a lot."

"Finish your sandwich."

Danny laughed, then sat back down. "What's in the bag?"

Gary A. Braunbeck

"In a second. Are you guys going to be home tomorrow morning around ten-thirty?"

"Yeah, why?"

"The tickets aren't the only present I got for you. Please don't go all macho-pride on me, okay? I know you and Lynn have been wanting to get a computer—"

"No way! You didn't!"

Robert nodded. "It's a really, really nice system, and it was on sale so don't go telling me that I can't afford it, because I can. I'm not rubbing your face in anything, okay?"

Danny shrugged. "You're on television. I'm guessing that pays a whole helluva lot better than construction work."

"And you work hard, Danny, and you goddamned well deserve to have things you and your family want. I got no one else to spend my money on now, so the three of you have been elected, okay?"

"Okay." Then: "A computer, huh?"

"With a ton of software and games and a DVD-ROM. It'll be delivered in the morning. I made arrangements with the store manager for a couple of the store's tech people to come over around eleven and hook up the system and get you guys started. They'll show you how to use it, get you set up on the Internet, all that fun stuff." What he failed to mention was that this special Saturday delivery truck would also contain a second computer (this one just for Eric), a new stereo system, a forty-two-inch color television so Danny and Lynn could *really* see the OSU football games, a new VCR and DVD player, about fifty different movies for everyone, a satellite dish (Robert had purchased a five-year contract with the service), a new microwave, refrigerator, stove, and assorted other goodies.

Christmas would come a little early to the Connor house this year. Robert was sorry he wouldn't be able to see their faces.

"Now, the bag," he said. "The third and last part of your gift is in here. This is where I need your help, Danny. I need you to stash this in that steamer trunk of yours and not tell Lynn

300

about it until Monday. Will you do that for me?"

"What is it?"

Robert grinned wider. "That would be telling. Promise me that you'll ask Lynn to come home for lunch on Monday, and that you'll do the same?"

"Sure . . . ?"

"Open it at lunch on Monday. Read the letter inside first. Okay?"

That letter went as follows:

Dear Lynn and Danny,

By now, hopefully, you're enjoying your presents. Don't give me any crap about this either, Lynn. It's my money and I'll do what I damned well please with it. I know this is stuff you guys have needed and wanted, but, sis, you're a little too practical and frugal sometimes—I know you'd probably never buy half this stuff for yourself, so I decided to it for you. Don't even think about returning any of it, dig?

There's a little more to this, though. I know that Danny told you I was going on a trip, and I am. Here's the thing, though; I don't know how long I'm going to be gone. At least a year, probably longer. I'll write and call as often as I can, so don't worry about me. I'm a big boy and will be fine. I've always wanted to take a cruise around the world. Denise and I had talked about doing it sometime. I need to do this not only for myself, but her, as well. For us.

Okay, the money. Remember last year when you borrowed three hundred dollars from me and didn't want Danny to know, so you made arrangements for me to electronically transfer it to your private savings? Well, sis, you never bothered to change that, so I still have access to your savings account. To whit: The envelope in this bag contains around fifty thousand dollars. That's for you and Danny—I've always thought everyone should be able to see that much money in one place at least once in their lives. Spend it, deposit, hand it out to bums in the

301

street—it's yours to do with as you want. Now, if you'll put down this letter and call your bank, you'll discover that your private savings account balance has increased by one hundred thousand dollars. That's Eric's college money. Period, no arguments.

Now for the deed to the house. I have signed ownership over to you and Danny and arranged for all taxes, utilities, etc., to be paid from a separate account that my attorney helped set up. You'll find his card attached to this letter. Call him as soon as you can. The house is paid for, and it's now yours. You guys can move into it, use it for weekend getaways, or sell it—same goes for whatever stuff I leave there. Whatever you decide will be fine with me. I know how much you always loved the place.

No, sis, I haven't crumbled my mental crackers. The last several weeks have shown me what is important in life and what's just window-dressing. This is only money and stuff, that's all. When I come back I'll either get a new place (I'm thinking a condo) or move in with you guys. I'll decide later. I've got time.

Please remember how much I love all of you. I hope now that you and Danny will be able to breathe easier about money. Money is a terrible thing to sacrifice any of your happiness and peace of mind to. If you decide to sell the house, the current market value of it's somewhere around three hundred and seventy-five thousand. If you do decide to sell, then the money from the tax/utility/etc. fund will be given to you. Whatever. I just want for you guys to have a good life. I love you very, very much and will miss you while I'm gone. Please remember to tell Eric about me so he won't forget his uncle.

That's about it. Keep me in your thoughts because all of you will be in mine. I'm sorry that I left so abruptly, but I got a great deal on the trip providing I left this weekend. I'll call you as soon as I can. Be happy.

Bobby

"Okay, the letter first."

"Danny?"

"Yeah?" replied his brother-in-law, looking more and more puzzled.

"Can you keep this a secret until then?"

"Sure thing."

Robert chewed on his lower lip for a moment. "Promise me *you* won't look in here before then?"

"Hey, I know Lynn says that I'm nibby, but I'm not *that* bad. Yes, of course, sure."

"It'd spoil the rest of the surprise if you did."

"I give you my word."

"Good. Here's the thing. I have to leave on a little trip later tonight, so I'm not going to be around when you guys open this. It's very important to me that this be done on Monday, no sooner. You won't let me down, right?"

"You ask me that again and I might take it personally."

"Good enough for me." He rose from the table, reached into his pocket, and pulled out four fifty-dollar bills. "Here."

Danny took the cash, counted it, and said, "Ah, Robert! Come on! You don't need—"

"Yes, I do. Clean yourself up, and when Lynn and Eric get home, take them out for a really nice dinner, then maybe go to the movies or shopping or something. You guys deserve a really great family night out. On me."

Danny stared at him a moment, then slipped the money into the pocket of his greasy jeans. "You sure are some piece of work, Robert."

"Yeah, yeah, yeah—they broke the mold." He made a show of checking his watch. "I gotta scoot. Packing and all that—besides, I don't want to be here when Lynn gets home."

"Yeah, she was a little irritated that you didn't want her to take you home from the hospital."

"She'll get over it." Robert opened the back door, then turned to Danny once again. "You're a fine man, Danny. I'm glad my sister had the good sense to marry you."

"Hear her tell it sometimes, she was suffering a bad fever and hallucinating when she said, 'I do.'"

Robert laughed. "Yeah, well, don't let her fool you. She's crazy about you."

"She'd better be. I'd hate to be this head-over-heels and have it be just my little secret."

"See you later."

"Thank you, Robert. For everything."

Robert winked, closed the door, then got into his car and drove away.

He would never see Danny, Lynn, or his nephew again.

Chapter Nine

In the basement, a new *matryoshka* doll had taken up residence in Denise's work area. This one came from inside the doll that bore Robert's likeness. During his stay in the hospital, his doll had been cut open, and this new one placed within. It showed the face of a man Robert did not recognize. Everything about the likeness was generic: the shape of its face, the color of its hair, the expression on its face, even the clothes it wore. It was the likeness of a man you would pass on the street without a second glance.

It was only as he was setting the doll back down on the table that Robert noticed something like a small scar on the figure's left temple.

He reached up and touched the bandage on the left side of his own head.

He quickly reassembled both sets of dolls, placing one inside the other inside the other inside the other inside the other, then carefully packed them into a box along with all of Denise's art supplies. He placed the box in the trunk of the car, then went back inside and sprinkled kitty treats inside the two cat-carriers he'd purchased earlier that day. Tasha and The Winnie sniffed around the carriers, not sure what to make of them, then, eventually, the lure of the treats was too much and each chose a carrier for itself. He'd also purchased two very comfy-looking pillows and placed one inside each carrier. He wanted the cats to be comfortable for the trip. It was important that they get used to the carriers and pillows. He had a feeling that when it happened, it was going to happen very, very quickly.

His guess proved to be correct.

But before his last hours as a part of humanity unfolded, there was only waiting.

Friday night: a pizza and several DVD movies, then some painkillers and a little sleep.

Saturday morning: cartoons and Coco Wheats, something he hadn't done in years. Most of the programming struck him as sloppy and greedy—they weren't so much cartoons as badly animated thirty-minute commercials for action figures available at a department store near you. Almost on the verge of giving up, he flipped around one last time and came across a channel that was running cartoons from his childhood: *The Groovy Ghoulies*, *Scooby-Doo*, *Spider-Man* (the good one, with that great theme song, which Robert found himself singing along with), and, of course, the original *Johnny Quest*. For a couple of hours, he was six years old again, and it was great.

The waiting continued.

Saturday afternoon: a Robert Mitchum double feature on AMC (*Night of the Hunter* and *The Friends of Eddie Coyle*, two of Bob's best), then more painkillers and a nap. He heard the phone ringing at several points as he drifted in and out of sleep (no doubt Lynn calling to see if he'd changed his mind about the trip so she could yell at him) and for a moment was gripped by panic when he remembered that Lynn had an extra set of keys and might very well come over and let herself in, but then dismissed the idea. She was probably too busy trying to pull Eric and Danny off the ceiling when they saw all the toys that had been delivered that morning.

He slept, then awakened, and waited.

Saturday night: leftover pizza and a Kurt Vonnegut short story collection. Robert chuckled throughout, and was touched, and given some food for thought. Old Kurt never let him down.

He decided then to pack all his Vonnegut books for the trip, as well as his Stephen King and Carson McCullers and Jonathan Carroll and Russell Banks and Mark Twain and, before he realized it, it was two-thirty in the morning and he'd packed up all the books in the house.

It took him four trips to load the books and few records and CDs he'd decided to bring (*One Foot in History* being the first music he grabbed). He was impressed with how much trunk space the car actually had. There were six boxes there, and room for three midsized boxes more . . . or two bigger ones.

He filled one midsized box with the files from Denise's cabinet and loaded it, as well. Something told him that it would not be a good idea to leave those behind.

He came in through the back door after the last load and washed his hands, then grabbed a soda from the refrigerator and sat down at the kitchen table with a peanut butter sandwich. His head was starting to throb again but he held off on taking any more painkillers.

He sat in silence for a few moments, closing his eyes and trying to relax. He drifted off for a minute or two but did not actually fall asleep.

The sound of a key being slipped into the front door lock startled him to full, anxious consciousness. He looked at the clock: one fifty-five A.M. Jesus H! Lynn had finally decided to come over and see if he *had* actually left. She'd waited until Danny and Eric were asleep and then snuck out.

Robert jumped to his feet and turned off the kitchen light,

then pressed himself against a shadowed wall and held his breath.

The door opened, closed, and was locked again.

Soft footsteps crossed the entryway and came into the living room.

He listened, and could clearly hear the sound of Lynn's breathing as she sighed, walked around the room, then took off her coat and sat in his chair.

Robert moved slowly and quietly to the kitchen doorway.

He could see the back of her head . . . but the hair was the wrong color. It was too dark to be Lynn.

Then he caught a whiff of the perfume the woman wore, and though it wasn't Lynn's perfume it was, nonetheless, one whose scent he recognized from long ago.

He walked into the living room and came around the front of the chair.

She was thumbing through the current issue of *Columbus Monthly*. "You always did take a really great picture, Rob."

Rob. Only one girl had ever called him that—because, she said, he reminded her of Dick Van Dyke and she could do a mean Mary Tyler Moore as Laura Petrie; God, how many times had she pulled an "Oh, *Ro-o-ob!*" on him while they were dating?

Cathy Pope looked up at him and smiled. For a girl who'd been in her grave for over twenty years, she still had a smile that could melt him. "Hi, Robert."

"Hello."

"Did you see me on the bus that day?"

"Yes. You blew me a kiss."

She put down the magazine and stood up. In high school they'd been roughly the same height; now Robert had a good three inches and nearly as many decades on her.

She put her arms around his neck, leaned up on tiptoe, and kissed him. "Miss me?"

"Who are you?"

"You know *who* I am. I think maybe there's another question you wanted to ask instead."

Robert pulled her arms from around his neck and stepped back. "What are you?"

"Horny as all get out. I'm still a virgin, remember?"

Robert began backing away from her, suddenly terrified. "What happens now?"

"Am I still the same, Rob?"

"Yes . . ."

She moved toward him. "Look closer. Am I *really?*"

He examined her face as part of his mind flipped back to her photo in his high school yearbook, as well as her *matryoshka* likeness.

"God," he whispered, then began to touch her cheek but pulled back his hand at the last moment.

Most of her was still the Cathy Pope that he had loved and dreamed of, but something about her face . . . its size was smaller, her cheekbones a tad sharper, the point of her nose harsher, and . . . and . . . what was it?

"Your freckles," he said. "What happened to your freckles?"

"Damn it!" she snapped, turning away and pacing back and forth. "Damn it, I *knew* there was something missing! I mean, the nose and the cheekbones and all that, minor stuff—did you notice my lips are fuller than when you knew me?—but, Christ! How do you forget something like all those freckles?"

"Your eyes are a different color, too."

She threw her hands in the air. "Terrific! Anything else?"

"No. You look . . ." He shook his head. "You're still just as pretty as I remember."

She stopped her pacing and smiled at him. "Good. I wanted to look pretty for you. Pretty is important."

"Not really."

"Like hell it isn't."

"Like hell it *is*. Pretty is an illusion. It took me most of my life to learn that."

She froze. "Do you mean that? Do you really mean that?"

He nodded.

Her wrong-colored eyes glistened with pride. "That's wonderful, Robert. You don't know how happy that's going to make—" She cut off the words. "Come on, then. Let's get the cats in their carriers."

Tasha and The Winnie were already there, both of them curled up on their respective pillows and sleeping warmly. Robert fastened the door to Tasha's carrier, Cathy took care of The Winnie's.

"Do you have everything you want to take with you?" she asked.

"Yes."

"Are you certain? Once you leave, you can't come back. Ever."

"I'm certain."

Cathy looked around. "This is a really beautiful house, Rob. If I'd've lived, I would have wanted us to get married and live in a house just like this." She wiped something from her eye and picked up The Winnie's carrier. "Let's go."

Chapter Ten

She gave him directions as he drove. It wasn't until they turned off Sharon Valley Road, took a couple of side streets, and were passing Weathervane Playhouse that he realized where they were heading.

"We're going to Utica, aren't we?"

Cathy nodded. "Ye Olde Mill. Best ice cream in the known universe."

"Why there?"

"Because," she said, looking back to check on the cats, "it

was the only old college hangout of yours that you ever shared with Denise."

It was everything Robert could do to get the next words out: "Is she waiting there?"

Cathy checked Robert's watch. "All I know is that's where I'm supposed to take you."

Fifteen minutes later they pulled onto the entrance path to the Mill grounds. Robert eased down on the brake as the car descended the steep drive, then put it in park a few feet in front of the locked gate.

Looking over his shoulder and out the rear window, he said, "I don't know how I'll explain this if a cop drives by and spots us. A thirty-nine-year-old man parked with a high school girl at two-thirty in the morning."

"You're still thinking in *chronos* terms, Rob. No car—police or otherwise—is going to drive down this road until a little before six A.M."

"How do you know this?"

"Because I looked through one of the places where the walls aren't squared, okay?"

"Okay."

She took off her seat belt and moved closer to him. "Will you put your arm around me?"

He did. She laid her head against his shoulder and place a hand on his chest. "God, Rob, your heart's beating a mile a minute."

"I'm scared."

"There's no need to be." She rubbed his chest. "What a wonder the flow of blood is, the feel of life pulsing through your body, each cell remembering everything that makes you specifically yourself. When you stop to think that the probability of any one of us being here in this form at this time is so *small* . . . it's a wonder people don't stumble around in a daze of wonder. We're all alive against stupendous odds of genetics and infinitely outnumbered by the alternates who might have taken our place if things had turned out differently." She pulled back and looked at him, her eyes full of fire. He remembered how once that fire had kept his young heart beating.

"Why don't people realize," said Cathy, "how amazing they are? To live as they do, catching electrons at the moments of their excitement by solar photons, swiping the energy released at the moment of each jump, and storing it up in intricate loops for themselves! Humanity violates probability simply by its physical nature. Somebody should sit everyone down and explain to them how effing *random* matter is, and how statistically improbable it is that *just one* of them exists at all, let alone billions of them . . . and that people have survived for so many thousands of years in this improbable form without drifting back into randomness is nearly a mathematical impossibility." She lay back against his chest, holding him.

"Every one of them is a self-contained, free-standing individual, completely original, singled out by specific protein configurations at the surface of the cells, or whorls in the skin of the fingertips, or even a special mixture of fragrances only the body can produce. Each one of them is one in five billion, as unique and majestic as a snowflake. You'd think they'd never stop dancing."

Robert remained silent, content to hold her and fill himself with her scents.

"Sorry about all the Rael-isms," she whispered. Then: "Not to change the subject, but to change the subject—we never did go parking like this when we were in high school, did we?"

"No."

"Ah, well . . . this is nice now, isn't it?"

"It sure is."

She took his hand in hers and kissed its palm. "Would you have married me if I'd lived?"

"I don't know, Cathy. Maybe. We were so young."

"Maybe you were . . ." She began to tremble.

He pulled back and looked at her. "What's the matter?"

311

She pulled her hand up to her face. "I forgot for a minute."

"What? What did you forget?"

She leaned forward and kissed him on the lips; deeply, moistly, lovingly. "I forgot that two of us can't be in the same place at the same time. She doesn't have the strength for that." She kissed him again, more quickly this time. "I'm sorry about this, Rob, but you have to be the one to do it."

"To do what? Cathy, please, tell me what's going on, what happened to your—"

She pressed his fingers against her face.

Her skull collapsed inward almost instantly, followed by her shoulders, torso, arms, and legs. The sound was so dry, paper cups tumbling in the wind, then being gently crushed under a sneakered foot.

Within moments, Robert was sitting next to a pile of dust and empty clothes.

He tried to turn his head away but his eyes were locked on the sight.

When he was finally able to compose himself, he reached down, turned the key, started the car, and turned on the headlights.

She appeared in the beams like an image in a time-lapsed photograph.

She looked so much older than she had when he'd passed her downtown; older even than when he'd awakened from what he thought was a dream to see her riding him in bed. Looking at least seventeen now, she'd dyed her hair black, and was thinner and pale-skinned in her Goth-chick outfit, black leather and lace and silver metal from neck to ankle; her hose were fashionably torn and her lipstick was dark as a bruise, just like her eye makeup and fingernails. Around her neck hung a bright silver cross on a heavy chain, and around her wrists were black leather bracelets dotted with several small metal spikes. Her left biceps was tattooed with a coil of barbed wire that encircled the flesh there, and she sported a nose ring on the left side from which hung a thin chain that connected to another silver ring that dangled from her pierced left ear.

She came around to the passenger side of the car and opened the door. A wind pulled at the ashes inside, swirling them around her. The ashes fell on her skin and were immediately absorbed. She closed her eyes and smiled as this happened, sighing as if a lover were softly kissing her neck.

"Ah . . . that's a little better." She opened her eyes, smiled at him, then climbed in, tossing Cathy's clothes onto the floor behind the seat. "Don't gawk at me like that. I think this is a cool look." She leaned out the door and whistled. Suzy came running up to the car (or executing the high-speed waddle that was her chubby basset hound version of a run), leapt into the girl's lap, slobbered all over her face, then jumped into the backseat between the cat carriers.

Neither Tasha nor The Winnie was disturbed in its slumber.

Robert stared at the nose ring and the chain that led to the girl's ear.

"I didn't know if you'd like this or not," she said. "Judging from the look on your face . . ." She removed the nose ring and chain. "Better?"

"Yes," said Robert.

She shrugged. "In order to blend in, you've got to be either generic to the bone or so effing outlandish that people see you without really looking. If anyone were to see us, all they'll remember about me is the pale skin and black leather and this cross."

"Don't you *know* whether or not we'll be seen? I mean, the places where the walls aren't squared and—"

She shook her head. "That ended with Cathy. At least for a while. For the next few hours, we have to deal with *chronos* head-on and all by our lonesomes." Her expression became grave. "She's very sick and very weak."

"Denise?"

"Yes."

313

"Then are you Emily?"

She smiled. "You can call me by Rael's nickname, Persephone, though I prefer my own version of the name, Sephera. It sounds like 'sapphire.' "

"Are you my daughter?"

Sephera played with a large silver ring on one of the fingers of her left hand.

"Are you going to answer my question?"

"It's not as simple as a 'yes' or 'no,' so I'd rather not answer it right now. Later. I promise."

She continued playing with her ring. As she did, Robert saw that her right hand was missing its ring finger. He held her right hand up between them and looked more closely. The finger had been severed at the knuckle, leaving a pinkish white stump of scar tissue that looked several weeks old.

"What happened?" he asked.

"My parents."

Robert felt his stomach tighten. "They did this to you?"

Sephera pulled her hand away. "We need to get going. Please."

Robert started the car and backed slowly up the driveway and into the road. "Which way?"

"Left."

As he drove, Robert's mind filled to bursting with questions upon questions, each one seeming to hold a seed from which the next one blossomed. Since Sephera wasn't volunteering much, he decided to take a chance and ask her a few more things.

"Look, I understand that there's a need to get back to Rael and the others—"

"There are a couple of more urgent things we need to take care of first."

"Will you please tell me what?"

She blinked, exhaled anxiously, gave her silver ring one last twist, and said: "We're . . . I mean, Denise is pregnant."

314

Robert was surprised he didn't lose control of the car and wrap them around a telephone pole. "How is that possible? I haven't . . . I mean, she's . . . I don't—"

"So what I'm hearing is how can *she* be pregnant when I'm the one who had sex with you?—and by the way, I'm sorry about hitting you with the lamp. You weren't supposed to come awake and you scared the hell out of me and the lamp was the first thing I saw and . . . and I didn't mean to hit you so hard. I could have killed you." She turned her face toward him. "Forgive me?"

"Of course."

"If it helps, I know a lot about acupressure and herbal remedies for pain. Once your meds run out, I can help a lot. I can help you *instead* of having to take the meds, if you want."

Robert's mind sputtered, then he laughed softly.

"What?" said Sephera.

"That's very good."

She parted her hands in front of her, shaking her head. "Okay, I must've wandered off the highway somewhere—*what's* very good?"

Robert went with it, a bit of the banal, an old argument he and Denise used to have, to act as a final thread holding him together; his last defense against fully accepting that he lived in a physical form that statistically should not have existed, the drowning victim's last fighting gasp before succumbing to randomness. "The evasion tactic. Denise used it on me all the time—she was a lot more subtle, which is why it took so long for me to catch on to it, but even then she still managed to get it by me more often than not. I ask a question about something she doesn't want to talk about, so in the midst of *appearing* to answer, she introduces some item or incident that has close ties to the original subject—so much so that for a few moments I start to think that *it's* what I'd asked about . . . and by the time I realize I've been misdirected, we're deep into a conversation on the red-herring subject and my original question seems a little fuzzy and distant and not worth repeating."

"So all women are manipulative?"

"*Again,* very nice try. No, all women aren't manipulative, but Denise could be when she wanted to avoid a subject, just as I can be manipulative, just like you were manipulative when you made that slick misdirection about hitting me with the lamp, which led to your telling me about you expertise with acupressure and herbs, which was supposed to make me ask more questions about your healing abilities, which was supposed to make me forget the original question, which I didn't: How can Denise be pregnant when you're the one who—"

"Turn right."

Robert almost missed the little side street but managed to make the turn before it was too late.

"Slow down," said Sephera. "Okay, pull over here and turn off your lights but don't shut off the engine; I'll be damned if I'm going to freeze my ass off while you're gone."

They were parked near a grade school playground.

Robert rubbed his eyes. "What now?"

"You can't see it from here, but if you walk across this section of the playground and go right, there's a small cluster of picnic tables where the kids eat their lunch. Go there."

"And . . . ?"

She played with her ring again. "You'll figure it out soon enough."

"Don't try this bullshit with me, please? I had enough of it with Rael and—"

Sephera suddenly and violently doubled over, pulling her knees up toward her chest and quietly shrieking. Robert moved toward her and placed a hand on her back. She was soaked in sweat.

"What's wrong?" he pleaded. "Is there anything I can—"

"*Shut up!*" She crossed her arms over her middle and began to rock gently back and forth, pulling in deep, slow, steady breaths as she leaned forward, releasing them as she pulled back. "Put your . . . your hand on the back of my neck."

He did as she instructed.

"Okay . . . now, put your thumb behind my ear so its tip presses against the earlobe . . . good . . . stick your index finger straight up so it's right against the base of my skull . . . a little more to the right . . . okay, now . . . imagine that you're trying to press the tip of your index finger against your thumb . . . and *squeeze*.

"Now . . . release . . . squeeze again . . . release . . . oh, yeah, that's it, again . . . again . . . once more, really hard this time . . . oh, yes. . . . okay, now . . . keep that hand right where it is, and press your other hand against the small of my back . . . yeah, just like that . . . okay, okay . . ." A wave of pain, less severe, it seemed, than the first, washed through her and she shuddered. ". . . Push down toward the seat, then pull that hand up again, up, down, no more pressure than that, good . . . now do both at the same time, squeeze, push down, squeeze, push up . . . there you go, feel that rhythm? Keep going, a little more . . . wow, that feels nice . . . just a little bit longer . . . again . . . o-kay." She pulled his hands away and sat straight up, the tension and pain dissolving, it seemed, into the heavy sheen of perspiration that made her flesh glow. "Not bad for your first time."

"Are you all right?"

She smiled slightly, began to shake her head, then gave a nod instead. "As good as I can be under the circumstances." She placed a very moist palm against his cheek. "I'm not trying to play Rael's head games with you, all right? It's taken me a very long time to figure out just how to explain everything to you and . . ." She winced a little as a small aftershock of the attack rippled through her body. "And you have to trust me, Robert, please? I promise you you'll understand everything by the time the sun comes up. Now, please, go over to the picnic tables."

He stared into her eyes for a moment, then—on impulse—kissed her cheek and sprinted over to the playground, past the monkey bars and teeter-totters and merry-go-round, turned right and saw the picnic tables—

—and the figure that sat very still on a wooden bench just to the left.

He walked slowly toward her. The diffuse glow of a security light at the far end of the school building held her half in the light, half in shadow, but even if he hadn't been able to see her clearly, the regal, almost arrogant way she sat would have betrayed her.

He stood before a vacant-eyed Amy Wilder and stared at her. She was still dressed in the same absurd Joan Crawford outfit that she'd worn at the cemetery when she'd handed him the note in Denise's handwriting.

He looked over his shoulder, half expecting to see Sephera walking toward him, but then the ghost-echo of Cathy's voice returned to him: . . . *Two of us can't be in the same place at the same time.*

He looked again at the mannequin-still woman on the bench, then at his own hand.

I'm sorry about this, Rob, but you have to be the one to do it.

He remembered the way Rael had taken hold of his hand down in Chiaroscuro and pressed it against the body of the woman from the bus, as if touching her were something Rael himself wasn't supposed to do.

He reached out and brushed his fingers across Amy's face.

Her skull collapsed inward with the same sick-making dry sounds the others had made, her clothing dropping into a heap as the rest of her hollow body disintegrated.

Robert stepped back as the night wind stirred, cold and steady. The dust swirled upward from Amy's clothing and twisted in the wind, a funnel cloud no bigger than Robert's forearm; it danced and twirled on the breeze and then—so quickly that he barely had time for his mind to register what was happening—came right at his face, was in his eyes, nose, and mouth; he tried to wave it away but that did no good. He was momentarily blinded by the dust in his eyes until it mixed with tears it had caused, ran down his cheeks, and was absorbed into his skin. The dust that he had inhaled through his nose mixed with that choking his throat and he staggered backward into one of the picnic tables, tripped over a leg, and fell back-first onto the ground.

The remaining dust followed him down.

He nearly lost consciousness from the lack of air, but as quickly as the dust had choked him, it began to *strengthen* his breathing, mixing with the frosty night air as he filled his lungs deeper and more fully than he had in years, feeling decades of damage from cigarette smoking dissolve away as the lung tissue was rejuvenated, and as he pulled in yet another deep, crisp, full breath, a breath as strong and healthy as the one he breathed the second after he was born, he rolled onto his side, pulled his knees up toward his chest, and began to cry.

A few moments later he felt Sephera's hand touch his cheek. He tried to turn over but it seemed his entire body was gripped in the midst of a metamorphosis; he could *feel* himself physically altering from within: muscles, cartilage, bone, tissues, everything was changing, strengthening, healing.

"Shhh," whispered Sephera, stroking his brow. "Just lie still and let it happen, there, just let it happen, breathe in, hold it, now let it out slowly . . . that's right . . . shhh, there . . . there . . ."

He could hear little pops and cracks issuing from deep inside his body, could feel his muscles spasming, cramping, expanding, then relaxing into their new and better shape.

He had no idea how long it took, only that when he at last had the strength to sit up he no longer felt like the same man. He looked at his hands and saw that the few dim liver spots that had begun appearing on them a couple of years ago were gone. The flesh was no longer as deeply lined as it had been. He felt his chest, his arms, his face. The shape of him did not feel all that different than before, but what existed *within* that shape . . . dear God, he was changed.

As was Sephera. The seventeen-year-old girl he'd left back in the car was now a young woman of twenty-one. Some of her clothing now strained against the new fullness of her body.

He reached out with an unsteady hand and gripped her arm. "Do I look any different to you?" Even his voice had changed; nothing dramatic, but its timbre was stronger, deeper, and more mellifluous; it was the voice he'd had ten, fifteen years ago, before cigarette smoke and alcohol had harshened it.

"You look pretty much the same," she said. "A lot of the gray is gone from around your hair and you've already seen that the liver spots have disappeared. The scar on your nose isn't quite as noticeable; were you to remove that bandage from your head, the wound wouldn't be as severe—but don't take it off, okay? It would still bleed if you messed with it. The stitches have to dissolve, remember?"

"Yeah . . ." He looked back at the pile empty clothes on the bench, then held Sephera's damaged hand up between them, transfixed by the stump of her missing finger.

"That missing finger became my parents, the people you saw walking with me downtown. I had to cut it in half in order to make the two of them. Physically, their forms are much more fragile than Amy's or Cathy's. Cathy was a wild card. Denise took a big chance with her—that's why she wasn't quite the way you remembered her . . . the missing freckles were a stupid mistake—but you still needed convincing, and she thought Cathy would be enough of a shock to bring you around. She didn't count on just how deep *chronos* had its hooks in you."

"But how—"

Sephera placed a finger against his lips, helped him to his feet, and began guiding him back toward the playground. "Cathy was recreated based on Denise's memory of what she looked like when you knew her in high school. It's the only time Denise has had to repeat herself."

"*Repeat . . . ?*"

Sephera's eyes glistened as she spoke, her words coming out in a rapid, intense cadence: "Before Amy Wilder there was Debra Jamison; before Debra was Linda McDonald, the computer technician; before Linda was Tammy Franks, the art gallery manager; before Tammy was Vanessa Long, the legal secretary you met at a Buster Keaton film festival; before Vanessa was Penny Duffy, who you dated a few weeks before graduating from college; before her was . . . You wouldn't remember the names because most of them were one-nighters, women you met in bars or at concerts or football games and then fell into bed with . . . but not all of the women were part of the progression. That woman who came at the end of your boozing days, that thirty-five-year-old, the one you woke up with in the middle of your sophomore year in college and couldn't remember her name, you have only yourself to blame for that . . . but before college was Cathy, and it doesn't stop there, Robert, not by a long shot . . ."

Sensing that he was still shaken from the metamorphosis, Sephera helped him to sit on the merry-go-round, then—as his weight and the night wind set it to slowly turning clockwise—proceeded to list the names of nearly every girl Robert had been involved with before Cathy; short-lived romances with girlfriends in ninth and eighth grades who let him get to second base, girls from sixth and seventh grade who liked to hold hands and maybe kiss once in a while, Sephera knew all of their names, what they looked like, how Robert had met them, and as he listened she guided him down through the years, through all the women and girls who had at some point staked out a claim on part of his heart, however briefly (he'd forgotten all about Tracy O'Rourke, the east-end girl who was the first to ever stick her tongue in his mouth), ending, at last, with Yvonne Carlson, who at age eleven was the awe inspiring paramount of femininity to eight-year-old Robert (forget that she never wore a dress and was missing a couple of lower teeth and cussed when there weren't any adults around and was a better baseball player than any boys in the neighborhood); she was Robert's very first and, until Denise, sweetest kiss, the kiss that all others had to measure up to throughout the rest of his childhood and teenage years.

The merry-go-round came to a stop. Robert stared up at Sephera and whispered, "Were all of them . . . all of *you* . . . an outgrowth of the one who came before?"

"Not at first, no. Do you remember when you sometimes went as long as two years before getting involved with a woman? That's when Denise returned to Chiaroscuro so she and Rael could replenish their strength. After a while, it became more difficult for her to make that journey back and forth. About ten years ago, right after Linda McDonald, Denise decided to hide herself from Rael and stay in this world until the two of you could be one.

"When you first met her, when you were a child and she was whole and chose you, it was a simple matter of a finger or toe, a digit here and there. But God has a nasty sense of humor, especially where the Hallowers are concerned, and those pieces did not grow back. As a result, over the years she's become less and less—when no fingers remained on her left hand, she cut it off; when no toes remained on either foot, she cut those off, as well, using them to grow the women who moved in and out of your life, each of them a direct outgrowth of Denise, each carrying the knowledge of you that had been gathered by those who came before. Though each new outgrowth took care to fit in to this world, they remained connected to Denise; what they experienced, she experienced; when they wept, the tears were Denise's, as well; when they made love with you, Denise savored every delicious, life-affirming moment." Sephera smiled and touched her chest. "I carry inside me the memory of nearly every romantic experience you've shared with a woman. If we were to make love right here, right now, I know all the things you like, I know every way to please you. If you were to be grieving, or frightened, or uncertain or sad, I know exactly, *precisely* how to ease and comfort you; heart, mind, body, and spirit. I know all they knew, and Denise knows even more than she has shared.

"There were other men each of these women knew before coming to you, that was necessary in order to learn the ways of a man; his prejudices and fears, his dreams, his pettiness, his grandeur, his strengths and weaknesses, all of the tender nuances, the infuriating behaviors, every last endearing, perplexing, magnificent, selfish, contradictory, *human* imperfection that all men share and that gives them their worth. But always, they ended with you, for you were their goal. They learned from the other men as you learned from those women—and there were several—who *were not* an outgrowth of Denise. But each time, as you met these women created from Denise, the two of you came *that much* closer to achieving and *sustaining* the one thing that has eluded most of the human race since its first learned to stand upright.

"True Love. Denise would settle for nothing less for the two of you. Now I can understand why. You're a much better man than you give yourself credit for." She bent over and kissed Robert softly on the lips, smiled, then gave the merry-go-round a counterclockwise push. "Denise had to extend the reach of her powers over the last ten or so years, as the *chronos* flies. Call it a lack of raw materials, if you will. The number of outgrowths she could produce was never infinite from the beginning, but it's grown dangerously small now. She's had no choice but to pass on a little bit of her Hallower's power to those of us you've know this last decade—that's what I absorbed with Cathy's ashes, that's what entered you when you breathed in Amy's remains: a bit of immortality. Sort of the ultimate recycling program.

"So, Penny Duffy cuts off her little toe to make Vanessa Long; Vanessa cuts off her thumb to create Tammy Franks; Tammy severs a digit from her foot and from that grows Linda McDonald, whose ring finger became Debra Jamison, whose toe then formed Amy Wilder. But with this last cycle of creation, the limits of Denise's power started making themselves known. If Amy had not been wearing her gloves, you would have seen that the pinkie was missing from her right hand. She cut it off in order to create Cathy Number Two, and Cathy Number Two cut off one of her toes to make the woman you met on the bus . . . but it ended there. Denise's power could not extend itself any further. She knew, after the woman on the bus, that any outgrowth she created from what was left of her body would only be able to repeat the process once; that's all she had the strength for."

Robert swallowed with great difficulty, talking over his shoulder as the image of Sephera spun slowly past. "Then my *wife* . . . she was an outgrowth of who?"

"The woman you married was made from what remained of Denise's left arm between the elbow and shoulder. Your wife's missing toe was used to create the woman she introduced to you as being her mother—she had to do that because you insisted on meeting your mother-in-law; after all, the woman wasn't at the wedding, was she? 'Mom's' death and funeral were simply window dressing to get her out of the way and out of your lives so Denise wouldn't have to spend any more strength than absolutely necessary."

The merry-go-round again slowed to a stop. Sephera gripped the safety rails and leaned in until her face was only a few inches from Robert's. "That woman, your wife, was the last *direct* outgrowth of herself that Denise could create. Unlike the others, she was physically human, inside and out—veins, organs, bodily functions, all of it. She was *supposed* to be the last in line, the Vessel of Becoming. Everything that's happened since—me, creating my window-dressing parents from my finger, and now our—*Denise's*—new pregnancy *should not* have happened. Why do you think your wife kept having miscarriages? She was only an extension of Denise; *Denise* should have been the one to become pregnant. That's how she knew her powers were weakening, because the transference of memories and knowledge and all physical phenomena between her and the outgrowth that was your wife became more intermittent. She had to fight tooth and nail for what little control she *did* have. Finally, she became so weak only the most tenuous of connections could be sustained. That's when your wife became pregnant with me. But the physical process of human birth has been and always will be forbidden knowledge to the angels, and that's why your wife died."

"But you," said Robert. "You *came back!* I held your dead body in my arms. I *buried* you, for chrissakes!"

"But before Rael took me, you gave me part of yourself, remember?"

The image of that single globule of blood dripping from his nose and into her open chest cavity replayed itself in his mind. "Yes . . ."

"If that hadn't happened, if Dr. Steinman had not taken you down to the morgue . . . I would have been truly dead, and there would be no hope for Denise or Rael or the children of Chiaroscuro now. One drop of grieving blood, Robert, one drop that held your longing, your hopes, your love. But Rael had to be certain that the process had taken hold, that's why he returned me to you. Remember what he said about the power of Home? It's true, sentimental as it may sound." Holding tightly to his hand, she whispered, "You can't imagine the scope of the suffering that would have occurred if you had just left that hospital without saying good-bye."

Remembering Joseph Alan Connor and the faces of the children of Chiaroscuro, Robert said, "I think you're wrong there."

They began walking toward the car. Robert noticed that there were no emissions from the tailpipe and for a second feared that the car had either stalled out or run out of gas.

"I turned it off before coming after you," said Sephera, holding up the keys. "We can't afford to waste gas, not with all the traveling we've got ahead tonight."

They got back into the car and started driving back toward town. Sephera gave Robert an address in the Morgan Manor area, one of Cedar Hill's richest housing developments. Robert decided to take the I-70 on-ramp; it would cut their traveling time in half.

"Why do you suppose it happened?" he asked Sephera. "I mean, if Denise—if *my wife*—wasn't supposed to get pregnant with you, then . . . how? Why?"

"I'm not sure, but my best guess is that heaven has momentarily turned its back on us—God *does* blink from time to time. I have no idea how long it might be before someone figures out that the last two Hallowers have managed to survive and are laying groundwork for the race to be reborn, so Rael and the children of Chiaroscuro aren't the only ones living on borrowed time."

"But how . . . how can you be certain that you'll be protected against . . . *whatever* once Denise and Rael are reunited?"

Sephera shook her head and smiled sadly as she touched Robert's arm. "Because *kairos* is neutral territory. It exists at the place between heaven and hell where the walls aren't quite squared, and neither God nor Satan can trespass there without ruining it for *all* children for the rest of time . . . and the children have to be protected. The balance of Good and Evil in the cosmos must be maintained, and destroying *kairos* would tip the scales in one direction or the other. Believe me when I tell you that neither one of them wants that to happen."

"But Ian *died!*"

"Rael's powers are weakening, as well. He can only hold back *chronos* for so long without Denise. Every force in the universe, from the light of a photon to the cataclysmic blast of a supernova, has a counterpart that enables it to be. It's that way with Denise and Rael's powers, and it's the same with *chronos* and *kairos*; one cannot exist without the other, so both are neutral territory—which, by the way, is one of the big reasons that neither God nor Satan intervenes in human affairs, regardless of what you've been told: Trespassing in *chronos* would be just as destructive as interfering with its counterpart, so humankind has been left to its own devices." She sneered slightly. "And just look where that's gotten it." She gripped his forearm. "It could all come crashing down on our heads before the sun rises, Robert, so you have to promise me something. Swear to me that, regardless of how soul-sick some of it might make you, that you *will not hesitate* to do what has to be done. Will you promise me that?"

"I'll do whatever's necessary, I swear on my life."

"What a coincidence—that happens to be what one second of hesitation will cost you, will cost all of us."

They drove on in silence, save for the purring of the cats and Suzy's wet, comfortable snoring. Robert took the exit to Cherry Valley Road, maneuvered the car through the countless twists and winds there, came to the fork five miles down, and turned left onto Morgan Way. "I've never really been here before," he told Sephera. "You're going to have to guide me."

"Drive toward that house that's under construction and turn right."

As he did, Robert saw the empty lot beside it and thought of his mother-in-law's house.

"How did—"

"Denise's mom, right?"

He was startled by her knowing what he was about to say, then realized that he shouldn't have been. "Yes."

"You know that pad and pen you used to keep by the phone for writing down messages? Did you ever notice how when you removed the top page and began to use the one underneath that the impressions of what you'd written on the previous page were embedded there?"

"That's how I once found a phone number I'd lost. I saw its impression on the new page, so I took a pencil and lightly colored over the area until the number appeared."

Sephera nodded. "There's a physicists' term for the effect but I don't remember what it is. Anyway, that's how your wife was able to take you to a house that had burned down six years before. Just like words written on a piece of paper whose impressions are left on the sheet below it, a structure will leave its impression on the space it once occupied." She shrugged. "Then it's just a matter of—how'd you put it?—'coloring it in.' Or as Rael would say, ' . . . performing a goddamn parlor trick.' " Her imitation of Rael was dead-on, and both she and Robert laughed.

"Can I ask you something else?"

Sephera nodded.

"Why did Denise—why did *my wife* invent such a troubled relationship between her and her mother? Why not just have them be the best of friends?"

"Because you wouldn't have understood a genuinely loving relationship between a parent and a child, having never really known one yourself. It was a way to connect with you.

"Okay, make a left at the stop sign, and go all the way down into that big-ass circular driveway. There are three houses that share it. The one you want is right smack in the middle."

The descent was much steeper than it looked. The carriers slid forward and bumped against the back of the front seat, startling both cats awake. They immediately began to yowl in irritation. Suzy jerked her head up, sniffed the air, then offered a short, phlegmy rasp that was her version of a bark. Sephera turned around, lifted her hand, then whispered, "*Shhhhh*," and slowly brought her hand back down. At once, all three animals fell back asleep.

A large, new-looking Jeep Cherokee sat in the driveway, its front end facing up toward the road. Robert barely had room to park beside it. As he looked around, it quickly became obvious that there was no way in hell he'd be able to turn his car around, which meant having to back the damn thing up that Kilimanjaro of a driveway, which meant that a quick exit wasn't in the cards.

Before he could give voice to any of this, Sephera said, "We need to transfer everything to the Jeep. The keys are under the sun visor on the driver's side and a license and registration are in the glove compartment."

It took them only a few minutes to move everything from the car to the Jeep. Not once did any of the animals stir. As Robert closed the hatch door, an upstairs light came on in the house to the right. He stood there, frozen and afraid to breathe, as a shadow passed by a window, paused, then—just as the light was turned off—pulled back a corner of the curtain.

"I think you've got a nosey neighbor," he whispered to Sephera.

"Yeah, well . . . they're under the impression that me and my family are in the process of just moving in. So far, we haven't struck them as particularly friendly." She took his hand and led him around to the side of the house and up a short set of wooden stairs to a door. Once inside the house, she closed the door and peeked out from behind the curtain. "Shit."

"What is it?"

"The light's back on and now two of them are looking."

"We made almost no noise."

"Doesn't matter. That's not what worries me." She glanced at Robert and made a downward sweeping gesture at her clothes. "The last time they saw me, I was a little girl of twelve and with my parents. They've never seen either of *us* before."

"Do you think they'll call the police?"

"No. If anything they'll call Morgan Security first and have them come out for a look. If the cops have to be called, then the Morgan guys'll do it." She let the curtain drop back into place. "Which gives us roughly twenty minutes. Come on."

She led him through the downstairs of the house. Scattered about were several boxes of various sizes and a baker's half dozen of small furniture pieces: a coffee table, a couple of chairs, a small television set atop a wooden crate, other pieces that made the house look like its new owners were still waiting for the rest of their furniture to arrive.

"How long have you been here?"

"Long enough that I've had no choice but to make my parents interact with the neighbors—nothing too dangerous, a 'hello' in the morning, maybe a conversation about football when they run into each other while taking out the trash, stuff like that. The houses at this end of the development have been around the longest—this place is about twenty years old—and there's not a lot of traffic."

"Is that why you picked this house?"

"That, and because it was the only empty one with an insulated subbasement." They crossed through the living and middle rooms and were now in the kitchen. Sephera opened the refrigerator door, bent down and removed the vegetable drawer, and removed a set of keys that had been taped to the bottom. "Basement door's through there," she said, pointing to an arched doorway. Robert followed her, anxiously looking over his shoulder for the glow of headlights as she unlocked the basement door, turned on a dim stairway light, and gestured for him to follow.

The basement was divided into two sections by a thin paneled wall. Sephera used a second key to open the door there and they entered the room where the washer and dryer would have been. Turning on the single bulb that hung from the middle of the ceiling, she took hold of Robert's hand and squeezed it. "You can feel it, can't you?"

"Yes."

From the moment they'd entered the basement, Robert's entire body—especially his head—had thrummed.

Memory. Ancient and tired. In this place. Deep within it. He knew it. Felt its imprint all around him. Recognized it. Was part of it. Wanted to know it. Be it. It wanted him. Wanted to give to him. The need to merge. Calling. Come. Please. Hurry.

Sephera led him to a third door, unlocked it, and flipped the light switch on the other side. "Remember your promise, Robert. You cannot hesitate one second."

Not waiting for a response, she started down the cement stairs toward the subbasement. Robert followed. To keep himself calm he counted the steps. Nineteen. Nineteen steps that seemed to go on for an eternity, ending at a fourth and final door. Sephera unlocked it, turned the knob, and pushed it open.

The room was surprisingly large, nearly as wide and deep as the entire house. Robert's shoes echoed eerily against the cement floor as he stepped inside. The lights down here were dim but warm, giving the whole place an atmosphere of intense restfulness. It was like the viewing room at the funeral home.

He was positively terrified now. It wasn't so much fear for himself, although that might have been a footnote to the greater terror that threatened to engulf him, but he knew that he was standing in the middle of a great, ancient secret, one that on the physical level wore the shape of the blackest, most mind-crumbling nightmare, something that crushed even the most primitive notions of what constituted humanity.

Lining the walls on both sides of the room were bodies. Some lay on their backs, glassy eyes staring up at the beamed ceiling; others sat with their backs against the rough stone wall, arms and legs akimbo, marionettes whose strings had been cut in middance. These, too, stared out at nothing, unblinking. Some were women, some were teenaged girls, others were children, and all of them were naked. As he moved forward, looking at all the ladies from his life, sweat beading on his forehead and upper lip, it was not so much their nakedness that Robert noticed but their faces: Penny Duffy, Debra Jamison, Linda McDonald, Tracy O'Rourke, Yvonne Carlson, others he recognized but whose names had long ago been forgotten, abandoned with the detritus of youth and its cynicism, drinking, selfishness, and the easy promiscuity of a failed romantic.

At various points between the bodies were metal racks of women's clothes. There was a purple dress that Robert remembered as sliding slowly off a pair of creamy shoulders, a set of children's sneakers whose soles he once saw Yvonne slam into a catcher's gut when she slid into home base during a back-lot baseball game, a thin, off-white blouse that he'd bought for Linda as a birthday present, a pleated beige skirt that Penny Duffy had worn on their first date, jeans and dress slacks, business suits and nightgowns, winter coats and autumn windbreakers, the wardrobe in which love had entered his life and followed him throughout all of his days.

At the far end of the room was a wide folding partition decorated with painted birds resting on summer branches. From behind this came a muted symphony of sounds: whirring, clicking, dripping, buzzing, thumping, and something that sounded like an amplified breeze. To the left of the partition was another group of bodies, these piled haphazardly against and on top of one another. There were children here, and young girls, and women of Robert's age . . . but there the similarity between them and the ladies of his life ended.

Here there were babies with the full breasts of grown women, young girls with vertical mouths on their cheeks, women with fleshy animallike limbs in place of their arms or legs; there were heads with two overlapping faces, torsos with eyes, vaginal cavities that were three times too wide and filled with circular rows of teeth; hands with a dozen fingers; feet that at first glance looked to have been crushed, but on closer examination more resembled hooves; another face that was no face at all, only a hollowed eggshell of skin filled to overflowing with eyes and tongues.

Robert lost track of how long he stood there gaping in revulsion. He lost track of his own body, fully realizing for the first time in his life how impossible and miraculous the human form was, how easily it could be perverted—though perversion was not the intent with these piled bodies. He was now merely a pair of eyes attached to a brain that floated in the oppressive air like a lost balloon whose child-owner cried loudly in the lonely distance. When at last the horror of the sight threatened to send him flying away like a spray of vapor, Sephera touched his arm and he fell back into the cocoon of flesh and tissue and bone that was his body. It was *his* body, wasn't it? Yes—he touched his chest, throat, face; yes, it was his body.

"Early on," whispered Sephera, "Denise had to make the forms from memory. Creation was difficult and painful and the results . . ." She looked at the piles. "The results were horrible. She almost gave up once. These aren't even the worst of the mistakes."

Robert's voice crawled out as if it were afraid of the light. "Where are the rest?"

"Buried or burned. Some were lost on the way to being disposed of. A few years ago, a couple of them turned up in jars of formaldehyde at a carnival freak show. I don't like to think about what kind of person would dig up something like that and then put it on display and charge people to gawk at it. Even mistakes like these deserve to have dignity in death."

Robert nodded, then looked back to the forms of the women he'd known. Tears welled in his eyes but he held them back. "My whole life," he said softly. "She was with me for my whole life."

"She's loved you for your whole life. From the moment you met, she's loved you."

Robert blinked, then cursed silently as a stray tear spilled down his cheek. "God, Sephera, I wish I could remember when I met her."

"She remembers."

"Does that mean *you* remember?"

"Yes. But I promised not to tell." She faced the partition and took a deep breath. Robert locked on her face, looking for a sign, an emotional touchstone, something that would prepare him for what he was about to see, but the look on her face was one of ferocious intensity that said nothing. Or maybe everything.

"Okay, Robert. Time for the formal introduction." She spread her arms, grabbing each end of the partition and folding the halves together.

"Robert Londrigan, meet the love of your life." Her voice cracked on the last two words. She gathered the partition in her arms and carried it off to the side.

Robert stood alone.

There was so much to absorb that comprehension was beyond a simple, all-inclusive glance, so he focused on details, working from the outside in.

To the left were a set of EKG and EEG machines, buzzing and blinking as their black screens displayed waves and lines of green and red. To the right stood a respirator unit, lights blinking, engine whirring, interior pump pounding away. A long, ribbed plastic hose extended from the upper portion of the unit, snaking through the air before splitting into a Y shape; the upper tube ran past two metal IV stands, each of which held two clear plastic bags of solutions varying in colors and density; one bag held a clear liquid, another something that resembled skim milk; the third bag bulged with a semithick substance the color and consistency of gravy; the last and largest bag, now two-thirds empty, held something that looked like jellied blood. The four thin IV tubes followed the path of the respirator tube, all of them emptying into an incubator that leaned at a slight angle against the back wall. Its positioning reminded Robert of those lidless coffins you often saw in movie westerns, propped outside the undertaker's shop, tilted backward so passersby could get a good look at the body of the outlaw inside as the photographer's camera flashed and smoke rose.

Almost without realizing it, he began to move slowly toward the incubator and its occupant.

Inside, the glass walls of the incubator were decorated with copies of the photographs from Denise's files; here was Andrea; next to her, a boy with an impossibly large head; beside this boy was Ian's baby picture, and seeing this pulled Robert's grief dangerously close to the surface, but he refused to cry—not because he didn't miss Ian, but because tears would blur his vision and it was very important to him that he see everything.

In Silent Graves

Taped toward the top of one of the walls, positioned so that the occupant could easily turn its head and read it, was a sheet of paper with a quotation written on it: *Fear not your friends, for they can only betray you; fear not your enemies, for they can only kill you; fear only the indifferent, who allow the killers and betrayers to walk safely on the Earth.*

Inside the incubator was something that bore only the most distant resemblance to a human being. A small light installed over its head glowed down, a grotesque halo illuminating every detail of its body. It hung in the center of the unit from a special harness, swaying slightly. It was naked except for a leather-and-rubber dressing that was fitted to its lower area like a diaper.

It had no legs and only one arm—the right. The stumps pulsated moistly in rhythm with the respirator pump as if they too were breathing, occasionally discharging a few globules of something that looked like a mixture of blood, pus, and water. These discharges dripped down into one of six plastic bowls positioned in a circle around the figure. Each bowl had a little something in it.

Robert moved closer.

Its skin was gray, slack, and pallid, spotted with chafing sores where the diaper and harness worked against it. The small top portion of its head, covered with electrodes, was rounded, smooth, and hairless. Dark veins bulged against the flesh in spiderweb patterns. Its nose jutted out from the rest of its face like a hybrid of snout and beak. Its face began to widen at the cheeks and jaws, then angled back inward to form the sharp, small chin. Part of its lower face was obscured by the medical tape that held the respirator tube in its mucus-gummed mouth. It was only as Robert began to look up into its eyes that the shape of its head found a point of reference within him: It was a diamond.

At first the expression on its face seemed to be that of the damned, forever banished to the bowels of hell to writhe and scream in hideous, unspeakable agony, but as Robert eased toward it he saw that its expression was not one of anguish but

335

relief; a long journey, one filled with terror and sorrow and false hope and little triumphs, a journey that often seemed futile if not doomed, was about to end in grace.

Robert's gaze moved to her crusted eyes, which stared at him in wonder.

"*Denise . . .*" he whispered.

She blinked once, very slowly—so slowly that at first he thought she was falling asleep; but then, as she opened her eyes in exhausting degrees, she began to lift her remaining arm. The tendons popped and the muscles writhed under her skin as she did this, fighting atrophy; Robert imagined the muscles shredding apart like a sheet of dampened tissue paper, and wondered what she was trying to point at.

She did not point; instead, she held out her seven-fingered hand, silently beckoning.

Robert did not hesitate. He stepped forward and took her hand in his.

Its touch. There was something familiar about this, the sensations of her too-many fingers against his flesh, and for a moment he had an absurd thought, familiar, from the dust of the past: *It's a spider made of skin and it's missing a leg.*

And then it returned to him in crystal clarity. He began to tremble. Denise tightened her grip and Robert his. He did not want to let go; in her, beauty and hideousness were intertwined, at once compelling and horrifying, as something as miraculous and terrible and majestic and unknown as her must be. Before him was something that had never before been seen on earth, and he began now to weep. As did she. What passed between them next did so in a series of silent, painful sputters. Tears fell from her eyes, slipped by the second respirator tube that was inserted in her chest, and fell onto her bulging belly. Were absorbed. Drawn in. Like a sponge. Her tears made it shine. Glisten. Moving. Was it love? Transference. Loneliness? He didn't know. She made a sound. Warm. Comforting. Secure. Their child. Inside her. Growing under glistening flesh. Her need. Her memory. Her hand in his. Soft. Smooth. Constant. The flow of blood. The miracle of blood. The mystery of blood. Resonating. Sighing. Vibrating. Within her. Inside him. Within them. The sound of her loneliness. The taste of his need. The kiss of her desire. To return. To heal and be healed. Her longing. The children. Chiaroscuro. Laughter in the chambers. Their songs. The children. A child. A boy. So young. Above her. His hand. So big. So tender. He remembered. Their meeting. Hello, there. Are you—

—the thought was never finished, because the man I once was nearly vanished at that moment and I nearly took his place, but then—

—a shock like an electric current jolted painfully through Robert's body. He let go of her hand and dropped to his knees, doubled over, and wrapped his arms across his stomach, rocking back and forth, pulling in strained breaths as he tried to force the pain away, away, away. He managed to turn his head and saw that Sephera, too, was on her knees on the floor, arms crossed over her center, rocking.

"Wh-what's happening?" croaked Robert.

"A con . . . contraction," replied Sephera weakly.

It took several moments more before the pain subsided enough for either of them to relax; when it did, Sephera was the first to move, crawling slowly over to Robert's side and rubbing his lower back.

"Better?" she asked.

"Yes."

"I was watching your face when you held her hand." A smile. "You remembered when you met her, didn't you?"

"Yes. Jesus, this hurts."

"Now you know why I got so bitchy in the car earlier."

"Tell me about it."

As the last waves of pain ebbed, they took a few extra moments to steady their breathing. There were no windows in the subbasement, so there was no way either of them could have seen the headlight beams pass across the front of the house as the car marked MORGAN SECURITY SYSTEMS swung around and stopped at the top of the driveway. Two security guards got out and were met by the man from next door, who hurriedly explained how he'd gotten up to use the bathroom and saw Robert's car pull in, how a man and woman he'd never seen before got out, moved some luggage into the Jeep, and then proceeded to break into the house. The security guards told him to go back inside his own house and they'd check it out. After the man left, both guards checked their radios and side arms, then one of them radioed in their location but did not call for backup because they didn't think they were going to need it (guy was probably half asleep and didn't recognize his own goddamn neighbors). They separated for their approach; one went to the side door while the other went around back.

Their car radio crackled a few moments later. The guard at the side door ran back up to answer the call. The dispatcher informed him that, according to Manor records, that particular house was supposed to be empty.

Both the side and back door of the house were unlocked. Flashlights in one hand and firearms in the other, the guards entered.

In the subbasement, Sephera was helping Robert to his feet. "Sure you're okay?"

"Yes, I'm fine," he snapped. Then: "Sorry."

They both looked at Denise.

"Something's wrong, isn't it?" asked Robert.

Sephera slipped her arm through his and squeezed his hand. "She doesn't have enough strength left to finish the two things she wants to do. She can either carry the baby to term or transfer her life force into a different Vessel of Becoming."

"Oh, no . . ."

Sephera turned him to face her. "You know what her choice is, Robert. Close your eyes and think. Somewhere in that torrent of thoughts that she shared with you, she told you which. Think."

He closed his eyes.

Above them, the security guards finished their sweep of the upstairs; finding it empty, they made quick work of searching the downstairs rooms.

Then one of them spotted the open basement door.

Robert replayed everything that Denise had shared with him. And within the torrent, he found her answer.

Later, he would allow his heart to break; for now, there could be no hesitation.

He opened his eyes. Tears ran down his cheeks. "Transference."

Sephera froze, then released her breath. "Okay then."

He touched her cheek. "You?"

She nodded. "It's an odd feeling, being the last in line. C'mon, we've got a lot to do and not much time left. We've been down here for over ten minutes." She led him back to the bodies that lined the walls. "You have to touch all of them. Quickly."

The guards were just finishing their search of the basement proper and walking toward the door to the subbasement stairs.

Robert began with Penny Duffy and made his way down the left wall, crumbling the bodies into dust. As he did, both he and Sephera breathed in the remains and grew more powerful. Some of the flesh-dust wafted over their heads, fell on Denise's body, and was absorbed into her system, giving her a last, small, extra reserve of strength for the final task before her.

It was as he was moving from the left wall to the right (where Sephera's parents had been sitting off to the side so he hadn't see them at first) that the guards began their cautious descent down the nineteen steps that seemed to go on for an eternity.

He crumbled the parents, then Yvonne Carlson, and was just about to lay hands on Tracy O'Rourke's face when the first guard stepped through the door.

In the hours since, when I remember the next ninety seconds,

I try to imagine what it must have looked like from the security guards' point of view; here they were, at four o'clock in the morning, in the subbasement of a house where no one was supposed to be living, facing a man who stood over a basement filled with naked and seemingly dead bodies.

Is it any wonder the reacted as they did?

"Jeezusfuckingchrist!" shouted the first guard, dropping his flashlight and leveling his weapon at Robert's chest. "Hands over your head, now!"

Robert moved away from Tracy O'Rourke and slowly lifted his arms.

"Middle of the room and on your knees. Do it!"

Though both guards had their weapons drawn, it was only the first who was looking at Robert; his partner was staring at the bodies that lined the wall to the right.

Why haven't they seen Sephera? thought Robert as his first knee touched cement. Then he remembered the folded partition she had leaned against the left wall. She was probably hiding behind it, waiting for an opportunity.

"I said *on your knees! Both of them!*"

As Robert's second knee touched the cement and he folded his hands behind his head, the flashlight dropped by the first guard stopped rolling; it now lay less than two feet away from Robert.

The first guard took one step forward, narrowing his eyes as he examined Robert's face. "Holy shit," he whispered. Then, to his partner: "You know who this guy is?"

Not looking away from the bodies, the second guard gave a short, sharp, "No."

"It's that guy from the news . . . Londrigan. Holy shit." He moved forward another half step. "I never would've pegged you for a freak. Take a look at him, man!"

The second guard looked away from the bodies, over Robert's head, and saw the incubator and its occupant.

"*Oh, God!*" he cried out.

His partner looked away for only a second, but it was a second in which Robert did not hesitate. Throwing himself forward and down, he scooped up the flashlight, spun sharply, and hurled it at the first guard's head. He missed the head but managed to make a solid connection to the gun hand. The guard cried out and dropped his gun. The gun discharged into a nearby body. The second guard whirled around at the sound of the shot and that's when Sephera made her move; grabbing the partition on either side, she leapt up holding it over her head, charged forward, and threw it. It sailed across the room in a straight, deadly line, hitting the second guard in the middle of his chest. He too dropped his gun as the momentum of the hit walloped him against the doorway. Robert was on his feet then, bent over, head down, running forward. He slammed the top of his skull into the first guard's stomach and kept going until they were out the door and tumbling onto the cement steps. Behind them, Sephera grabbed up the second guard's pistol, jumped onto the partition that was pinning his legs, and struck the side of his head with the butt of the gun; once, twice. The guard lost consciousness as she was pulling back for a third blow, which she decided against delivering. On the steps, the first guard was trying to get his hand down to his side to grab his stun gun. Robert tried for the hand, couldn't get a grip on it, and so took a fistful of the guard's hair and pulled his head up. The guard twisted underneath him, jerked to the side, and both of them rolled. Robert again pulled on the guard's hair, yanked his head up, and tried to slam it down against one of the steps. The guard freed his stun gun and snapped his hand up. The weapon made a hideous *buzz-snap-buzz* sound that warned Robert what was coming; releasing the guard's head, he twisted himself around and grabbed the hand holding the stun gun. He pulled it up, then slammed it down hard against the edge of the step. Bones cracked and the guard screamed, dropping the weapon. Throwing all his weight into it, Robert rolled on top of the guard, grabbed both sides of his head, and cracked the back of the man's skull against the step; once, twice, three times. The guard's eyes suddenly turned to glass and he went limp. Robert fell backward onto his ass and realized with a profound, sick-making certainty that he had just killed another human being.

"*Fuck!*"

Sephera was in the doorway instantly. "What is it?"

"I j-just . . . I think I killed him. Oh, God, I didn't mean to! I didn't. I w-w-was just trying to knock him out, that's all."

Sephera stepped over Robert and touched two fingers to the side of the guard's neck. "He's dead."

"*Goddammit all to hell!*"

Sephera whirled on him. "Calm down. We don't have time. It was an accident, it couldn't be helped. We'll cry about this later." Pulling him to his feet and pushing him back into the room, she looked down at the second guard. "He's going to have one hell of a headache and probably need stitches."

". . . recognized me," whispered Robert.

"What?"

"The guard I killed. He recognized me. He said my name."

"So what? You're done with this world anyway. It doesn't matter if he recognized you and it matters even less that the other guy's going to tell anyone who'll listen. Get over there and finish the rest of the bodies."

Robert did not so much walk as stumble quickly down the line, brushing his fingers across the faces like a child with a stick in hand rattling it along a picket fence in summer. They crumbled into dust, were breathed in and absorbed, becoming energy.

"What about those?" asked Robert, pointing to the piles of mistakes.

"We have to leave them. I'd hoped there'd be time to dispose of them properly but that's not going to be possible."

Robert elbowed past her and began touching the bodies. Dead, cold, clammy flesh that did not crumble under his touch.

"Damn it, Robert, I told you, they were early attempts, mistakes, they're not the same as the others. *Leave them.*"

Already Sephera was disconnecting the EEG and EKG electrodes from Denise's body. "There's a blanket over in the corner, get it."

Retrieving the blanket, Robert ran back just as she was removing the IV needles from Denise's arm and covering the wounds with Band-Aids she yanked from her pockets. "The respirator's attached to the stand, unlock it. It has to come with us. Hurry."

Robert fumbled with the locks but finally got them open. The respirator was no larger than a suitcase—it even had a carry handle on top—but weighed at least ninety pounds. He lifted it from the stand and set it on the floor. Sephera called for him and he joined her by the incubator.

"Slip one arm underneath her like I'm doing, okay; now, lift her a little, just like that, good. We have to unhook the harness straps from up here; back ones first, then the front. On three: one, two, *three*." They removed the back straps from their hooks, then did the same to the front straps. Being careful not to accidentally tear either respirator tube away from her body, they lowered Denise onto the blanket. Robert quickly wrapped her in it. Sephera looked around, spotted the black medical bag under the EEG machine, and grabbed it.

"Okay, I'm going to unplug the respirator. It has an emergency battery inside that's good for fifteen minutes. We need to get her and it into the back of the Jeep. There's a small portable generator already in there, fully charged. It should provide power for at least twelve hours—not that we'll need that long. Wait here." She made a fast sweep of the basement, grabbing up both of the pistols as well as the guards' stun guns and stuffing the lot of them into the medical bag. Then she was back at Robert's side. "I'll carry the respirator, you take Denise. Move."

Robert climbed the nineteen eternal steps with his back facing the door above; his muscles cramped slightly from having to walk in a stoop, but the tubes were only three feet long. Sephera trailed behind him, the muscles in her arms bulging as she kept the respirator at chest-level. Once they were in the basement proper, she told Robert to hang for a sec.

Setting down the respirator, she sprinted through the doorway into the first section of the basement and returned a few moments later with a large hand cart. She placed the respirator on the bottom, then laid a pillow on top of it. Robert gently sat Denise on the pillow, then—following Sephera's lead—used the harness straps to secure her in place.

"I'm sorry," whispered Sephera into Denise's rodentlike ear. "A being as wondrous as you should not have to endure such indignities." She gestured for Robert to grab the handles of the cart.

They moved quickly through the basement. Sephera grabbed the bottom of the hand cart and help Robert to move Denise up the second set of steps with as few bumps and jostles as possible.

"Do you think your neighbors heard anything?"

"They're jerks, Robert, not deaf. Let's assume they called the police, and that we've got maybe three minutes before they get here."

Through the downstairs rooms to the side door, then out into the chill air. His breath misting as he and Sephera maneuvered the cart down the last few steps, Robert looked around for the telltale whirl of approaching lights. The police would be on silent approach; no sirens, then kill all lights once they were two blocks away. Sephera threw open the hatch, then helped Robert to slide the hand cart into the back before climbing in herself. Denise and the respirator lay facing the ceiling like some absurdist totem pole.

Sephera reached into the medical bag and shoved one of the pistols at Robert. "Remember, you mustn't hesitate."

He stared at the gun as if she'd just shit in his hand. "I don't know if I can bring myself—"

"Whatever is necessary, Robert. I don't like it any more than you do, but there's no choice. It's 'them or us' time." She reached up and grabbed the inside latch, pulling the door down. "Go."

He ran to the front of the Jeep and jumped inside. Flipping down the sun visor, he caught the keys as they dropped, then started the engine. He hit the lights and saw the empty Morgan Security Systems car that blocked the top of the driveway. "Shit!"

Sephera crawled forward and looked over his shoulder. "So much for a quiet exit." She patted his shoulder. "This thing's built like a tank and has pickup like you wouldn't believe. Put it in gear, then floor it."

The tires squealed loudly as the Jeep shot up the steep drive, hitting thirty by the time its front end flew over the top and crashed into the security car, smashing it out of the way in a shower of broken glass and crumpled metal.

Robert looked into the rearview mirror. Lights were coming on from both the other houses, as well as several along the street they were now on. He checked the mirror and saw that Sephera had the generator going and the respirator hooked up and running. Denise breathed easily.

"Where the fuck am I going?" he shouted.

"Straight, then left at the intersection. We're heading for the side route that they use for the construction equipment. It's going to be rough as hell because the road's not paved, but I don't think the police will think to take it."

Robert nearly missed the turn and for a moment thought about hitting the brakes, then decided *Fuck it* and jerked the steering wheel to the side, spinning the Jeep's back end around and burning a set of skid marks that followed them for the next twenty yards as he straightened the vehicle, hit the gas, and tore off down the street. He checked the digital clock in the dashboard: four forty-five A.M. Lights came on in houses as they screamed by.

"Right at the corner, then a left past the 'Construction Vehicles Only' sign."

She was right, the road was covered in potholes and large bumps and was alternately slick with ice and thick with mud, but Robert slowed down and managed to plow through. By the time the road emptied out onto a paved street it was a little before five A.M.

"The sun will be up in a little while," he said over his shoulder.

"We'll be okay now . . . at least for another twelve hours."

"How's she doing?"

"Believe it or not, she slept through the whole thing."

"Good."

"Take the on-ramp up ahead."

"Where are we going now?" When there was no answer, Robert looked in the mirror.

Sephera was kneeling next to Denise, holding her hand and staring straight ahead as if in a trance.

"Sephera?"

"Rael . . ."

"What about him?"

"He knows . . ."

"What? What does he know?"

Sephera shuddered, blinked, then slowly sat down. "He knows that you've found her. He's on his way to meet us."

"Where?"

"I'm not sure, I caught only pieces of his intent."

"What are we supposed to do, just keep driving until Suzy picks up his scent?"

Sephera laughed softly. "No. We need to head toward Indiana. So go West, young man."

"Sephera?"

"Yes?"

Robert glanced at her reflection in the mirror. "Are we going to make it?"

She looked down at Denise, then laid a hand against her slumbering face. "We have to, Robert; it's as simple as that. *We have to.*"

Chapter Eleven

They had to pull over three times during the trip because of Denise's contractions; not only was she experiencing the pains, but Sephera and—to a less severe degree—Robert as well. It was during the third stop, after the pain had subsided and they were able to breathe easily again, that Sephera put her hand on Robert's shoulder and said, "She won't survive the next series. We have to find a place to stay."

Swallowing back the sorrow that threatening to gag him, Robert continued the drive.

They were on the outskirts of Montrose, Indiana, when he spotted the motel VACANCY sign. He parked the Jeep as far from the office as he thought safe and went to get a room. He looked over the layout as he approached the office; three, possibly four one-floor buildings, each with about a dozen rooms that he could see. The parking lot had maybe a dozen cars, all of them parked a good distance from one another. So they spaced out the guests when it was possible; that was good.

The clerk was a young man of perhaps twenty-one who looked to have just gotten out of bed and didn't give a damn if his manner and appearance betrayed he was definitely not a morning person. He was on the phone when Robert came in. After nearly two minutes of waiting for the clerk to finish his conversation, Robert checked his watch—it was nearly a quarter past ten—then hit the bell on the check-in desk. The clerk glared at him, told whoever he was talking with to call back in five minutes, then racked the receiver and proceeded to perform his duties with all the enthusiasm of a hemorrhoid sufferer looking for a seat in a proctologist's waiting room.

"Single or double?" he asked, yawning.

"Double."

"Sign the register."

Robert could feel his center starting to twist again; another series of contractions was on the way. Without thinking he signed his own first name, began to panic, then did a quick shuffle through his mind for the rest of a name.

The clerk turned the register around and handed Robert the key. "You're down in the second building, Mr. Nitzinger. Room 207."

Robert looked up at the MOTEL POLICY sign and saw number 7: NO PETS ALLOWED.

He had two choices; he could either not tell the clerk about the pets and chance having another guest hear Suzy or the cats and report them, or . . .

"My sister and I have pets with us."

"No pets, sorry."

"We've been on the road a very long time and she's not feeling well. We need to rest."

"I can't help you, dude."

Robert quickly sized up the clerk; his shirt was well worn but clean, just like his pants and tie, but it was the man's shoes that sealed the deal, severely scuffed with badly worn down heels; the clerk had used a lot of elbow grease and shoe polish to try and cover up the sad condition of his footwear.

Robert reached into his pocket and removed a roll of bills, tearing a crisp Ulysses S. Grant from the bottom and slapping it down on the counter. "Would this make it worth your while?"

The clerk did an admirable job of concealing his surprise. "Look, dude, I don't make the rules here and I can't afford to lose this job right now. We don't take pets."

The clerk was studying Robert's face with more than passing interest now. In the few seconds before he made his next move, Robert quickly scanned the table and desk behind the clerk and felt his heart skip a beat when he saw the small stack of magazines on the desk; even though most of its cover was concealed by copies of the recent *Time* and *Newsweek* that lay fanned on top of it, he could clearly see that the most recent issue of *Columbus Monthly*.

He tore another fifty from the roll and put it on top of the one already on the counter. "How about now?"

"I already answered your question. Now give me back the key, please."

Knowing that he was taking an awful chance but realizing there was no time and therefore no choice, Robert quickly peeled off two one-hundred dollar bills and added them to the ante.

This time the clerk wasn't so quick to rebuff the offer.

"My sister is not well," said Robert, amazed at the ease with which the lies poured from his mouth. "She has breast cancer and for some reason has not been responding well to her treatments. We're on our way to Indianapolis to meet with some specialists there. My sister's only comfort these last several weeks has been her pets. We'll be staying in Indie for at least a week and she refused to be without them. I love my sister very much but this trip is really taking it out of her and she has to rest now. Just a few hours. We'll be out of here by this evening."

The clerk stared at the money on the counter, then slowly lifted his eyes to meet Robert's gaze. "She must be in really bad shape."

"She is." *Jesus Christ, kid, come on!*

"I understand how you feel, dude. My mom died of breast cancer. Left me and my dad with a lot of medical bills."

I don't fucking believe this.

Robert peeled off another hundred. "I'm very sorry to hear that."

The clerk nodded, then took the money from the counter and slipped it into his pocket. "The room is forty-seven fifty."

Robert handed the clerk another hundred. "Keep the change."

"I'm here until seven P.M. That's when the manager comes on duty. The Pacers are playing the Buckeyes tomorrow night

349

at home, so this place is gonna start filling up this evening. I'd really appreciate it if you—"

"We'll be gone before seven."

The phone rang. As the clerk turned to answer it, Robert said, "Can I look at your magazines there? I'm not particularly tired and—"

The clerk answered the phone and then, without looking at any of the covers, tossed the pile onto the counter. Robert grabbed *Time* and the new *Columbus Monthly* and left. Hopefully the clerk hadn't seen the cover of the *Monthly*.

Still, he'd really been *looking* at Robert's face for a moment . . .

Room 207 was on the left side of the second building. Only one other vehicle—a shiny pickup truck with a gun rack and a Pacers bumper sticker—was parked on this side of the building, four doors down.

Robert backed the Jeep into the parking space, then unlocked the room and left the door open. Checking to make sure no one was coming from either side, he opened the hatch and Sephera jumped down. They quickly removed the hand cart and took it into the room. Untying the harness straps, they moved Denise onto the bed nearest an electrical outlet and hooked up the respirator. Then Robert brought the Suzy and the cats inside.

"How's she doing?" he asked, closing the door and engaging the dead bolt.

Sephera looked at him and sadly shook her head.

Robert made a quick check of everything and discovered that the door that led to the right-side adjoining room had a broken lock and would not close all the way. At least the other door was securely locked in place. He'd have to keep an eye on that.

Standing behind Sephera, he placed a hand on her shoulder and said, "What happens now?"

"Nothing you can help with, so do me a flavor—whoa. A *flavor?*"

Robert grinned. "Denise used to say that a lot."

"Well, it's a first for me. Keep the cats in their carriers a little while longer, okay? There's a can of kitty treats I put on the nightstand. Suzy's fallen asleep again, so that's something." She closed her eyes, took a deep breath, and folded her hands together. "I need for you to go sit on the other side of the room and be quiet, all right?"

Something caught in his throat. "So th-this is . . . this is it?"

"This is it."

He stared down at Denise and was stunned by the depth of affection he felt toward her. It didn't matter what she looked like, she was his true love. His heart ached with the thought of how she must have felt all these years, isolated within her glass-walled prison. Even with the connections to the other women she'd created from herself, she must have longed to experience *something* firsthand. Like *this*—had she ever wished, even once, briefly, that she could feel herself be held like this, as she truly was?

"I can't . . . I can't do this just yet."

Sephera opened her eyes and glared at him. "Sit *down*, Robert."

"No." He pushed her aside and gently sat on the side of the bed. He touched the side of her face, and Denise opened her eyes. There was such *need* in them, such pain; her eyes reflected intimate knowledge of a loneliness so profound Robert could not begin to imagine it.

"*Robert* . . . " whispered Sephera impatiently.

"No, not yet. Go stand over there and leave us for a minute."

"But—"

"*Do it!*" He was shocked at the violence in his voice. Sephera moved away from the bed, her eyes shooting bullets into Robert's back.

He turned on the bedside light so as to see every detail of her face clearly, then leaned down and—as best he could without jostling the respirator tubes—kissed her cheek, her eyes, her forehead, then slid one arm under her back and draped the other one across her center.

Gary A. Braunbeck

"Listen to me, my love: This guy's involved in a terrible traffic accident, right? Totals his car and breaks both his arms and crushes one of his legs. He comes to in the hospital later on and the doctor's standing at the foot of his bed looking really upset. 'What's wrong?' asks the guy. 'Well,' says the doctor, 'I've got good news and bad news. The bad news is that we amputated the wrong leg.' 'And the *good* news?' the guys asks. Then the doctor looks at him and says, 'The good news is that your bad leg's getting much better.' "

Denise made a sudden crackling sound from deep inside her throat.

"Jesus," said Sephera, coming closer. "Is she choking?"

"No," said Robert, slowly working at the tape around the respirator tube. "She's laughing. I never told her that joke. I always meant to."

"What the hell are you doing?"

"The chest in her tube will be able to keep her breathing for a few minutes, right?"

"Yes, but—"

"Please go away."

"You can't—"

"Go. A. Way."

He finished working the tape loose, then gently and quickly pulled the tube from her throat. She tried opening her mouth but the gummed mucus had hardened in several places, making it almost impossible. She exhaled a slow, ragged breath, filling the air between her face and Robert's with the scent of an ancient rose suddenly released from the vase where it had been sealed five thousand years ago. Unlike the man in Siempre's story told to the Prince, Robert *did* know the gift of the rose; he pulled her breath into him, savoring it, recognizing it for the treasure that it was, one that had existed since the beginning of time only for this day, this place, this moment: He took it in and felt his weary heart both awaken and sorrow, but there was

352

grace here, and glory, and the true beauty that comes from time's gift of perfect humility.

"Thank you," he said, touching her cheek, then her lips. "All my life you have loved me without condition. You're the only person who ever did, and I'm sorry that it took me until now to realize that. Imperfect as I am, you loved me without question." With his thumb he wiped away a small tear from her right eye. "I'll never be able to put into words what you've meant to me. I was an idiot, Denise. I was afraid to lift my head and look up from the world because I was sure the light would hurt my eyes, because that's what dreams did to a person; they hurt. And the brighter the dream, the deeper the pain when you couldn't reach it." He laid his head next to hers on the pillow, whispering in her ear. "But I can do that now, because of you. I can look up into the light and not be hurt by what it shows me. I understand what you've tried to say to me, and I *do* despair, but I know that my despair is also my strength, and I can be strong now, my love. I can hear the voices and laughter of the people from my past and not crumble inside from regret. I can remember everything good and bad and know that each was necessary." He kissed her cheek, her eyes, her chin. "I now know that a man can grow old without giving up the songs and laughter and summer afternoons of calliope music and back-lot baseball games that make childhood eternal. I promise you, I *swear to you*, that I will protect the children of Chiaroscuro with everything I have. There will be no more sorrow for them, no more pain. I can do this because I am strong now, you gave me the ability to see that." He traced her lips with his index finger. "I wish I could have known you as you were when we first met. But I was not the same then. You have changed me. And I will love you forever because of that." He lifted his head and looked into her eyes. "Right now, at this moment, I think you are the most beautiful woman ever to grace this world, and I am honored to hold you in my arms. Thank you for loving me. Thank you for giving me to myself, and for sharing my life. I want you to know

Gary A. Braunbeck

how much I love you just as you are at this second: I have never loved anyone more. You are the dream in the light; you are my heart and spirit; you are the gift of the rose."

Despite the obvious pain of the effort, Denise tried to smile but could not, and so simply gave a short, slow nod of her head.

Robert wet his lips and lowered his head. It was the softest, most tender kiss he'd ever given or received, and he never wanted it to end. Denise lifted her arm and placed her hand on the back of his head. No jeweled crown could ever feel grander.

Then her chest hitched and she began to sputter and cough. Grabbing Robert's hair, she pulled his face away as something thick and black spattered down her chin.

Sephera yanked Robert from the bed and shoved him to the floor, sat beside Denise and cupped her face in her hands, then pressed their foreheads together.

Robert watched from the floor as the Transference took place.

The atmosphere thrummed. Both Denise and Sephera became less and corporeal.

The world proceeded backward, forward, downward, sideways.

Denise was there/not there.

Sephera was whole/incomplete.

They were both children/old women at the edge of life's final breath.

Denise was alone/a succession of ghosts.

They were whole/other women, some older, some younger, each dimly visible, each more diaphanous than the last.

. . . one used a walker, one didn't; one wore tattered clothes that looked to have been purchased at a Goodwill store while the next was adorned in sable and pearls; after her, so confident and healthy that her bloom was still visible, another woman, younger than the others, laughed with sparkling energy, her eyes filled with mischief and wonder; the next woman, pitiful and emaciated, shambled slowly forward, brittle hands knotted against aged, sagging breasts, eyes unfocused, lines on her face harshened by shadows and age spots; sauntering dreamily behind her . . .

The Transference continued.

The world became another world looking into another world that shifted and changed and faded into shadows to be replaced by another, firmer possible world. There were children laughing, playing, growing old, dying, turning to ashes, blowing away with the snow; there were trees growing, toppling, rotting, turning to ashes, blowing away; mountains rose and crumbled before his eyes, and with them races of beings so hideous and fantastic Robert nearly wept at the sight. He was back at the house, an old and bitter man, broken by grief, yet he also stood across from this old man, young and alive and bright-eyed at the Possibilities; the two of them met each other in the middle of the room, whispered, "Denise," then became one, grew even younger, became shrunken and pink-cheeked, an infant vanishing back into the womb of its mother who spun back into time and vanished.

He thought he would be lost here forever, shifting, turning, rising, falling, becoming old and young at once, a babe and an invalid, longing for her touch, her voice, her laugh, then he felt Sephera's hand grab his shoulders and shake him and—

—and he was rooted firmly in the moment, *this* moment, on his ass on the floor in a motel room somewhere outside Montrose, Indiana.

"Robert? It's okay now. I'm here, it's over."

He blinked several times, then looked up into Sephera's shadowed face. She looked no different than before; same full lips, same black-dyed hair, same nose and cheekbones and—

—her eyes.

He looked into her eyes and saw all of them: Penny, Amy, Linda, Yvonne, Tracy . . . but most of all, Denise: his love, the prism, the rose.

"Denise?"

She parted her hands. *"Ta-da!"*

At once he ached for her. He jumped up and took her in his arms, holding her against him so tightly the flesh of their cheeks burned from the friction as he pulled his face around to kiss her. She grasped his back, her nails digging in. They both breathed heavily through their noses, not wanting their lips to be apart. His hands explored her body. She rubbed against him. He flicked his tongue against her lips and she responded by opening her mouth and slipping the tip of her tongue against his, then ramming it in so deep and hard he nearly choked. She slid her hand down between his legs as he reached under her blouse and bra and squeezed her breast, then began tracing slow circular patterns over her areola, growing more excited as he felt her nipple engorge. She squeezed his hardening cock and gave a low moan of pleasure, then pulled at his shirt from his pants and ran her hands up to his chest underneath. He worked at the buttons of her blouse; at first with the clumsiness of a virginal schoolboy, then with the skilled hands of a lifelong lover. She began to unzip him. Her blouse fell open and he pulled his face away from hers, running his mouth wetly down her neck until he reached her exposed breast and took her hot nipple in his mouth, flicking it, sucking it, licking it, tongue and teeth in perfect play. Her soft moaning then became a louder shriek of pleasure as she gripped the back of his head with her left hand while her right unbuckled his belt and pulled it free. Robert moved his mouth from one breast to the other, then trailed his tongue to the sweet bowl between her clavicles, then up along the sweaty ridge of her throat to her chin. She shuddered against him, her moans growing longer, deeper, louder. She unsnapped his pants. He took her tongue into his mouth. She began to push him backward until he was pressed against the wall. This was crazy. They shouldn't be doing this, he knew, but was possessed by a wrenching hunger for her. He managed to pull his head back and took a breath through his mouth, feeling the sweat soaking his back. "We . . . oh, God . . . we can't . . . we shouldn't . . ."

"Shhh," she said, placing a finger damp with his juices against his lips. "I *need* to . . . don't you . . . mmmmm, don't stop . . . don't you remember what day it is?"

"No . . . I . . ."

She kissed him, then smiled and said, "Happy anniversary, Robert."

And then he remembered. Their first anniversary, right after she'd given him the watch, they'd gone at each other just like this, standing up in the living room, and she'd pushed him against the wall and said, "Let's see if that . . ."

". . . treadmill's doing you any good," she finished now. His pants were down around the middle of his thighs and she'd worked her underwear off. Hooking one arm around his shoulder as she bent her right leg and tucked it under his elbow, she stroked his erection for a moment and then took him inside her. They fought each other's speed and rhythm for a moment, a delicious, teasing war of desire that had both of them at a screaming pitch in seconds. Robert pressed himself hard against the wall and bent his legs, then drove himself up deeper inside her, wanting to bury himself up to her throat. The force of their coupling shook the wall; a painting hanging near them began to bounce against the imitation paneling; the edge of the television stand smacked against the wall; and the door that led to the adjoining room clicked slowly open, though neither of them saw or heard it. It swung inward and was stopped from opening farther by the next door.

Denise moved her hips faster, plunging against him, sighing, growling, her face glistening with sweat, the joy of it making them both cry out as he grew bigger and she wetter, sliding down, then up, faster, so much heat between their bodies, and she pressed her hand against the wall and drove herself down onto him and Robert threw back his head and closed his eyes and felt himself explode inside her, felt her own orgasm shudder through her body in sweet, hard, merciless waves as both of them came, their juices running down the insides of their legs as she groaned and he cried out and they began a slow, hot, moist slide down the wall to the floor where she fell against him and, just as it had happened on their first anniversary, they rolled to the side, her leg still draped over his, their bodies covered in heavy rivulets of sweat.

As their breathing slowed, Denise ran a finger down the length of his nose, then gently flicked its tip as if ridding it of a mosquito. "Well, hello, you."

"Hello yourself. God . . . I can't believe this."

"Believe it," she said, then kissed him again before moving her leg and slowly, with one last shuddered sigh, slipping his cock from inside her.

"Think you can get yourself into that chair by the dresser?"

"Think I can manage that."

"Go on, then. There's something we've got to do while there's still time."

They both fixed their clothes. Robert staggered over to the chair and sat down. He saw his reflection in the chipped and dingy mirror and laughed. He was a mess. A wonderful mess. He scratched his neck and, as he pulled his hand down, felt the piece of paper in his shirt pocket. He removed, then unfolded it.

And there was her handwriting: *Send me a picture of the daughter we never had . . .*

He suddenly went cold all over as the echo of an unanswered question came back to him. He reached out and slipped the note into a corner of the mirror where he could see the words, then turned around in the chair and looked at her.

The weight of the question made his stomach twist. "Are you my daughter?"

She smiled at him. "Only at the level of the flesh. Your seed helped to create this body."

"Oh, God . . ." Robert felt like he was going to throw up.

"Hang on, you're stronger than that." She lifted her blouse, exposing her creamy skin. "Do you see an autopsy scar?"

"No."

She lowered the blouse back in place. "I needed a body that was equal parts human and Hallower. There was no other way. But if you're thinking that some part of me might be Emily . . . no. She never lived to breathe in existence. Feel better now?"

He nodded his head.

"Good. Now don't make a sound. If this is too much for you, look away." She turned and reached down into the dead, deformed, mutilated body on the bed, her hands passing through its bloated belly as if into water. When she pulled them out, they held a small, bloody, perfectly formed fetus.

The body on the bed began to quickly deteriorate, its flesh discoloring, becoming semiliquid, falling from bone, staining the bed, trickling to the floor. The stench was strong but not overpowering. That would come later, causing the first police officer to enter the room to whirl around, drop to his knees, and vomit.

But for now, it was a sickly sweet stench of something old and decaying.

Robert looked away. Denise placed the infant body on the bureau, then picked up the medical bag and opened it. "I don't know how much farther we'll have to travel or how long it's going to take, but your face has to go, my love." She removed a small glass vial and a hypodermic needle.

Robert stared at the needle. "What are you going to do?"

"Collagen for your lips and cheeks." She laid the hypodermic to the side. "Dr. Steinman told you the truth: Fetal tissue *is* the perfect transplant material. It bonds instantly and the body won't reject it." She looked at the infant. "This first part has to be done the messy way—the *human* way, I'm afraid. The rest of it will be as the Archons did when they assisted in the creation of Adam." She scooped some placenta off the corpse, licked it, then held the rest out to Robert. "Eat this."

Do not hesitate.

He swallowed it in one gulp. Its taste was thick and meaty but not unpleasant.

Gary A. Braunbeck

Denise ran her hand along the body, then removed a scalpel from the bag and proceeded to cut away the tiny face, exposing bone. She used the bone-saw and something that looked like small tongs (only these with teeth) to work loose a section of skull. "Close your eyes, Robert."

He was more than happy to do so; the sight of the baby's blood and exposed tissues was more than he could handle.

Denise began to apply pressure at various points on his body. His head went numb.

"Shhh, that's it, just take steady breaths and keep your eyes closed."

He lost track of how long he sat that way; her every touch was a gentle caress, soothing and sensual. He was aware of slight pressure, of muscle tissue being manipulated and reshaped, of sections of his skull being cracked apart and added to, of the prick of a needle against his lips and cheeks, of something being scooped from around the inside of his throat.

"Done," she said in a very self-satisfied tone of voice.

Robert opened his eyes and turned toward the mirror.

Though the face in the mirror was not his, it was one he recognized, nonetheless.

It was the face that had been painted on the last *matryoshka* doll he'd found, the one that came from inside the Robert-doll.

It was a different face, but a good one.

A kind face.

It was my face.

And that is when the man I once was closed his eyes and gave up his existence to me.

I saw my new face and smiled. Denise had straightened those two lower teeth that had always bugged me. "Good grief," I said. "I look like the young Fredric March."

"He was always our favorite movie actor, so I figured, why not? It was either that or Robert Mitchum and, frankly, Mitchum always sort of gave me the creeps. Guess it was because *Night of the Hunter* was the first movie of his I ever saw. After that . . ." She gave a mock shiver. "Even when I saw *Ryan's Daughter*, I kept expecting him to whip out a knife and start slicing away at everyone."

I started to respond but was stopped by something large walloping against the wall of the room next door. Someone let fly with a loud "Whoo-ee!" and then hit the wall again.

"What the hell . . . ?"

Denise shot an irritated glance to the right. "It's six-thirty. The Pacers Parade has started."

I rose from the chair and pulled back the curtain. Outside it was growing dark, the streetlights surrounding the parking lot were beginning their slow rise to full brightness. I looked left, then right, and saw that well over half of the parking space was now occupied.

The wall slammer next door was at it again, but this time I realized what he or whoever was doing: bouncing a basketball against the paneling.

I turned and looked at the room. Blood, organs, and tissue from the fetus were scattered on the bureau, a chair, and the second bed. The body where my true love had once resided was losing its battle against decomposition; I could see a loop of gray intestine pressing against a thin membrane. I moved to cover up the body and accidentally bumped it. The membrane burst and the loop of intestine popped free, uncoiling like slick rope.

"No use in trying to clean up," said Denise, gathering up the cat carriers and shaking Suzy awake. "I know where Rael is now. We have to leave. The children need us."

I began to take one of the carriers when the basketball next door hit the wall with five times the force it had before and the second adjoining door came open, swinging out into the next room and allowing our door to swing.

There were three men and a woman in the next room, and they had a clear line of sight into the slaughterhouse next door.

The woman was the first to see it; noticing that their door had opened, she rose to close it, laughing through her apology for having bothered us, she hoped that we hadn't been scared when—

—she saw the bloody, mutilated monstrosity on the bed and screamed.

One of the men jumped up and pulled her away, then got a clear look for himself. "*Oh, goddamn!*"

The other men yelled for him. The woman was shrieking and babbling incoherently. One of the unseen men screamed, as well, and then a door opened. I could hear footsteps outside, the door of a truck being opened and something large and metallic pulled from inside the cab.

The first man charged into the room shouting, "You sick *fucks!*" but Denise tripped him. He fell face-first into the body on the bed, scrambled to regain his balance, and rose with a face covered in the moist flotsam of death.

"Jesusjesusjesus, *Jeeeeeezuuuuusssss!*" he screamed, clawing at what clung to his cheeks and chin. Denise grabbed the lighted lamp from the table and smashed it against the back of his skull, sending his unconscious form back down onto the bed. His face and chest sank into the corpse as if it were a down-filled pillow.

I could hear the other man yelling into the telephone at the police, trying to make them understand what was happening. I grabbed something from the medical bag, moved past Denise, and stormed into the other room. I used the stun gun on the woman first, then yanked the phone cord from the wall and zapped the other man. He and the woman lay on the floor, two glassy-eyed mannequins but still alive.

I turned toward their open door just as the third man stumbled into the doorway, trying to load a pump-action shotgun with trembling hands.

I started toward him. He pumped a shell into the chamber and was raising the shotgun but I was faster, lifting my foot and bringing it down on the barrel. Why he didn't panic-fire anyway I'll never know.

I heard a couple of doors opening on this side of building.

Confused voices tinged with potential panic began spilling out into the encroaching night.

I grabbed the barrel of the shotgun, pulling it and him into the room. I swung him around and slammed the door closed. The man and I did an insane, twirling dance for a few seconds as he held on to the trigger and stock and I held on to the barrel with one hand. I didn't want to hurt anyone but there was no choice on that point.

I dropped the pistol, gripped the barrel of the shotgun with both hands, and shoved it back into the other man's groin. He doubled over, releasing his grip. I spun the gun around and brought the stock down hard against the middle of his back. His face was the first thing to hit the floor, breaking his nose. Denise was right on top of him with the stun gun—*zzzzipht!*—and he was still.

She and I stood looking at each other, listening as the people outside—three, maybe four of them—milled around and asked questions of each other. "Did you hear someone screaming?" "I thought so, what'd it sound like to you?" "Maybe somebody's getting laid and she's a real screaming meemie, huh?"

We stood there, silent, not daring to move.

Finally someone knocked on the door. Denise, much to my shock, walked over and answered, pulling the door open only a few inches; enough for her and the person on the other side to see one another without the person able to see into the room.

"Hi," said Denise, sounding embarrassed.

"I don't mean to be nibby, miss, but is everything all right? Some of us heard a scream and—"

"That was me, I'm sorry. I was using the bathroom and a cockroach crawled up my leg."

The man on the other side groaned in sympathy. "Oh, that's awful. Did ya at least kill it?"

"My husband did; he's the exterminator in the family."

This got a laugh. "Well," he said, "glad to hear it's nothing serious. Doesn't surprise me that this place'd have a roach or two, though, being so close to the creek and all."

"Thanks for checking," said Denise.

"Could I ask a favor? Would you and your husband mind not bouncing that basketball off the wall quite so hard? It's making my wife a little grumpy."

"I'll tell him," replied Denise cheerfully. "He gets a little over-excited right before a Pacers home game."

"Don't we all?"

The man said good-bye and, "Go, Pacers," then returned to his room next door.

I finally released the breath I'd been holding.

Denise closed the door and locked it. Then her shoulders slumped. "*Now* can we go?"

"Way ahead of you."

We loaded the pets into the Jeep (after all three of them insisted on being taken into the foliage outside so they could relieve themselves), then closed the door of the room.

I am more sorry than I can say that I did not think to move the man who had fallen into the body on the bed. It never once crossed my mind that he might drown in the sour juices of that corpse.

I never meant to kill anyone.

Denise got into the backseat of the Jeep with the animals. I figured she wanted to sleep while I drove, even though I had no idea where I was going. I climbed in behind the wheel and damn near jumped out of my skin when I saw someone in the passenger seat.

"Some pretty snazzy wheels you got here, Willy. How's the mileage? We have a bit of traveling ahead of us."

Denise reached over the backseat and gripped Rael's hand. I sensed what was passing between them because I could hear, somewhere in the distant night, thousands of children sigh, as one, with relief.

"What a long, strange trip it's been, huh?" I said, dazzled by my originality and eloquence.

Rael looked at me and, for what I think might have been the first time, genuinely smiled at me. He clapped a hand on my shoulder and said, "Thanks for not letting us down, Willy. I think we're gonna be okay now. Is there anything you want to do before we—"

"Yes," I replied immediately. "There's one thing I *very much* want us to do before we go home."

Rael gestured at the steering wheel. "Then let's hit the road, Jack."

"It's Willy to you, handsome."

"Don't be a smart-ass."

I pulled out of the motel parking lot and turned onto the night road. The sky was clear of overcast and a million silver stars guided us with their light.

The world of man fell into memory behind us as I drove on. My center was full and strong and new, with compassion and despair and hardened with anger to a shine. What a tale this would make for the children. I could hardly contain my excitement.

When the four of us returned to Chiaroscuro with the pets, I was stunned at the grandeur of the mountain as it opened to receive us. The children flowed forward from the depths of their chambers. They smiled and laughed with healthy bodies no longer threatened by *chronos*. They kissed and embraced us. They told us about what they'd been doing while we were away. They looked upon Denise with wonder. They spoke to Rael with a new respect. Andrea held my hand and whispered happy stories about Ian. Suzy was already a fixture here and found everyone wanting to play with her. The cats were a bit wary of their new home but eventually came around; thousands of pairs of hands to pet and feed them? You bet they came around.

As the mountain closed behind us and we moved toward the deeper chambers, a group of very small children formed a circle around me as we walked. Those who could not reach my hands held the sleeves of my jacket; those too small to reach the sleeves of my jacket held on to a pant leg. They told me how happy they were to see me. They had missed me since I left. There was lots and lots to tell me about. They had some secrets to share. They had stories to tell. They asked if I knew any stories.

They called me Father.

This place has been my home for a while now, though the more I learn about what I have Become, the less I think about the man-made concept of Time. Denise and Rael have grown very strong, stronger than either of them has ever been before. We still journey to find other children who need a home like this, where they can be safe and loved and unafraid, but since there are now *three* of us who carry Hallower strength, *chronos* cannot infect us during these trips.

I thought it best to write down everything that had happened so that you will have answers to your many questions. Andrea gave me Ian's old typewriter, and I used it until the ribbon ran out of ink. That is why some of these pages are typed while others are handwritten. The writing is not all mine. I have been teaching Rael proper penmanship, so he has been helping me. (He's doing very well, by the way.) Denise also has written some of this as I dictated it, as has Andrea and several of the other children. It is, after all, *our* story.

As I sit here at Denise's writing table finishing these last few pages and listening to *One Foot in History*, the thought occurs that you who find this may label everything the ravings of a lunatic. It's very important that our story not be dismissed, that you know what's been written here is true, so I am going to perform a parlor trick for you (as my powers have grown, Rael has taught me a thing or two, as well).

When the last of this tale has been written down, I am going to slip through one of the gaps where the walls of the infinite and finite are not quite squared and leave this manuscript in the very Montrose motel room where my True Love was returned to me and the man I once was gave his life so that I might live in his place.

I will put the manuscript in an envelope and tape it to the bottom of the drawer in the writing table.

I will do this during the four seconds that elapsed between Detective James Anderson's leaving the room and Officer Greg Harrison's entering it to find Denise's note tucked into the corner of the bureau's chipped and dingy mirror.

I can do this because Time is your prison, not ours. So to all those who read this after it was found, ask yourselves this question: With so many police officers and detectives searching so small a room, how did you manage to miss something as glaringly large as the envelope that contained this manuscript?

You missed it because when Officer Dale Wilkins ran his hand under that table at nine forty-seven P.M. this manuscript was not there; however, when Detective Anderson—purely out of habit—checked under the table at nine-fifty P.M. . . . there it was. No one else was in the room at that moment—check Wilkins's and Anderson's reports.

If you still don't believe what you've read here, I will enclose something that you will not have the courage to make public, and which will prove the truth of our tale.

There will be seven fingerprints on the last sheet of this manuscript: a top row of three, then one print all by itself, then a second row of three. They were taken from seven different children—as I'm sure your fingerprint experts will quickly deduce. All of them have been missing for no less than ten years, and all of them came from homes where abuse was strongly suspected but never proved. If you dismiss this by saying I could have stolen or copied the prints from police or hospital records, then I draw your attention to the print that is all by itself. It belongs to Nicholas Roger Dawson (who likes for all of us to call him "Nick" because it sounds like such a grown-up's name), who vanished from his home in Whitby, North Yorkshire, England, on January 17, 1874. He was nine years old at the time of his disappearance. Nick was born with Down's Syndrome (called "mongolism" on his birth certificate) and was rarely allowed to leave the house, except to visit with his favorite aunt (the only member of the family who showed him any degree of kindness), Rachel Dawson, the sister of Nick's father, Harry. Rachel taught Nick how to read simple words and sentences, taught him how to write his name, showed him the proper way to clean and dress himself, and, in short, provided him with the only education he was ever to receive. Rachel Dawson was a nurse, and during one of Nick's visits escorted him to the hospital and took two sets of fingerprints. One she placed in the official files, the other she kept for herself.

Nick was remembered as being a shy and quiet boy who only seemed to smile when not with his parents. There is a reason for this. Harry Dawson, his father, was a brutal man who often drank and beat Nick into unconsciousness while "Mumsy" sat at the table and watched, urging Harry to "give it to" the "idiot beast" God had cursed them with. When Harry wasn't beating Nick, "Mumsy" was burning his arms and buttocks and genitals with cigarettes her husband left burning around the house after he passed out. Nick would never scream or cry out, because any sound meant that he would be locked in the cellar and not allowed to eat for a week. (He kept himself from starving by hiding table scraps in the cellar for these times. For water, he would lick condensation from the walls.) He learned to endure the pain. Then one night both Harry and "Mumsy" got stinking drunk and fell on him at the same time.

They tortured Nick for nearly two solid days before he fully lost consciousness and could not be revived. They put him in a cloth sack. Sometime between midnight and one A.M. on the morning of January 14, Harry left their house, threw Nick into the back of his wagon, hitched up the horse, and left the city.

Nick isn't sure where his father loaded the sack with heavy stones and then threw him in the river; he can only remember the feel of the water forcing itself down into his throat. Nick—

who had regained consciousness a few hours earlier—freed himself from the sack (Harry could never tie a strong knot) and swam to the surface.

Rael was waiting for him onshore.

The Dawsons waited three days before reporting Nick's disappearance. Scotland Yard had very little to go on and the search for Nick lasted only four days. The Dawsons happily wallowed in the attention and sympathy they received from friends and neighbors. One year after their "poor, sweet little boy" vanished inexplicably from his bed in the middle of the night, Harry Dawson went on a drunken rampage and murdered his wife with a sharpening stone, then stumbled around and fell down the cellar stairs, breaking his neck.

Rachel Dawson kept the fingerprint card that she had made for herself. She put it in a small, tasteful frame, along with a photograph of herself and Nick that she'd had taken during one of their days out. It became a Dawson family heirloom, as did the sad story of sweet Nicholas's tragically short life. Rachel eventually married, and gave birth to a daughter, Cynthia, who was to later marry and have a son, Graham. Graham would marry, and himself be the proud father of a little girl, Emma—

—and I am starting to wander off the highway here; you need only know two other names in the long succession of Dawsons.

That framed photograph now sits on the mantel in the home of James and Elizabeth McCarrick of Green Bay, Wisconsin. Elizabeth McCarrick is the great-great-great-great-granddaughter of Cynthia Dawson. Contact the McCarricks, as well as the Green Bay Police Department, and then have the Green Bay authorities get in touch with the Metropolitan Police and New Scotland Yard. Nick's fingerprints, taken from the set that Rachel filed at the hospital, has been in their computer systems since 1990. That's when several sets of records from 1897 were discovered and deemed to be of "great educational and research value," and so were entered in the Yard's system.

Go ahead, see for yourselves whether or not it all checks out.

Gary A. Braunbeck

Dismiss this story *then*.

I can hear the children beginning to gather in the Story Chamber. It's my turn tonight. I think I shall tell them about an elephant named Horton and how he one day heard a Who.

Rael just stuck his head in to inform me that everyone is waiting, and if I want him to make cheese-boogies (using Ian's recipe, of course), then I'd damned well better get my "back-door half-breed ass" out there.

I think he's getting used to me. I have, believe it or not, grown quite fond of his ugly mug.

Oh, wonderful; now he's got the children chanting, "Cheese-boogies! Cheese-boogies!" His idea of subtlety.

We are happy here. The little ones are safe. That is all we ever wanted.

I leave you, then, with this: Believe me when I tell you that there will come a morning when the world will be awakened by the sound of a lone child crying somewhere in the wilderness, and on that morning it will realize once and for all that its children, *every* child, must be loved, cherished, protected, and healed at any cost. When this happens, when the world of man at last assumes responsibility for the small ones, the weak ones, the innocent and trusting ones, then those children who did not live long enough to see the dawning of this day, whose tortured, raped, mutilated, burned, abused bodies lie in secret graves, will rise up together and speak the names of those who did this to them, and the world will exact justice on their behalf.

And if the world doesn't, then I will. Make no mistake about that.

Raise no fists; don't touch where you should not; and, most of all, never ignore the pained shrieks from next door. For I will know, and I will remember.

Do you despair?

Perhaps you should.

For there will come a morning when the world at last cherishes its little ones as they should be cherished, and when that happens the mountain will then open up for the last time; on that morning a melancholy, crippled, weary old man, who as a little lame boy was so lonely since all his friends went away with the Piper, this old man will look up at the distant hillside and watch in wonder as these friends return to him, dancing toward the home and friend they left so long ago. Then I will walk out of the wilderness with my True Love by my side, and the children of Chiaroscuro will follow us from the shadows to forever remain in light.

And that morning we shall begin to tell our stories.

Just like this one. Will you remember it?

Shhh, listen then.

Ready?

Good.

Once upon a time . . .

The day after police and detectives discovered the bodies in room 207 of the Montrose Motel, the following news item appeared on page 12 of the *Cedar Hill Ally*:

SUSPECTED CORPSE THIEF DISAPPEARS FROM HOSPITAL

A man being held for observation in connection with the theft of several infant bodies from various morgues and funeral homes has been missing since late last night.

Joseph Alan Connor, 26, was under police guard on the sixth floor of Cedar Hill Memorial Hospital, scheduled to begin the second in a series of psychiatric interviews to determine if he is competent to stand trial.

According to hospital and police sources, Connor was secured in his bed by hospital staff at 10:30 P.M. A bed check performed at midnight reported that he was still in bed and asleep. Connor has been kept under moderate sedation since after his arrest by Cedar Hill police last week.

One sixth-floor staff member remarked, "I just can't figure how he managed to get himself free of the restraints.

Those things are locked in place. When we found that he was gone, we checked the restraints and they were still secure. I don't know how a body could do such a thing, unless he was Houdini."

Connor, who was taken from his home by Children's Services after the scalding death of his sister when he was seven, was frequently seen at the Cedar Hill Open Shelter in the company (Continued on Page 14)

GUEST FAXING SERVICES

February 19

From: Ben Littlejohn
Cedar Hill Division of Police
Burglary/Homicide Unit

To: William Emerson
c/o Victoria Grosvenor Hotel
101 Buckingham Palace Road
ENGLAND

Dear Detective Hand Model:

Hope you and Eunice survived your hop across the pond; I know how you hate to fly. I'm sorry to have to bother you with this, but a couple of things have happened since you left that I figured you'd want to know about. I was just going to mail this but then I got a call that's left me kind of rattled.

I finished reading through everything a few of days ago. Did some of it creep you out as much as it did me? Cheryl kept asking me what I was reading; no way in hell I was going to tell her about it. She was, to put it mildly, unhappy with my refusal to share. I've been sleeping on the couch for the last two nights, and for that I want to thank you.

I contacted the Green Bay police, who put me in touch with the McCarricks (come on, you had to know I'd be too curious). Elizabeth McCarrick is a very sweet woman. (I think she was really excited to be taking part in an "unofficial" investigation; I'm guessing she'll tell her friends this story until the day she dies.) She confirmed Londrigan's claim; she did have that photograph and the fingerprint card. Guess what? She also has Rachel Dawson's diary. It seems that Rachel strongly suspected Nicholas was being "mistreated" by his parents but could never get the boy to admit anything to her. Mrs. McCarrick's going to send me a xeroxed copy of Rachel's diary; she said I'll find it "fascinating from a historical standpoint."

Anyhoo, she faxed a copy of the prints to me, and I had good old Latent George run a quick comparison, then I faxed everything to the London Metropolitan Police.

I got a call this morning from a Detective-Sergeant Terrence Johnson of New Scotland Yard. You might want to pop open one of those room-temperature beers and sit down for the rest of this.

The print from Elizabeth McCarrick's card not only matched the one from the manuscript, but also matched the one in the Yard's system on *sixteen* reference points, including two rare abnormalities in the whorl pattern. There is no doubt that it belongs to Nicholas Dawson.

Hang on, Pard, it gets better.

I contacted the Montrose lab about the paper the manuscript was written on and the ink used for the fingerprints. The paper stock is from a mill in Seattle. According to the tests, it's not quite two years old. The ink used for the fingerprinting is manufactured—guess where?—Cincinnati. I was on the phone for three hours and was transferred about a million times, but I finally found out that the formula for that particular ink has only been in use since 1991.

Think about that for a second, Bill.

When Johnson and I talked on the phone (he may be contacting you during your visit, by the way), I could hear that he was as stunned as I was. I asked him what he thought, and he quoted Sherlock Holmes: "When you eliminate the impossible, whatever remains, however improbable, must be the truth."

Which means there's a nine-year-old boy out there who's been alive for over a hundred and twenty-five years. And if that, however improbable, is the truth, then how can we write off the rest of what Londrigan claimed?

Just thought you'd like to know. I'm guessing there's a long conversation in our immediate future. Kisses to Eunice.

Ben

Reliquary

Uh, okay . . . hi, everybody. Rael said that tonight it's my turn to tell a story. I think I got a good one. It's one of Father's stories, but he says that I tell it better than he does, so here goes.

This doll belongs to Father. He says it's just like the vase where that old rose was sealed, only instead of a rose, it's got this memory inside. The babies used to tell me the same thing whenever I found them in the rain. They said everything has a story inside it.

You see the face on the doll? It's that woman Father met on the bus. Do you remember when he told us about the two old people who were on the bus that night? How he thought the old woman looked familiar?

Well, we're sort of ghosts now, all of us, and we're back on that bus. Father is sitting in his seat and watching the old woman. She's talking to her husband. Since we're like ghosts, they can't see us, so the old woman doesn't know we're listening. Can you see her face? Now you know why she looked so familiar to Father. I mean, she's a lot older and she ain't as big as she used to be, so maybe that's why he didn't know her right off. Her name's Alice Rutledge and she

375

Gary A. Braunbeck

used to be a nurse. She took care of Father when he was a little boy and in the hospital. He used to call her something that made her laugh.

Okay, we have to be quiet now, because she's telling her husband about something.

Listen:

"It's the strangest thing, hon, but I just now remembered something about that little boy who used to call me 'Nurse Claus.' Don't know why. Lord! I'll bet I haven't thought of him in twenty-five, thirty years. Remember that deformed baby that was abandoned at the hospital all them years ago? Well, that little boy, he used to like for me to take him to see all the newborns, and one day when we was up there, he asks me about the door to the ICU and I told him that was where we had to keep the babies who were really sick. Well, he just stood there for a minute looking at the door, then he said something like, 'I hope they get better.' I thought that was just the sweetest thing! He was like that, real gentle, you know?

"Well, a couple of nights later I stopped by his room to check on him and he's not there. I asked Janet Tyler if she'd seen him but Janet'd been busy with the charts so she didn't know. I got to worrying, so I went looking for him. He wasn't looking in on all the newborns like I thought he'd be doing, then I remembered how sad and worried he'd looked when I told him about the babies in ICU.

"That little stinker had snuck in there without anybody catching him. Can you imagine? I go in, and I see the nurses all gathered around the window looking at something. That little fellah had not only snuck into the ICU wing, but he managed to get into the isolation room where we was keeping that deformed baby! I got it out of him later, how he managed to get in. He just walked through the doors into the ICU and went right up to the window and saw her. They didn't have all the fancy electronic security they got nowadays, and the gals on the ward were making their rounds so there wasn't nobody at the desk to see him. He tried to get into the room but the door was locked. The gals started coming back from their rounds, so he hid behind a cart one of the orderlies had left in the little hallway that ran alongside the door to the isolation room. He waited there, pulling this IV stand along behind him the whole time on account he was still on a lot of antibiotics because of his spleen and all.

"He waited while the nurses unlocked the door to go in to check on her, then as they were coming out he made real quick-like and snuck in before the door closed again. He walked right up to that baby—and I tell you, Douglas, I still just want to cry when I think about what that poor baby looked like! And then to have been treated like she was, starved and half froze and all cut up . . . makes me wonder about some people.

"So he goes right over to her incubator and picks her up in his arms. Well, by now the gals on the unit have seen him in there, and they go in to try to get him out and he pitches a fit, won't let go of the baby or nothing. The nurses didn't want to try and take the baby from him, because she was still recovering from her surgery and they didn't want to chance hurting her, so they left him, in there and called Security.

"I saw him in there and I knocked on the glass and he looks up at me and smiles.

" 'You know him?' asks Marge Cooper.

" 'Sure do,' I said. 'That's the little fellow who calls me "Nurse Claus." ' "

" 'Think you can get him to lay her down?'

" 'I bet I can.'

"So Marge lets me into the room. Little guy's trying real hard not to cry. 'She's so sad,' he says to me. 'She's pretty sick,' I told him. 'You really should put her back down so she can rest.' 'Is she gonna be okay?' 'I think so, yes,' I said. 'Will you help me?' he asks. So I go over to him and hold out my arms, but before he gives her to me he takes hold of her hand and leans his face down real close to hers and says, 'You'll be okay, don't be scared. I hope they find a nice place for you to stay when they let you go.' Then he kisses her forehead and hands her to me and I put her back in the incubator, but before I close the lid he put his hand down on her.

"Her heart's beating real good,' he says. Then he looks at her and says, 'I think you're a great baby. I think you're really pretty, too. I hope you have a home with lots of brothers and sisters and that your mom and dad love you. You have to promise me something, okay? I want you to promise me that you'll never forget me. If I had a baby sister like you, I'd take real good care of her. So you go to sleep now, and remember that I love you, little baby. Wherever you go, I'll always love you.'

"Oh, Douglas, I'll never forget what happened then. That little baby, she opened her eyes, and he told her again that he loved her and hoped she felt better. Then she held up one of her awful little hands and he squeezed it.

"You should have seen how her eyes lit up then, and the way she smiled at him, like they had some kind of secret. . . ."